THE FOOTBALL FACTORY

John King was born in 1960 and lives in London. He is currently working on his second novel.

JOHN KING

The Football Factory

JONATHAN CAPE
LONDON

First published 1996

7 9 10 8

First published in the United Kingdom in 1996 by Jonathan Cape,
Random House, 20 Vauxhall Bridge Road, London SW1V 2SA

Random House Australia (Pty) Limited
20 Alfred Street, Milsons Point, Sydney,
New South Wales 2061, Australia

Random House New Zealand Limited
18 Poland Road, Glenfield,
Auckland 10, New Zealand

Random House South Africa (Pty) Limited
Box 2263, Rosebank 2121, South Africa

Random House UK Limited Reg. No. 954009

A CIP catalogue record for this book
is available from the British Library

Papers used by Random House UK Limited are natural,
recyclable products made from wood grown in sustainable forests.
The manufacturing processes conform to the environmental
regulations of the country of origin.

ISBN 0–224–04302–1

Typeset by Deltatype Ltd, Ellesmere Port, Cheshire
Printed and bound in Great Britain by
Mackays of Chatham PLC

TO MUM AND DAD

Thanks to:
Anita Nowakowski for the kick-start,
Kevin Williamson and Irvine Welsh for encouragement,
and Robin Robertson for taking me on

COVENTRY AT HOME

Coventry are fuck all. They've got a shit team and shit support. Hitler had the right idea when he flattened the place. The only good thing to come out of Coventry was the Specials and that was years ago. Now there's sweet FA and we've never had a decent row with Coventry. The best time was two years ago in Hammersmith with a bunch of Midland prototypes looking for a drink down the high street. About fifteen of them. Short cunts with noddy haircuts and tashes. Stumpy little legs and beer guts. Looked like they should be on Emmerdale Farm shafting goats for a living. They clocked us coming the other way and took off. You could smell shit over the petrol fumes, which is saying something in Hammersmith.

It was a stupid move. They should've piled in the nearest pub and sat tight. We weren't looking for them. We don't expect Coventry to perform. We were on our way to King's Cross to meet Tottenham coming back from Leeds. Saturday night battering yids. But the Diddy Men were running into the precinct and when you see something run you follow. Pure instinct. They were moving fast as their little legs would carry them. Red faces reflected in shop windows along with the hi-fi gear and baked beans special offers. We were right behind as the bloke at the front took them into the car park. Like those sheep who lead the flock to slaughter. You'd think they'd smell blood and hear the knives being sharpened. Not this lot. Straight into the car park with the last of the Saturday shoppers standing aside to let us through. We had them boxed in and gave them a hiding, working fast because someone would've called the old bill. We had the numbers and kicked them into next week.

Harris was there and opened up some cunt's face with his hunting knife. Said later he should've signed his name, so if the bloke ever managed to get his end away his kids would know the old man had been to London. That he wasn't just a goat fucker. But he was joking. That's just the Harris humour. He's not one of these sadists you read about who torture kids and give them chemicals to loosen their arses. Time was short and we were in and out of the precinct. Straight down Hammersmith tube before you could chant Harry Roberts. The Coventry boys would know next time. Don't walk around taking the piss. If you want a drink after the game, fuck off out of West London.

It's one o'clock and we're having a pre-match pint. It's been a hard week at the warehouse and the lager gives me a kick-start. Stacking boxes five days solid takes it out of you. Cardboard rubbing against your hands eight hours a day takes away the feeling. You go into remote control and the brain goes numb. Worst of all are the forty-footers full of pressure cookers. Four thousand of the bastards and you sweat your life away for three hours stacking pallets for Glasgow Steve the Rangers fan driving the forklift. A tall, thin bastard who spends his days shouting Fuck The Pope as he buries each pallet in the racks. He's one of those Ian Paisley Rangers fans who talk politics all day and wish they'd been at the Battle of the Boyne. Thinks he's King Billy. He's got a sense of humour and comes down Chelsea sometimes now he's exiled from Ibrox. Says Chelsea are a good Protestant team. Doesn't know any of the names but comes along anyway. Not with me though.

It's a closed shop round this table because since the old bill got serious with all those undercover operations you have to watch yourself. It's not like the old days. Not like when I was a kid sitting in front of the telly watching football riots with Jimmy Hill or some faceless cunt giving us a commentary and slow-motion replays. Today there's surveillance gear and you have to remember the cameras. But it's all a bit of a joke, because pitch invasions and riots for the cameras never compared to the trouble away from the ground. Your actual nutters do damage miles from the stadium in a tube station or down a back street, not behind the goal with a telephoto lens shoved up their noses. You don't stop that kind of thing. You can't change human nature. Men are always going to kick fuck out of each other then go off and shaft some bird. That's life. Mark's always going to get his end away.

– That bird last night was well dirty, he says, scratching his bollocks for emphasis. I got back to her flat in Wandsworth and she gave me a can of Heineken, then told me to go sit down in the living room. I'm sitting there with the telly on pissing about with the remote and she walks in tarted up in suspenders and crutchless pants. She's only shaved herself and walks straight over, kneels down and takes my knob out.

He looks at a couple of lads as they walk in the pub. Jim Barnes from Slough and someone I don't recognise. A tall bloke with a silver earring who looks knackered with a bruised right eye and cuts along his knuckles. Must've had a good Friday night.

– She starts sucking me off and there's this bald presenter on the box talking to a sex therapist. One of those stuck-up slags who've probably never had a decent shag in their lives. Talking about safe sex and how queers are taking the blame for Aids.

Barnes goes to the bar and orders. There's a few of his mates on the piss and he gets lumbered with a round. Takes it in his stride. Slough's well the drugs town but it's a Chelsea town as well. Shit hole basically, but a Chelsea shit hole. Croydon's another new town with Chelsea credentials. West Ham have Dagenham and Spurs have Stevenage. They're welcome to them.

– There's this bald TV head nodding up and down as he listens to the woman and this bird's head banging up and down giving me a blow job. A bald head and a bald cunt, and I'm sitting there with my Heineken resting on her shoulder. The TV personality is making a couple of thousand quid, but I'm getting the business off some dirty old slapper from South London.

Mark's a mouthy bastard and who'd want a bird sucking them off with a sex therapist on the screen watching? Those studio experts are ugly cunts and if Rod's description of Mark's woman last night is anything to go by then she was no oil painting either. Rod had to make do with a hand job and a large donner from the kebab van off the Hammersmith roundabout. Just down from the Palais where the freaks and niggers hang around. All those stroppy little cunts acting smooth in one of those fun pubs where a pint of lager's only worth the price if you're looking to get your end away fast or make do with smacking up a few kids. Rod wasn't impressed with Mark's bird. Reckons she was a bit dodgy. Off her head he says. He walked her mate back round the corner.

– She was only on, wasn't she? Rod's aggrieved. We go back and she lives with the old girl near the flyover. We're sitting there waiting for her mum to go to bed and when she finally leaves I think right, I'm in now, but the mouse was in his hole and she just tossed me off over the couch. She got angry when I shot my load over these cushions with pheasants on them. Indian she said. Bought them down Wembley market. I couldn't be bothered with all that bollocks and she stunk of blood. I just told her to leave it out and walked off. I mean, why hang about when you've dumped your load? I went down the van and nearly got in a ruck with these Shepherd's Bush raggamuffins. Chains and leather jackets and patterns shaved into their heads. They were young enough, but I thought next time you fucking black bastards. You've got to watch it on your own. Any of them could've been tooled-up and I'd be dead now and you lot would be listening to Mark, believing he pulled himself a stunner.

– Fucking did mate. Why waste time with pig meat like that bird of yours last night when you can get some woman dressing up for you and buying the rubbers. She had her bedroom kitted out with a mirror and all these different condoms to choose from. Not that I bother usually, but all the packs were open and she takes out this gel and the tube's half empty so she's been a busy girl. If we'd been playing someone tasty today I'd have left after the blow job and got a decent night's kip. It's only Coventry so I put myself through the grinder. She was a dirty cow. Swallowed it like a trouper. Not a moment's hesitation. The only downer was she kept biting me. Put big teeth marks into my arms and back. Bloody painful it was. Woman needs to go on a diet.

I go to the bar to get a round in. The service is always slow and you'd think they'd get more staff in when Chelsea are playing at home. It never changes. It's a captive audience so they make us wait. The lager tastes watered down and they serve it in plastic pints so no-one gets glassed. It makes sense I suppose, but the plastic means the lager smells like piss. It's another fun pub and it got done up after Chelsea and West Ham clashed a good few years ago now, during the peak of the original Headhunters.

Eleven o'clock in the morning and the ICF are turning up in Chelsea pubs. It was a golden age back then. West Ham hate Chelsea like we hate Tottenham. They reckon we're all mouth.

That East London is the real London. That Chelsea's mob is full of wide-boys and new town delinquents. They come in, get a warm welcome, and we're lumbered with an amusement arcade. They all think they're related to the Krays. Bill Gardner with your cornflakes and *Sun*. They'll be down here again in a couple of weeks. Tottenham one week, West Ham the next. You couldn't ask for better.

Dave Harris stands at the bar moaning about the six-month sentence handed out to a mate for fracturing a copper's cheek down in Camberwell. Says he didn't know the bloke was old bill because he was off duty outside a club. When he started acting cocky his mate nutted him. Thought he was a cockney Yosser Hughes. Broke the bloke's nose as well and the old bill made the effort to find him. Wouldn't normally have bothered. They take care of their own. Six months isn't a death sentence but it's long enough. Harris says the bloke's Millwall. That he's sound. There's grudging respect for Millwall and a few names have been known to grace Chelsea in the past, but when we play them it's war.

Funny how it works. It's like blacks. People say they hate niggers but if they know one then he's okay. Or if he gets stuck in then he's a Chelsea nigger. Or like when you watch England away all the English get on, although there is occasional trouble, between Chelsea and West Ham say, because some riffs run deep. Generally you're broken down into people rather than mobs so somehow the whole thing works. But no-one gets on with Tottenham because they're yids and the scousers are all thieving little cunts. Talk to a Man U fan and they'll tell you about scousers.

Harris turns to me as I wait to be served. He's a nutter, but friendly with it. His head's together which is something you can't say about one or two of the blokes who hang around this pub. He's got a brain and uses it to good effect. Runs a roofing company, or something like that. Must be in his mid-thirties and he's been around.

– It's half-eleven in King's Cross for Tottenham, he says. Flash yid cunts coming down here last year having a go at our pubs. It'll be worse than usual next Saturday. You don't come down here and take liberties like that. You lot will be there, won't you? I'm running a coach to Liverpool as well, so tell me if you want seats. We'll stop in Northampton on the way back. It's a good town to go on the piss in and you can get back to London in an hour or so on the motorway. We've got a bog and video, and the driver's an original Shed skin from '69 so he'll hang around till Northampton closes down. Quality travel and we'll be getting tickets lined up. Let me know. Fifteen quid for the coach and the price of the ticket on top if you want one.

There's a lazy cunt behind the bar serving and some of the lads are getting pissed off waiting, telling him to get his finger out. Coventry never pull a big crowd and the pub's half full, but still they take their time. Try and make the punters wait. We're only football fans after all, but if we decided to turn the pub over they'd get it sorted quick enough. But you don't piss in your own lift. Or if you do, you've got to be a bit slow. Finally a bird with black hair in a pony-tail serves me. She looks at the glass she's filling or over at the wall the whole time, as though I don't exist, so I just stare at her tits so she knows I'm alive. She goes all red, the dozy cow. I take three pints of lager back to the table and Mark's into one about the Liverpool game.

He's got a cousin Steve who lives in Manchester and says we can stay with him after the match. Manchester sounds better than Northampton if you've got somewhere to doss and you don't have to worry about the trip back to London. We've been to Old Trafford and Maine Road enough times but not seen much of the city centre. That's the way with football. Unless you get it organised and get there early you just see the train station or coach park, the old bill waiting to escort you to the ground, and all the local slums. The natives do their best to have a go at you and, if you're smart, you get away from the escort and find them. Usually that's about it. You go up, see the game, have a punch-up if you're lucky, then get out.

Old Trafford's a smart ground and when they write about Man U being a great club you know deep down they're right. Going to places like Old Trafford and Anfield gives you an extra kick. Football's all about atmosphere and if the grounds were empty and there was no noise, there'd be no point turning up. Chelsea have had some good rucks in Manchester. Piling out of Maine Road when the old bill haven't got it together. Running fights along the side of the ground. Last year, walking back to the coaches, a mob of Moss Side niggers started lobbing bricks and we were straight after them. They just ran further down the road, then started chucking more bricks. We'd chase them again, but they'd just move on. We had to give up in the end because we were out of breath. There was only twenty of us by that time and they could've been leading us into a trap. There's a lot of ways and places to die but hacked up by Man City fans in Moss Side isn't a chart topper. Niggers don't fuck about. They can't afford to and if you see one in a white mob you know he'll do the business.

– If we take the Harris coach up we can get a train to Manchester from Liverpool, says Mark. Or if my cousin comes to the game get a lift back, have a wash and some mushy peas and go into town. Steve says it's more than just Coronation Street. Some of those places are mental. You can get a cheap pint and northern birds are friendly. Mind you, that bird last night was friendly enough with her mirror shaking as I gave her one from behind. Banging her head into the wall waking the neighbours. I had to shut my eyes after a while and think of England, because the way the street light was hitting the mirror it looked like I had my cock wedged into the wall. One day that mirror will come unstuck and there'll be two dead strangers found shredded in Wandsworth.

Coventry at home is always a bit of a letdown compared to Man United and Leeds. There's a lot of boring home games but you turn up because what else are you going to do? We sit around a bit hungover from last night, then at twenty to three drink up and leave. There's a crowd building up along the Fulham Road heading for the ground. We wait for the traffic to stop at the lights and avoid the police lined up outside Fulham Broadway. There's the smell of horse shit and hamburger meat, coppers on horseback telling the crowd to go separate ways when they get to the gates.

A van full of coppers moves slowly, eyeballing everyone under the age of forty. Outside the church hall tables sell fanzines and souvenirs. Kids with blue and white scarves hold the old man's hand. More vans are positioned outside the entrance to the North and West Stands, though fuck knows what they think's going to happen. A pissed up old geezer stumbles off the pavement and three coppers go over. They're young and mouthy and if there was a decent sized crowd and there weren't those fucking cameras up on top of the flats maybe they'd get the kicking they deserve. But they've got uniforms and overtime and they nick a harmless drunk. Bundle him into the back of the van well over the top with their attitude.

– I went round Andy Marshall's this morning, Mark says, handing his ticket to an old boy behind bars on the turnstile. Haven't seen Marshall for a good two years, but he lives near that bird in Wandsworth and I thought I'd find out if he's still alive. He's got a beard and long hair. Right hippy. Sits in front of the telly watching old Arnold Schwarzenegger videos. Thinks he's half man, half machine. He's just started lifting weights. Says it kills time as he waits for a job to come along. He wants to join a gun club and kill twenty chinks with one bullet.

– They should sign him on and send him off somewhere, Rod says, leading up the steps, weaving through railings. Marshall was a Special Constable. Wanted to become a copper but they wouldn't have him. Even the old bill have standards. He's the kind of bloke who sits in front of the box all day and then goes out and does a Hungerford. Imagine that cunt with a shooter down Wandsworth shopping centre. Just walk through the crowd and think he was Arnie on patrol in the jungle.

We're at the top of the steps leading into the West Stand. It's a clear day and I turn and look over the surrounding scene. It's a good view and I remember a clear evening with a gold sunset and West Ham turning up outside the North Stand. We were already inside the ground when it went off along the Fulham Road. I can hear the police megaphones. Visitors keep moving. North Stand to the right. Everyone stay on the pavement. There's more vans coming along the road and coppers giving it the big one.

Cameras are busy recording life. Videotape rolls and faces are saved for future reference. We go for a slash and wait for space. The bogs are full of piss and this is the kind of Saturday you have a few pints and don't worry about aggravation. We show our tickets to a wanky-looking steward and are in the West Stand. We look towards the visitors to see how many have turned up. There's a few hundred Coventry in small groups. There's empty spaces all around the ground, though there's still time before kick-off. But the price they charge nowdays what do they fucking expect?

We're in our seats and all the usual faces are here. Harris sits two rows in front flanked by a couple of evil cunts I know from sight, sipping a cup of tea. He isn't a big bloke but gets things organised and is always looking for trouble. That's all you need. With a bit of common sense and the confidence to make people believe you know best you can impress. The old bill know his face and he's been done a few times, but he manages to escape the kind of sentences the lads who got done in Operation Own Goal were lumbered with. He's careful and learns from past mistakes.

The camera under the roof records our sins and it's only kids and pissheads who step out of line. You've got to be daft to do anything else, though occasionally things boil over and then the papers are clocking faces and running witch-hunts. It's hard to believe there was a time when you could go on the rampage inside the ground and get away with it week after week. Like the Chelsea North Stand when I was a kid. They steamed in every chance they got. Went mental regular as clockwork. Millwall and West Ham in the Shed and the whole place went up.

– That bird last night, says Mark, her head's banging into the wall and she's telling me to go deeper. What does she think I am? Some kind of marathon man? A deep sea diver? It's not the fucking Olympics. If she wants that kind of treatment she should go and see Marshall. The bloke's in need of some serious sex. If he doesn't do the business soon he's going to start killing.

– He used to have a big porn collection. Rod's thinking. Had over a hundred films. Used to sit there for hours after the pub closed with the pause button at his fingertips freezing the action. I mean, I like a dirty film like anyone else, but after a while you get sick of watching other people doing what you should be doing yourself. The more films he watched the more he bought. It was all Dutch and German stuff. Hardcore you'd get done for bringing through Dover. Customs only wants to watch the hard stuff.

It was when he lived in Hammersmith. We know him from school. He was an upright kid. Looked like a miniature bank clerk. I ended up round there with some of the lads one time and he puts this film on of a girl getting gang-banged by a bunch of squaddies. No sound, just classical music, Mozart or Beethoven, someone like that. Some dead German cunt. The girl was trying to fight them off. There were four or five blokes taking turns as their mates held her down. I was into my chow mein takeaway and wasn't interested in that kind of sex, but Marshall was laughing. They couldn't act but the girl was alright. It made me feel a bit sick though, seeing some bird getting treated like that.

When it was over Marshall said it was the real item. Paid a hundred quid for the video. It was made in Aldershot. Authentic rape. Authentic squaddies. The lads just laughed, but you knew they didn't like that kind of scene. You have to be a fucking nonce to get off watching rape. Just sitting there with your camera trained on the barmy army waiting for them to do the business. Get them going, pay your money and then send them down for ten years. I made my excuses and pissed off. After I left John Nicholson threatened him with a knife from the kitchen. Kicked him in the head and told him he was a cunt. Then he put a chair through the screen. Only honest bloke there.

The tannoy pumps out Liquidator, the Sixties Chelsea anthem from Harry J And The All Stars. It's a ska classic and belongs to the skinhead era. Next up is Blue Is The Colour with Peter Osgood and Alan Hudson in the Top Of The Pops studios. The teams come onto the pitch and we stand to clap. The players wave and the pre-match kickabout begins. The crowd looks a bit more respectable. Men coming in from the pubs. A zigger zagger chant starts up, echoing through the West Stand, video camera capturing the image. Coppers sit at the controls. The pitch is a brilliant patch of green catching the sun. Harris laughs with Billy Bright. Mark reads his programme moaning about the price, while Rod skins up and adds a bit of blow. I sit back and wait for the captains to toss up and the game to start. Coventry get a bit of a chant going and half the West Stand looks their way. We raise our right hands and give them the wanker sign.

DOING A RUNNER

You're well fucking pissed on ten pints of lager, with a decent jukebox and a bit of fluff knocking about, mostly slappers in mini skirts, black cotton wedged up their arses, just what you want after a few sherbets, wide-boys and tarts with wide open thighs, spread easier than margarine, telling them to wait a while because you're drinking with your mates, downing the cheapest lager like nobody's business. Eight, then nine o'clock, evening's steaming past, end of the week job with two days off, and the lager tastes like heaven. Cold and sharp against the throat. Chemical bubbles brewed quickly for lager louts. All the lads on the piss talking bollocks, nothing you'll remember tomorrow, and the music's cranked up so you have to shout, but the electric beat is what counts, gives the place a bit of rhythm, drowns out the need to think about what you're saying and means you don't have to make any sense, just keep talking, moving the tongue, and the more pissed you get the more you find the words in the brain aren't what come out through your mouth. You could be saying anything. Fuck it. Drop your money in the slot, press a button, flick the pages and choose your songs. Dead simple. A fucking idiot could do it without thinking. But it's hard getting in at the bar if you're not half cut, fucking difficult, but it's easier now because you're pissed and don't give a toss about fine edges, just blunder your way through, push and stumble towards the barmaid with big tits bursting through her blouse, pouting painted lips and a bit of a stroppy method, knows she can afford to act like she's something special because there's enough pissed-up blokes looking her way, fucking loves it, time of her life, and you tell her you'll have two of those darling, you with the blouse at breaking point, tits knocking forward, showing your wares getting the hormones going, and if some cunt doesn't like you piling through they shut up anyway because you're pissed, but mostly because you're with a tidy mob of blokes who'll put a man through a plate glass window for looking at you and your mates. No fucking strop steaming into ten o'clock, evening flashing by, all those faces under the lights, blending together, skin tone changing with each pint, waxwork reflections and suddenly it's last orders, always comes around too fast after ten, white faces melting through the smoke haze, the smell of perfume in the air, a sweet smell, but you want another drink, getting double rounds in, a couple of pints to knock back, and the cunt behind the bar wants you out of his pub sharpish now he's got your money and the till is loaded, he wants to fuck off upstairs and watch his new surround-sound TV, that till full of cash, your cash, you should rob the place, smash a few windows, that slag of a barmaid on all fours getting shagged by the landlord's dog. Lot of laughter from the lads imagining the picture. And the landlord's got a Rottweiler out back so drink up lads, drink up gentlemen PLEASE. Otherwise you'll get the dog set on you, that's what he really means, nice little warm up for the mutt before he slips the woman a canine length. And in the street it's cold and you're hungry, fucking starving because the drink gets you going and it's only poor cunts go down the burger van to stand in the drizzle, it's a long hike for a burger made from cat food and you're all agreed, it's straight down the curry house. Can taste it now. Red velvet wallpaper and Ravi Shankar sitting out back tuning up the sitar, and though you don't admit anything you know it's a fucking good sound, magic music when you're pissed and staring into the pilau rice doing an acid turn in front of you, buried deep in the plate, multi-coloured spin washable, the original bangra sound without the electrics, just the old rishi on a mountain top job stroking passing tigers. Like fuck. But you've got to get inside the curry house first so you have a few minutes making the effort, acting sober though the waiter giving you the table isn't convinced, you all know the real state of affairs, the cunt must be able to smell the hops or whatever shit they put in your drink nowdays, who knows, imagine that, not having a fucking clue what you're drinking, same goes for your food down the supermarket, it's dangerous thinking about that kind of thing, but so fucking what anyway. Money's money and the waiter knows your face. It's the easy option. Better than an argument and there's hard-earned cash into the bargain. The curry boys can't lose. You're wedged in ordering a stack of papadoms and six pints of lager, and you know it's going to be Carlsberg, that it's always Carlsberg in curry houses, that it tastes wrong if your Indian isn't accompanied by a bit of Danishhhhhhhhh. Maybe it's down to bulk buying or something. Brewed by Danes for Indians. Fucking right. What else does Europe give you apart from a few dodgy lagers? Not like the Commonwealth, shunted out the back door, you'd rather have a curry any day of the week, none of that French muck the rich bastards eat, fucking wankers, if they want to be French fuck off to France. What have the frogs ever done for the English? The cunts come over in 1066, stick an arrow in someone's head and build a load of stone churches. Then they make the rich cunts speak their language while the rest of us are told our words are filth. Fuck off. And they fucking sided with the Germans when they rolled into France in the war. No bollocks those cunts. No fucking pride. Hang on to the curries and JA sound systems. But the place is packed and you're lucky to get in because there's blokes being turned away a few minutes later, mobs of geezers, not taking it well, stroppy cunts can see there's no tables left, too fucking bad pal, and there's four birds at the next table, right old slags by the look of them, fit bodies a couple of them but fucked-up faces, all shagged out, cunts like the Mersey Tunnel most likely, what was that Stranglers song, something about making love to the Mersey Tunnel, you can't remember, kiddie memories, fuck it. They're pissed-up looking over and you start giving it the classic chat while you're waiting for the papadoms and they're dopey cunts, know fuck all about curries, just looking for a length, then they get their kormas delivered, and what's the fucking point coming for a feed if you go and order a korma? Should be embarrassed with a full tandoori menu in front of them, but that's women for you, and they're going on about it being hot, how the fuck can it be when it's full of yoghurt or whatever the bastards put in it, probably spunk, have to laugh, telling them the korma's full of it, a line of waiters wanking in the sauce. The birds look disgusted but only halfway, and then the lager arrives and you're straight into the papadoms giving the main order, bhajees all round, digging into the chutneys, lime pickle and mango, chopped onions, fucking beautiful, the business, talking with your mouths full, then the various vindaloos and Madras dishes, Bombay potatoes and bhindi bhajee side orders, ladies fingers wrapped round your knob, but the girls next door are no ladies, no chance, and you order a stack of nans, half plain, half Peshwari, then the waiter fucks off and your mouth's like a dam. Peshwari nans, fucking beautiful, and you're telling the lads about your Irish mate who went overland down through Iran and Iraq, hard trip through the desert but good people, sound people, and he ended up in Peshwar during the war against the Russians, and the town was the base for the Mujaheddin, fucking hard cunts, a real wicked place on the North West Frontier, the Golden Crescent, and he spent a couple of weeks there out of his head. Some cunt says he should watch it because those Muslims would have him, specially the desert warriors, they have no qualms about shit-stabbing a bloke, and your mate said they were good people, no hassle. Still, you don't want to take chances. Not in Pakistan anyway. And the slappers next door are giving it the big one, always some mouthy cow leading the charge, some body-builder slag with a wet pair of knickers, always those birds have the biggest mouths to go with the biggest leg muscles, telling you they're putting it on a plate for you, eat your curry lads and come back with us for a drink, for a fucking shag you mean, but you're hungry, really fucking hungry, and you just want them to shut up so you can concentrate on the food. Either that or fuck off girls, go and pick up some other cunt. Doesn't matter who it is, but the food's important, watching the trolleys get rolled out, tandoori chicken sizzling for the mob a couple of tables along, look like off-duty squaddies, shaved heads and straight clothes, smart wearing blazers, none of the crisp Fred Perry gear, must be soldiers, can't read the words on the blazers but know it's some kind of crest, fuck them, you're not getting involved because the army's always on the lookout for a bit of aggravation, a couple of hours out of the garrison and the cunts need a ruck, it's essential to their training, Queen and country and kick some cunt's head in, basic training is what decides a soldier. Shut the old brain down and learn to obey orders because the Eton wankers in charge know best, just do as you're told, follow orders, and one of the lads says his great granddad was a soldier on the North West Frontier, up on the Khyber Pass, must have been fucking mental and you wonder what it was like being a soldier in the Empire, keeping the Commonwealth together, and the old boy saw a donkey one time loaded down with bricks or whatever, and the poor fucker was breathing fit for a heart attack, about ready to explode, and the soldier called the man over, the cunt who owned the donkey, and cut the rope holding the bricks and told him not to overload his donkey, because the English love their animals. No fucking cruelty mate. Or not much anyway, except for the scum who burn cats and drop dogs off high rise blocks. Cunts you read about in the paper but never see, because if you did you'd be straight in and break their fucking necks. Cunts. Just eat your curry when it comes and the lager's sliding down a treat, the onion bhajees arriving with a sweet mint sauce, salad arranged around the sides. There's a slice of tomato, bit of cucumber and lettuce. You get stuck into the bhajees, order more lager from the waiter, call him Abdul, he's Abdul and you're Mustafa Curry, bloke just laughs because he's heard it all before, every fucking time. You're starving and there's four prats to the other side, away from the birds, two couples with their food positioned in front of them, and you're looking all envious, then the big cunt with you, always the big bastard who's one hundred per cent beer monster, gut spilling over the front of his jeans, old lager drenching his hair, the kind of bloke who'll never get married or have kids, you know the one, he's fucking famous and you meet him all over the country, he's everywhere you go whether it's a city centre or village high street, wherever you go he's there after the pub's kick out, rain or shine, well, the big cunt leans over and sticks his hand in the middle of the nearest plate, pilau rice and dhansak, and you laugh and feel for the bloke who owns the curry, because he's not exactly Henry Cooper, splash it all over, or Frank Bruno, first of a new generation of black boxing heroes, and the prat can't do a thing about it, just hope his woman isn't the kind who demands honour gets defended, one of those cunts who think they're the fairer sex and should be fought over, fucking slags, and he takes it well when the big cunt leans over with a smile on his face, stopping with his hand in the bloke's food, saying YOU DON'T MIND DO YOU MATE? like he's worried, really worried he's gone too far, and maybe he is because the messages are getting delayed on the brain-to-tongue trip, but you know he could go a lot further, fucking headcase that bloke after a few sherbets over the top, but he's your mate and you forgive most things if it's your mate. Poor bloke just laughs a bit and shakes his head and the fat bastard lifts a hand full of Persia and stuffs it in his mouth. You're so fucking pissed you're cracking up, start pissing yourself but keep control of the old bladder, mind shifting round all the time, watching the squaddies getting in a bit of an argument with some long-haired cunts at another table, trendy wankers or something, you don't mind a bit of dub-smart drumming and synthetic magic but you don't fucking dress up for it, slags to one side moaning the fucking korma's too hot, stupid cows, forgetting about the happy foursome with the wrecked dhansak. The onions in the bhajees are harsh as fuck and you wash them down with more lager, feeling a glow inside, get up to go for a piss, stumbling along between the tables, the racket must be turned up but you don't register because you've drunk your fair share. The door slams and cuts off the Ravi Shankar tunes, fucking tunes mate, Toon Army, geordie bastards, and you unzip and rock forward against the wall, piss bouncing against the marble, solid marble like the Taj Mahal, that picture above your table sticks in the mind, real love story behind that, the waiter told you once, a few months ago when you weren't so pissed, and the marble's being destroyed by pollution and the Government wants to close down the factories in the area, save the Taj Mahal, fucking beautiful building, but more for the tourist money it brings in, and the factory owners say they'll bomb the cunt, jobs are jobs, fucking right they are, and you think of your head leaning against the wall and how some sick cunts wipe their snot there when they're pissing, you've just washed it as well, rock back too fast and nearly fall over. What a way to die. Back of the skull cracked by a sink. Sad. You zip up and wash your hands and wipe your head, squaddie coming through the door, doesn't fucking see you, walks like a prize bull, fucking animal, Stone Age man in slacks and blazer, hard cunt you wouldn't fuck about with unless there were some very good odds, ten onto one. You've grown up in the Slough-Windsor area and seen plenty of aggravation with the army, fucking wankers, and this bloke's not exactly a raw recruit, more like a career soldier, well into his thirties and you reckon he's killed his way round the globe, cutting throats in the Falklands and shooting his way through

Northern Ireland, all over the shop, and you get out of the bog because it smells like fucking death in there, you don't want to get on the wrong side of the bloke, by standing too close or sneezing, breathing too heavy, it just needs an excuse. You're back at your table and the waiter's come along and taken away the plates, put out the heaters, and you down a third of a pint chatting with the tarts next door who've finished their meals and ordered ice cream, congealed spunk this one lads, ha fucking ha, telling you to hurry up with your food, they're waiting, and you tell them they can wait as long as they want, they just laugh, playing hard to get are you lads, the mouthy slapper, real pig meat, though the bird next to her's nice enough, jet black hair and massive eyes, but when she opens her mouth the teeth are rotten, fucking horrible, you don't want that wrapped around the old anti-tank missile do you, and then the main meal arrives and they can fuck off home for all you care. It's the business this and you're getting stuck in, everyone sobering up fast, sharing fair and square, and the two couples next to you ask for the bill and are on their way, and you're lifting the first few forkfuls into your mouths, heaven, fucking beautiful, the meaning of life, Ravi Shankar going into one in the background, the strings vibrating like they're about to snap, listen to the fucking music you silly cunts, real music, none of your mechanised bollocks you long-haired cunts, did you say that, the squaddies laughing and the long hairs looking round, don't know where it came from, the birds are laughing too, one of them leaning over rubbing your leg. You tell her to leave it out, all good things come to the slag who waits, and they don't like that, what do you think we are, common or something, fucking right darling, flat out on the parade ground with a queue of squaddies in line like that video you heard about, that's not nice boys, but so what anyway, fuck them, and the couples have gone leaving their money on the plate with the bill and one of your mates leans over and pockets the lot. You see what's what and keep the momentum, cracking a joke with the slapper acting aggrieved, they haven't seen a thing and neither has the waiter who comes over, looks round, asks his brother, then one of them goes to the bar, they're confused, talking among themselves, arguing, Abdul going outside looking up and down the street. There must be some kind of mistake, decent citizens don't do runners, not respectable little men and women in their best clothes who go to the theatre and have nice jobs in finance. Not those cunts. And you're trying not to laugh because this is what it's all about, all that wealth distribution bollocks, this is what makes the country tick, petty thieving and sharing the cost, money safely tucked away, bunking the trains and being ready to pocket the difference. You order more Carlsberg and it's there in front of you, nice white head, the Danes know what they're doing, most of the time, like when they won the football and voted no on Europe, but then they fell apart on the pitch and were forced into another vote, and said yes, silly cunts. Just had enough of the old pressure politics and let the businessmen have their way. You're washing the food down, throat burning, magic this, and there's a bit of a commotion as the squaddies and a mixture of acid casualties and other lads start fighting. It's a right fucking grin because it's all slow motion and the bull soldier tries to smack someone in the face but he's too pissed and the other cunt jumps up on a chair and kicks him in the chest, more like a push with the bottom of his trainer, and the bastard falls back through a table letting the regiment down, then a couple more soldiers in casuals who aren't as pissed come over and the whole lot of them are into it, waiters running behind the bar taking cover, you wave to Abdul and he half smiles, not sure this time, what a way to make a living, and the phone will be going for the old bill. You're sitting there watching the show, everything moving out of time, punches missing their mark, talk about a drunken brawl, like something from a Carry On film, Carry On Steaming, you can't remember the name, but it was that Western, Carry On Cowboy, something like that, with Sid James, the great British hero, a fucking Aussie or South African one of the lads reckoned, part of the Commonwealth, a bunch of convicts shipped off for fuck all, raped on the ships, not a bad job if you're a sailor, it's not fucking funny though if you're one of the women or children. And your meal's nearly finished and you've only got half a pint left, lift the glass to the lips and there's a table emptying across the room, all the waiters out back now, the bar end of the restaurant a big fucking bundle, playground fight, hasn't got that nasty edge yet, not vicious or anything, just because they're all so fucking pissed, though it won't be long before someone gets hurt, and more people are joining in, a little cunt who must think he's a karate master or something, chopping some scruffy pissed cunt, his bird jumping on the bloke's back, ski pants and legs wrapped round his body, cunt wedged up against the base of his spine, like something from those karma sutra cartoons, smacking his head with her fists, fucking lovely, real laugh, and the old bill won't be long and maybe she'll get a cell all to herself. Fucking wicked. Rakes her nails down the man's cheeks. Long red slashes. You wipe your mouth and the whole table's up on its feet heading for the door, a right fucking laugh, and the cunt with the nicked money says next time lads, next time we pay nothing, though you're paying nothing now, but it's always good to have something to look forward to, something that's planned, you've got to take your chances in life, don't ignore the opportunities when they crop up as you don't get that many, every little helps, the small victories are important because that's your lot, and the half of the curry house not involved in the punch-up is doing a runner, eighty per cent anyway, a few dozy cunts too honest or thick, what's the difference anyway, they stay where they are, but you're outside in the street and the lot of you are doing a runner, saving your hard-earned cash for the future, out in the evening air shooting round the corner, out of sight. You're pissed and running and soon you're fucked, leaning against a wall, panting, breath gone, laughing and wheezing at the same time, and when you catch your breath you know you've been a bit silly, that you'll have to tread careful next time you go to that particular curry house, maybe leave it a few months, go back when you're pissed and think you won't be recognised, but fuck it anyway, and there's always one cunt who thinks with his knob and wants to fuck the girls at the next table. Did anyone see where they went, did they do a runner as well, who fucking knows, who fucking cares, and a couple of the lads piss off home with the sound of sirens in their ears as three cars flash past and you shout that they've got a major disturbance to worry about. They don't give a fuck about a bunch of wankers who've just done a runner, they're interested in the ruck demolishing the curry house. Problem is, the running got your head straightened out a bit and the curry's soaking up the drink, you've got your breath back and you decide to take a wander, should have got it lined up with those slags at the next table, so you start walking back in the general direction, get near and see the wagons pulled up outside, blue lights pulsing like bedlam, setting off epileptic fits, fucking video games, playing police and thieves nicking a load of blokes, some short-haired figure, not a squaddie because he's not thick enough, he hits a copper and the bastards have him on the ground and start kicking the shit out of him. Battered to fuck outside the tandoori by the old bill. The waiters are looking through the window. The English are a race of barbarians and the Indians get their revenge, like the time down that curry house at the seaside, well pissed, and the bastards only laced the fucking meal, you thought it tasted a bit iffy at the time but put it down to the heavy water beer up north. You remember it well, have to laugh, you deserved it trying to throw a table full of food across the room, and you got the train back early the next morning shitting fluid the whole way. If you ever go back the lads are going to wreck the place, put a fire bomb through the window because your arses were burning all the way back to London, talk about the big smoke, then the tube home, but credit where credit's due, those northern waiters were smart. And you're no fool either saying enough's enough, turn and take another road, no point being spotted, making it easy for the old bill, more cars steaming past, looks like World War Three has broken out, Islamic fundamentalists on the rampage, more like Christian militiamen. You walk down by the station and there's two of the tarts from the curry house by the taxi rank trying to pull soldiers, three blokes from the tandoori, one the white buffalo soldier from the bogs, they must've done a runner as well, woke up half way through battering some cunt and realised they were in trouble and got out before the old bill turned up. And the mouthy slag is giving them some chat, but the blokes are too pissed, you can see it in their faces, jaws hanging down dribbling over their clothes, no chance, rough bastards who'd give the girls a hard time of it, but they're going to be suffering brewer's droop soon as they get back, and the only hard things left will be their fists when the girls start laughing, pissed, too much vodka, too much something, but they work it out and they see you coming and blow the squaddies out, leave them for the taxis and come over and it's getting late and a bit cold and they're inviting you back for a drink, a shag, whatever you want lads, bit of music, don't have anything but shitty sounds, nothing worth listening to, who cares, it's somewhere to go, something to do, better than nothing, just standing around idle. But the squaddies are up and moving and there's a bit of an argument about nothing in particular, the sound of a police car nearby, they say you can have the women boys, you're welcome to them, and the squaddies return to the rank, jump in a taxi, fuck off back to barracks or wherever they came from, and you're standing against the wall, listening to the siren cut off, knowing you've got off lucky. The two birds are telling you not to worry about it, those squaddies mate, those fucking squaddies are bred to kill, trained to inflict brain damage and other serious injury and the mouthy slag is looking a bit more human now, her perfume is strong and doesn't let her down, makes her warm and female, but she's a pig, you know that, a pig in knickers, though her mate's not bad, but those rotten teeth, rough as fuck both of them, be honest about it, you're well pissed, and your best mate has just walked off in disgust and left you to fend for yourself, you can't believe it, the smell of perfume and warm breath, wet pants and a beer gut, rotting teeth and a dose of the crabs, you've got to make a stand, show a bit of class, all you've got to do is say no, but you know you're going to hate yourself in the morning.

TOTTENHAM AWAY

HALF-ELEVEN ON the dot and we're in King's Cross, standing at the bar in our North London local. The city's wide awake and there's a good mob packed into the pub. I'm sipping a pint of lager. Taking my time. Making it last. Mark's making do with orange juice and Rod holds a bottle of light ale. Harris is by the door watching people come in. Seeing who's who. He's got his usual firm on hand and there's small crews from all over West and South London. We're exclusive. There's no room for part-timers. The landlord must think it's Christmas because he's in the right place at the right time.

We usually use this pub before a game in North London, or when we've come back to King's Cross from up north. It always works like that. You find somewhere in a handy location where you can get together without the owner calling the old bill. You keep using it till it gets sussed. When there's a police van sitting across the road you know it's time to move. We just want to be left alone. Dress sensibly and leave the army fatigues and funny haircuts for school kids and sillies. You have to be casual and blend into the background.

Tottenham away is a cracker. There's always been a healthy hatred for Spurs. They're yids and wear skullcaps. They wave the Star of David and wind us up. We're Chelsea boys from the Anglo-Saxon estates of West London. Your average Chelsea fan coming up to Tottenham from Hayes and Hounslow is used to Pakis and niggers, but go up Seven Sisters Road and it's all bagels and kebab houses. Greeks, Turks, yids, Arabs. The Spurs mob like to get us going and it works both ways. Tottenham have always had a reputation for being flash. Silver Town yids. They're the rich spivs to West Ham's poor dockers. At least that's how the story goes. You go through Stamford Hill and Tottenham and you wouldn't think you're in the same city as Hammersmith and Acton. We've got our Paddies down in West London, but none of these yid ghettoes. I'm no Christian myself, but still Church Of Fucking England.

Tottenham sent us down to the Second Division in the mid-Seventies and most of the Chelsea mob got locked out of White Hart Lane before kick-off. It went off inside and there were battles all over the pitch. Spurs had the numbers and though Chelsea put up a show they gave us a kicking. Tottenham won 2–0. Chelsea went down. They've been paying for it ever since. Talk to other clubs' supporters, whether they're from up north or London, and everyone hates Tottenham. But we're Chelsea and proud of the fact. Harris has had the old brain ticking over since last Saturday and we're working to a plan. Know where to find Tottenham before the match. There'll be a good turn out for this one because Chelsea always show up in force for Tottenham away.

Black Paul is next to us at the bar. A Chelsea nigger from Battersea. He lives in a tenth floor flat looking over the river and sees the Stamford Bridge floodlights every morning when he gets out of bed. David Mellor shagging some bird in Chelsea gear's nothing, because Black Paul knocks them off with a view of the fucking ground. You can't get much better than that. He's no mug, Black Paul. Built like a concrete bunker and works on a building site. None of the lads wear colours because club shirts are the mark of a wanker, but Paul always has a kit top under his sweat shirt. Gets away with it because he's a mean cunt and nobody's going to say anything. He must be six-foot four in his bare feet and his hands are full of scars. Building walls for the white man.

He makes up for this by shagging the white man's women, winding us up something chronic with stories of the blonde birds flocking round his big black cock. It's always the same kind of birds. Blonde hair stacked up on their heads listening to digital drum beats. Your typical ecstasy girls from the inner city estates. Kids who won't touch a white bloke. They look us over like we can't compare with Black Paul and the niggers from Shepherd's Bush and Brixton. Like we're not up to scratch and it can cause bad feeling. Paul gives them a dose of jungle spunk but he's a

Chelsea nigger first and foremost. Do the business for Chelsea and that's all that counts.

I fancy a decent drink but take my time. Last night was quiet. A hard week at the warehouse. It's a boring place to work but you've got to do something. Didn't want to shag myself out with Tottenham next day so had a couple of cans and watched this film about some smooth cunt who makes a fortune buying and selling property. Knobs everything in sight, jacks up on heroin to help him cope with his millions, but gets a bit careless and shares his works and then finds he's got Aids. This makes him look up his old man who he's ignored for the last five years and they become the best of mates. The bloke dies and the old boy gets the cash. Rags to riches tale. Pile of shit basically, but there was nothing else on.

The lager tastes good but there's no point getting pissed and nicked for mouthing off along Tottenham High Road. You have to keep your wits about you when you're looking for a ruck. Get pissed and you're on for a kicking, not to mention a threatening behaviour charge. Assault if the old bill are around to see you in action. The cream of every club knows the score and leaves the pissheads to make lots of noise, jump up and down, and generally create a show for the TV cameras. It's a mug's game. Like the older chaps dressing for action. Like they're out on parade with their boots and fatigues.

We call them sillies because it's all about melting into the background. You can be twice as tasty without the show. Just do the business and piss off before you're spotted. It's all about calculation. Think before you pile in. Use your brain. Don't rant and rave and give yourself a heart attack. Look after yourself and stay healthy. Find the opposition and batter them into the concrete. You don't have to march in with a brass band playing. Do it on the quiet and you get the same result with none of the comeback. It's basic politics. It's great though, because the papers and television always miss the point. There's no reporters down Kensington High Street when we pull scousers off the train and kick them into next week. The cunts are in the East Stand rubbing shoulders with the money men, hoping a politician will look their way. The commentators don't sit in a block of flats with their camera crew zooming-in when we steam geordies at King's Cross

They're editing highlights and pocketing the wage packet. Suits us fine. Who needs the hassle?

One o'clock we start moving. It's a fair old walk along the Euston Road. We're out in the open then safe underground flooding the northbound platform of the Victoria Line, clockwork soldiers moving in time. Wind rushes down the tunnel and a Walthamstow train piles in. It's packed with Chelsea heading north. There's small mobs, kids and decent citizens. Older geezers with lion tattoos and granddads who remember Bobby Tambling and Jimmy Greaves like it was yesterday. There's nothing aboard to compare with us though and we get a few nervous looks. No colours. No sound. We wait for the next train a couple of minutes later, watched by London Underground lenses.

Video cameras see everything. You have to be sharp to achieve your ends because there's a market for Peeping Toms. Like this crime programme on the box hunting a serial killer wiping out sado-masochist queers. They took the cameras to a grubby flat in East London. Inside a bedroom with a body wrapped up on the bed. They were everywhere. Even went upstairs to talk with a granny who said she saw the victim and another bloke come home on the murder night. Said her eyesight wasn't too hot, but if the bloke's a nutter, which by rights he has to be, then he could well top the old girl as well.

They fucking loved it in the studio. Letting the country get off on the forensic team checking the flat. Pointing out old condom packets and an empty tube of KY. Then a camera at Waterloo picks up the killer with another bum bandit on their way to Putney and another murder. Cameras have a lot of power, but they won't stop anything. If you've got the urge to do something then it takes a special kind of strength to resist the desire. You don't have to get caught just because London's turning into a surveillance arcade. Not if you're clever.

The second train's half full and we spread out and take over. It's sauna conditions in the carriage with Mark and Rod pressed up against glass and Jim Barnes sweating last night's curry, moaning about some pig he shagged. Harris is in the next carriage down. I can see the back of his head through the door. Black Paul's against the wall, eyes to the ceiling. The train picks up speed. Curves through tunnels. There's a few women caught on the wrong train obviously worried, but we're Chelsea, not fucking Tottenham. We're not interested in bothering women. True, there are wankers about who'll get pissed up and give them a bad time, but they're nonces who wank their days away and spend their evenings telling everyone how hard they are.

We stop at Highbury & Islington and Finsbury Park. We check the platforms for Tottenham. If they're out looking for us and we get them underground that's their mistake. But the platforms are empty. Finsbury Park's Gooner territory, but Arsenal are away today, though there's a few memories of that particular area. The doors close and there's reflections in the windows. The next carriage starts singing Spurs Are On Their Way To Auschwitz and our lot joins in. A gang of kids in their late teens smell of too much drink. They start pulling at a seat. Flash a knife. One of them puts his hand on the emergency lever. Rod tells him to leave it out, we don't want the old bill fucking up our Saturday. Little hooligans showing off is okay when they do it away from us, but we don't need that kind of behaviour. You have to have standards. Would have done the same when I was their age, but I'm not. Now is now. There's no room for nostalgia. The kid does the sensible thing. Puts the knife away. Rod's not a bloke to annoy.

When we arrive at Seven Sisters the platform is all Chelsea. There's jokes about what will be first on the menu. A launderette or kebab shop. Harris is ahead now and the rest of us filter through the crowd trying not to draw attention. Tottenham offers a bonus because the tube's so far from the ground. It's a long way down Tottenham High Road and the old bill can't police all the different routes properly. Gives us the chance we're looking for. The crowd spills through barriers into the street. There's a kebab house opposite and a queue forms at the counter. Fair dodgers get pulled at the barriers while we move onto the main road. Keeps the old bill busy. Makes them feel needed.

There's traffic clogging the street and men run for buses to save their legs. Harris is on the other side of the road with Black Paul and some of the Battersea lads behind him. There's Hammerhead, a fat cunt from Isleworth who never runs because he's too fucking heavy. He got a bad kicking at Leeds last season and reckons he didn't suffer permanent damage because of his weight. Sixteen stone of blubber. He's more a mascot than anything and heads for the kebab house saying he needs a feed. He's a funny bloke. Lot of humour about him. Not the kind of bloke who deserves a kicking. Leeds are scum doing him. Ten onto one. It's not the odds, just Hammerhead doesn't want to know when it comes to a fight, which is fair enough.

Tottenham's a dump. There's holes in the pavements and more fumes than Hammersmith. Pensioners sit on benches looking into space and an old black woman pushes a supermarket trolley packed with flattened cardboard and empty cans. There's a heavy smell of kebab meat and even the niggers look different. The streets are wider. Derelict flats boarded up against squatters. These are the areas kids from up north head for when they come to London. Cheap accommodation. But there's plenty of builders looking to do them up and make a few quid. Plenty of nutters around who'll carry out the eviction. You've got to look after yourself. Nothing comes free and you've got to do the other bloke before he does you. That's what the pensioners on the bench don't realise. They might be owed something but there's nobody left to cough up. It's a different world now. The war spirit is dead and gone, packaged and sold off to the highest bidder.

We cross over and follow Harris, the crowd from the tube stretching along the High Road. We're dedicated in our mission. Getting in tight behind the leader. Black Paul telling us he's going to have a Tottenham nigger. Makes the lads laugh. His mate Black John with him. A smaller bloke with a shinehead and a way of making you nervous. His eyes are always darting around and you know his mind's working overtime. Only turns up for big games. Usually the aways. Paul told me on the quiet John makes a packet flogging crack in South London. Five hundred quid for a couple of night's work in Camberwell and Brixton. He's worth having along because you know he's always tooled-up. There's enough full-time, would-be yardies around who don't like him hanging out with the white man. He has to watch his step. Loves going up to Tottenham and Arsenal. Gets to deal with his North London rivals, or at least their brothers.

There's a few yids hanging around further down the road. Half white, half black which means they're Spurs. They're scouting and move away all stroppy like. Look back and we're together now, spilling off the pavement into the road. They turn a corner and the wanker at the back disappears sharpish, as though he's running. They're trying to play it cool, at least till they're out of sight, but we're looking for their mob and they're off to give the warning. Harris moves a bit faster now, telling some of the younger lads to hang back, take it calm, don't spoil the party. We come to the corner and the yids have disappeared, a pub further down the street on another corner the target. We turn right and spread across the road. You can feel the tension and I'm buzzing. Been looking forward to this all week. Washes away all the boredom and slaving over hot cardboard boxes.

Some of the lads start kicking at a broken wall, breaking away chunks of brick and masonry. Harris is trying to keep things together. Black Paul's handing out halfbricks. A professional who knows his trade. Makes me laugh. Rod and Mark's eyes shine. A chunk of concrete with wire sticking through the middle rests in my hand, and then we're running down the street and there's that noise that comes from somewhere deep down inside when you steam in. No words, just a roar like we're back in the fucking jungle or something, and the bricks are flying through the pub windows and I can see shapes inside already heading for the door, vital seconds lost with indecision as the scouts got back and made their report. Tight cunts should try investing in a couple of mobile phones.

My hand's in the air and I see my lump of concrete among the bricks caving in windows, the sound of glass shattering a soft noise in the din of voices, and Tottenham are breaking through the doors but we're there to meet them and Harris is leading from the front with Black Paul and a load of other blokes, pulling the first yids into the street, weight of numbers piling out of the pub so we spill everywhere, Harris copying his mate from Camberwell, nutting a big cunt between the eyes, bridge of the nose job, no copper this one, and Black Paul kicks him in the bollocks, and as he stumbles forward a few of the blokes start kicking him in the head and gut, driving him under a parked car.

Rod's laying into some bloke with a Tottenham shirt on, silly cunt, and we're shoulder to shoulder, smacking a nigger in the mouth feeling the pain in my knuckles as I don't catch him right, try to kick him in the balls, but Mark's in first and we're in a position by the door of the pub, more yids inside trying to force their way out, but we've got the strategy and I do the geezer now, he falls back against the wall, Chelsea piling in and he sinks into the pavement, feet catching him in the head and for a split second I see his eyes glaze then he's fighting to survive, panicking in the crush, but they're piling into the street now because someone's lobbed tear gas into the pub, and we back off because it makes you choke and you feel like you're going to suffocate.

There's a split in the road and we're further back, those of us near the front rubbing our eyes, all the pub windows smashed, just long shards left, a pint glass flying through the air catching Mark on the side of the head sending blood down his shirt over his jeans, and the yids are getting it sorted out, a few of the cunts dazed on the pavement, others helping them away where they can half walk, half crawl, and we get ready to steam in again, the noise cranked up, car windows kicked in as the energy has to come out some way, held back by the gas, and there's a fucking giant Irish-looking geezer with red hair and pasty white skin coming through, and he's with a nigger with a machete and nobody's going to tangle with that cunt, the only weapons bricks which batter him and then Paul's saving face taking him out and the mob piles in kicking the bastard to fuck, paying him back for their fear, head on a stick, everyone reads the papers, and I'm in there feeling the sheer joy of kicking a deserving bastard in the bollocks, head, gut, anywhere we can get the cunt, in among the wrecked cars in this broken down North London slum.

The two mobs clash again and this time it's less frantic, trouble flaring across the street, mostly punches and kicks, a couple of blades coming out, flashing in the early afternoon sunlight, sparks of silver fear which make you pull back and everyone mob together and do the offender. Martin Howe's in there, only got let out two weeks ago, did four months for smacking a bloke who cut him up at a set of traffic lights, and he's bleeding from his leg, pig stuck by Spurs, and it's slower now, picking our spot, and I'm after a mouthy cunt shouting insults and he goes for my head and misses and I do my kung-fu impression because he's small enough and split his mouth open, Mark following through trying to do his knee like a kickboxer, Rod the man in the know using his karate to bruise his throat, sending the cunt spluttering into the crowd, choking on his words.

The battle moves along the street, the pub empty, scared faces watching from behind net curtains. A shitty street with broken walls and small rundown gardens. Piles of rotting rubbish left uncollected. Rusted bike frames on the pavement. Place smells of curry and decaying big ends. There's pale kids on doorsteps shitting themselves and you have to feel a bit bad for them, because when you're young you don't need this, not with your mum and dad at each other late into the night, but they'll get it from somewhere and we've all been through that shit ourselves anyway.

There's sirens screaming in the distance and one by one we take them in, know where they're heading. The sound sends us moving back towards the main road and there's a van flashing blue murder, just one of the cunts, and a brick sails through the windscreen, back door opening and the old bill are looking for aggro. They're tooled-up and Tottenham have scattered into the back streets. I turn round and Mark's holding his head together okay, Rod next to him, and I'm with Harris and his mob, looking further up the road. There's only the one van, and the old bill are sizing the situation up even as they pick on a young lad nearby and crack his head with their truncheons, one cunt with stripes smashing his head into the side of the van, another one kicking him, splitting his lip with the truncheon, screaming abuse, voice and siren together, fucking Chelsea scum. Somehow knows we're Chelsea.

The other coppers are lashing out and trying to nick some of the younger element, but they know they've fucked up and we're mobbing together and the cunts are on for a kicking. I want to laugh and shout because this is Tottenham. A fucking shit hole and the old bill don't put cameras down poor people's streets. They're only interested in protecting City wealth and the rich cunts in Hampstead and Kensington. Fuck the scum round here. There's no cameras this distance from the ground. No fucking chance. The old bill know they haven't got the numbers and there's no videotape deterrent. The road's jammed with traffic and we can see flashing lights further down the street blocked by buses. You couldn't ask for more.

There's a few seconds of quiet and everyone knows the score. We run towards the van and the coppers are shitting themselves.

Even the sergeant leaves the kid alone. The boy murmurs to himself on the pavement. They've all got their numbers covered so there's no chance of identification and you know that any complaint you make against police brutality comes to nothing. They love football fans because they can do what they want. We're lower than niggers because there's no politician going to stand up for the rights of mainly white hooligans like us. And we don't want their help. We stand on our own feet. There's no easy place to hide. No Labour council protecting us because we're an ethnic minority stitched up by the system. No Tory minister to support our free market right to kill or be killed. The old bill are the scum of the earth. They're the shit of creation. Lower than niggers, Pakis, yids, whatever, because at least they don't hide behind a uniform. You may take the piss out of the bastards occasionally but you have some hidden respect somewhere.

But the old bill? Leave it out. We have the cunts in our sights. We pile in and the bastards don't have a chance. The sergeant takes the worst of it because he's all stripes and mouth and we've seen him batter the kid. Somehow he's worse because he's got a uniform and authority and we've been trained to respect uniforms and believe in the idea of justice. He shouts out as he sinks to the road, pulled to his feet by Black Paul, and a few of the Battersea mob take turns kicking him. His eyes are shut and bruised. Blood spews out of his nose. His head snaps back and opens up on broken glass. He's getting his reward and we're so frenzied we couldn't care less if he died.

The sirens are louder and police vans mount the pavement. We move off. Another train has arrived at Seven Sisters spilling more people onto the pavement, the vast majority of football fans who hate violence. Content to sing songs and have a few pints. We're evil bastards in their eyes and it gives us a special position. We split up and leave the battered coppers and the old bill unload their vans and block the road, a few coppers going over to check their mates, the rest piling into the crowd fresh off the train. They tug the nearest blokes and start laying into them. We look back and they've got some kids under a bus stop, kicking them black and blue, and a black woman's screaming at them to stop, that they haven't done anything wrong. A copper turns and lays her out with a single punch. Calls her a fucking slag.

The old bill are going mad and there's a couple of thousand people along the road now, and they lose it and start fighting back, defending themselves, and that's how you get a riot going. It only takes a few of you to start things off and the old bill are so fucking thick they whip everyone up. There's a helicopter above and more coppers piling down the road. They've got their shields out and try to form a barricade as Chelsea move forward, covering the area, kids and older blokes joining in. It's paradise this. A great way to spend your Saturday afternoon. There's a few bottles bouncing off shields and snatch squads running out to pick off young lads who look the business but are just caught up in the spectacle. We're ahead of the main lot now, nearing the ground, trying to suss out yids among the onlookers, but doing it from habit more than anything.

There's people in the street watching the battle. It's turned into a stand off with the crowd singing and smashing the odd car window. They've missed the nasty part and it's turning into a show. Something to put the shit up Spurs. Mark and Rod catch up and we're on our own approaching the ground. I feel great inside. The rush is there and my body tingles. Sounds funny but it's true. It's better than shafting a bird. Better than speeding. Mark's head's a mess but the bleeding has stopped. My knuckles are bruised and Rod's eyes have gone a bit mental looking. We join the crush trying to get in the ground. The crowd's already buzzing inside and we can hear the constant chant of CHELSEA. This is what life's all about. Tottenham away. Love it.

WORKER'S DREAM

SID CHECKED HIS watch and wiped the sweat from his forehead, annoyed at his aching muscles. He smelt of salt, and the close atmosphere of the lorry he was unloading made him feel as though he was working with a surgical mask over his face. Tom was by the doors stacking boxes for Steve on the forklift. It was hard work, and boring, very boring, so Sid just daydreamed the morning away, imagining he was playing centre-forward for QPR in one of the finest football teams the world had ever seen.

He was having an excellent game. It was the Cup Final at Wembley and he was on a hat-trick. His first goal had come just before half-time as he finished off a long run, which had seen him cover the length of the pitch, by rounding the Man United keeper and slotting the ball into the back of an empty net. The second was scored midway through the second half, a diving header from a pinpoint cross from the left wing, Sid ducking his head in among the flying boots in a magnificent display of sporting bravery.

Now he was considering the options on how to complete the scoring. Leaning his back against the cold metal of the lorry's wall, he hitched faded jeans over a sweltering beer gut and decided on another pitch-length sprint with a pile-driver of a shot which burst the back of the net and sent the commentators into a frenzy of familiar football clichés. The voices of Brian Moore and John Motson echoed through the living rooms of a watching nation, the praise of Alan Hansen and Gary Lineker hailing the young West Londoner as the greatest living footballer since that Argentinian hand-of-God merchant Diego Maradona. Sid was a George Best for the modern game. A worthy QPR addition to the Rodney Marsh/Stan Bowles hall of fame. He closed his eyes to stop the flood of sweat from blinding his view, watching his own celebrating run towards the royal box, where Princess Di cheered her favourite player with a look on her face which meant one thing and one thing only. Romance.

– You want a cup of coffee Sidney? Tom asked.

– No sugar or milk. I'm trying to watch my weight. I'm up to seventeen stone again.

– Right.

The Chelsea bastard pissed off to the hot drinks machine and Sid was left with the image of a beautiful princess spread out on his bed in a silk negligée, looking seductive. Her elegant fingers were covered in diamond and sapphire rings, and she wore a sparkling tiara. Sid had other things on his mind though. He was running around the room making sure there were no journalists hiding in the wardrobe, sticking their lenses through his dirty washing stacked up in a corner. Once the bedroom got the all-clear, he tried clicking back to the expectant royal awaiting his plebeian touch, but he wasn't much good with pure fantasy. There had to be a bit of reality to make the daydream work. He had too much respect for Lady Di. Anyway, he'd read somewhere that she'd had that illness girls got sometimes, where they stick their fingers down their throats and make themselves sick so that they can stay skinny. It was disgusting. All that skin and bones. They'd never catch him making himself sick just so he could lose a bit of weight.

Sid wondered if he was pushing it a bit by scoring a fourth goal in injury time, just so he could rub Man U's nose in shit. Why not? You only lived once and he'd got his second wind after completing the hat-trick. Steve was busy messing about with that last pallet they'd loaded, trying to work the forklift into the grooves, the sound of creaking wood and nails vibrating through the trailer. Sid switched back to the Cup Final, immediately setting off on an intricate dribble, a slimmed-down vision of his former self, ten years ago as a twenty-year-old, twisting and turning this way and that, nutmegging the centre-half and chipping the keeper. He ran to the QPR fans and sunk to his knees, enjoying their hysteria. Grown men spilled onto the pitch and hugged him. Sid was a hero.

– Here you go, Tom said. You look fucked. Out on a bender last night were you?

– Seven pints of London Pride and a couple of cans of Tennants when I got home. I was only planning a quick one, but it was Kevin the landlord's birthday and he had a bit of a lock-in to celebrate. You can't be rude.

– I thought you were going to lose some weight?

– I was. I am. Starting today. There's no time like the present.

Steve finally got the troublesome pallet up and moving, and soon had it stacked in the shelves. Tom dragged a new one into the trailer, as far as it would go up against the boxed pressure cookers rising above them, and they started the process again. Sid pulled boxes out and threw them to Tom, who formed precise rows. On the next pallet they would change over. It was a shit job, unloading these big efforts, but it did make the time pass if you could keep your mind busy, and Sid was having no trouble there.

He had won the pools and was signing on the dotted line. He was the biggest winner the competition had ever known, a cool forty million pounds topping up his savings account, which at the moment stood at a modest seventeen pounds and fifty-six pence. He had decided to buy up Queens Park Rangers Football Club, thereby fulfilling a childhood dream which showed no sign of fading. He would invest in new players and assume the managerial role. True, he had not played the professional game himself, though he'd had trials with Watford and Orient as a kid, but so what? He was an innovator ready to break the rules. He was rich. The rules didn't mean a thing if you were loaded.

– Slow down a bit will you Sid, Tom said, grinning. There's no rush. You're getting a bit excited up there. You're not imagining yourself in the cab with that French bird are you?

– I just won a fortune and bought Rangers, and was planning my first signing, he said, slowing down. He liked Tom.

– Hear that Steve, Tom shouted, turning towards the forklift driver. Sid's just bought your club and he's going to sign a team full of Catholics. He's signing Fenians behind your back.

– He fucking isn't.

– QPR, mate, QPR. I'm not interested in your Jock football. It's all haggis and kilts in the centre circle at Ibrox.

Sid had his say and didn't wait for a reply. He was back at Loftus Road with Rodney Marsh and Stan Bowles sitting on either side of him in the director's box. Chelsea were getting hammered 5–0 and he'd tipped the old bill off. He laughed as Tom and his nutter mates were led down the tunnel for a good spanking. He didn't approve of hardline policing, especially at football grounds, but neither did he like trouble-makers spoiling things for everyone else. He was a football fan. A programme collector. A third of the way to being a trainspotter. He was busy building a team the fans would love to watch and he had already halved admission prices. Soon he would redevelop the ground and crowds of fifty thousand would be common. The whole of White City and the surrounding area would flock to see his team of stars perform. Rodney, Stan and Sid would wave to the punters and share an after-match pint or three with Gerry Francis and Ray Wilkins.

– That new bird in the office is well nice, Tom said, watching Janet walk past on her way to the foreman's office.

She was. Very definitely. Sid couldn't disagree. But he was too busy in the director's bar to bother about fanny, sitting at a table with Rodney and Stan and Gerry and Ray. It was Gerry's round and he was on his way to the bar as Tom spoke. Rodney and Gerry had become best of mates and it was turning into a good evening. Gerry came back with five pints of the new Dave Sexton Best Bitter which Sid was having brewed on the premises. They were a bit pissed and talking about going for a sitdown curry when the bar closed. Terry Venables was coming along a bit later, when he'd got his England squad sorted out, as there'd been important matches played that evening and there was bound to be five or six players reporting themselves injured.

– Hurry up Gerry, you grey-haired tosser, Rodney shouted.

– Oh Rodney, Rodney . . . Rodney, Rodney, Rodney, Rodney, Rodney Marsh, chanted Ray, obviously unable to handle the Dave Sexton Best.

– Shut up you bald sod, Stan mumbled. You'll get us kicked out and we'll have to fuck off down the Springbok.

– Baldness is a sign of virility, I'll have you know, Ray said. Remember that next time you're doing the business. Anyway, how many caps did you win for England?

– It's you wearing them every night in the bath that's turned you into a baldy bastard, Stan laughed, secretly cursing the former midfield maestro for highlighting his own lack of international recognition, simultaneously comforting himself with the knowledge that he had just been too talented for the limited thinking of the England set-up of his day.

Sid thought about telling the lads not to worry about getting kicked out because he owned the bar, the ground, everything, but he didn't want them to think he was a bighead. He kept quiet. Gerry was downing his pint in one and Stan was smirking to himself as he watched the former England skipper, at the same time trying to open a pack of salted peanuts he'd been saving since Sid bought the first round. Good old Stan. A great player. Unique talent. Sid was in heaven. A rich man surrounded by the greatest players he'd ever seen. All of them QPR men. He wished the night would last for ever, but knew time would pass quickly and they'd have to get down the curry house fast before the Indians locked the doors in the vain hope of keeping out the drunks who treated every tandoori house like an assault course. Sid was well used to eating his prawn vindaloos surrounded by rambling men, but tonight he preferred a quiet corner where he could talk the lads through the four goals he'd scored at Wembley, then tell them how he'd felt lifting the FA Cup, and how Lady Di had slipped him her number on a piece of paper torn from her autograph book.

– I heard about you and the princess, Stan whispered when they were outside the ground, waiting for their cab to arrive. She's a fine-looking woman, though I heard she sticks her fingers down her throat and makes herself puke.

– That was years ago, Sid said, keeping his voice down, because although he respected Ray and Gerry and Rodney, he was a discreet character. There were no kiss-and-tell betrayals falling from the lips of Sid Parkinson.

– Lovely princess, Stan whispered again, nodding his head thoughtfully. I remember the day of the Royal Wedding. A fine event. A day of celebration for the entire nation.

Sid thought of their first meeting. It was in McDonalds in Shepherd's Bush, just after midday, and they'd spent the afternoon window shopping before Diana had hopped on a bus back to her own manor. She'd had two hamburgers, small fries and a large strawberry milkshake. He timed her when she went to the Ladies, but she'd been quick, too fast to make herself ill. She really was cured. He had made the decision that their relationship would remain purely platonic. He was at the peak of his football career and in the finest physical condition. He couldn't afford rampant unbridled sex sessions with a member of the aristocracy. He knew Di wanted more, but he remained firm and knew that his moral stance was understood. She was a class act.

– I've got to be honest lads, said Rodney, once inside the taxi and racing towards the White City Balti, I don't fancy the old ethnic food much. Let's go to Tel's club and have a few sherbets there.

Sid felt a bit disappointed at first, but then reasoned that Rodney had been in the States so long that he had fallen behind in his understanding of British culture. Anyway, it would prolong the meeting of five great footballing brains, and Tel was bound to turn up sooner or later. Sid leant forward and told the driver the change of destination and, with the screech of tyres and a few choice words, the car was on its way to El Tel Palace in Camden Town. They raced along the Westway at seventy miles an hour, passed Baker Street tube and then cut past Euston to Camden. Once safely inside El Tel's, the Rangers contingent pushed their way through the hordes of blonde-haired Page 3 girls crowding around them to a private table boxed in with mahogany wood panelling. A bouncer stood nearby deterring the beautiful women pestering Sid and his mates, while El Tel's favourite hardcore beats blasted from an adjacent sound system. Sid thought he recognised Mixmaster Incie playing the England manager's CD collection, but knew he must be mistaken.

– It's five past eleven, Tom shouted, obviously narked.

El Tel's vanished in a sea of cardboard boxes and Sid was sweating in the back of a forty-foot lorry. He had lost five minutes of his precious tea break and wasn't too pleased. He left Rodney and Stan and Gerry and Ray without a word and went into the warehouse, swore as he had to return for his cup of coffee, then entered the tea-room. The rest of the warehouse crew were either playing cards, reading their papers or staring through the glass partition towards the loading ramp, waiting for something to happen.

– That driver's been in his cab with that French bird the whole time we've been unloading, Tom said.

Nobody answered. A couple of card players looked towards the lorry and then returned to their hands, a stack of small coins piled in the middle of the table waiting for a winner.

– There should be a law against us working our bollocks off while he's on the job emptying his, he added.

Still nobody answered. Why torture yourself with visions of female beauty and the joys of sex when hours of mindless warehouse tedium was the best you could hope for from the rest of the day?

Sid stood up and took his sandwiches out to the ramp; round the corner and out of sight of his fellow workers. He had to graft with these men five days a week and wasn't in the mood to share his tea break with them as well. Good luck to the driver if he was getting his end away. He watched cars and people arrive and leave the car park. He saw Janet getting into her company car. She waved and he smiled. Then she was off. Heading to El Tel's midday ambient room perhaps. He shook his head sadly. What would he really do when he won the pools? He liked to think he'd make QPR a power in the land, but would he when it came to the crunch?

First off he'd buy himself a flat and move out of the dump he rented at the moment. He'd tell the landlord what he really thought of him, the arrogant bastard. He'd spread a bit of wealth around to family and friends, maybe one or two blokes in the warehouse, though he wasn't sure about that one. He'd have a holiday and go somewhere interesting. He fancied Brazil. A trip down the Amazon and the street carnival in Rio. Maybe meet Ronnie Biggs and discuss the talent crowding the Brazilian beaches. He'd invest his millions, but then what? Money for players? Wages of fifteen or twenty grand a week? He didn't think he could justify the expense. Professional footballers were overpaid as it was. Would he really want to meet Rodney and Stan and the rest of them? He'd gone to the Rodney Marsh–George Best roadshow at the Beck Theatre in Hayes, and much as he loved Rodney and those childhood memories of genius with a ball, the bloke was a bit disappointing, with his comments about British passports and the Indians in Southall. Most of the crowd laughed, but Sid thought it was all a bit naff. He expected more. Footballers were just that, footballers.

When he had his millions invested, perhaps he'd look into

doing something with the homeless. Or start up an organisation to help people with psychiatric problems. Buy up some old houses and turn them into homes for the kids who ended up on the streets of London and were forced to sell their bodies to paedophiles. If he had all those millions of pounds in his account he'd help the doctors and nurses struggling against Government cut-backs, or aid protests against vivisection and the veal industry. He'd pour funds into a non-aligned progressive programme for the prisons which would re-educate people rather than drive them to suicide and a hardening attitude to the world. There was a lot Sid could do with the cash and when he heard the foreman shouting that it was time to get back to work, that there was work needed doing, he knew he had a good line of thought which would take him right through to dinner. Then there would be the short walk to the bookies, for a fiver on Sir Rodney, running at Cheltenham. Sid was feeling lucky.

ROCHDALE AT HOME

I'M LATE MEETING the others. Had to finish off the lorry from France we started in the morning. A late delivery arrived at two which needed seeing to and then it was back to the French job. Untold pressure cookers and the driver's a flash cunt with a tasty blonde bird he takes into his cab and gives a good shafting while we're breaking our backs in the trailer. Couldn't exactly hear him doing the business, but it wasn't hard to imagine. Specially when you're knackered and just want to get away, and Glasgow Steve's going slow on the forklift because he's angry with the foreman.

It's six o'clock and there's a crowd building up on the Wimbledon-bound platform at Earl's Court. There's a fifty-fifty mixture of Chelsea going to the Rochdale cup game and smartly dressed wankers from Fulham and Parsons Green. Always makes me laugh the rich cunts who live around Stamford Bridge. They must hate us lot coming along, messing up their Saturday afternoons. The blokes act like they're lord of the manor and the birds all think they're the Queen. They look down their noses at the world, but it's a doddle staring them out. Every single time they look away, shitting themselves.

A train shows on the board and the coppers standing by the stairs check their watches. The attendance will be low tonight which translates as easy money for the old bill. A grey evening and it's been raining on and off all day. A midweek League Cup game against Rochdale isn't going to stir up much passion and I need a drink to warm my spirits. I'm on edge. It pisses me off when the warehouse interferes with Chelsea. Beggars can't be choosers, but I do my duty and want to leave on time when there's a game on. Steve can rant and rave about Glasgow Rangers, but the Scottish cunt should learn to move a bit quicker when Chelsea are at home.

The train pulls in nearly empty and it's a quick ride through West Brompton to Fulham Broadway. I flash my ticket and dump the *Standard* I've been reading since Hammersmith in a bin. There's print on my hands and I'll get rid of it in the pub. Paper says Chelsea are in the market for a goalkeeper. I wait for the lights to change and cross over. The kebab house on the corner stinks. Reminds me of Tottenham. Mark and Rod are by the door with FA Henry, a funny-looking bloke with thick glasses and FA Cup handle ears. Only comes along to the midweek games because he works on Saturdays.

– Alright Tom, lager? Mark says as I walk in and he empties his glass. Perfect timing. Henry's getting married next week, aren't you Henry? Lucky bastard.

– Congratulations Henry. I mean it too. He deserves a bird in a white dress even though it's all a big con. He's a romantic bloke. Wouldn't hurt a fly. We've known him since we were kids.

– Who you marrying?

– Lisa Wellington. Henry's chest puffs up with what I imagine is pride. You remember her from when we were at school, don't you?

– Course I do. Thought she moved away. Ireland or Scotland. Something like that. Somewhere with their own language and drinking laws.

– She did. Married an Irish bloke, but it didn't work out. Gave it a couple of years then packed her bags and came back here. My old girl knows her old girl. That's how we met up. By accident really, or maybe it was fate. One of the two.

I remember Lisa when we were teenagers. She was a good-looking girl and I wonder what she's like now. Black hair and Slav features. Her old girl was from Bucharest and came over in the war. Hated communists if I remember right. There again, who doesn't? But the woman was always on about them whenever I saw her. Fucking hated yids as well. Them and the gypos. Well over the top on the subject. Lisa was all right, even if she was a bit laid-back and into hippy drugs when everyone else was speeding. Makes sense her marrying FA Henry. He's a sound bloke and has never done too well with the birds. As well as the FA Cup ears he's Fuck All Henry. Women like him well enough, but most of them are looking for a quick length, not Henry's thoughts on creation.

– Where you having the stag night then, Henry? Let us know and we'll come along. Give you a good send off before you disappear into the twilight world of sweat and tears and supermarket trolleys.

– I'm not having one, he says, looking a bit nervous. I'm not bothering with all that. I've never been into those sort of things. Rod's was enough for me.

Rod has the decency to blush, and he should as well, the dirty cunt. Speeding through space like the Starship Enterprise at the time, hitting warp factor 700. A hall off the Fulham Palace Road and there was this stripper on stage. Dirty-looking tart with a fit body and I don't know what the fuck she was stripping for because she could have done better for herself. Real cracker. She got Rod up there on stage with her and he was out of his tree. Let her strip him stark bollock naked, spread him out on a table and shag his brains out. Mark had a camcorder and Rod was shitting it long after the wedding came and went. It was surprising he managed to get it up he'd drunk so much, but he says it was the drugs.

– It was enough for Rod too, wasn't it mate, and I slap him on the back and he's looking a bit uneasy. Sometimes you do things under the influence you just don't want to admit.

– Don't remind me. I remember it well enough but it was like someone else on that table. Like I was in the operating theatre getting my balls stretched or something. That bird was leaning over telling me she'd had five Taffies on stage in Cardiff the week before. Five of the bastards for a hundred quid. Talk about bulk buying. Told me I had to compete with five Cardiff City leaks. That she was full of Welsh spunk and wanted to see what a cockney could do. It got me going at the time, but looking back I must've been mad to dip my winkie in that old slapper.

– I don't want that kind of thing happening to me. Henry's face is bright red, his ears a very dark purple. Looks like he's about to explode. Suspect device primed to go off with a two-minute warning.

– You're right Henry. That's what tradition does for you. But what about Lisa? Hen nights are worse than that. Birds get together and they go fucking mental.

– Lisa's not interested either. She's not that sort of girl.

Don't believe it mate, but you can't blame Henry, knowing how he runs his life. Rod let his standards slip and it wasn't a pleasant sight watching one of your mates on the job. I felt sorry for Mandy more than anything. Mind you, she was probably up to no good on her night as well, so there you go. It all evens itself out in the end. You can't trust anyone. Certainly not women. They're at it like fucking rabbits then act all coy when you swear in front of them or turn up with a black eye. It's a load of shit, but you'd be a miserable cunt if you didn't hold out hope for people like Henry. Let him have his dreams and believe in love and romance. Suppose we all do deep down if we thought about being honest.

– Here you go Tom. Get that down your throat and give us a smile you sad cunt.

Mark hands me a pint. I smell the familiar football mix of plastic and lager. The bubbles feel good down my throat even though it's cold outside. It's a depressing evening and the place is dead. Couldn't be more different than Tottenham. Days like that don't come along very often. Still, you have to make the effort. Just like the Rochdale fan walking into the pub. Must be well into his fifties and wears a scarf round his neck. A few of the lads look his way but he's an old geezer and harmless. Why fuck about with civilians? You just make yourself look a cunt if you start having a go at old men and kids. Leave that to the yids and scousers. They go back to their drinks and conversation. The Rochdale man buys a pint and stands nearby. I wonder if he's carrying a wooden rattle. Probably an engine driver or machine minder. Looks like something out of the Fifties. Thick hands and steel under the nails. Northerners are all the same. Dopey cunts the lot of them. I tell him he'll get a decent pint now he's in London.

– Not bloody likely son. He appreciates the humour.

Northerners are always moaning about the beer in London. They reckon it's piss. Expensive piss. The cunts up north don't believe it's a proper pint unless it's got an inch of froth on top. Can't handle that kind of head myself. They're right about the prices though. It's a scandal what they charge for drink down here. We're getting shafted left, right and centre, but there's nothing you can do. You just have to get on with it, otherwise you'll end up doing fuck all because you're looking at the price tag the whole time. It's not fair, any of it, but that's life. You work hard and the more you earn the more worthless cunts are after you for a slice of your wage packet. Mouthy wankers in suits acting big, but when it comes down to it they're bottle merchants to a man. Get rid of their suits and give them the options and they'd disappear up their own over-mortgaged arseholes.

– We've got a good team coming through, lads. We might beat you tonight. How do you fancy a trip to Rochdale if we get a draw? Chelsea won't like a replay.

– I'd rather we had an away game against you lot than play at home, says Rod. Gives us a chance to get out and about. It's more of a laugh. Small town like Rochdale would suit Chelsea fine.

– Same here. I like going away. I'd go watch England, but it's all young hooligans who go overseas and spoil things for the rest of us.

– You shouldn't believe what you read in the papers. Those blokes writing the stories know fuck all. They're too busy getting pissed to leave their hotel bars and discover the truth. Too scared. If you don't want to get involved, you don't have to.

– True enough, but you can't trust the Frogs or dagos, or whoever else you're playing. You pay for the sins of others.

My glass is empty. The others have hardly started. I go to the bar and get a refill, remember I need to wash my hands and go to the bogs. The water's freezing but I get rid of the shit. There's no towels but at least the print has been washed off. I've never seen a decent pub toilet. It's all shit, piss and graffiti. Not surprising really. The bowls have flooded so I stand in the cubicle and undo my buttons. My bladder burns as I piss and splash the plastic seat. Fuck it up for the next cunt. There's a bog brush with white bristles. It's got *Ken Bates* written in felt pen along the handle, a face drawn at the end. I button up and go back to the bar. The Rochdale fan's already pissed off to the ground. Should have stayed for another drink. I was even planning to buy the old sod one. There's not exactly going to be a crush getting in.

– Tom was on the pull Saturday night after Tottenham, weren't you mate? Rod's filling Henry in on the details. Aims to get his story in and whitewash the memory of his stag night. He can do what he wants. It was him on that stage performing for the lads, not me.

– We had a skinful in the Unity and went to this party in Hounslow. The three of us got a taxi down with this nigger playing jungle shit all the way. Tom was hanging out the window puking down the side of the car, but he couldn't say anything otherwise he'd have been on for a kicking.

– I don't remember Tom doing that, Mark says, trying to picture our journey down the Great West Road. Remember that fucking jungle nonsense though.

I can see bits as Rod tells the story. It's those few pints over the top, when you steam into the shorts like there's no tomorrow morning and next thing you're fucked for the duration. I was leaning out the window watching the road thinking we must be near Griffin Park and my guts were churning. Didn't need to hold back because my head was outside picking up the sweet smell of Brentford. Splattered the back wing. All the time there's some tape playing and it was making me think of Nelson Mandela with a spliff wedged in his mouth, for some strange reason, and of how the last thing I wanted now was my lungs full of poison and the brain mixed up. But once you clear your guts you're okay and ready to live again. The bloke driving wasn't too impressed but so what? It's all part of the service. What does he expect?

– We get to this party and there's this geezer on the door telling us we can't come in without bringing some drink, but we're not bothered with the small print and Tom's lining up to take the cunt out. He's too far gone to do the job properly and it's all getting a bit iffy. It's about to go off with the bloke on the door and a load of his mates when the bird having the party turns up and we're in without hassle.

There was fuck all drink around but I got hold of a couple of cans from somewhere and at least there was a bit of talent knocking about. Makes a change. Some places you end up it's full of pissed-up wide-boys, which is okay because you can wind someone up and give him a hiding, but it's not the same if you've been steaming yids all day. It works both ways. Either pull a tart and fuck the arse off her or fuck up some arrogant pisshead with a kick in the bollocks. The easier option is to get hold of an old slapper and give her a seeing to, specially after a good day out like Tottenham. Get in a ruck in a house when you're pissed and chances are you'll be on someone else's manor where the numbers are too heavy, or some bird'll phone the old bill. Try doing a runner at two in the morning when you're pissed. It's a big mistake. Like we tried it once at this house in Acton. Rod nutted some bloke who was getting lippy and the whole place went up. We got a bit of a hiding and next thing there was the old bill kicking the door in and everyone scattering out back. We did a runner over the fence and down an alley. Nicked a vintage Rover and I'm driving to Hammersmith whizzing trying to keep my thoughts together. Mark was chewing a lump of dope mixed up with gum. Laughing like a psycho in the back seat. It was bad news all round.

Nick a motor when you're fifteen or thereabouts and go joyriding, fair enough, no-one's going to think bad of you, but when you're working you need to show a bit of class. Nobody wants to get done for thieving a car for a two-mile trip down the road. If you're going to get nicked then get nicked for something major. Best off, don't get done at all. I mean, we've all got previous, but not for petty theft, at least not since we left school. You have to move up the rankings. It's all about respect.

– We're standing round listening to this fucking greatest hits shit, says Rod, going back to the party, and Mark's giving this tall cunt the eye looking to start a bit of trouble and we're telling him to leave it out because there's loads of skirt walking around waiting for three Chelsea boys to give them a good servicing.

– Fucking was as well, says Mark, waking up. All a bit young, but if they're old enough to bleed then they're old enough to shag.

– Tom pulls straight off, says Rod, and this bird's into him like nobody's business. Wasn't bad after a skinful and she's pissed or stoned or both, fuck knows, and she's giving him the come on so obvious even we could see it clear enough in the dark with this fucking android music breaking the eardrums.

– They're only talking a few minutes and they're off. Cunt doesn't even stop to say goodnight.

This bird comes up all confident and asks am I the romantic type? I nod my head and say nothing. Never commit yourself. Never give a statement. Deny everything unless it's going to serve the greater good. She looks alright and I can see the curve of her tits through a tight T-shirt she shouldn't be wearing if she wants to keep them to herself. Purple with patterns and snug enough to show off her nipples. She's made up like a fucking doll and her hair's dyed a mix of red and brown, but she'll do, can't complain. Her body's well put together and she's in jeans, baggy round the waist showing the shape of her arse. Probably bought them a couple of sizes too big to make her look thinner. Says I look like a romantic and her breath stinks of fags and gin. I agree, remembering the romance of turning Tottenham over and seeing those coppers get a kicking. That's pure romance, natural justice. Next thing we're outside walking down the road. She shares a place with four other birds and it's one of those big West London houses, rundown with bay windows to let in the light, overgrown front garden and peeling paint on the front door.

There's the sound of the telly in the front room and we have to walk quickly but quietly up the stairs. Her mate's watching a video and is expecting in a couple of months. The bloke's done a bunk. Gone to sea or prison. Can't remember the specifics. The sound the video's making it's one of those love stories women like watching. A girl with a fat belly and box of chocolates wishing life was like it is in the videos. Not abortions and stitch-ups. We get up to this bird's bedroom and she turns on a lamp by her bed. The place is a mess and the bed's unmade. Pisses me off a bit, but if that's how she wants to live it's up to her. Can't stand dirt and mess myself.

I go for a piss because if there's one thing worse than going home with your balls loaded it's trying to shaft a bird when you need a slash. The bathroom's a state with bras and pants hanging everywhere, a year's supply of tampons in with a couple of hundred toothbrushes and almost as many empty containers. I go back into the bedroom and this bird's only lying on the bed asleep. Didn't take her long to forget what she was supposed to be doing. Right dead loss. I think about waking her up, but I'm knackered myself so just pull a blanket off the floor and go to sleep in a chair. The bed's too small for two people unless one's on top of the other and Tottenham has made me tired. A good day all in all and next morning I take a look at the woman and she seems like the sort who'll want to talk and I'm not in the mood for idle chatter.

I call a taxi and let myself out. It's early, the streets are empty and

I'm freezing. I feel dirty and my neck's stiff like I've been strung up for murder. The cab arrives and I'm on my way home listening to some chirpy cunt on the radio telling me what a fucking great life it is and how we should appreciate the time we've got before God calls us back up to heaven. Cunt must be doing some serious drugs. What does he know?

– Tom disappears and we don't see him till Sunday night and he looks shagged, says Rod. Which he obviously has been. He only goes through her handbag and nicks twenty quid. Says she was so pissed she'd think she spent it, that he needed to get home and was skint. But he's just a fucking tea leaf on the quiet.

Rod and Mark like winding me up. Henry looks on a bit disgusted. Fucking idiot. This isn't Alice tripping through Wonderland. There's no magic bus back to Hammersmith at eight on a Sunday morning. It's a long hike from Hounslow and I'm not in the mood. The bird looks like she's got a bit of money so she won't miss twenty pounds. Spent enough on the fucking make-up. Henry wants to grow up sometimes. What's he going to do in a couple of years' time when he finds his wife's been shafting the plumber, dustman, local fire brigade? You have to be careful. Look after yourself. Fuck them before they fuck you.

Henry drinks up and he's off. I ask him what's the hurry. Have another drink. But he wants to get down the ground. Rod goes to the bar. I tell Mark he doesn't like being reminded of his stag night. Mark agrees. We should wind the cunt up a bit more. The image sticks in the head. Spread out on a slab and this old tart on top, tits hanging into Rod's mouth. She was tasty all right, but rough as fuck. Mark says he gave Rod the videotape in the end it was causing the bloke so much grief. Mandy would have done her nut if she'd found out. Of course, Mark would never have shown her, but Rod was worried and you can't really blame him.

I can just imagine the wedding reception. Mark's had photos made and they get passed round with everyone pissed and Rod's old man making his speech about his son turning out okay in the end. Has another drink and says he had some difficult times when his son was a teenager growing up, but that's understandable because he's a young lad getting to grips with the world, sowing his oats, no offence Mandy, moving into manhood, all the usual bollocks. The blushing bride who Rod met pissed one night and when they went home together he couldn't get it up. Probably made them, that lack of a hard-on. Something special as the films say. Pulling a bird and not shafting her right off.

The old man's giving it the big one about the reformed young hooligan with a good job as an electrician, making a bit of cash, buying his own flat, still into his football. Rod the good son taking out yids and shooting his load over Indian wildlife. Rod the honest lover stripped off ridden half to death by a whore with a cunt full of Cardiff City fans, Chelsea tattoo coming out well in the video, face dazed and distorted in artificial light. Everyone wants to have something to look back on. That period of being a bit rebellious then growing out of it and turning into a nice boring citizen. Fuck that for a game of soldiers. Talk to people like that and they've done nothing. They just like to think they have. Blokes and birds. They're all the same. Wankers the lot of them.

– You know, Rod, I've probably got a copy of that tape knocking about somewhere. I'll have to give it to you. Mark starts winding him up.

– You gave me everything you had. Rod holds his pint still, stuck on its way to his mouth. That's what you said. I got rid of it straight off. Obscene propaganda. You're a fucking pervert taking those shots. You're not an iron by any chance? Keeping it quiet because you know you'd wind up on the end of a serious kicking rather than some queer's joystick.

– I didn't give you the copy, just forgot about it, but it's got to be somewhere. I'll dig it out and pass it on.

– You sure? Rod looks worried. Then starts laughing. You're winding me up. I know you are. Why would you make a copy? It wasn't exactly a pro job. The picture was out of focus half the time. It's not like you're going to make a packet selling it to Marshall.

– Just forgot about it, that's all. Mark's voice has an edge. If you don't want the tape I won't bother.

– I was pissed and did the business when I shouldn't have. So what? Rod tries the big bluff but he's looking bad. Poor cunt. Why crucify the bloke for making a prick of himself?

So he shagged a whore on stage in front of his mates. He was out of it and everyone makes mistakes. Better than going out and raping someone. Or watching squaddies doing it on video for you. We've all followed the urge and serviced things that didn't need servicing. Why have regrets? There's no place for sentiment, though Rod's only bothered because he's worried about Mandy somehow getting a glimpse. Who cares. None of us are into being a spectator. Leave that to the pundits on telly. All those noddy gameshows. The cameras looking for a bit of football violence, getting off on the lads steaming in. But it's a con. If you want something like that go out and get it yourself. Don't sit at home flicking channels expecting someone to live your life for you. We may be cunts but we're not hiding the fact. Unlike the docile majority. So silent you can hear their thoughts quivering with outrage. I tell Rod we're joking and he says he knew it all the time. We start laughing. There's twenty minutes till kick-off but bollocks, we'll have another quick pint. It's cold outside. We need the warmth.

Shame it's not someone like West Ham tonight. It would be good to have a bit of a punch-up. We don't have to justify ourselves to anyone. Like those wankers running the army or killing grannies because they won't give them enough money to pay their heating bills. Kicking fuck out of someone is excitement. It gives you a buzz. You can dress violence up anyway you like but it's still there. Why play games and try to justify your actions? All these plonkers with their politics and moral outrage are kidding themselves. The kick is seeing your first ruck, a mob of Cardiff chased down Fulham Broadway and battered by Chelsea when I was a kid. Pure and simple. No explanations. I ask Rod if he remembers Chelsea running Cardiff that time. He does. Says it was justice. Paid those five Taffs back years before the event. That he was looking ahead even in those days.

HOOLIGANS

POWERFUL WINDS BATTERED the multi-million pound structure, yet for the assorted players, officials, sponsors and media personnel cocooned inside the East Stand it could just as easily have been a warm summer's evening. The last spectators had left the stadium, driving rain forcing hunched shoulders deep inside coats, the visiting contingent facing a tiring trip north, clothes soaked and a heavy defeat for cold comfort. The glow of floodlights had vanished, brilliant illumination replaced by deep shadow. Stamford Bridge stood out against the rolling clouds, light from a near-full moon catching the angles of the towering main stand.

In a corner of the bar, Will Dobson was educating Jennifer Simpson, a rather attractive young hopeful, in the wicked ways of the press. Will was a good teacher who knew the football world inside out, all the gossip and a few of the facts, filling his belly with bottled bitter and a steady stream of double vodkas. It was humid and sweat stained his white shirt, every now and then his eyes straining for a peak at Jennifer's slender legs.

– It wasn't how I thought it was going to be, Jennifer said, learning the lesson and downing half a glass of white wine in a single gulp. There wasn't much of a crowd and those who came were pretty quiet. The game was very boring as well, don't you think? Where were the hooligans we read so much about?

– In here, Will laughed, tapping his temple. A figment of the imagination. An editor's wet dream. Sadly our hooligan friends are a thing of the past.

Jennifer let her eyes wander to the bar, allowing Will an escape route from any embarrassment he might feel at the sexual reference, watching casually-dressed young sportsmen rub shoulders with older, heavier men in suits. Will didn't seem bothered about such niceties though. He probably thought a new man was a type of service robot, and in a way he would have been right. Jennifer congratulated herself on the humour, and determined to use it some time in the near future.

The bar blended athleticism and new money, its own small world lost in the enormous concrete structure, an almost unique aura of big pay cheques and wholesome job satisfaction. Jennifer was aware of Dobson's occasional glances under the table but not averse to letting the old boy get a glimpse of her legs. She knew she was good looking and didn't believe in false modesty. He wasn't a bad sort and it did no harm. If she was going to make a career for herself in journalism she would need all the help she could get. Connections were vital in every walk of life, probably more so in this particular line, and even the likes of Dobson might prove useful in the future. She wondered what he had meant by a figment of the imagination.

– The hooligans faded away after Heysel, Dobson confided, lowering his voice because the subject was a taboo which turned off the sponsors. Before that they were a bloody nuisance, but they shifted papers and journalism's all about circulation figures. My theory is they either got into drugs like ecstasy which destroyed their violent tendencies and/or organised crime, or got married and settled down, and the kids today can't afford to go very often which means there's no new blood coming through to fill their shoes, Dr Martens if you like, so the hooligan drifted towards extinction, just like the dinosaur. The police became experts in the field of crowd control and introduced video cameras and the yobs decided enough was enough. A few tough sentences and they handed in their Stanley knives and started new lives. There's a pitch invasion now and then, but that's just a handful of idiots pissing in the wind, if you'll excuse my French. Football violence is dead and buried. Society is much better balanced these days. The Tories have eradicated the class system. The angry young men of yesteryear are either sitting in bed smoking cannabis or wandering around their local homestore trying to decide what shade of paint to buy for the baby's room.

– What about the trouble at that England game? Jennifer asked, remembering the televised pictures and endlessly reproduced face of a frightened child, the wide eyes sticking in her mind, the media's innocent-victim line of emphasis working a treat. There always seems to be a riot of some kind when the national side plays overseas.

– I'm not saying there aren't one or two bad boys around, but they know to behave themselves, more's the pity. I had my best bylines during the hooligan era. All you needed was a half-decent photo and it didn't matter what you wrote. There was a lot of glory to be had back then. You couldn't fail. But that's progress I suppose. Then there was the Taylor Report and the clubs aren't stupid you know, they've increased their prices and blocked out a lot of people, priced the hooligans out of the game. When they go to Europe the policing's not up to scratch so the thugs see their chance and go on the rampage.

– Well, if they do that, then they must come from somewhere, surely?

Will had given up looking at the girl's legs and was concentrating on the alcohol situation. That was the trouble with these bloody women, they never got their round in because they were always too busy asking pointless questions. Things changed and he was the first to welcome progress, sound investment and all that, and a lot of people were getting mega-rich from the beautiful game now it was adopting sensible business practices. His own match-day experience was vastly improved, but women should remember to move with the times as well and get the fucking drinks in. He liked Jennifer's legs but wasn't sure about the rest of her, the knowledge that she was studying at university a major turn-off. They thought they knew everything, these further-education people, and he wasn't conned by her mild manner. She was an arrogant bitch if ever he'd seen one. He had only brought her along as a favour to the editor, who was a lifelong mate of her father, a bigshot in the armaments industry with serious political clout. Then he remembered he was drinking at the paper's expense so didn't need to worry about enforcing equal rights, but he was too late.

– Would you like another drink, Jennifer asked, standing and walking through the crowd to the bar once the experienced pro had delivered his order.

Will was feeling tired, what with filing his report, walking to the bar and drinking his fill. Chelsea were on his patch and the old hooligan-heavy days really were a thing of the past. It *was* a shame as well, because apart from the opportunity to file some fine moral outrage and amuse the sub-editors, a punch-up was an exciting distraction from the dire games he'd been forced to watch through the years. As much as he loved football, and he honestly did, he wouldn't have paid to see more than five or six matches a season, and with so much football on television now he would probably just stay at home. The atmosphere wasn't like it used to be, whatever the vested interests said, and if the major clubs kept alienating ordinary fans and trying to attract a so-called upmarket clientele, they would eventually go bust. There was no loyalty in money. Even Will Dobson realised that much. But football was his livelihood and he had done very well for an ordinary lad from Swindon. He couldn't complain. He preferred to go with the flow.

– How many games do you watch during an average season, Jennifer asked, carefully placing Will's order on the table, not waiting for a reply. Did you go to the Tottenham match at the weekend? Everyone seems to be talking about it at the bar.

Will's eyes widened. The Spurs-Chelsea fixture of the previous Saturday had shown the sport at its very best, a great advertisement for the modern game. There had been plenty of goals and goal-mouth action and the crowd had roared its appreciation. In the old days that particular London derby meant trouble, but now the spectators were as well-behaved as a party of boisterous school children. True, there had been a few anti-semitic songs which the club was trying to stamp out, and the usual gestures, but nothing particularly violent.

– Mind if I join you, David Morgan asked, arriving on the scene and taking a chair between Jennifer and Will. Bloody terrible match wasn't it? They should refund our money.

– But we don't pay, Will laughed.

Morgan worked for a rival paper and was a full-time shit-stirrer. He had been widely accepted as having his finger firmly on the pulse in the mid-Eighties. While he'd never pushed himself more than his contemporaries, he always seemed to be in the know. Will suspected that this was because he was a little more liberal with the truth than the others, which in turn reflected the attitude of the title paying his wages. A readiness to shell out hard cash for dramatic pictures of supposed hooligans was legendary. He had his story and the subjects of the photos were generally well pleased with the extra cash and fleeting fame. The lads had welcomed the attention at first, treating the hacks as an amusing sideshow, pissed old geezers chasing ghosts, always a mile or two behind the action. Professional football journalism was a small circle and they were doing very nicely thank you. If people on the outside took some of their stories a little too seriously, then whose fault was that? Will raised his glass for a toast, eyes bleary from the blend of beer and spirit.

– Here's to the next round.

They drank up and Jennifer felt part of the gang. She had accepted the chance to get involved with the sports desk even though her eventual aim was to write celebrity features for a better-class newspaper. It was all worthwhile experience and would stand her in good stead when it came time to send off job applications. Looking around, she had to admit that they were a bit oikish, the lot of them, and the hooligans had rather let her down, but at least she would be able to tell her friends that she'd been to a football match. She could always lay it on a bit. She thought of her part-time boyfriend Anthony, assistant editor on a trendy style magazine which was forever pushing imagined left-wing credentials. Jennifer was always taking the mickey out of poor Anthony, asking him what expensive clothes, consumer pop and an obsessive interest in bisexuals had to do with socialist politics.

Jennifer smiled as she remembered Anthony's warning that same afternoon, delivered via his company mobile from a champagne-lunch CD launch party in Soho. He really cared for her and had insisted that the Chelsea crowd revelled in indiscriminate violence. He firmly believed Stamford Bridge was a breeding ground for white supremacists, where black players had been hounded off the pitch and black spectators went in fear of their lives. She should watch herself. Chelsea fans were brain dead and even capable of gang rape on terraces which no longer existed, rambling on about the notorious Shed and those metal kung-fu stars which would blind her for life, a backing soundtrack of synthesised music filtering its way down the phone line.

Anthony was drunk and had tried to talk her out of attending the match, but Jennifer had been determined. It was a shame he had been so mistaken, though she would lead him on all the same.

She had a vindictive streak and enjoyed his discomfort. He was rather childish sometimes, possessive and even hinting at love, yet was little more than a convenient London stopover. He came from money and was well-meaning, but lacked the calculation Jennifer found so attractive in a man. She was meeting him after the game, although her thoughts were with Jeremy Hetherington, who she had recently met at university. She was visiting his parents' manor house in Oxfordshire the following Saturday and was looking forward to following their initial drunken coupling with something a bit more satisfying. They would make the most of the countryside during the day, then attend the local hunt ball in the evening. It would be an experience.

– How did you find the game? Morgan asked. Will says it's your first time inside a football ground.

– It was interesting.

– You should have taken her last week against Spurs, Morgan said, turning to Will. Now that was football at its best. Passing and movement from two teams dedicated to the art. But you know, those bloody little North London sods only scratched the side of my Volvo. I managed to squeeze a line into the end of my report concerning the state of today's youth, but those moronic subs chopped it out. The politics of envy I'm afraid to say are alive and fermenting. It might not have been football fans of course, just the local population moaning about its lot, but it's going to cost a bit to get fixed. I'm taking the car to the garage tomorrow for an estimate. The paper will pay the bill but it makes me angry when the havenots take their petty frustrations out on me. It's a bloody nuisance more than anything else. I'm a busy man.

They had another round of drinks and Morgan took over in his usual way, bending Jennifer's ear with the story of a politician who had been discovered in Brompton cemetery with a thirteen-year-old rent boy, a young lad from Burnley whose homelessness was a direct consequence of Government cutbacks. Apparently they'd been caught at it in one of the crypts, a family vault with ripped coffins stacked on shelves along the walls. It was an excellent story, and Morgan had toyed with the idea of somehow introducing vampirism and Aids, but due to political considerations the papers were hushing up the affair, and even if there had been a decent left-wing paper it would have ignored the story, dealing as it did with homosexuality and the individual's right to privacy. If they could just get hold of something similar on a high-ranking Opposition figure they'd be away.

As Morgan talked, Will started drifting. He vaguely heard his colleague listing the buzz-words and phrases which made for a good hooligan article – 'scum', 'mindless yobs', 'thugs', 'ashamed to be English', 'not true fans', 'bring back the birch', 'give them a good thrashing' and 'now is the time for the courts to hand down tough custodial sentences'.

– Just shuffle that lot around and you're there, Morgan laughed, subtly checking the girl's legs under the table, marvelling at the texture of her skin and deciding the stockings she was wearing went right up the crack of her arse.

– First comes the titillation and gory details, then the condemnation which masks the pleasure the reader's had from the story. Call for the return of the cat o'nine tails and demand some good old fashioned square-bashing and everyone's happy. It makes the public feel secure.

He had little call for such specific vocabulary now, with the death of the hooligan and his own shift to more meaty subject matter – the general moral decay afflicting society, spongers living off the taxpayer and any kind of violent sex or sexual violence involving the rich, famous and/or politically unsound. Homosexuality within the clergy was another favourite. It was an interesting job and if Jennifer ever fancied discussing her future career she should give him a call and perhaps they could meet for lunch. He had seen everything during his time as a roving reporter and could share some interesting stories which had never made it into print. There was an excellent Italian restaurant he frequented in Knightsbridge. It would be his treat. He handed her his card.

– Perhaps I'll take you up on that, she replied, smiling, and adjusted her legs so David had a better view of her upper thighs, filing the old lech's face in her memory and his card in her purse. He would certainly be more useful than Dobson who was an old duffer in comparison.

When Morgan offered him a lift home, Will gladly accepted. Jennifer was meeting Anthony in a restaurant on the Kings Road and David was more than willing to drop her off on the way. They drank up and left the bar, surprised by the ferocity of the wind when they got outside. Jennifer sat in the back seat as the two journalists talked about mutual friends, a Frank Sinatra CD playing in the background. They pulled away from the stadium and Jennifer checked the streets for life. A couple of nearby pubs were doing good business with groups of men staying on till closing time, features distorted through the windows. The streets were windswept and empty. It was a pity. A gang of hooligans on the rampage and a quick exit in a fast car would have made up for a wasted ninety minutes watching the football.

– There it is, she said, spotting Bo-Bo's halfway down the Kings Road, purple neon lights above the door, flickering white candles inside. Just drop me off anywhere. Thanks for the ride and I'll see you tomorrow Will. Thanks for taking me. Nice to have met you David. It was fun.

– Phone me about lunch, won't you?

– I will. See you soon.

Jennifer waved at the Volvo as it drove away and looked for the scratch but saw nothing, then she pushed herself forward through the gale, opening the door to the restaurant. She was greeted by a burst of warm air, cigarette smoke and excessively loud laughter. She immediately felt at home, the clientele class-conscious and suitably confident. Looking around for Anthony, she flushed when she thought of those toads sneaking glances at her legs. Then she was angry at the boring game she had witnessed, the loss of a good evening, and not a thug in sight. At least she was on familiar ground in Bo-Bo's and could act normally again. The common people really were common as muck. You could give them money, but couldn't fake breeding.

WEST HAM AT HOME

THE PUB'S MAKING a racket and the old bill have pulled a van up outside. Everyone's trying to get a view through the window and there's a lot of movement in the street. Mark reckons they're bringing a train straight through from East London. Don't know how he knows this, but that's how football works. It's all rumour and speculation which fast becomes fact. The two blend together and in the end it doesn't really matter where they meet. It's logical enough though. We've already been down Victoria looking for them and come back with nothing. You never know with West Ham. They could turn up anywhere at any time and Victoria is a good place to meet up and sort things out. There again, they want to get into our streets and take the piss so why waste time messing about in the West End?

The tension's been building since early this morning. Mark banging on the door at nine telling me to get up. That I'm a lazy cunt. A cup of tea and some toast and I don't feel too bad after eight pints in the pub last night. He looks happy enough. Got his end away with some spaced-out blonde kid who couldn't have been much over the legal limit. Looked like she knew the score well enough and Mark confirms this as I get myself a second cup. Thin legs and small tits but was on all fours in the hall with her mum and dad asleep upstairs. Says she had a cunt so tight he thought he'd got the wrong hole. Had to take a look to make sure, though she wasn't complaining so doesn't know why he bothered.

We walk down the station and Rod's already there getting impatient. We catch a train to Victoria and there's a mob hanging around looking for West Ham, taking the tube to Tower Hill, then back along the District Line. Harris doesn't know where West Ham will turn up and we start getting worried in case they've gone straight down the ground. They could be turning the place over while we're stuck on the tube. We decide to go back to the ground and stop off in Earl's Court. There's fuck all going on there, so we head for Fulham Broadway where we've got a view of the tube and are guaranteed to find them in the end. We're on edge the whole time because West Ham's no joyride. Not like having a go at Arsenal or Tottenham.

Now we're out of circulation. There's dogs barking in the street and the hollow echo of horse's hooves on concrete. Traffic is diverted away from the run between Fulham Broadway and Stamford Bridge. There's a pub full of needle bottled up and confined by coppers ready to steam in at the slightest provocation. There's fuzzy police radio messages and a flashing light, Harris talking into his cellphone, scouts out and about, then we hear the West Ham anthem Bubbles coming up from the tube into the street and we're pushing towards the door, but the old bill know what they're about and they're laughing, pretending they're in control, and they are in a manner of speaking because they've got us locked up safe and sound.

I can see the scene through the window as West Ham pile out and the old bill have them contained well enough, but the Hammers breed lary cunts and the main faces are at the front, older blokes and nutters from Bethnal Green and Mile End, fucking headcases the lot of them, and they've no respect for coppers, taking the piss, trying to push past the British bobby looking towards the pub. There's psychos in leather jackets and a kid in dungarees and flat cap. The ICF and Under Fives mean more around Upton Park than Ron and Reggie Kray. History stays around for years. But who cares about names.

West Ham are forced towards the ground and they're letting everyone know they've arrived. The pub's singing as well but we feel like a bunch of wankers locked up out of contention. West Ham keep coming out of the station trying to turn right, forced left, and they've come down from the East End mob-handed, strolling along taking their time, but Stamford Bridge is one of the safest grounds in the country these days and the old bill have got everything tied up. Those cameras on rooftops record the scene but most of the faces are well known. These blokes are professionals. Not your average snotty-nosed hooligan. There's vans across the street, flashing lights through glass, horses helping the crowd along, shitting everywhere, the familiar mix of horse shit and hamburgers.

A few harder cases try to push their way back down the road towards the pub. The dogs go mental straining at their leads keeping things civilised, walking on two legs. Two legs good, four legs bad. Like they teach you in school. Lights flash and more horses come along the street. All those coppers think they're the business. They're keeping the lid on things and West Ham are moving reluctantly towards the ground.

Harris is near the door and we're getting wound up locked away, freedom of expression denied for the duration, but know it's the wrong location. Talk about civil liberties. West Ham are walking our streets, controlled it's true, but we're at home and it's up to us to do the business. If they can walk in here then it's half a result. Turn us over and we'll never hear the last of it. East against West and it goes back decades. Something you grow up with. It's all about territory and pride and having a laugh. They're fast disappearing down the street and the police will shepherd them into the away section, unless some of the cunts have tickets for the West Stand and are looking to have a go inside the ground. But it's unlikely. What's the point?

When West Ham are out of harm's way the old bill pile into the pub and empty the place. They're in a stroppy mood and line up outside the door. Think they're a firing squad except they've got no guns. One day that will change though and they'll walk more cocky than ever. A fat bastard punches me in the gut as I go past and I stare straight into his face asking him what the fuck he's doing, let's see your number, then he's telling his mate to put me in the van and nick me, but I get lost in the crush leaving the pub and they're thick cunts with the attention span of a goldfish and are already into someone else. Mark gets a knee in the bollocks from a copper which doesn't connect properly and I hate the bastards worse than West Ham and Tottenham combined.

Fucking scum the lot of them hiding behind uniforms, licking the paymaster's arse. A van escorts us towards the ground and when we get to the West Stand we're trying to bluff our way further down the street but only half heartedly because there's video cameras burning on overtime and West Ham are probably inside by now anyway. I'm well narked and have to remember Tottenham and the old bill getting a pasting just to calm things down and look on the bright side. I try and see it as a bit of justice but it doesn't work. We've all seen enough of them in action to realise the score. The old bill are just another mob but they're getting paid for their Saturday entertainment while we fork out for the privilege. They're hiding behind some kind of fucked morals where they're right because they've got a uniform and we're wrong because we haven't taken the oath. We're our own bosses and they're working for the courts. It's enough to turn you into a fucking Trotskyist, except they're a bunch of bent student wankers who spend all their time making placards and shafting your ordinary white bloke.

They're all the same those kind of people. Politics is a load of shit basically and you'll find little of it around here. True, there's a few blokes into the fascist bit, but the old men at the top would wipe us out if they got into power. Line your football hooligans up against the wall and blow their brains over the pavement. That's their idea of law and order. But it's a crack winding up scruffy rich kids selling Marxist papers and fuck knows what other dodgy reading matter. Give them a Nazi salute and watch the bastards boil up inside knowing they'll do fuck all back.

We're soon in the ground and West Ham are into another round of Bubbles. Chelsea are singing around the ground. The game kicks off but we're watching West Ham. They're a fair distance off and there's little chance of it going off, but they fucking hate Chelsea. Reckon we're mouthy bastards. They fire a rocket into the stand and it bounces off the roof. Lands a few seats back. Flares for a second and I wonder if it's about to set the place alight. I think of Bradford and all those people burnt alive. Then of Hillsborough and the scousers killed by fences.

Thing is, the people who wanted the fences put up never admitted it was the fences responsible. Just shifted the blame onto terracing. Give us seats and we'll all behave. Some chance. Your harder cases have been going in the seats for donkey's years. It's another mark of class. We're no grubby paupers. No lippy hooligans mouthing off doing fuck all to back up the words. We're the business. The people who run football are redundant. Clueless the lot of them. Hillsborough was one big scam from start to finish. They were all in it together. Politicians, papers and the old geezers running the show. But what can you do? Fuck all at the end of the day.

– Bunch of cunts aren't they? Harris turns to me. We'll have them outside if we can get hold of them. Kick them all the way back to their East End plague pits.

There's a lot of the bastards and they're no pushover, but you've got to have belief. West Ham and Millwall are always the bad ones. Must be something in the water. Some strain of infection which affects the brain cells. Rabies is alive and well and flourishing in the East End. Probably came into the docks before the area fell apart, then stayed in the bloodstream. Some people don't fancy having a go at West Ham but if you're in a mob you can't afford to bottle against anyone. West Ham are hard, true, but they don't bother me. If you can get everyone to stand firm and the odds are even you've got to have a good chance.

It's all about presentation. If you've got a reputation then half the job's done before you start. It's everyday propaganda. Make yourself believe something and it's easy to persuade everyone else. There again, you end up getting every cunt in the country wanting to have a go and prove themselves when the odds are stacked. If you get picked off and cornered and you're on the receiving end then there's no mercy. It's survival of the fittest and the law applies everywhere. The weak don't last long in this country. There's no help for those who can't look after themselves. It's primitive man talking. Real Stone Age society where the biggest lump of rock wins. That's why you have to stick together.

– East London cunts. Rod's giving them the wanker sign. I fucking hate those bastards. Reckon they're so fucking hard with their cockney coons and Brick Lane Nazis. Fucking cunts the lot of them. Muggers and Paki-bashers. Same fucking gene working overtime.

– Scum, that's what they are, and Mark's got a soft spot for West Ham, bad memories from when he was a kid seeing his old man having the piss ripped out of him outside Upton Park. A split lip for the old man and a kid's blue and white scarf in the gutter.

The game kicks off and Chelsea cut their way through the West

Ham defence at will. We're knocking the ball around with style and it's great watching the Blues when they play like this. A reward for all the bad performances. The rain's hammering down and the players have trouble keeping their feet. We score twice before half-time then add a third near the end. It's a dull day with heavy clouds and a vicious wind but we don't care. We're stuffing West Ham on the pitch and it's good to see the bastards getting their noses rubbed in it. The rubbish they write about West Ham being a football academy is all in the past. More television nostalgia. They're more Billy Bonds than Trevor Brooking. We know the truth. They're cunts and they'll be twice as wound up by the time the ref blows the final whistle.

We're making the most of the score winding the Happy Hammers up and they're not taking it well. Even from this distance I can see the expressions on their faces. Sullen and narked as fuck, the Irons are simmering under the surface. They're like a pan of boiling water waiting to spill over and melt some cunt's face. They're all in there. Just like Rod says. The lads from Bethnal Green and all the other bomb sites stretching to Upton Park and on to Dagenham. But we're stuffing them on the pitch and enjoying the chance to take the piss.

The final whistle blows and most of Stamford Bridge is celebrating a good game, cheering victory over London rivals. For the majority of people the football is everything and they don't want to know about what's going to kick off soon as we get the chance. I can feel the pit of my stomach getting tight. I follow Mark, Rod and the rest of the lads up the steps and West Ham are moving towards their own exit.

Behind the West Stand there's a bit of a crush and the light covering the pitch is shut out. Floodlights burn high above but they're pointing the other way. That's the stage the media focuses on and once we're out the back of the West Stand it's just another Saturday night. There's a few small lights burning but more shadows and the smell of piss and dirty rain water. We get to the steps and there's a bit of singing and we can hear West Ham coming down the road already. We're moving down the steps with Harris getting everyone together. We've got to keep tight and act together once it goes off.

We're out in the street with police vans everywhere and we're looking into where we think West Ham will be, but it's all decent citizens and the old bill are moving Chelsea along, serving the community keeping the scum in line. There's a tense silence and everyone's giving everyone else the eye and we're getting down towards the tube. It just needs a spark. There's a few lads hanging around the flats and we start moving over as well but a couple of horses come up the steps and the old bill are moving everyone on again.

We're getting pushed down by the tube but we don't want to go home yet. We follow the happy supporters down into Fulham Broadway station. It's all Chelsea in here now and the tube pulls in and we take it up to Earl's Court, check the platform which is full of old bill, and continue to Victoria. We get off and hang around the platform, doing our best to blend in with the Saturday evening crowd. It's all backpackers and shoppers. We've clocked the cameras and Harris tells a couple of kids to smash them when West Ham pull in. We're taking a chance but acting camera shy. Just put a cross on the coupon and take your chance. No publicity and no video evidence. We're waiting along the eastbound District Line platform knowing West Ham will come through sooner or later.

Trains pull in and we scan the carriages, taking the piss out of a few civilians with West Ham colours, but their firm is nowhere to be seen. It's getting on for six when the tube we've been waiting for finally arrives. We know right away it's West Ham and the cameras are put through with bottles and before the doors open we're kicking the windows in. The mob on board are booting the doors trying to get out and there's the vague sound of crying from women and kids. The doors open and the bastards are on the platform, and it's real toe-to-toe stuff and we've picked a good mob here, a lot of older blokes but not too many of them, more or less equal odds and Harris kicks a squat bastard first off the tube in the bollocks, and Black John kicks another cunt in the gut. Rod kicks him in the face and the front of the train empties, a running battle now along the platform because out of nowhere the old bill have appeared.

Transport police on the platform and it's chaos and I can't believe they've got here so fast. Both sides are trying to get out of the station. Get above ground and the old bill have got no chance. There's coppers piling in forcing us through tunnels and up the escalator. It's all gone wrong somehow and then we're in the flush of Victoria jumping over the barriers, mingling with the crowds. We're out and about and move into the bus station waiting for West Ham to find their way. We move back as police vans arrive, doors flung open and coppers heading underground, sprinting to get stuck in. Then we see West Ham across the station and we're running into them but the bastards just stand there laughing like fuck and it goes off again in a big way, people running everywhere and it's a bitter punch-up this one and Black John's getting the shit kicked out of him when he goes down on the floor. We try to get over to the bloke but a mob of West Ham are around him and he's down for the count.

Some West Ham cunt lumbers into me, fist connecting, and I feel a numb throb through my jaw as I kick out at him, missing any decent kind of contact, then he's back in the crowd and my head's spinning. I focus myself and get my mind in gear, but I don't see anything now, just hear the racket of shouting men and alarms, then mad barking as the old bill get into the battle again, dogs on the rampage, always one step behind, and we're moving across the bus station, lobbing bottles and whatever else we can find at West Ham who are busy having a go at the old bill. I look over and Black John's on his own on the ground and a couple of coppers are looking down at him, and we've got to keep moving because there's vans and cars coming in from every angle and the last thing we want is a ride in a meat waggon. There's a few running fights with West Ham but everyone's getting split up and the old bill are nicking everyone they can get their hands on. I jump on a bus with Mark and Harris and a few other blokes. Rod's got lost in the commotion. Victoria's a no-go zone now if you're looking for trouble and we're on a bus heading for the West End. We're well pissed off at the old bill turning up so quick and just sit back and go with the motion.

– Black John was getting a hiding last I saw of him. Harris is leaning back over the seat in front. I tried to get to him but there were too many West Ham.

– The old bill were helping him up. Dusting him off making sure he was still alive. Mark scratches his bollocks. Hope that bird I shagged last night was clean. Last thing I need is a dose. Specially off some juvenile delinquent.

I reckon Black John's going to be visiting a doctor before Mark. He got a heavy duty kicking and I hope he wasn't tooled-up like normal. Coppers don't like knife-carrying black boys and any sympathy they might feel calling an ambulance would disappear once they got him for carrying an offensive weapon. But there's no finding out now. Not tonight. We've just got to fade away and old Rod's going to be a bit pissed off losing us in the chaos. But John's a cunt and a wicked bastard. Wouldn't want to cross the man but you can't feel too sorry for him because he's done enough bad things in his time. Couldn't cut a bloke myself, but I wouldn't knock him on that score. Just as long as we're on the same side.

– John'll be alright. Harris is laughing. It'll take more than West Ham to put him out of action for long. It'll just make him meaner next time around.

– Like a short sharp shock to the system, Mark backing him up. Give someone a dose like that and they're twice as bad in the future.

I lean against the window and watch the plush rows of houses pass. There's money in these streets, home to gun-runners and oil merchants. Millionaire flats full of Stock Exchange cunts with acne-free upper-crust birds choking on the property developer's plum shoved half way down their throats. But we're just passing through. We're content getting away from our battleground in Victoria. Fighting among ourselves. East against West. But West Ham's over for us now and when we get up to Oxford Street we decide to go for a few sherbets.

The centre's lit up for tourists and everywhere you look there's Arabs selling plastic police helmets and models of Parliament. It's all bright lights and fast food hamburger meat. An amusement arcade full of dagos. It's a black hole in the middle of London. We walk along the street and turn into Soho. Another fucking abortion with its fake reputation for sleaze, but it always pulls in northerners down for the football because they haven't got a clue where they're going. They see this area and no wonder they think London's full of queers and posers, rich slumming bastards and fashion queens. It's a magnet for scum. We go to a couple of pubs but they're dead so we move down towards Covent Garden, find a pub. There's eight of us in all and Harris says Derby played in

London today, away to Millwall. Maybe we'll pick up on a few of the bastards.

– Where did you get that tan from darling? Mark's into a small bird with dyed hair and a skin colour which means she's been abroad flat on her back shagging dagos or spics for a two-week break from the routine of shagging white men in London.

– What's it got to do with you?

She's a stroppy bird that's for sure and we're all laughing because Mark's gone red in the face. Obviously embarrassed and not pissed enough to take it in his stride. He's made a bad move here, that's for sure, and I can only see it getting worse.

– Who do you think you're calling darling anyway? Her mate's telling her to be nice, that Mark's only being friendly, but Mark snaps back.

– Fucking dyke.

– Macho wanker.

– Don't call me a wanker.

– Then don't call me a fucking dyke.

– I was only being friendly. Like your mate said.

– Well go be friendly with someone else.

– What's the matter with you anyway?

– I don't like being called darling for a start. And I'm talking with my friend and don't need you butting in.

We're cracking up laughing and tell Mark to leave it out. Fair play if the girl's not interested and, anyway, we're on the lookout for a few Derby fans, or even West Ham strays if we get lucky. There's a long way to go till closing time. What's he going to do in the meantime? Spend the whole night chatting up a couple of dodgy birds. Mind you, the dyke's mate seems game enough. Same suntan so must have been on the same holiday. But Mark should sort himself out. There's a time for shagging and a time for fighting. He should think twice about mixing the two. He'll just end up getting himself confused.

NEVER NEVER LAND

DAD IS HOLDING Mum's hand and I run ahead of them along the beach and Sarah is trying to keep up, yelling in my ear, and I'm a year older and a bit stronger and I don't want her to start crying so I slow down and let her catch me, but don't let her know what I'm doing because that would spoil the race for her. We get to the water together and stand there out of breath and we're holding hands like Mum and Dad. I look back to where they are and they're laughing about something and Mum's waving to us and Dad's kicking sand up which blows back because of the wind and then Mum's turning away so it doesn't get in her eyes, and then she's got her hand through his arm and they're getting nearer.

– Put your foot in the water, Sarah says.

– I don't want to, I'll get my trainers wet, I answer.

– You're just scared.

– I'm not scared of anything.

– Yes you are. You're scared Dad'll tell you off and Mum'll smack you.

– Dad wouldn't tell me off. He doesn't care if my trainers get wet because we're at the seaside and it doesn't matter at the seaside, nothing matters at the seaside.

– Mum would smack you though.

– Maybe.

I run on a bit further and Sarah follows and then we stop and look over the mud to where a big black dog is running out towards these wooden boats that are sitting on the mud. He runs very fast towards a load of seagulls floating on top of the water and when he gets near they all fly away and they're skimming across the water and this dog is doing his best to catch them and then they're up in the air like magic and I wish I could fly as well. I'm a bit worried in case the dog gets the birds and tries to eat them but they aren't stupid and just let him get near enough before they take off. I watch them go up in the air and the dog does a big circle with the water over his paws and then he's coming back to the sand and at first I think he's coming for me and Sarah and I'm moving in front of my sister because boys have to walk on the outside of girls to protect them from traffic so they don't get knocked down and hurt by cars and lorries and I'm stronger than my sister and other little girls and must never hit them because it's a bad thing to do, but then I see a man in a black jacket with a metal dog lead calling him and the dog changes direction and speeds up a bit and when I look back to where the seagulls were they've come back again and now they're sitting in the same place.

– You both won the race together, says Dad, and he lifts me up in the air above his head because my dad's big and strong and the strongest man in the world apart from boxers and people like that, though maybe he's even as strong as them, I don't know.

– You're both winners, he says, putting me down and lifting Sarah up in the air and she's laughing but looks a bit scared at the same time, not sure what she's supposed to do next.

– Mind you don't drop her, Mum says, and she looks worried as well.

But Dad's like Superman with his muscles though Superman doesn't have a West Ham tattoo on his arm and Dad doesn't wear a suit and cape. He says he can fly like Superman high in the sky and visits planets in outer space when we're asleep but I don't believe him, I think he's joking, and if I could fly like a bird I could fly with Dad as well but birds can't go to the moon and planets and I wouldn't want to go too far away because there's no air in space and I would choke and maybe we'd meet aliens and spacemen who would use us for experiments, like people do with rabbits and dogs and other kinds of animals. Anyway, if he could fly then he would have carried us all down to Southend on his back instead of in the car and we would have got here much quicker and Sarah probably wouldn't have been sick all over the back seat, but she might have fallen off or something and then Dad would have had to move fast and catch her again before she hit the ground and broke into small pieces.

– Is anyone hungry? Mum asks, and Sarah says she's starving but

I'm thinking of her puking in the back of the car and shake my head no.

– Not even for chips? Mum asks, and I nod my head up and down because chips are my favourite food.

– Come on then, Dad says, and we walk over the sand to the pavement and climb up and go along the front to where there's a cafe. We sit by the window and we can watch the boats coming in and Dad says they're heading into London along the Thames and that they used to go all the way to the docks in the East End, but that was a long time ago now before his time and times change and people move on and there was a big war or something and later on there was unions which the rich people didn't like and then the rich people built big luxury buildings and the poor people got nothing.

– What would you like? asks a girl who Dad tells me is a waitress, and I have fish fingers and chips and peas and a glass of Coke.

Sarah has the same. So do Mum and Dad, and Dad asks for some bread and butter as well, and then all of us ask for some bread and butter, and it's warmer in the cafe than outside and Dad says we timed it right because there's more people coming in now and we wouldn't have been able to sit by the window if we hadn't hurried here and then we wouldn't have had such a good view of the water. I like watching the ships move slowly along and wonder how big the bottoms of them are because the smaller boats on the mud have big bottoms to them, to make them stand up in the water Dad says, and the small boats are painted in lots of different bright colours but the bigger boats carrying stuff for shops and factories are grey and black.

Sarah kicks my legs under the table and I kick her back and she makes a noise like it hurt and Dad tells us both to behave. He winks at us and when the food arrives he says he's starving hungry and asks the waitress if we can have some more ketchup because the bottle's almost empty and she nods and goes back to the counter and then she comes back and puts a new bottle on the table. Dad says he'll put the ketchup on our food but I want to do it myself because I'm a big boy now, seven years old, and he lets me but it comes out too fast and there's a load of ketchup on my chips but I don't mind because I love ketchup and Mum and Dad raise their eyes into their heads in the way which makes me look away because it looks like their eyes are going to disappear into the back somewhere and then they'd have to go to hospital for some help. Sarah has to have a go with the ketchup as well but Dad helps her a bit because she's smaller than me.

– There's a train we can go on later, Dad says. It runs right out into the water, to the end of the pier.

I start asking questions because I love trains and sometimes Dad takes me to Liverpool Street and we go and look at the trains coming in, but best of all I like Thomas The Tank Engine, though not as much as I used to because I'm getting too old for Thomas, he's for smaller children really, and I think Sarah likes trains as well now, and I'm looking forward to going on the train over the water, but I like the fish fingers and chips and will think about trains in a minute.

– I'll be a train driver one day, I say. If not I'm going to be a policeman or a doctor.

Dad coughs and says a doctor would be best, but being a policeman is tough work, and he laughs and says a train driver would be best of all, but not a policeman, anything but a copper, and laughs some more, but Mum frowns at him and says that the police are good, that they protect us from bad people, and if there were no police we would soon miss them. I scrape ketchup off my chips and cut bits of fish finger and put it in my mouth and chew with my mouth shut when Mum tells me, and when I've swallowed a mouthful I have a drink of Coke and it has ice in it which makes it hard to drink, and I have to wipe my nose on a piece of toilet paper Mum gives me. I keep looking out over the water at the boats coming in and wonder what it would be like being a sailor living on a boat and I think I would be scared because if the boat sank I'd get eaten by sharks or at least have one of my legs bitten off and I can't swim properly yet though Dad has started taking me on Sunday morning.

– Don't play with your food, Mum tells Sarah, and she's full up and has only eaten half her dinner, and I'm almost done and so are Mum and Dad.

We walk along the front and I'm thinking that I'd like to be a policeman and help people, I suppose Superman's a sort of policeman, then suddenly I see a pirate ship next to the pier and I try to run towards it but Dad's got my hand because of the cars along the road and he holds me back and I've forgotten that, and I want to go see the pirates and he says okay, but first we're going on the train because it might start raining soon and it could get more windy, so best to get the train ride done first because it goes out over the water and we don't want the kids getting a cold or sore throats.

I'm sitting on the train which doesn't look much like Thomas because Dad says it's a big children's train and I wonder what the driver calls it, and Sarah keeps looking back at the pirate ship, but once the train starts moving it's more exciting and I'm looking down at the water and I don't like it much because what if something breaks and we fall in and Mum and Dad and Sarah and me get eaten by sharks or crocodiles or submarines or something even worse. I don't say anything because I shouldn't be scared and have to be a brave man and boys don't cry either, though I did at school last week when that kid hit me with a lump of wood because of some black man who got beat up by white men but that wasn't my fault and I told him that but he just laughed and ran off and the teacher asked what happened but I shut up and didn't tell because telling is the worst thing you can do.

There's a man driving the train and he has a whistle and blows it every now and then and I like that and I feel safe because the driver's in charge and knows what he's doing, that's what Dad tells me when he puts his arm around my shoulder, and I like the ride now, so does Sarah, and then we're at the end and have a look around and see the ships coming in a bit closer and Mum says that one's from Russia and another one's from Africa. There's wolves in Russia she says, and bears, and there's all kinds of animals in Africa like lions and elephants and giraffes and other things I don't know about, but some people are bad and kill elephants for their tusks and Sarah starts crying and Dad says it's okay it doesn't happen much now and he buys us both crisps from an old man with a box of different stuff.

We get the train back and I can see the pirate ship ahead and wonder when the pirate ships come down the river into London, though Dad says there aren't pirates any more, only in the sea around Vietnam and places like that and they've got new boats now and it's not like the old days. We get off the train and hurry to the pirate ship because it's starting to rain a bit more and Dad pays the woman some money and then we're walking onto the ship that's made of wood and has a mast and bits of rope and loads of other stuff and some big guns on wheels which Dad says aren't real, but then he says they are but not dangerous so don't worry, and I'm glad they're not toys and they don't look like toys either.

There's writing when we get inside and Dad tells us that the pirates wore baggy trousers and they were covered with tar to protect them against the cold and their buttons were sometimes made from the backbone of a shark or pieces of cheese that had gone hard. He says that the pirates often ate their food in the dark because the food was horrible and they drunk lots of rum and suffered from a lot of illnesses like things called scurvy, typhus, typhoid, dysentery, malaria, yellow fever and another kind of disease to do with men and women. Pirates liked gold and silver and even though they'd been around for a long time before, it's for what they did in the seventeenth and eighteenth centuries that they are best known. They were mostly Dutch and English and French and at first they robbed Spanish galleons coming back from America which was called the New World at that time and took their treasure.

Dad says the pirates lived mostly in a place called Tortuga near Haiti and in the Bahamas and in 1663 there were about fifteen ships and a thousand men who lived around Tortuga and Jamaica and though they started off working for the kings and queens of their countries after a while they just attacked anyone and became their own bosses and then the kings and queens didn't like them any more because it was alright when they were robbing and killing for their countries but they weren't liked much when they did it for themselves. Francis Drake was a pirate and that's why the Spanish sent their boats in the Armada to stop his attacks on their boats and he was sent by the first Queen Elizabeth.

Pirates were called buccaneers and corsairs and filibusters and freebooters and gentlemen of fortune and privateers and sea wolves and Henry Morgan was one of the best and everyone was scared of him. Dad says that all the sailors on a Spanish ship killed themselves rather than get caught by Henry Morgan. He was captured and went on trial in England but Charles I made him a knight instead of killing him and then he was made Governor of Jamaica. Woodes Rogers was another pirate and he later became Governor of the Bahamas and there was Edward Teach who was also called Blackbeard and he was a giant who swore a lot and had a long beard that had ribbons twisted in it and this looked like dreadlocks and Dad says he liked to put gunpowder in his rum. Calico Jack had two women in his crew, Anne Bonny who was from County Cork in Ireland and was his girlfriend, and Mary Read who had been a soldier. Dad says one of the fiercest pirates was a Welsh man called Bartholomew Roberts who often killed people and he had a dandy look and wore a red feather in his hat.

We walk through the boat looking at guns and pictures of big ships with sails and drawings of pirates drinking and fighting. Sarah says she doesn't like it much and it's boring but I wouldn't mind dressing up like a pirate and having sword fights but I don't think I would want to kill anyone or make them walk the plank and get eaten by sharks because I wouldn't want that to happen to me. Dad says there was Captain Kidd who was Scottish and there was a flag called the Jolly Roger which he points to on the wall and it's a skull and crossbones and not very nice and when the pirates put it at the top of their mast it gave the ship they were after the chance to surrender but if the ship didn't give up then a crimson flag was put up instead and it meant everyone would be killed with no quarter given.

The captains made their own versions of the flag and we walk up some steps onto the deck of the ship again and look over the side at the water and there's big ropes everywhere and Dad says a pirate's life must have been tough with storms and hard conditions but it must have been exciting because they got to live in the West Indies where the weather is nice and different to England where it rains all the time and they were their own people and didn't have to worry about electricity bills and gas bills and taxes and paying for the phone and local council charges and they didn't have all the insurance people and rule-makers after them all the time making their lives a misery. Dad says maybe he'd have been a pirate and smiles at Mum, with all that drink and beautiful women with big earrings and necklaces and stacks of gold and sword fighting, and she could have been a pirate as well like Anne Bonny and Mary

Read who they didn't hang because they found she was going to have a baby. There would be no more laws to tie them down and steal their wages for stupid reasons and someone is always after Dad's money, trying to take it away from him, making him pay lots of money for the rent and they just have to make a law and he has to pay what they say otherwise he goes to prison.

I can imagine Dad being a pirate with pistols and a sword and baggy trousers and he's got a big black eye where he got punched by a Chelsea fan when he went to see West Ham play there and I bet he would make the men who punched him at Victoria station walk the plank. Sarah wants to go to Never Never Land across the road so we walk back through the exhibition and I have a final look at the pirates and the guns and then we're waiting to cross the road.

– That's the sixth Rolls I've seen since we've been here, says Dad. I wonder how many millionaires live in Southend.

I look and there's a black Rolls-Royce along the road and this is where the people who get rich in East London come to live and there's a cartoon picture of a man in a coat with a funny look on his face and I ask Dad what that is and he says it's a police warning about flashers and he says that flashers are men who show their willies to people who don't want to look at them, and Mum says that's one of the reasons we need policemen and Dad nods and agrees. I laugh because it seems a bit stupid showing your willy like that and it must be freezing with the wind blowing and we cross the road and Dad gives the old man some money and we go into Never Never Land.

Mum leads us through the big cartoon pictures and says it's all about Peter Pan who was a boy who never grew up and I say that's strange because I'd like to grow up and be like Dad, but he says not to rush because he'd rather be a child again, that's the best time in life because you don't have to worry about anything and you can just play and go to school and be yourself. He says if he could have his childhood again he would learn stuff at school and he's always saying this to me, that it matters when you grow up, and Mum tells us about Wendy and Tinker Bell and Captain Hook and a crocodile. Sarah wants to be Wendy and I'll be Captain Hook because there seem to be pirates all over Southend and I could carry a sword and I'll tell them at school and maybe we can play it in the playground. Sarah likes Never Never Land and wants to see Tinker Bell and Mum says it's just folklore, there aren't fairies and little people any more but Dad says yes there are, and they laugh, maybe Mum says, but not around where we live, we'd have to go right out into the country somewhere, or across the sea to Ireland, and even then we might miss them because we're not used to seeing this kind of thing. There's a shop with books and toys, and Mum and Dad buy Sarah the Peter Pan book and I get a sword.

When we get outside again it's not so cold as before and we walk along the seafront. There's more people around now and we get some donuts from a little shop and watch the lady making them and they're brilliant when I bite into them. Mum says she'll read us Peter Pan tonight when we get home and I keep thinking of pirates and would like to see a real pirate ship sailing towards us and I'd wear a patch over my eye and have sword fights if I had the chance. Dad says we'll walk to the end of the wall and turn back. Then we'll go back to the car and drive home so we miss the traffic and we'll see Bobby who'll be waiting for her dinner, and Mum says she just hopes that bloody dog hasn't been in the bin again.

LIVERPOOL AWAY

LIVERPOOL ALWAYS BEAT us at Anfield. We don't expect anything result wise, but the team generally puts up a good performance. It's a funny ground. Gets a lot of good press but I've never liked the place. There's a cold atmosphere. I don't go for that chirpy scouse wit bollocks. Unity in poverty. All that shit. The real Liverpool is gangs of scrawny scousers with blades trying to pick off lone cockneys on their way back to Lime Street. Shitty streets and piles of rubbish. Under-age scallies throwing darts and dropping concrete slabs on the trains back to London. Indiscriminate scum.

They can put Brookside on the box and try and bring the place upmarket like they try and do everything else, but Liverpool's just forgotten housing estates, Toxteth riots and the scousers moaning when they lose a game. Cilla Black and all those professional scousers make money out of the myth. But you never believe that kind of stuff. You believe what you see and Liverpool can be a nasty bunch of knife merchants and there's never been press about what it's like to get bushwhacked on the streets of Merseyside. Trophies count and nobody wants to know.

The ground's emptying and we've lost again. Mark's cousin, Steve, is with us. Met him outside the ground. He's parked up by Stanley Park and we're driving back to Manchester. It feels like half a day out this one, because there's Harris and the regulars trying to work out a way to find the opposition, but they know the old bill have the situation tied up. They picked us up coming into Liverpool and we didn't get a look in.

We shuffle our way to the exit and now we're out in the grim Liverpool night, dark streets and a flood of coppers. Same scene as London. The bastards on horseback carry long sticks and serious attitudes. The old bill are scousers themselves and hate Chelsea like everyone else in the country. They don't take any lip in this part of the world and if you step out of line they'll have you. It doesn't impress the harder element but makes them wary. Harris tries to con his mob away from the coaches but the old bill aren't daft. He's got fifty or so blokes hanging back. No chance. Vans block their way. They smell of trouble and they're caught in the trap.

We follow Steve and persuade a copper we're going to the car. It takes some doing but we're walking along the side of Anfield, large areas of concrete and men and kids hanging around talking. We feel obvious. There's paranoia because all we need is a mob of scousers to come round the corner and we'd be cut up in seconds. They'd fucking love it finding four Chelsea boys on their own. We're keeping our voices down because there's no point being careless and getting overheard. My fists are clenched and the first scouser who mouths off is going to get his nose broken into tiny bits of shrapnel. Drive the bone into the brain and maybe it'll sort out that whining scouse accent. Steve better know where the car is because it'll be a sprint job.

There's no hassle though and any interested scousers must be waiting towards Lime Street, mobbing up down one of their concrete tunnels. The thieves I've seen watching England are human rats. Pale white skin and that fucking accent which nobody understands. They brag about being good robbers and they did the business following Liverpool around Europe nicking expensive gear from Switzerland and Germany, starting a designer trend with stolen property which dozy followers of fashion, missing the point, went out and paid through the nose for years later. But when it comes to doing a few Dutch equal odds in Rotterdam the scousers would rather turn over a jeweller's. Thieving little cunts the lot of them. We're in the car and I've got a thirst and a hard-on. Some Manc bird's going to have a good time tonight.

– Turn on the radio, will you? Mark's in the front seat with his cousin. Let's hear the other scores.

It starts to rain outside and our glimpse of Liverpool is huddled figures and street lights, bricks and mortar shining under artificial lights. Tottenham have lost and we cheer. Steve's windscreen wipers sweep side to side clearing a path through dirty streets, chip shops packed with scouse kids and old men. Mushy peas and chips with curry sauce. It's a fucking sad place and as much as I hate the bastards I have to feel a bit sorry for the young kids in thin rain-soaked shirts. This is bottom of the shit heap this city. They can keep their Boys From The Blackstuff and Derek Hatton. I'd die in a place like this after growing up in London. I mean, London's shit, but it's home and nothing like Liverpool. This city has to be the arsehole of England. I don't blame Yosser Hughes nutting everything in sight. I'd do the same.

– Fucking zoo this place, says Rod, following my train of thought like he's a mind reader. No wonder the bastards come down to London just to sleep on the streets. At least in London they get to suck a rich man's cock and earn a few quid. What are they going to do round here?

– Fuck all, says Steve, keeping his eyes on the road. Liverpool's a dying town. It's gone. There's too much Irish blood and Toxteth's full of kids left over from the slave ships. Liverpool was the original slave town. They bought the bastards here from Africa before shipping them to America. The past has caught up with this city.

– I don't know about all that, but the place should be bulldozed and the scousers sold off to the highest bidder. Rod stops to think. Not that anyone would want the bastards even as slaves. Wouldn't get much work out of them. He starts whistling the tune from the Hovis advert.

– Manchester's class in comparison, says Steve. Mancs and scousers hate each other's guts. You've never seen anything like it. It's worse than what you get in London. You go see Man U play Liverpool and it's evil. Real hundred per cent hatred. Only thing worse is Rangers against Celtic. Total civil war that one. It's religion tips the scales. Protestants and Catholics living like they did a hundred years ago. There's even a bit of that kind of feeling left over between Liverpool and Everton, Man U and City.

We start picking up speed and soon we're on the motorway to Manchester. The results come through the radio and we swear and cheer as our prejudice takes us. We're feeling good now leaving Liverpool behind, even though Chelsea got beat. We're in a relaxed mood. You get out of the situation, away from the mob, free from alcohol, and you're not bothered. We've done our bit for the Blues and I just fancy some food, a few pints and maybe a decent woman. Steve's putting his foot down and the rain's coming heavy now. We're steaming along surrounded by lorries and cars, dim outlines which could be anywhere in England but somehow we know we're up north. There's a definite smell and feel to the place, even on a stretch of motorway. Go into a service station and it's all fry-ups and strong tobacco. Like going back in time. You get spoilt living in London. It's a different world up here. A primitive world full of primitive people. Different tribes for different parts of the country.

When we get to Manchester, Steve parks up outside his flat. It's a dead area but only a short ride into the city centre. We haven't brought any gear with us, so pile in the nearest pub. It's early yet and there's a few locals staring into their pints, all laid back and reflective, which makes us feel noisy till we've downed three pints and calmed the nerves, and it's going to be a good night. I can feel it somehow. You go through the routine all week, keep your wits about you down the football, maybe do the business, maybe not, but now we're relaxed and out to destroy a few brain cells.

We end up having six pints in an hour and a half and Steve is pissed. Can't make my mind up about the bloke. Whether he's alright or a bit of a cunt. There's something not quite right about him. He's not a full shilling. Not thick, but not all there. Not sure what, but there's something. He goes off and calls a taxi. The pub's filling up now. Mostly middle-aged couples. A good laugh most of them, dressed up smart like Northerners tend to do. They're sound people, and I suppose if we were sitting in a boozer full of scousers they'd be alright as well. We make the last pint stretch and the taxi arrives to take us into town.

– There's a fair bit of crumpet knocking about, says Rod as he pays for the drinks in a done up pub with glass mirrors and leather bar stools. One of them's going to get a strong dose of Chelsea tonight. A dose of London infection.

I have to agree with the bloke and the pub we're in is packed solid. They all seem a bit sweet somehow, students or something probably, and I'd rather get hold of a real chunky northern girl than one of these inflatables. A hundred per cent Manc. The music's okay though and the lager's cheap so we stay a while and try sussing out some Man U or City fans but this lot are more into their clothes than rucking. Poor little babies wouldn't want to get their costumes messed up. Fucking idiots all think they're Peanut Pete and it's daft really because wankers like these deserve a kicking just to bring them into the world with a bang. Slap their bottoms and force them to breathe in the fumes of an English city, but when there's no resistance you don't bother. You want a bit of conflict, not one of these docile wankers who hate violence yet use it in their language and manners.

I pinpoint a mouthy cunt near the bar with some of his mates. Dressed up like a clown obviously thinking he's some kind of Saturday night special who's going to show his bottle down some flash club impressing birds who reckon being hard's a haircut and expensive gear. Cunt. I'm going to take the bastard out no problem, but my head's still together enough to know it's early in the evening and I'd get tugged within ten minutes. I've got to keep things sharp and pick the right moment. No point making a prat of myself. This one's personal and not something to share with an audience. I know the time and place well enough. Piece of piss and the bastard's going to have a split head the next time his bladder starts hurting him.

– I only go down the clinic and the bloke there tells me to drop my trousers. He has a bit of a look and then starts scratching round my knob. Mark's pissed going into one about his visit to the STD clinic.

– I'm thinking whether to nut the bloke, whether he's a fucking iron or something, and he must have the problem all the time because he starts talking about his wife and kids. How well his young ones are doing at school and all that family stuff. How he hopes his kids will go into the medical profession like their old man.

– You're better off dying of the clap than having some doctor playing with your balls, less it's a bird of course, and Rod's laughing into his drink spilling lager down his front, over the floor, everywhere. Scratch your own bollocks. Least you don't have to give up drink.

– It's professional, isn't it? It's different than some queer trying to get to grips with you and I was clean enough first time round, though I've got more tests coming back next week. Said I should watch where I dip my todger, not in those words exactly, but I started thinking about that skinny bird I had and what a tight fit she was. That's a real blood job. That's where you get your Aids from.

The mouthy cunt I've been watching puts his bottled lager on the bar and fucks off to the bogs. I follow him across the pub. Music's loud in my ears, some old Happy Mondays wank, I don't know, but I can hear the bloke's voice and see the cockiness in his face. Cunt. Reckons he's something special. I go in the bog and he's having a piss, leaning over the bowl admiring himself. There's another geezer zipping up ready to leave and I pretend to wash my hands. When he's gone I walk over to the wanker at the bowl, grab a handful of his golden locks, pull his head back and slam his skull into the wall hard as I can. There's a heavy thud of bone and concrete. I pull his head back and slam his face into the tiles. I feel the shudder through my arm. His knees go and he's sliding into the piss down below, blood splattered across the wall. Fucking lovely pattern. Poor little darling's fucked and his clothes are fucked as well. Blood and piss, the great British cocktail. A national institution. I walk out and tell the others we're leaving, that I've just done some Manc cunt. We get out of the pub sharpish.

Manchester's buzzing and there's a real flavour to the place. I feel better. Brought things to a natural level. Cunt deserved a bruising. Hope his fucking head's split in half. Hope the stitches dig in deep. That the doctor fucks them up first time around. But it's no time to linger so we get walking and ten minutes later we're in another pub better than the last one and there's a couple of tasty girls at the bar. They're well moulded. Built for one thing. Remind me of Letter To Brezhnev, but then I remember that those girls were scousers, that there's a difference, that Mancs hate scousers, and scousers reckon they're the business when it comes to thieving. Have to watch my money with these two.

I'm leaning across one of the girls ordering four pints of lager. She smells strong of perfume and she's laughing with her mate making no attempt to move away. I lean into her a bit more a little unsteady on my feet from the drink, using it as an excuse to test her and she doesn't shift an inch and I know I'm in. I can feel her tits through the thin material of her top and know she's wearing a low cut bra. It gives me a boost just getting the scent and texture.

– Get any nearer and you'll be sucking my nipples, she says with a smile which spreads lipstick across her face, and her mate's laughing, choking on her drink.

They hear our accents and know we're from London, but it doesn't phase them. They've been down a few times themselves but reckon it's a shit town full of posers. It's expensive and the clubs are full of silly little kids. The girl with the strong perfume and willing nipples will be no problem and Steve's straight in with her mate. Doesn't waste any time, I'll give him that much. He's giving her some nonsense about how much he loves Manchester. How London's a dump and even though I should be concentrating on the bird next to me who's flashing her eyes in that way pissed girls tend to do, he's winding me up without knowing it, all in the cause of getting his end away.

I can take a bit of a pisstake from the girls because at the end of the night I'll be doing the business and it's all in good fun. But Steve's got nothing to offer. I mean, if it was a mob of blokes in a pub I didn't know and they were taking the piss out of London, or worse than that, Chelsea, then we'd just steam in without a second's thought. But with the girls I can take the joke, basically I suppose because they're women and there's some kind of inbred respect deep down inside, buried under all the insults and jokes. Steve's a relative of a mate so I have to play the game, but he can go too far with the slagging. He's a bit of a smarmy cunt, but he's Mark's cousin so I keep my mouth shut.

– I was glad to get out of London and move up here. The people are more genuine and you don't get so many madmen walking the streets. Up here people talk to each other and everything costs less so you can afford to go out more. The people are real. They're not so bothered with their image and how much they earn.

I notice Rod giving Steve the eye, picking up on his line of chat. He looks my way and I know we're thinking the same thing. I mean, he might have a point about some of the things he's going on about, but at the end of the day you don't slag your own kind. The truth's often hard to swallow but you don't abandon your culture whatever anyone tells you. Steve might have lived in Manchester for the last six years, but he was born and raised in London and he's always going to have a bond with the place.

It's like the Indians in Southall. You might take the piss

occasionally but they're not just going to come over and ditch everything because they're in England. They're not going to give up their curries and start eating beans on toast every night. They can mix respect with their own ways. You're always going to push your way of life, but deep down you understand what's what and Steve's just making a cunt of himself in my eyes. He's like those wankers who are always slagging off the Union Jack. Say it's a symbol of fuck knows what. They all have the same accents. All follow the same kind of politics. Posh accents, posh politics. Intellectuals they like to call themselves, but they're just outsiders who don't belong in their own culture.

Maybe Steve's one of those misfits, but he hasn't got the accent and I doubt he's got any politics other than the politics of dumping his load. But that's just as fucked as the tossers who deliver lectures on something they've never experienced. Steve's following the politics of promising anything and slagging everything off just to shaft some pissed bird who'll knob anything she can get hold of because it's Saturday night. Steve's just fulfilling a social obligation. Saturday night. Bloke shags bird. Girl shags bloke. Says anything to achieve that goal. Basically, the man's got no pride. No self-respect. No nothing. He's one of those people you meet who needs to impress and has no solid foundation. He'll say anything, do anything. Another cunt in a world jam-packed with them.

I finish my pint and Mark's at the bar ordering. I think his cousin's a wanker and I'm wondering whether to let him in on the secret, but we're not pissed enough yet. Steve's like a fair weather football fan. He'll go along with the atmosphere when the team's doing well but you won't see him for ten years when they're losing. He'll come along to Anfield because it's a short drive down the motorway, and he'll rant and rave because everyone else is doing it, but that's as far as it goes.

– The worst thing about London is places like Brixton. You go down there and you might as well be in New York. It's a dangerous place not safe for a woman to walk around once it gets dark.

I'm looking at the back of his head as he rambles on and he's giving her a long line of shit because he's been slagging off Moss Side and Hume for the same reasons when we were at Anfield. I don't know, maybe I shouldn't get so wound up about things. Maybe it's just me. He's pissed and talking shit. I should let it go. Not worry about what Steve has to say to shag a tart. But then I think of football and how you go everywhere through thick and thin and it represents something, like being faithful maybe, but he just doesn't understand the notion. I go for a piss.

I'm standing with my head against the wall pissing away the lager. I think of that smarmy wanker in the last pub. Must be down the hospital at this very moment. I could have killed the bastard and I start thinking what it must be like to go down for twenty years. To find yourself banged up slopping out every morning. Shifted around the country from prison to prison, trying to keep your nose clean so you can get time off your sentence, but the whole time bottling everything up just wanting to kick fuck out of someone and release the tension. I do my buttons up and wash my face in the sink. I'm wound up worse than normal and I don't know why. I'm on for a shag, seen Chelsea, even though we got beat, and I've had the bonus of smacking some wanker already tonight. Even so, I want to nut Steve, but know it's not on because he's Mark's cousin and Mark's a good mate. A diamond. We go back years. Same with Rod. Another diamond. Both do anything for you. We stick together and help each other out. I let the cold water wake me up and I feel in control again. Go back in the bar and take the drink Mark's just bought.

– Are you coming back then? The girl I've been chatting with leans into me, rubbing against me. She's already sorted things with her mate. We could go on somewhere if you want, but I'm pissed.

– You can come back to my place, Steve says, interrupting. It's not far. We can get a cab. I'll pay if you're short.

– No, I don't fancy odds of four onto two. I look at the woman wondering if she thinks we're sick or something. Rapists or gang-bangers.

– Nothing personal. She looks me square in the eyes, a serious expression on a nice face. A girl's got to be careful these days. There's a lot of weird men around. Make the wrong choice and you could end up hacked to pieces with bits of your body scattered around Greater Manchester.

Steve shakes his head and turns away.

– You coming or what, and the woman's on her feet leading me to the door. I tell the lads I'll meet them tomorrow at twelve at the train station. Follow her outside.

She bundles into me and we start walking. It's a cold night and I forget about the rest of the lads and she's not bothered about her mate either. Too pissed to think. Too pissed to argue with another drunk. We walk for what seems like ages, but it's only ten minutes and I'm climbing up two flights of stairs in the dark. The light doesn't work, but when the front door opens we're in a warm flat with nice wallpaper and purple carpet. I don't have much time to enjoy the surroundings, though, because the woman's leading me into the bedroom without bothering to offer me a drink or go through the normal routine of coffee and dull background music. We strip off and before I stop spinning from the excess lager flooding my brain we're banging away with the bed threatening to cave the floor in.

She's a good ride, no doubt about it, which is unusual when you're pissed and maybe the lager has an effect because it's a fair old while before I finish and collapse in a sweating lump of rubble. We're both fucked by drink and sex and next thing I know it's morning and she's handing me a cup of coffee. Tells me I've got to drink up and get out in fifteen minutes. Nothing personal, her mum and niece will be round soon. I'm not feeling bad and, to be honest, wouldn't have minded another pop at the girl with a clear head, but you can't have everything in life and it was a good bit of sex last night so that's a bonus over the usual drunken effort.

I'm sitting on a bench, reading the football in the papers for half an hour before Rod and Mark turn up. They look rough and eye me with suspicion. Must have got rid of something more than the standard with that bird last night. I feel good. Set up for the trip back to London. Rod goes to get a cup of tea and Mark sits on the bench next to me. He's shaking his head. Doesn't look too happy with life.

– I'm fucking dead when we get home. He stretches his legs out and kicks at an empty fag packet. Misses and stubs his toe. He swears.

– My cousin, Steve. Fucking did the bloke last night. He only persuades that bird, the one whose mate you went off with, to come home with him. Me and Rod kip down in the living room and then he comes in about three in the morning with a towel round him, wakes us up and tells us to come in his bedroom and fuck her.

– I tell him to piss off. I'm not some fucking pervert. Anyway, I think he's joking but then I hear this crying, like a kid, and I get up to have a look and he's only battered her. She's shivering in bed with bruised eyes and blood on the sheet. He's shouting that she's a fallen angel and deserves everything she gets.

– I just went mental. Kicked the shit out of him. I hate that kind of thing. I mean, the girl was suffering. He was a wreck the time I got through with him and we just sent the bird home in a taxi. Left Steve this morning and told him to get himself an ambulance. I'm not helping the cunt. If he comes round my place again I'll kill him. Talk about bad blood in the family.

Rod comes over and sits down. Sips at his tea blowing the steam away. Looks my way to see if I've heard the story. I raise my eyes. I knew there was something dodgy about the bloke. Makes you wonder what else he gets up to if he goes that far when he's got witnesses around. The first time I've met the bloke and hopefully the last.

– You missed a bad night, Rod says.

– I'm history when I get back to London. He won't tell the old bill but I wouldn't put it past him telling his mum. Maybe he won't, I don't know. It's sick though. I've known him since we were kids, though we didn't exactly see a lot of each other. I never had a clue. I hope he keeps quiet about me having a go at him. My aunt Doreen's a strange woman. She'll set God on me if she finds out I touched her Stevie.

SWEET JESUS

SHE KEPT HER mouth shut most of the time and just spoke when she was spoken to, which was quite often really, considering, what with people wanting to leave their washing and needing change for the machines, maybe poking their heads around the door to ask what time the launderette closed. And this suited Doreen fine because it meant she didn't have to talk about the weather and how bad the Government was unless she wanted, though working in the launderette meant being discreet and knowing when to speak and what to say to a particular person at a particular time, judging their moods, but generally life panned out fine, only now and again one of the old girls, older than her, would come in and spend her time getting in the way, talking to herself or some invisible friend, more mumbling really than talking, they'd gone a bit dotty and, because they'd been through it all, the war and everything, they thought they didn't need any answers, so Doreen had to bite her lip when she wanted to warn them of the Devil's influence, of the salamanders in the heat spitting fire, salvation a short walk away at the altar of the Protestant church she attended twice a week.

It was too much time on their own that did it. Usually their husbands were dead, a lot of them killed by the Germans in France, or else run off with a younger woman though, to be honest, the state of most of the men around the neighbourhood you wouldn't think they'd be able to attract anyone decent, but life was full of surprises, none of them that surprising. Like Walter, wandering around the streets on his own all day, then he'd visit the launderette on Friday afternoons with his plastic bag, the same plastic bag which gradually fell apart until by the end of the month Doreen had to give him a new one from the supermarket, one that they used to make you pay for, stronger than the rubbish given away free, but they wanted to switch back again, or so she had heard, nothing was free in a man-made world, only the air and sunlight, and they belonged to God. She would tell Walter that the bag was sitting around forgotten, doing her Good Samaritan act, not letting on that he was in her thoughts and he should think about a conversion for the good of his soul.

Walter did his own wash and whistled old Dubliners tunes, and occasionally he would shout out loud about the tears of Ireland and how the Catholics had been downtrodden for centuries, mourning those who had died fighting the English. Then Doreen would have a quiet word because nobody wanted politics in the launderette, it scared the mothers in with their kids, or at least she imagined it did, and there might be a man in reading his paper who would have his own views and then there would be a fight, and blood, and damnation. Politics worried Doreen. It was a bad word and life was hard enough anyway thank you very much. God was watching his flock and the men in new suits kept getting in His way. But once she'd had her say, smiling all the time and talking in a soothing voice, Walter was quiet and she would hear nothing more from him. He just kept his head down looking a bit embarrassed and sometimes Doreen would feel uncomfortable, that she should have let him get the ideas out, that he was from a different people who didn't have the ability to bite their lip and take everything on the chin. When she felt this kind of guilt she was stern with herself and knew she had to enforce some kind of standard.

Walter couldn't come in ruining things for everyone else, making the launderette an unpleasant place to visit. Business would fall off and Mr Donaldson might be forced to close down or cut back and that would be Doreen on the dole with her begging bowl pleading for charity. She paid her taxes and gave generously when the collection came round at church. Calm was restored and it was always the same youngsters who came in with the family wash, because their mums and dads were saving pennies and didn't put it in for a service, and boys sulked and girls talked too loud, really irritating it was, swearing sometimes because they wanted to be noticed, but they were seeing things through their own eyes only and hadn't learnt about other people's feelings, not yet anyway, and when it got too bad Doreen had to put on a stern voice and tell them to watch their tongues or they would be banned.

Most of them were fine though, like young Ronald who came in every Saturday morning, only eight or nine years old, and he shouldn't have been doing the washing, but he always had a smile on his face, like a lot of darkies, though not the youths with anger in their faces and shiny cars with that music all tinny through open windows, but real darkies, the ones that came over when she was young, guest workers from the Caribbean, and Ronald's smile was the same, real ray of sunshine whatever time of year it was, summer or winter, and Ronald came from a good Christian family who went to church regular as day followed night. He wasn't aggressive like some other children she could mention and Doreen would tell him to leave the wash for her, to go and play on the swings but watch out for the older boys selling drugs, remember to avoid temptation, and he would go off and she would do the wash for him, it was a pleasure, no charge, a labour of Christian love, just did it along with the rest. And when he returned he was always nice and polite and said thank you Mrs Roberts, it's very kind of you Mrs Roberts. Off he would go to his mum and dad, and children should play more, like she had done when we was a little girl.

Things were different now and some of the things she had heard about, the stories she read in the newspaper, all these men who molested children and mutilated their bodies. That monster who killed a child and buried the body in Epping Forest, then went back and dug the poor little thing up, took photographs, it was so hard to understand that kind of thinking. It proved what the vicar said, that there really was a Devil lurking in the shadows, in the dark recesses of the human mind, a monster preying on the defenceless, the old and the young, small boys and old ladies, the raving lunatics turned onto the streets for some care in the community. It was really shocking, as though the world was going mad, people turning in on themselves and falling prey to wicked thoughts. Doreen hadn't slept properly for months. She just didn't understand the frantic scramble that surrounded her.

Children had forgotten how to enjoy themselves and they shouldn't need lots of computerised toys to be happy, video games and cartoon superheroes, and their parents were to blame dressing the girls up like painted dollies and the boys were turned into miniature soldiers. But there again their mums and dads were copying what they saw on television, in the adverts and shop windows. Some of the things Doreen saw in the windows of toy shops made her wonder where it was all going to end, how far God would let His children go before He lost His temper. All that money spent on plastic guns when so many of the people who used the launderette were dressed like scarecrows. Doreen never got near their clothes because they did their own washes, but it was obvious, the colours gave it away. Drab and worn out colours faded because they'd been washed too many times. But it was their own business and during the winter it was a good job in the launderette, with the door closed and the radio going and the machines and dryers working flat out.

It was so warm, it was a job, and Doreen felt sorry for the down and outs living on the street at this time of year, the boy who slept in the Post Office phone boxes at the end of the high street. The first time that she saw him she'd thought he was a bundle of rags, a pile of lost washing, but then the legs moved and he couldn't be more than twenty or so, poor little lad, and she'd seen him the day before sitting there in the twilight with a pair of sunglasses covering his eyes, staring at the wall. In winter the launderette was a haven and every time the door opened and a gust of cold wind came in she remembered how lucky she was to be inside out of harm's way, the Lord watching over her. The window dripped with condensation and the heat from the dryers made her perspire, those tumble dryers spinning round and round, with the clank of motors and steam from the washing machines and the strong smell of powder. In the summer, though, when it was really hot outside the windows sweated as well and Doreen wished that her customers would take their wash home and hang it out to dry instead of wasting good money on the dryers. It became so hot in the launderette at this time of year and it would be better for the ozone layer and the polar ice caps wouldn't melt, bringing on another Flood. It would save energy as well, but they still got the dryers rolling and Doreen had to go to the door and stand on the pavement for some fresh air, but when there was a lot of traffic the carbon monoxide fumes were over-powering and her skin itched, though it could have been the powder she was using, but most likely it was the poison in the atmosphere.

Doreen's back ached more in the summer and she felt lazy, but her job was important, she couldn't complain because she was fit and healthy and working, and at least she didn't perspire as bad as some people. It could be horrible at times, the state of some of the clothes she had to wash. It just showed how different people's sweat glands operated, or the food they ate perhaps, herbs and garlic and spices, and then there would be bags of washing where the clothes seemed clean already, she just didn't understand why they bothered, maybe they thought they were the Queen and wore something different ten times a day. Not the English Queen, of course, because the older generation knew all about recycling and making things last, they wore their skirts and trousers and shirts longer than the younger people, they weren't so regimented, they made things last, made do with what they could get.

Now and then Doreen would wonder whether she had developed her own smell after twelve years working in the launderette, because people did, and their odour came to match their occupations and lifestyles. She could tell the bankers and solicitors who came in because their blouses and shirts smelt sharp, as though all that frustration and paperwork created a build-up of acidic sweat, a really disgusting smell, and the people who did manual work, whether stacking shelves or digging the roads, they had a heavy kind of smell which wasn't so unpleasant somehow. Then there was the girl who worked in the pub across the road, and she smelt of drink, quite a nice smell really, Doreen had to admit that much, and the Rastafarian who came in, his clothes were so sweet, lovely colours as well, and his hair was all knotted and clean and sometimes she just wanted to run her hands through it and let her cracked fingers get snagged on the knots. He had bought her a yellow china teapot at Christmas, a present he said, for being so nice to his nephew Ronald, and she made a cup of darjeeling on Christmas Day morning, such a lovely man, about the same age as her Stevie. She used to run her hands through her son's hair when he was a child, such lovely hair, and sometimes she wished she could move up to Manchester and see him every day.

Everything Stevie told her was honest and true, he was the best son a mother could have, so when he had that trouble with the drugs she knew it couldn't be wrong if Stevie said it was okay, what did she think helped Jesus with his visions and miracle cures, and she loved Jesus and her son Stevie, he was almost holy in his sweet innocence, such a good boy, and it was a good job James was away visiting his sister when the police came to the house about that horrible girl who said Stevie tried to touch her in the park, a wicked vicious lie, because her husband never loved Stevie like she did, no mother could love a son like she loved that boy. James had always been hard on poor Stevie, said the lad wasn't all there, and it was the only thing they had ever argued about.

Certain drugs were better than beer and didn't do so much damage to the body, it wasn't like drink which led to violence and caused death, it all made sense that time when Stevie was younger and sat her down and explained things in his special way, and she ran her fingers through his hair which needed a wash, but he was so innocent he didn't realise that appearances were important. But if she was honest with herself, Doreen could see the other side as well because if someone took drugs every day there was no way they'd get into work on time and it would be a quick walk to the social. It was the same for everyone. Punctuality was important. Even Mr Donaldson was a businessman first and foremost, and though his favourite worker got on with him she knew he would send her on her way without a second thought if he felt she wasn't doing her job properly. Life was like that, making choices and putting things in perspective, and some of the people who came into the launderette were all nerves and misery, crushed by society, right across the scale, from the poor to the not so poor, they all had their problems, doesn't everyone, though Doreen understood that she had less than most, but it was the rich ones who had moved into the area, the estate agents and insurance brokers, all those men and women under thirty who were power dressers or whatever they called it, they just gave her their underwear and talked like they owned the world, which they did really when it came to property and bank accounts.

Doreen had never known that only twelve and a half per cent of money actually physically existed, that the rest was just numbers in computers, until Stevie told her, when she caught him going through her purse that time, a difficult period of his life, it wasn't his fault, the power of the Devil trying to work its way into God's finest creation, and it was handy to know, something they should put in Christmas crackers, because she looked at the arrogant little so-and-so's with their expensive clothes and upturned noses and wondered if they realised what that meant. Did they? They moved into the neighbourhood for a couple of years and then sold the property for a profit, and the locals couldn't afford to buy a home in the area in which they'd grown up, that was greed for you, Jesus just turned their table over and threw them out of the synagogue. If Stevie had been born two thousand years earlier he would have done the same, died on the cross for suffering humanity, and the Son of God might return one day, the vicar didn't know everything, good man though he was, and she could see Stevie in the desert through the mist coming off a pile of shirts, and hear his voice above the roar of the dryers telling a crowd of people to love thy neighbour.

Sometimes she felt guilty for her good fortune, but James always told her to enjoy life while she could because they would be dead one day, it all ended in the grave, and that's why it was good to have a religion, it didn't really matter which one she supposed, though she couldn't imagine being anything but a Protestant, and she would have liked Walter to convert for the good of his soul, but it was just what you were raised with, and it was best to get on with it because if she looked at what the vicar said too closely maybe she would find some of the ideas a little bit suspicious, and then where would she be? Doreen hoped she wasn't being blasphemous because she knew God was listening to her thoughts, but surely he would understand, because she was a good woman really and she knew that God loved her.

James was away again visiting his sister, poor Kate was ill, the air in Wiltshire didn't seem to be doing her much good. She was lucky to have such a dedicated brother, they'd always been close, both their families were close and the children were always around on Sunday for their dinner, though not Stevie who was doing well in Manchester, they didn't see him very often, never anything but smiles, truth be told there were never many problems, a few when the children were teenagers and they were having trouble making ends meet.

Doreen snapped back to the launderette and she was watching

Mrs Atkins load a machine, the poor woman had lost her husband the year before and had apparently turned to drink though she never smelt of the stuff and was always well turned out, though they said she stuck to gin because it leaves no trace. Doreen hoped she would be okay and she was coming towards her suddenly, swaying a little, asking for a twenty pence piece, and Doreen went into her little room and took the two tens she handed over, gave Mrs Atkins the coin, exchanging pleasantries about their respective children, what good people they had turned out to be, free from the drugs which destroyed so many youngsters today, nothing wrong with a little cannabis now and again Doreen told herself, hearing Stevie's voice, and the dryers were spinning behind her, the door opening and closing, the hatch a nice addition, thank you Mr Donaldson.

Then Mrs Atkins turned back towards the washing machine and Doreen was wondering what she would eat that night, perhaps she'd treat herself and have a couple of samosas and a big bag of chips, maybe a pickled onion, that would be nice. She started thinking about the man who ran the kebab house, she could never pronounce his name properly, but how the place smelt of grease and meat, and when she met him in the supermarket and said hello he smelt just like the kebab house, all that fat and frying oil, a mix of kebab meat and battered fish, it was awful, made her stomach turn, it was as though he had no personality, like it was swamped in bubbling oil, doused in vinegar and chilli sauce. It was disgusting, the poor man, with a wife and children and maybe that's why his sons were always in trouble, fights and drugs, his eldest son was in prison for beating up a policeman, because kids could be cruel and violent when they got into their late teens, just look at her nephew Mark, though he'd straightened himself out now and was good as gold.

Doreen wondered if the other children had made fun of their father, because he really was foul-smelling and she felt terrible because he was such a nice man when he was in the kebab house, so friendly, and he gave her big portions when she went in, a Greek or a Turk, she was never sure which and didn't want to ask because she knew the two countries didn't get on, but she never saw him in the launderette and she was quietly and guiltily pleased because she would hate to have to handle his clothes, poor man, what a terrible thing to carry around with you, and it started her thinking, making her a bit nervous, that parable about casting the first stone. He had been behind the counter for such a long time that he had picked up the smell of the place, and Doreen wondered if the same thing had happened to her.

She thought of the clothes that she washed day-in day-out, and how each bag had its own unique smell which told everything worth knowing about the owner. But what did other people think of the woman from the launderette when she passed them in the street? Did they smell dirty clothes? Perhaps all the rotten fumes she dealt with through the years had worked their way into her pores and mutated her glands. Maybe she turned heads when she passed, her odour one of dirty socks and smelly underpants, curry-stained T-shirts and bloody jeans. She had been in the place so long now that she was used to the stench of dirty laundry when opening bags left for a service wash, pushing their contents quickly into the machines, washing away the sins of the world, turning her head away, turning the other cheek, giving her customers the chance of a clean start in life though she knew well enough they would never learn from the past but make the same mistakes all over again and then come back to her looking for one more chance. Like Stevie. She was just another cog in the machine, her purpose in life the cleaning of soiled shirts and dirty hankies.

The poor man in the kebab house probably smelt her coming and thought poor Mrs Roberts, she reeks of other people's dirty washing, she has no identity of her own, a faceless woman in other people's clothes, washing and drying and folding shirts and towels in neat little piles, and if that was what he thought then Doreen told herself that it was only right, a just desert for thinking the same about him, poor man. She looked up and Ronald was trying to cross the road with his washing, the bag heavy over his shoulder, weighing him down, a police car stopping to let the boy across, and he pushed the door of the launderette open and looked at Doreen uncertainly. She knew what he wanted but was too polite to ask, such a lovely little boy, perfect manners, no trouble to anyone, and she smiled at Ronald and told him he should be off playing, that he was a child and children should play games, that they should sit on swings and climb slides. He grinned and handed

Doreen the bag, said thank you Mrs Roberts, and Ronald was an honest boy, a good boy, all children were honest up to a certain age when it all got too much and they became confused, poor Stevie, God's suffering children, but this boy was different, she knew he was a good boy, and he would tell nice Mrs Roberts, the woman who went to the same church, the truth, he would tell her the truth so she asked him what she smelt like, and he didn't flinch at such a strange question, and it was best to be direct with children, no point hanging back keeping her mouth shut with this little boy, the salamanders in the heat digging their forks into the launderette lady, some kind of punishment, heaven and hell on Earth. Ronald said she smelt clean. Like nice new clothes. Then he turned and left the launderette and Doreen smiled as she watched him walk along the street towards the children's playground.

NORWICH AT HOME

NORWICH ALWAYS BRING a lump to the throat. It's like some old fossil in power has decided to bring back hanging. That's what happens when you look back. You stitch yourself up. Get all emotional. Pensioners live off memories because they get nothing from the Government. Enough for light bulbs, but forget about the electricity to make them work. But I've got my own memories. None of those wartime stories of the Blitz. Chirpy cockney bollocks about sticking together in times of trouble. It doesn't work like that. Not these days. Not outside a few good mates. Not in Norwich.

We were kids at the time. Seventeen or eighteen and a bit slow. It was me and Rod after a game and we took the wrong turn outside Carrow Road. We were talking about nothing and not looking where we were going, like you do when you're a kid, and suddenly there's twenty Norwich fans in front of us. Just our dress sense must've told them we were Chelsea. They asked more for effect and I told them straight out because I knew we were going to get a kicking, but didn't realise how much it was going to hurt.

They didn't hang about. I dodged the kicks at first as they went for my balls, then looked to Rod, but he was on his knees in the street with his arms held out like he was being crucified and there were three or four farmers taking turns kicking him in the head. I went back and smacked one across the side of the face, then some cunt bundled me forward and my head hit a concrete post. I was on the ground and just remember being dazed. They were soon busy kicking seven shades of shit out of me and I must've been down for a good while.

Don't know how, but we managed to get up and stumble along an alley. It was a real panic job. My legs were fucked and Rod was swaying from side to side. Couldn't see much as we went. There were no pretty sights, just wood and bricks, though I remember the smell of rain on concrete. A strong, stale smell. We were on a slope which helped us along and we jumped over a fence and sat on the ground surrounded by stinging nettles, breathing heavy like we were old men choking to death.

The Norwich lads didn't follow us and we looked over the fence after a while and they'd fucked off. Melted away like they never existed. We just sat there. Didn't even get stung too bad which would have been the final insult. Rod was lying back against the fence saying fuck fuck fuck to himself like the needle was stuck. His eyes looked a bit mental. I thought his brain had gone, but was more bothered about myself. Must've sat there for half an hour and my body was beginning to ache and my head cracking in two. We were shitting ourselves because it was a fair walk to the station and we didn't fancy a second helping.

Eventually we got the bottle together and climbed over the fence. Walked up to the street and turned back along the side of the ground. There were people buying tickets for the next game. Young boys with Norwich souvenirs. Men, women and kids. The great farmer support playing happy families. I wondered if they'd seen us get a kicking. They weren't giving anything away. Just living their lives. Maybe they watched the show, maybe not, I don't know. But nobody came to help us when Norwich were trying to inflict a bit of yokel tradition.

Can't blame them, of course. Scared people living shit lives aren't going to help a couple of teenage Chelsea boys. But they could've come down the alley and seen if we were still alive. They did fuck all. Left us to rot. Makes you think about all that decent citizen stuff. The public wants law and order and all the other stuff that goes with it, hanging and castration and short sharp shocks, but most of them are just small minded cunts who don't want to get their hands dirty. They'll have their say as long as it doesn't go against what everyone else says, but they'll do fuck all when it comes to the crunch. They flow with the tide. A great tidal wave flowing through the sewers. Shit and used rubbers. Maybe they were just embarrassed, or reckoned we deserved it being young and away from home, but after Norwich we realised the score and grew up. A bit of an initiation really.

I had a headache for a week after and, being a kid and thinking too much about mights and maybes, started getting worried I could be brain damaged. Imagined this blood clot spinning around my head waiting to kill me. None of it seemed worth the agony but once my head cleared I was fine and sense returned. Sometimes you need a bit of reason kicked into you and the whole thing raised the stakes. We realised there's more to life than being a cocky hooligan with a big mouth. If you're going to run the risk of getting a kicking it's better to get in first. Travel with a crew where you get maximum satisfaction and hopefully not too bad a hiding if things go wrong.

It's all about belonging and working together. Like in a war everything changes. Everyone pulls in the same direction and all the peacetime nonsense is knocked on the head. It's doing what's got to be done to survive the bad times, and when you're up against the wall you find all kinds of hidden strength. When he was still alive, my granddad called it war socialism. Said all the rich bastards bit their lips and reverted to a system they normally slagged off. It was different times and my granddad grew up with different notions, but the idea's the same, more or less. Makes sense that if you're going away looking for trouble you need a good mob that's going to get stuck in together. There's no point ten of you going somewhere like Leeds looking for a row because you'd last five minutes.

Flies around shit, those Norwich farmers saw us standing out and gave us a kicking like they were tenderising some of their pigs. We were mugs and it hasn't happened that way since. It's all a bit of a laugh, because if you've got a good firm together you can turn a place over and generally walk away without too much damage. Of course, things can go wrong, specially against big clubs, or when it's an important game. The locals make an effort and you turn a corner and find yourself up against a thousand psyched up Northerners determined to send you straight to Emergency. You shit yourself inside but the rush is so good you love it more than anything. You push yourself through the fear and you've done something that'll last you the rest of your life. They say it's adrenalin and that may be true, but all I know is that nothing compares. Not drugs, sex, money, nothing.

One day I'll be an old geezer pissed on a couple of pints and fuck knows what kind of world I'll be living in. I'll have some crippling disease and get mugged every time I walk out the door. There'll be no more pensions and I'll just be sitting around watching an endless stream of soap operas waiting to die. But at least I'll have lived a bit while I had the strength. And I won't be paying for my own funeral either. Dignity in death? Fuck off. I'll have stories to tell anyone bothered to listen and the kids will be surprised there was life in the good old days. They'll look at me a bit different.

I've done it myself. Listened to old geezers ramble on about their youth. But if you stop and listen it's not that at all. People are impatient and call a slow delivery rambling. The old people hanging around bus stops and libraries, the pub if they've got a bit of money spare, looking for something to do with their time, those are the ones who teach you about history. They can tell you about football riots. Or sex. Or drugs. Or anything you're into. Nothing's new. They just laugh and tell me we're nothing these days. That London's gone soft.

Nothing's changed. We're just more global and the village idiot gets a documentary made about him by all those people who want to be John Pilger. Everyone's in front of the screen watching everyone else. Listen to a pensioner and there was plenty of football violence in the old days. Look at Millwall. They were closed down enough times and nobody's seriously telling me that those boys didn't get stuck in on a Saturday afternoon. I've heard a few stories and I believe them. There's never been a golden age of love and peace. That's just down to the papers and television. Public exposure. Entertainment for the masses. One big fucking peepshow.

Despite the kicking we got at Norwich, I still enjoy watching them play football. A team's tradition gets handed down through the years and every club has its own approach to the game. It's the same as inheriting your dad's violent tendencies. Not that my old man got up to that much, or at least not as far as I can make out. Seems to have played it safe most of his life. Kept his head down and done his duty. But we're talking football teams and Norwich like to knock the ball about and entertain. Every football fan respects that. Whether it's your nutters concentrating on the movements of the opposition, or programme collectors guessing a player's vital statistics. I look over to the Norwich fans and wonder if those blokes who did us are there. I wouldn't recognise them and expect a few have fallen by the wayside through the years. Got married and stitched up with kids, mortgages, visits to the in-laws, whatever. But odds are there'll be at least one or two of the blokes here today.

Funny, really, I don't feel any hatred for Norwich. Not even those pig fuckers who gave us a kicking outside Carrow Road. They're just shapes without faces. I know it's nothing personal. It's all a dream now, like it happened to someone else, as though I'm watching it on a video with all the slow-motion replays and still-frames you could want. It's so long ago, but just yesterday when you think of the memories the Chelsea Pensioners must have sitting in the East Stand.

They line up in the middle tier, up the back, and you can just see this row of red jackets across the ground. White blobs where their faces should be. Same as the Norwich crew. It's a bit frightening thinking those blokes go back so far, the First World War probably. Don't know if there's any of that lot left now. Must've been kids at the time. But who's the mug? A handful of poor old sods get to sit behind the directors and politicians, but when half-time comes and everyone else is off for their drinks in the bar, the old boys are still there in their seats. Makes you laugh. A nation fit for heroes and they're the lucky ones because at least they've got a home and the chance to watch Chelsea play.

Then you think of their mates who didn't make it and ended up getting their heads blown off. Or fucked up with mustard gas. Bitten and infected by rats. Drowned in mud. Slaughtered by machine guns. It's a nightmare and my granddad told me stories about that one. I mean, I don't reckon I'm a coward or anything, but there's no way I'd have gone over in the First World War because some stuck-up cunts ruling the country thought it was a good idea. King and country and all that shit. If I want a punch-up I don't have to go and sit in a trench for a year up to my knees in diarrhoea. Making do with French whorehouses where every other British army cunt's been dumping his load. Beats me how they could let themselves get conned.

It's different times I suppose. The pressure must come when a war gets going and you had those women sending out white feathers to try and shame the sensible blokes who wanted to stay at home into wrecking their lives. A lot of them must've thought it was a bit of an adventure, but more probably they just didn't want to stay at home and have their lives made a misery. Everyone looking at them thinking they're bottle merchants. Better to die in the trenches than at home eaten away and tormented by vermin. Can understand that, but on my own terms. Sit in front of the TV watching war films and drama series, or get out and find your own excitement. Let everyday work and play grind you down to a dribbling video game boy, or open the front door and put yourself on the line.

With football you make a choice. It's no easy option. You don't want to bottle out in front of your mates, and the more your reputation develops the more pressure there is to perform. Still, it's freedom of choice because I'm doing it for myself, not because the wankers in power tell me. That's what they don't like. When it really goes off the show's so far beyond their control it's unreal. The fat bastards who think they're in control realise how much power we have. Mob-handed we can do whatever we want. That's why they make a big noise about it all. Spend millions on cameras and police bills.

Look at a war and they kill millions, but how many deaths have you ever had through football? Not from fences or wooden stands, but from the fighting that goes on between rival mobs. Everyone says look at Heysel, but if you get the story from scousers, blokes who were actually there, then according to them it's a lot different to what you're told back in England. Nobody wants to see people die at football matches, nobody, but at the end of the day they reckon Heysel was an accident. There was trouble inside the ground, it can't be denied, and anyway, so what, but the way it's painted is a con. The Italians have their own nutters and anyone who knows anything about football knows they're a bunch of knife merchants. Just like niggers, they're always tooled-up, and when you talk to scousers, like I do occasionally at England games, you hear that Liverpool fans were getting slashed before the game.

Add that to the match in Rome a year before when Italian mobs went mental attacking anyone English – men, women, children – anybody that supported Liverpool, something that the papers and Government conveniently forgot, and what do they fucking expect? Of course the scousers steamed in, but the dagos who were having a go when the numbers favoured them should take a bit of the blame. From the telly it even looked like there was a fence between the two sides. But who gets killed at the end of the day? It's all the people there to see a game of football who aren't interested in causing trouble. It's like everything, it's always the bystanders who get slaughtered. The old bill went mad trying to identify the scousers involved. They had the video evidence so why not check out the Italians as well? Because it's all down to public opinion, which is dictated. The whole thing's political, but people are too thick to understand. Talk to a Liverpool fan who was there and they'll go on about it all night.

Funny thing is, people look at football fans and think they're scum. But your regular football supporter, right across the board, from young kid to old man, nutter to trainspotter, has seen the propaganda machine in action through the years. First hand knowledge. You can go to a game and see a bit of trouble and then when you get home and read the papers, or turn on the TV, you think it's happened somewhere else. The amount of time and effort they put into minor outbursts, the way they exaggerate, makes you think seriously about what's true and what's a lie. The great thing is, though, that it's us lot, the scum, especially the major firms, who understand it better than most. We know the truth because we've been there.

When I was younger I was at games where there was supposedly major aggravation. While we enjoyed it, and it did get out of hand at times, it was generally more show than anything, happening as it did inside grounds. But the way it was painted you'd have thought it was an alien invasion. The truth gets twisted. There's always someone messing things up. Worse that that, your average person likes to believe the lies. Saves them making the effort. People don't think for themselves. That's why politics is such a load of wank. It's all about mindless prats standing in line obeying their masters.

There's this bloke Big Bob West, goes down the Unity regular as clockwork every Friday night, and every Friday night, regular as clockwork, he gets pissed. I'm not talking pissed as in drunk, I'm talking pissed as in out of his fucking tree. Gets as much beer down his throat as he can without puking then hits the double whiskies.

Doesn't get wound up or sad, or anything dramatic like that. Just sits in silence by ten o'clock and you don't know what the fuck he's thinking. Everyone else is generally pissed by that time as well, so to notice him acting unusual means something.

Big Bob served in the war against Iraq and reckons he saw enough sights to make any one of us sick. Says us lot back home know nothing about what went on. That tens of thousands of Iraqi kids got wiped out by the weapons we've been told to respect. It was high-tech warfare and the Iraqi army was useless. Conscript village boys and a few full-time soldiers trying to keep them in line. Says the Allies bulldozed thousands of bodies after the Iraqis abandoned Kuwait. That they slaughtered them as they withdrew. Shot the cunts in the back. Says the yanks called it a turkey shoot. Formed big queues in the sky lining their planes up. Everyone wanted to get in on the kill. Says we'll never know the truth.

First time he started going into one some of the lads in the pub were getting a bit narked. They knew he'd done the business and wasn't one of these pacifists, but still didn't want to hear news like that. I was the same. I mean, Hussein was a cunt doing what he did, even if he got started with British backing, but deep down you want to believe in all that bollocks about strategic weapons and smart bombs and fuck knows what else. It means you can have a couple of cans of lager, sit in front of the box and enjoy the special reports and newsflashes they put on TV. It makes it more like a film than anything else, and even though you're not there and it's got fuck all to do with your own life, you get a bit of a thing going because they convince you it's you and yours involved.

But Bob never bottles out. I look at his eyes when he gets going and they don't shift around like he's trying to impress people. He isn't one of these cunts you see who wants everyone to think they're different, or care about their fellow man, or something special like that bloke I did in Manchester. He talks to himself more than us. Isn't gutted or spaced out. Nothing emotional. He's just realised a few truths. Some of the blokes in the Unity were pushing it a bit first time, and I wondered if Bob was going to go all the way to Kuwait and come back with his health intact, and then end up getting glassed in West London. They were getting the idea he was a traitor or something, but I understood a bit of what he was saying when I got over my first kneejerk reaction. Maybe it was my granddad telling me about being a soldier, but more than that it was going down the football.

I know how the media distorts everything. I've been around when the law's making things heavy. But now it's supposed to have changed, as though you change anything in this world, and that's the ultimate revenge. They've taken away the shine but now we're so far underground they haven't got a chance. They say the harder cases from the Eighties grew up and built new lives selling drugs and running other petty scams. But there's always new talent coming through and a lot of the older chaps are still around anyway. When there's a big match familiar faces come out of the woodwork. Standing in the shadows using their experience, beating the cameras. A big black cross marks the spot. You do your time and who knows, in another five years I might have burnt out and be content to sit back and let the younger blokes have their say. But I'll still be down Stamford Bridge. That won't change.

Norwich hit a beautiful long pass that cuts through the Chelsea defence and the farmers bury the ball in the back of the net. We swear and tell the bastards to fuck off back to their cabbage patch as if they can hear us. Harris sits with Black Paul and Martin Howe shaking his head. Rod shouts abuse, talking about Wellington boots and the art of pig fucking. A copper's looking his way but leaving it alone. We all admire the goal, the forty-yard precision pass and the forward's instant control, then the first-time shot into the roof of the net, but you don't stand up and clap the other side. There's no room for that kind of behaviour. No chinks in the armour. You have to stand firm and dedicated, always loyal. Present the world with a united front.

Sometimes it can mean hiding your feelings, but not that often, and never to any serious degree. True, it's a good goal. Worth seeing. But none of us have any desire to be fair. We get no pleasure from the goal even though we recognise the skill involved. We're Chelsea and that's that. There's no place for indecision or dissent. It's something that doesn't come into the equation and as the Norwich players celebrate we're telling them to get on with the fucking game, illiterate pig-fucking farmers' sons. They can't read and they can't write, but at least they can drive a tractor. We all laugh.

Half-time comes and I go for a piss. There's a queue of blokes pushing their way in, lager held back. Nobody wants to go for a piss during the game and risk missing any of the action. Happens to everyone, of course, that moment when you think it's a safe time with nothing happening on the pitch. Then you get there, whip it out and feel that orgasm of exploding piss, and suddenly there's a roar that sends your bollocks shooting up into your body like some Millwall bastard's foot has just made the fatal connection. Chelsea have scored and you're a cunt missing it, and the pleasure you get from having a postponed piss is ruined and you hurry back with your jeans wet from a serious lack of concentration. When you get back your mates are calming down and having a laugh at your expense because you've missed out. It happens to everyone sooner or later and then you spend the next year holding on for half-time before you dare take another risk. Then it happens again. It's sod's law.

I get a cup of tea and go back to my seat. Mark and Rod are talking to Harris. He's telling them about Liverpool. How they had the coach windows put through by some scouse juveniles. Coach was making its way out of Liverpool and five or six kids came running out of nowhere and lobbed an axe through the window. The glass broke its flight but it still ended up in the side of Billy Bright. We laugh because he's just lost his job and things usually come in threes. What's next? The bloke had better keep his head down for a while.

He lost his right hand in woodwork class as a kid, but tells the lads he had his fist wedged up some black bird and she started contracting on him telling him what a fucking stud he was. Says he started pulling out because she was coming off and he had to remember his fascist principles. Didn't want to give pleasure to the inferior black race. But he pulled out too quick and was a hand short. The story always gets a laugh. Billy never says it when Black Paul or John are around.

Mark decides to have a bit of fun and rub salt in old wounds. He asks me if I remember that time at Norwich. When me and Rod got a pasting. I nod my head and he tells Harris the story. How Norwich sorted us out. Rod's a bit red in the face feeling embarrassed and I hope the blood's not showing itself with me. Mark knows he's winding us up. Harris is laughing out loud and so is Martin Howe behind him. They're laughing because Norwich are nothing. What a place to get a kicking. Insulting more than anything. Done by a bunch of farmers. It's a story that will spread quickly. I feel a bit humiliated. Tell Mark he's a cunt and try to laugh it off. Tell him that at least I was fucking there.

HAPPY EVER AFTER

ALBERT WAS GOING to be late for his appointment. He was due at the social in ten minutes. He had to get to the bus stop, wait for his transport to arrive and make the journey. If things went well he would only be fifteen minutes after the appointed time. He put on his coat and combed his hair in front of the mirror, then scrubbed his teeth and washed his hands. He dried them on a towel. He was ready to leave and checked his watch. Went into the kitchen to make sure everything was turned off. He looked at the taps. Counted them. ONE, TWO. Checked the knobs on the cooker. ONE, TWO. THREE, FOUR. All turned to OFF. He examined the knob for the oven. OFF. The control read HIGH. But that only mattered when the oven was ON. He couldn't smell gas. That was the confirmation for which he was looking.

Albert left the kitchen and put on his jacket. It had been expensive when new and he always made an effort when dealing with authority. It was part of his upbringing, something inherent in his generation. It made him feel clean and gave him added confidence. A person could never have too much confidence. He did up a button and walked into the bathroom. He looked at the taps on the sink. ONE, TWO. Both OFF. He wanted to tighten them but the plumber had already changed the washers because Albert tended to turn them too tight. He looked at the bath, squinting his eyes. ONE, TWO. He waited for the hot tap to leak. A lazy drop of water built up and fell. There was a vague sound.

Albert moved into the room and sat on the edge of the bath. He waited for the next drop of water. It took time to form. He moved closer so he could see the water gather. It swelled, then burst its skin and fell against the white bath tub. He looked at the plug and knew it was out of harm's way. The last thing he wanted was the bath to overflow and flood the flat below. The man who lived there was a nasty bit of work. Albert was too old to fight angry young men. His heart wasn't what it was and the doctor had told him to take things easy. His nerves weren't as strong as they used to be, and his thoughts had started turning inward. Confusion built up and he was a bit worried about the future. He had his faith, though, which pulled him through.

Albert wasn't a rich man and had to get to his appointment, but was worried about the tap. He argued with weakness and felt disgust at his lack of decisiveness. He had to get a grip and take control of his life. If not, he would lose his self respect, and once that went he was doomed. He reasoned with fear and knew that the bath wouldn't flood. The drop of water was too small and the plug far from the hole. He stood up defiant. Buttoned his jacket which had come undone. He held a hand under each of the taps. The taps in the sink left his hand dry. He did the same with the bath. The cold tap was tight and secure. He felt a drip hit his palm under the hot tap. It would be okay. He shouldn't worry. He checked the taps in the kitchen and made sure the cooker was safe. He went down the stairs and closed his front door.

It was a beautiful day. The sky was clear and though it was cold Albert didn't mind. He promised himself he would get out more often. He hadn't left his flat for four days and was missing a burst of crisp, clear weather. The winters were getting harder the older he became. He couldn't afford the heating bills and the doctor had told him to eat a high-protein diet. But protein cost money. He had three hundred pounds in his bank account and it would go towards his funeral. The winter months dragged and Albert was sure the temperature was falling each year. Perhaps another Ice Age was due. He wished he was a young man. He wished he could sit with his brother in the pub and drink and laugh like they did when they were young men. But his brother was dead. Everyone was dead. Albert was alive. He was living and should be making the most of his time. Things could have been worse. And he had that three hundred pounds set aside. They couldn't take it away from him. He would pay for his own funeral.

Albert Moss was no sponger and he didn't expect charity. He had his self respect. He made it to the corner and then stopped by the estate agent's. He felt water drying on his hand. Had the tap been secure when he left? Was the front door shut tight? Would the gas escape and destroy his home? He was late for his interview and needed the extra fiver he was trying to claim for heating, but he had to go back and check. He would hurry. He would walk briskly back to his flat and have one final run through the routine. If he was quick everything would be fine and everyone happy. That was all he wanted.

Michelle Watson was keen and sincere and working for the state. Albert Moss hadn't kept yesterday's appointment and she knew enough about the pensioner that it would be his condition more than anything keeping him away. It had happened before. As a dedicated socialist Michelle was appalled at the way working-class pensioners had been conditioned to regard their financial entitlements as charity. The idea was changing, but it should never have existed in the first place. She would write to him because he didn't have a telephone and line up another date.

At times Michelle despaired of the working-class people with whom she dealt each day, especially the younger elements of the community. They had no idea of directing their anger and aggression in the cause of class solidarity, preferring to drink themselves near to a state of coma and then fight each other over trivialities. There was no logic to this self-destructiveness when the people who crippled their lives with unjust laws and oppressive propaganda were so near in the Houses of Parliament. The young men kicked and stabbed each other at closing time, or in clubs, or when they were cut up at traffic lights, yet they allowed weak, chinless men in suits to rob them blind and tell them who they should hate.

If the joyriders and ecstasy users woke up and looked around they would find better ways of using their energy. Michelle could find no logic in drugging yourself up to the eyeballs and ignoring the realities of life. Everything that happened in society was political. Those football hooligans she'd read about were avoiding the issues, kicking lumps out of each over a sport. It was unbelievable. Sport was the ultimate indignity of a capitalist society, resting as it did on the importance of competition, the wastage of resources, concentrating people's energies away from the class struggle towards silly games. So many of these young men were reactionary right-wing thugs and she could well believe that a good ninety-five per cent were bordering on membership of extremist organisations. She had never been to a football match herself, though she had listened to gutter conversations in her local, but felt qualified enough to comment.

Michelle's great hope, as a radical socialist raised in deepest Hampshire but now living and thriving in London, was the black population. Downtrodden through the centuries they were the ultimate in crushed humanity. With the help of left-wing, educated whites such as herself the blacks would gradually fight their way up the scale, and in the black youth out on the streets there was potential for a political cadre of fit young men ready to overthrow the barriers of white capitalist racist oppression. She listened to gangster rap by the likes of early pioneers such as NWA and Public Enemy, though the violent and sexist lyrics were not exactly conducive to informed political struggle. Even so, they were talking about life on the streets of Los Angeles and New York as it appeared in the flesh and therefore a little slack could be allowed.

She shuffled the papers on her desk and opened the next file. Billy Bright. A deformed neo-Nazi by the look of the man when he responded to the raffle ticket he was holding in his one good hand. He had the short hair and black combat jacket she had seen on TV reports covering fascist activity in Brick Lane, and appearances while generally deceiving could easily be assumed correct in such right-wing instances. She studied his file, making the man wait. This was the kind of thing socialism was up against. He had been made redundant and expected the state to help him out.

Mr Farrell had become a gardener after the war. He loved plants and flowers and had been lucky enough to get in with his local park's commission. The seasons came and went and because he was outside Mr Farrell was able to appreciate the changes. The work kept him healthy and now that he was retired he benefited from a life of moderately superior health. He walked most places to keep the flow of energy circulating through his body and also because he appreciated the ability to move freely in a democratic society. He knocked on the peeling door and waited.

– Hello Albert, Mr Farrell said, when his friend opened up.

Albert Moss stood back and Mr Farrell entered. The flat was spotless and Mr Farrell marvelled at the order and control of Albert's life. He scrubbed the place weekly and kept the fittings and furniture in pristine condition. He walked down the hall to the living room and saw that Albert had everything ready for his arrival. There was a nice pot of tea on the table and the two easy armchairs had been moved from their normal positions so that they were now at an angle to each other.

– Would you like a cup? Albert asked, looking to Mr Farrell for the biscuits he always brought along.

– I'd love one. It's a nice day out, but turning a bit nippy.

The two men sat in the armchairs and blew on the tea to help cool it down. They said little and worked their way through the pack of biscuits. Mr Farrell enjoyed the calm atmosphere and liked Albert's flat.

His friend had gone to the trouble of framing old photographs and positioning them strategically around the room. Most were black and white, which worked well against the white walls, although Mr Farrell wondered what the golden pagoda in Rangoon would have looked like in colour. Albert had taken it during the war while he was serving in Burma and said that the original image was there in his memory and would never be dislodged. There was a colour drawing that stood out, a present from someone at the Spiritualist church he attended. It represented his aura. Mr Farrell didn't understand exactly what it meant, but found it interesting in its way, like a piece of abstract art.

– Are you ready then? Shall we get started?

The curtains were drawn and the two men sat in silence, their eyes closed. Soon Albert would begin talking and Mr Farrell would have some kind of contact with those he loved but who had passed over to the other side. Albert tried to relax his thoughts and let the spirits come to him. Leaking taps were the last thing on his mind.

Number 46 studied the woman interviewer in front of him as she examined his papers. She was a fair looker but he wasn't wanting female company at the moment. He was skint. Made redundant by the captains of industry who spent their time bleating on about national identity and then invested British resources overseas. He felt the hatred deep inside, shoved forcibly down his throat and left to rot and fester in the pit of his stomach. The woman looked like a right Trotskyist with her specs and clear skin, scruffy long hair and roll-up stained fingers; the kind of know-nothing outsider who came onto his manor and practised so-called positive discrimination for every minority that could ever possibly exist. These people talked about the working-class but didn't have a clue what the working-class was all about. Maybe he was wrong, but he doubted it. They all looked the same. Dykes and Marxist theorists with mortgages and framed university degrees next to the futon.

He wasn't saying anything though, because he didn't have a grievance with the woman and he wanted some cash to keep him going till he got a job. The cunts in charge of his firm had shifted their resources around to save a few bob and thirty people had ended up on the dole. Top management within the firm had awarded themselves big increases on the savings made. Fascism was an attractive proposition. Listening to speakers at local, clandestine meetings and their calls for the hanging of child molesters, rapists and the scum in the Tory party made a lot of sense. Blokes with the same attitude went along and the social workers and students with placards shouting Nazi at them from behind police lines just made him more determined. He wasn't into the Combat 18 bit but was gearing up for the push. He was white, Anglo-Saxon, heterosexual and fed up of being told he was shit.

The queers and Jews in the Tory party were shafting more than each other. They were stitching up the white population for the liberal wankers in the BBC and got all the plum jobs in the media. It was a cliché but true that Zionists controlled the media, and there was no need to look further than Washington's manipulation of the British establishment to understand the reasons why. The Klan had been making itself understood in the States and it was time nationalist groups in Britain became better known. It was like any ethnic or religious minority who wanted could walk straight in, get their benefits, shoot to the top of the housing list and the whites were expected to sit back and listen to the left-wing set up shop and slag off the native way of life.

Billy Bright hated the Tories even more than the scum on the Left. The Tories had taken charge of the patriotic stance, waving the Union Jack around while milking the common man as though he was a factory farm animal. He would gladly have seen the cabinet strung up in the street. They were con artists with their plum accents and even though they made subtle noises about race he didn't trust them. Jews in high places were talking double standards. Hitler understood what was what and while he didn't exactly go along with the mass extermination of a race he had to admit that he would probably have stood back just like the majority of Germans had done and said he didn't know what was going on. It was easier to let the subhumans in the East do the dirty work than get their own hands dirty. Sometimes, though, he got so fucking wound up by the whole thing that he could see himself out on the streets shipping the bastards off. He knew the official line, but would have preferred the bankers in the City and all the other public-school wankers to be on the first trains out of Paddington. He would have to change a lot himself, though, if the thing became official, because there would be no more drugs, drink or random violence. He would have to become a new man and hoped his deformity wouldn't count against him when it came to the crunch.

Everyone was as happy as could be expected given the circumstances. Albert Moss died peacefully in his sleep and his body was found four days later when Mr Farrell became concerned by an unanswered knock on the door. Mr Farrell was sad, but knew death came to everyone and that Albert would find things easier in the afterlife he so strongly believed existed. At least he had gone peacefully in his sleep and hadn't been forced to endure years of treatment for a crippling disease. He hadn't died of cancer or spent his last years paralysed after a stroke. He had gone with as much dignity as death allowed and had paid towards his own funeral. Prices had rocketed since Albert last looked into the matter and Mr Farrell was glad the tight-fisted bastards in the council were being forced to contribute.

Albert's neighbour downstairs was happy in his own way

because though he felt a bit sorry for the old boy, who had fought in the war in Burma and along the Malay Peninsular, he wouldn't have to listen to him moving around upstairs any more. It drove him mad at times, furniture being shifted at three in the morning, and whenever he said hello Mr Moss wasn't exactly friendly. He'd heard the old man was into Spiritualism and though he wasn't superstitious and didn't believe in all that ghost stuff, Mr Moss's neighbour didn't fancy his flat ending up haunted by a spirit which came for a chat and fancied staying.

Michelle Watson was happiest because Mr Farrell had discovered the body after four days. She could have found herself in trouble if the corpse had remained undiscovered for months on end and a local journalist had got hold of the story. There had been other well-publicised incidents in the national media and that kind of thing just did not look good whichever way it was explained. While the locals would get much of the blame, the social services would have come under scrutiny and it would have done her career prospects no good at all to be involved in something so messy. She was ambitious and knew she had what it took to make the grade.

NEWCASTLE AWAY

I'M PISSED AND hungry and telling the bird behind the counter to get her finger out. The coach will be leaving soon and we haven't got time to fuck about. The chinky's packed with closing-time pissheads but we're taking priority because it's Friday night and we're on our way to Newcastle. It's a daft time to leave but that's the way it's got to be when Chelsea play away and you're lining up a major beano. Mark's chatting up a couple of birds and he's obviously in with one of them, and her mate's going spare, but we'll just have to do without. A shag's a shag and no bird can compare with a trip to Newcastle. Would we rather take them back and give them a good servicing? Full lubrication job and a tank full of petrol? Wake up with a slab of freshly greased tart on the pillow tomorrow morning? Or open our eyes in Newcastle with the lads looking for geordies?

It's a cold night and these two sleep in beds kept hot with the flow of one-nighters. It's so fucking easy you want to laugh. No need for electric blankets with these two slappers. It's a long trip to Newcastle, uphill all the way. The inevitable hangover and a broken night's sleep. That or a takeaway girl. Number sixty-nine on the menu. No contest. The chink bird hands over a white plastic bag and the smell hits me full frontal. Mushroom noodles and sweet and sour. An away day special. I tell Mark to leave the slags for some other cunt and he smiles when they tell me to fuck off. Turns on his heel.

Rod's outside sitting in a doorway. Been mixing shorts with lager and it knocks him out. He should know better. We've got five minutes to get down Hammersmith roundabout and meet the coach. We start running and I'm huffing and puffing like a fat bastard, the night's lager rumbling inside, but I'm more concerned with spilling the sweet and sour because that's the fucker that always goes over. I get to the roundabout first and the coach is nowhere to be seen. Gary Jones and Neil Kitson sit on railings by the subway. We're in time.

– I'm going to have a fucking heart attack in a minute. Rod's the last one to arrive. I'm fucked.

– It's because you're Chelsea. Mark's quick with the oldest line around. Not used to running. Yids would have set a new world record. Don't know what I'm doing this for when I could be at home tucked up with that bird.

– It's because you're Chelsea. Anyway, it saves you getting a dose. They were well rough those two. Wouldn't have touched them with yours.

– Fucking unbelievable, Mark says. I can hear my heart beating.

– Least you're still alive. I was wondering for a while tonight. Mister fucking interesting sniffing round birds every chance you get.

– Leave it out. We're not at the football yet. It's just something to fill in the time. Let me think straight and get my breath back.

– You want to get on the weights. Do some running.

– Like you? I've really seen you down the gym pumping iron.

– I'm married mate. Nothing's expected once you put that ring on a woman's finger. Get married and it doesn't matter what happens to your body. Mandy loves me for my brain.

– What fucking brain? Only brain you've got is wedged between your legs.

– That's where I get my exercise. Fifteen times a night. Regular as clockwork. I'm a sex machine. Fuelled up on lager and ready to shag her rigid. Fifteen times a night, every fucking night without fail.

– Once a month more like. Once a month with Mandy anyway. You're a pig fucker on the quiet.

– Piss off. Only regular sex you get is off your right hand. And I hear that's getting fussy these days as well.

Ten minutes of Rod versus Mark banter and the coach pulls up. Ron Hawkins the retired skin is at the wheel with Harris sitting at the front, ship's captain, in charge of a select crew. We climb aboard and there's one pick-up left, at Hanger Lane, then we're off to the miserable north. We go to the back. It's a class coach with a toilet and video. Blade Runner's on the screen. I've seen it before but don't mind because it's a smart film. All robots and changing times. Specially the language and new breed of people. Bit like London really. Mutants in the underground. Harris says he's got a pirate Clockwork Orange for later if anyone stays awake past Birmingham.

I sit by the window and share out the food. It tastes good. The Chinese know how to cook. Them and the Indians. Best food you can get. I open a can of lager and watch London pass by. We roll through closed pubs, packed takeaways and pissed couples to the Western Avenue. Then down to Hanger Lane. There's ten or so blokes waiting across from the station outside a parade of shops and Harris has a full coach. Good news for the man's finances, though he always has a decent turnout for the aways because there's enough people around who respect his ability to sniff out trouble. We pile round the North Circular and pick up the M1 heading north. The engine pulls at the gradient. The coach is heated and slick, motor humming with confidence. Ron puts his foot down and Blade Runner replicants stick the boot in. It's man against machine and I want the replicants to batter Harrison Ford to a bloody pulp. Want the cunt to spit out bits of broken teeth. I know the finish but you always hope for something a bit different. Break the routine with a happy ending. Bit of magic.

Rod's head has snapped back and he's deep asleep. Dreaming of Mandy. I nudge Mark and get down on the floor. Tie his laces together. Silly cunt's out of it which serves him right for mixing shorts and lager. Mark hands me a lighter and I set a lace on fire. The flame takes off and in twenty seconds there's smoke spiralling up from his trainers. Still the cunt sleeps. Must be a good dream. Mandy getting her fifteenth portion of the night. Rod'll be so knackered when he finishes he won't be able to play fireman. He's the dummy on the bonfire laughing at death.

– Rod is burning, Rod is burning. Mark to the tune of London's Burning. Call the engine, call the engine.

– FIRE, FIRE. FIRE, FIRE. The back of the coach joins in.

Facelift, a headcase from Hayes or some other West London building site, leans over. Taps Rod on the shoulder. Tells him he's doing a Guy Fawkes. At first Rod doesn't understand. Looks around confused caught with his trousers down, Mandy asking what the fuck he's stopping for halfway. Finally he picks up on the smoke, looks down. Panics. Kicks his feet against the seat in front and he's going to set the whole coach alight if he's not careful. But everyone's laughing, even Facelift, though with him laughter could mean anything.

– You cunts. You trying to kill us all or what? Leave my darling wife a widow with five hungry mouths to feed?

– You haven't got any kids. Mark looks like his head's about to launch into space he's laughing so hard. Fifteen times a night and you can't even get your woman up the duff.

– Least I'm not some bent cunt servicing my hand.

– Could just be a cover. Marry a bird and it throws the rest of us off the scent. Closet bum bandit mate, that's what you are. Fucking iron on board a Chelsea coach. Doesn't look good, does it? That's a hanging offence.

– Piss off to the bog and give the five-fingered widow a portion.

– Fuck off.

Rod's swearing and banging his feet trying to get rid of the flames. They jump a healthy six inches in the air. Red and white whiplash effects. Stronger by the second. But he kills them with a bit of effort and starts having a go at me for some reason. How he knows it was me I don't know.

– Don't just sit there with that stupid grin on your face. Has that cunt sitting next to you been having a go at your arse? Is that what the smile's about?

Eventually Rod sees the funny side and the whole coach is cracking up. Even Harris and Ron the driver who have a stake in making sure we don't end up a burnt-out wreck on the hard shoulder. Just our luck. Coach wrecked before we get to Watford. But Rod's pissed and tired enough not to want revenge which is fine by me because I'm not in the mood myself. He plays the white man, takes stick, and goes back to sleep. I'm knackered and though I'm in the mood to hand it out, I don't fancy taking it as well. There's cans going round and Facelift's into a bottle of quality vodka. Tattoos cover his arms and his gut spills over his jeans. One of the few football stereotypes on board. The rest are nutters, but smartly dressed nutters. Facelift's pissed and moaning about Black Paul and John. Talks under his breath. But they're sound blokes and do the business. He'll learn soon enough when the geordies pile in. Geordies always get stuck in against Chelsea. They're no bottle merchants.

Have to admit I don't like Facelift but wouldn't want to cross the man. He did nine months for glassing his brother-in-law after a row in some snooker club over in Hayes so wouldn't hesitate with a casual acquaintance. Says he just lost it and cut the bloke up. Ran home and the victim's mates were round the house trying to kick the door down when the old bill arrived and nicked him. Said it was the only time he was glad to see the bastards, though he reckons his brother had a shooter stashed upstairs and he'd have used the fucker no problem. You've got to be a bit mental to take life so seriously and Facelift's the kind of bloke who'd do it all again. Prison just makes people like him worse. Makes everyone who goes down bitter and more fucked up than ever. It's not a pretty sight seeing someone's face sliced open, even if they're a cunt and deserve the grief, but you can half understand someone doing it in a blind panic to a stranger. But not your sister's husband. You've got to have standards or you're nothing.

Motorways are all the same by night and you don't get to see the rolling fields of England's green and pleasant land because the dark shuts out the housing estates and dead factories. Cities of the living dead; Derby and Wolverhampton and then up to Leeds and Huddersfield. England's full of shit towns. Places like Barnsley and Sheffield. They can't compare with London. We're out on our own and don't belong with the rest of England. Northerners hate us and we return the compliment. We're just a bunch of flash cockney bastards as far as they're concerned. They think we're all Mike Baldwin wide boys because we treat them like country bumpkins, even though they come from some fucking rough cities. It's two countries in one. Different ways of thinking. Though when you get to a football ground we're all the same really.

Mind you, go see England away and Northerners turn human. A bit like Blade Runner in a way. Android lads from Yorkshire take on new identities when you're in Poland or some other East European slave state. When you're facing a couple of thousand mad Poles aiming to kick you into the next world the sight of a mob of fat geordie bastards steaming in washes away all the problems. It's an odd experience and you have to push yourself at times not to lose the edge. You know you're fighting blokes with the same attitudes but it doesn't stop anything. If you sat down and analysed it you'd end up doing fuck all. You can't apply logic. Just blank the situation and enjoy yourself. Watching England's different and you have to remember your priorities. If you clock a familiar face back in England you're obviously not going to pile in. You'd avoid it somehow, though the situation's unlikely to come about. But no matter what, I'd have a word and save the bloke concerned. If I couldn't I might as well give up. That would be me ground down standing to attention. Sitting on this coach speeding north it doesn't pay to think like this too much. It serves no purpose. You want your fun and that's the end of the matter.

– Arsenal had their moment for a while. Facelift's holding court behind us with Martin Howe and some bloke who used to be in the Marines. Dave Cross I think he's called.

– They were never going to touch Millwall or West Ham, Dave says. Too many fucking niggers.

– They've had black faces in their time.

– Not like fucking Arsenal. It's all the kids from Finsbury Park and Seven Sisters. Paddies don't get much of a look in these days.

Black Paul's down the front of the coach. I can tell he's listening. Him and Facelift don't see eye to eye on a lot of things and it'll come out one day. At least Billy keeps his mouth shut. There's few niggers in this mob but the couple we have are here on merit, plus something extra. It's down to geography more than anything. Black Paul gets up and walks down the coach. Facelift sends him a look that gives nothing away. Their eyes lock on. Nothing's said. Black Paul goes for a piss. Facelift has a swig of vodka and says he's looking forward to doing a few geordie cunts.

I last through Blade Runner but fall asleep before Clockwork Orange gets going. Next thing I know the sun's making me blink. I never remember my dreams which suits me fine, but it makes the night go quick. Seems I've only been asleep a few minutes, but once I straighten my neck I'm feeling good. Rub my eyes and look out the window. Don't know what the time is and fuck knows where we are, but the coach has stopped and there's a green field and blue sky outside. Facelift stands in the middle of the field with his empty vodka bottle at his side, pissing away the dregs. Steam rises from the grass. A fucking slob that man. If he wasn't so hard he'd be an embarrassment.

– Piss stop lads. Harris looks fresh as a daisy, but all the daisies are getting pissed on by Facelift. Time for some fresh air. Last stop before Sunderland.

I get up and go outside. It's a crisp morning and it's a good piss. Maximum relief. Full bladder orgasm. Better than the chemical job on the coach which isn't working properly. I look over the fields and there's birds singing and mist rolling across lush grass. There's hedges and old oaks. There's a couple of houses in the distance surrounded by green trees. There's cows grazing on the side of a hill and when I look up at the sky there's just a dome of brilliant blue with all these weird little clouds floating around. And there's a tattooed Hayes cunt turning back towards the coach. He throws his empty bottle into a bush. There's the smash of glass and a couple of distant cows turn their heads and they're probably thinking the bloke's a right wanker doing that in such a beautiful bit of countryside.

– Could do with a good fry-up lads. Facelift wipes his face with the back of the hand. Set me up for steaming geordies.

Some of the lads standing around pissing in the grass laugh because he's like something out of a newspaper cartoon. Of course he plays along to the crowd at times because we all understand the difference between this bit of England and our own lives. It doesn't have to be spelt out. We stop, have a piss and get back on the coach. We leave our empties behind without a thought. There's no time to muck about with nature and romance. Start thinking like that and you'll be old before your time. Maybe we think we're shit and don't deserve something this good. The coach moves off.

The idea of the early start is to get to a pub in Sunderland where Harris has organised a get-together. The plan is to meet up with various Chelsea firms, have a few sherbets, then catch a train into Newcastle. That way the geordie bastards won't know where we're coming from and the old bill won't be there hanging around playing big brother. The Newcastle boys will be standing about with their noddy kit tops and Newcastle Brown beer guts when suddenly there's a flash of smoke and Chelsea steam in. That's the idea anyway. By the time the old bill get their truncheons out of each others' arses there'll be fuck all left except a few fat geordies to scrape off the pavement. Harris has got the day organised and if he pulls it off there's going to be some bruised heads by three o'clock. The cunts deserve it for all the fucking mouth they carry around with them. If the master plan works it'll be a tasty row.

I'm feeling great and there's not a hangover in sight. The chinky must have soaked up the lager and a few cans of piss water to wash it down beat off dehydration. Rod is awake and moaning about his footwear which doesn't look too damaged from where I'm sitting. Mark's just staring out the window watching the world pass. I feel fresh but wouldn't mind a bath. Don't like to do without. Can't understand those dirty hippy crusty bastards.

– Old bill ahead, lads. Harris calls back. Keep your heads down. Pretend you're asleep or something.

It's a turn-up for the books this one. Eight o'clock Saturday morning and there's a police car with a flashing light ahead and a copper waving us over. Could be chance, but this seems unlikely when a van pulls round the corner. A copper gets on and talks with Ron. He looks back and grins. We sit expressionless, good as gold on our way to church. Maybe we should practise a few carols. Ron switches off the engine and goes to talk with the old bill. Harris sits at the front boiling. I can feel the heat from here.

– That's all we fucking need. Mark's shaking his head. What are we going to do from now till three o'clock? I should have knobbed that bird last night. These bastards will probably send us back to London.

– We've got tickets, says Rod. It might just be a check. How would they know we'd be coming into Sunderland this time of day when Chelsea are playing in Newcastle at three?

It makes you wonder. The old bill must have had advance warning. Makes you think of undercover coppers and ten-year sentences. Things are tight these days and the serious firms have to watch faces and suss people out. You tend to know people over a period of time so anyone turning up on the scene is always treated with suspicion. You have to be careful. If you're not in the club you can fuck off. Ron is arguing with the old bill, raises his arms in the air, then comes back to the coach. He says something to Harris who tells us the bastards aren't letting us into Sunderland. They're taking us to a service station where we can have breakfast, then a pub outside Newcastle where they're holding all the Chelsea coaches till an hour before the game. Word's got out somehow and they're making sure Chelsea don't get loose in Newcastle.

There's nothing we can do and we're just sitting back playing it calm. We don't know if the old bill have got specific information about the meeting, or just know something's been planned. It's a bit worrying. Like you're being watched and your conversations taped. Seems you can't do anything these days without spies recording the event. If it's not a video camera watching you it's some undercover cunt keeping his head down passing on information. It's like being in a South American dictatorship or something.

The police car turns and we follow with the van behind. It's a fucking joke this. Their lights are flashing like we're some kind of virus that can't be allowed too near the locals. We're lepers. They think we're vermin and they can treat us how they want. We pass through green countryside and dead houses, and finally we're entering the services. Haven't got a fucking clue where we are. The day has gone seriously wrong.

– I should have shagged that bird last night, says Mark, who's talking bollocks going on about it because there's no way he'd miss a trip to Newcastle. Instead of some woman giving me a blow job I'm stuck with you lot and a motorway fry-up.

We take over the services and I'm sitting at a table getting stuck into a full English breakfast. It's expensive for what it is but we're no grubby paupers and aren't complaining. We're all making money and it has to go somewhere. There's a few families looking at us a bit nervous but fuck knows what they think we're going to do. True, we've had a couple of good punch-ups at services through the years, but service stations are easy for the old bill to police so you have to be careful. You can end up trapped. Even so, when another team's coach pulls in you have to do the business if they're interested, otherwise you look like a bunch of cunts. The old bill keep a lid on things. They know what they're doing.

We see a coach arrive with a police escort and look to see where it's from. Obviously Chelsea, but we're checking the name to see if it's a load of trainspotters or another firm. Turns out to be a Slough coach. A mixture of older blokes and younger lads. The men are well into their thirties and we know the faces and some of the names. They've been around years those blokes and don't take any lip.

– How's it going lads? Don Wright stands over the table. Must be forty if he's a day. Old bill picked us up like they knew everyone was mobbing up in Sunderland.

– Makes you think who's been tipping them off. Mark flicks beans across the table at Rod. It's going to be a long wait till three o'clock.

– All gone a bit wrong somehow. Don goes off to get his breakfast, eyes glazed.

– That bloke's a fucking schizo, says Rod. Used to work in a morgue, or so they say. You look at his eyes. Looks like he's pissed or stoned, but he's not all there. You've got to be off your head to work in a morgue with all those dead bodies.

– I heard he was a brickie. Mark leaves the beans alone. Even Don Wright wouldn't work in a morgue. You've got to be sick to get into that kind of life.

– I saw him jumping on some Leeds cunt's head one year. The bloke's out cold and he's using the man's bonce as a trampoline. Real brain-damage job. I don't mind giving someone a pasting, but trying to crack their head in two like a coconut is out of order.

I try to think what it would be like working in a morgue. They drain the bodies of blood and you'd see all kinds of mutilation from road accidents and that. You'd start dreaming of corpses and it would do your head in. Suppose you wouldn't think anything about jumping up and down on someone's head if you saw bodies being sliced up every time you went into work. Only thing I can think of worse than that would be working in a slaughter house. Least you're not killing them in a morgue. I watch Don Wright at the counter inspecting the menu and wonder.

Two hours later and we're bored to tears hanging around. Another couple of coaches have pulled in and the old bill are ready to take us to the pub they've been talking about. We get back on the coach and there's a delay as an argument gets going between the old bill and the driver of the Slough coach. Apparently a load of them have phoned for cabs and pissed off. The old bill are well narked. They want to know where everyone's meeting up but nobody says a word. They're pissing in the wind. Not sure of the facts.

We're up and running and kicking ourselves for not having the idea ourselves. Mind you, it would look a bit obvious the whole fucking services emptying and a convoy of cabs shooting off to Sunderland. We sit back and have to admire the nerve of the blokes. Fuck knows what they're going to get up to this afternoon. We arrive at a big pub set back from the road and within a couple of hours the place is packed with Chelsea. Everyone's getting pissed and the walls are vibrating. We have a few sherbets and watch the old bill outside in the car park with their vans and dogs. It's getting like an open nick in this country. Whatever happened to freedom of movement and choice? It's always been like this I suppose, but it pisses you off at times. About two o'clock they clear the pub and we're in a line of coaches with flashing lights around us heading into Newcastle.

Mobs of locals hang around giving us the wanker sign as we enter the city and approach St James Park. The coaches park up and we're on Newcastle's manor. There's a bit of geordie singing down the street, but no attempt to have a go at us. We're into the ground without aggravation and the Newcastle support is into Away The Lads. Don Wright and the others are already inside and the man's got a black eye and skinned knuckles. He's laughing and telling us we missed a treat. He's well pleased. Says they made it to the pub and a two-hundred strong firm got into Newcastle without an escort and turned over a pub in the city centre. The geordies were surprised, but got themselves together and put up a show. Says it was well worth the cab fair. That a bit of travel's good for the soul.

RUNNING THE BULLS

THE SUNSET DAZZLED as it creaked through trees and rock, a stunning orange Vince Matthews had never seen in London, though it could have been that he had never really looked. Whatever the truth, the sun was burning a path through the Basque country, and the hot sweaty trip up from Madrid was nearly over. Another half hour and they would be in San Sebastian and could enjoy a few days in the quiet of a friendly town away from the fumes and aggravation of Madrid, the capital's police and right-wing thugs out to batter the famous English hooligans attending the 1982 World Cup finals.

There were six of them in the compartment. Four Southampton lads and Vince's mate John. They were exhausted. The cheap beer they'd brought aboard was long gone and dehydration was taking hold. Only Vince was making the effort, watching the sleepy hills and scattered peasant homes drift away, the steady motion of the train a perfect complement for the country smells and waving children. It was a great trip and he was taking it all in because he would be back home soon enough. Back in London with its tower blocks and dead ends. True, London was better than Madrid, a nightmare city, but the Basque country was in a different league.

Madrid had been an experience, Vince had to admit that much, but it was too heavy by the end. Especially after the Spain match when they'd come out of the Bernabeu and the locals were lining up for the kill, pulling knives from glossy satin shirts. The English piled in and the Spanish scattered. Then the police arrived with their truncheons raised and set about cracking every English head in sight. There were hundreds of them tooled-up like they were extras in a sci-fi film, each man pushing for a starring role. They battered the English for the Falklands, showing the papers that the hooligan legend would crumble under the majesty of Spanish civilisation. Vince and a couple of others, isolated, worked their way around the ground, separated from the English mob which stuck together for protection as much as anything. There were kicks and punches from the Spanish, but they survived without a knife in the ribs.

Vince had a lot of sympathy for the Basque cause. They didn't want anything to do with the Government in Madrid. They were fighting for independence and Vince had learnt from his stay in Bilbao during the World Cup's first round that this was a different set of people, like the Scots, Welsh and Irish in Britain. The Basques treated the English as though they were people and not tabloid thugs, during the first round games, before England moved to the capital. Getting drunk and playing football on the beach was a great way to spend ten days. Vince had blacked out before leaving for Madrid. A local paid the fare and put Vince's wallet back in his pocket after taking the necessary amount. He woke up in Madrid, his only problem a hangover and some lost mates. Now they were heading north again, escaping the dust and hate of the capital.

While in Madrid, they stayed in a pension in the red light district, which was run by six identical women in their sixties. They were darlings really, with their grey hair tied back tight and always dressed in black. It was just how Vince imagined Spanish women. Either that or the younger Mexican bandit whore in a Tijuana-type border town, with her tits on the counter and hair soaked in cooking oil. Films and newspapers always had the same angle on foreigners. They didn't stretch the images, which was no surprise. The way the media represented the people who followed football was a mirror of their wider approach.

Vince was on a roll. He'd looked forward to the World Cup and saved for two years. It had been an eye-opener and he'd met some great characters. A lot of blokes travelled on their own, and everyone had a few drinks and stuck together. Some of the lads reckoned it was like the war, the spirit of the Blitz and all that, but Vince thought it was better. It was England away and the lads from Scarborough, Exeter, Carlisle, anywhere you wanted to mention, all had something to offer now they were outside the local scene. Club rivalries were for the most part forgotten. He wasn't saying the English were perfect all the time, and there had been a few people out to hurt as many Spanish youths as possible, but there was always a small number of headcases wherever you went. It was better than a war. There was no killing for a start.

He watched the villages pass and tried to imagine himself living in the mountains. There was so much scent in the air and the sun was warm and kept the forests full of light. It was a glimpse of a totally different kind of life and he had the bug. He'd get home, save for a few years, really make the effort and cut back on unnecessary expenses, and then he was off. Everywhere he thought about sounded good.

When he had the money he was going to India. In a few years' time. That was the place Vince wanted to see most of all. First he would go walking in Nepal. It was full of travellers, or so they said, but the Himalayas were the biggest mountains in the world, and even if Kathmandu was a bit commercial, what could they do to the likes of Mount Everest? He would acclimatise and get a bus to India, then he was going to Australia to work. It would be a culture shock, of course it would. Vince was no fool, but Spain was his first time out of England and it was excellent. He felt no pressure. Like the peasant's yoke you saw in school books had been chopped up and thrown away. The trains through France and into Spain, Bilbao, Madrid with all its aggravation, and now this journey to San Sebastian.

He was going to have a different kind of life. Friends and family would still be there when he got back. A year away, maybe two, three, four, five. His mates would be in the same pubs, pulling the same women, talking about the same things, and this gave Vince added courage because he didn't want to go away for ever. He wanted to see the world and come back to England and find everything the same. He didn't want great changes. Things could be better, they could always be better, but he wasn't one of those people who held a grudge.

The train was struggling to make it up a hill. The mechanism groaned and Vince listened for voices, the grumbling of an old man embedded in the system, a story from when he was a kid. He heard nothing. The other lads were sleeping and he was glad he hadn't gone full throttle with the drink. He left the compartment and stood in the corridor, window down, hanging his face through the gap. The air was warm but fresh. He breathed deeply and saw himself on one of those travel programmes, rambling on about paradise. Then the train was approaching San Sebastian, countryside giving way to the town, and Vince was back in the compartment telling the others they were a bunch of lazy bastards and it was time to get their gear together.

It took time to find a pension, a nice effort near the sea with blooming flowers in the garden and clean rooms, the only problem was that they were a bed short till the next day. The woman was middle-aged and efficient, wore a white cotton dress and didn't flinch when she saw the six English boys enter. That was nice. They looked rough in gentle San Sebastian, a mixture of beer guts, tattoos and dirty ripped jeans. One of the Southampton boys, Gary, carried a suitcase tied together with a length of rope. They were a mess, barbarians from the industrial slums of the freezing north. Vince laughed at the description. But that was what three weeks on the piss, staying in cheap pensions with cold showers and limited washing facilities and a long, slow train trip did for a bloke. The woman didn't care. Vince wondered if maybe she didn't even notice, but then she told them to give her their washing and she would have it cleaned. That they should have a hot shower.

When it came to a decision, Vince opted to find somewhere else to stay that night. He left and arranged to meet the rest of the lads in a nearby bar. He couldn't be bothered finding a pension and, anyway, he needed to save money. He was near enough skint and a night on the beach would do him no harm. The fresh air was still a novelty after the clinging, polluted atmosphere of Madrid. It was a warm evening and he went down to the sea. He crossed the sand and took his shoes and socks off, then followed the golden curve. There were a lot of people walking, mostly families and couples holding hands, stretching their legs before an evening meal. Vince was hungry. He didn't care if he was out of place and had none of the expensive gear worn by the Spanish. Fair enough. No complaints. England was all about poverty, and he was very definitely English.

He chose a place to sit at the far end of the sand and watched the sea gently sway back and forward. Most of those on the beach obviously had money, and he tried to distinguish the holiday-makers from the locals. This wasn't difficult, but he didn't feel the same anger he had for the rich bastards at home. He couldn't understand the language for a start, so couldn't make out the different accents. Most of all, he wasn't that bothered. He was on his own and had shed the responsibilities stacked on his back in London, where the class system was becoming so confused and distorted it took a full-time academic to break it into accurate categories. It was something Vince had never taken time over. He had an Englishman's distrust of politics and intellectualism, yet his life and behaviour was ground in a hatred of wealth and privilege. Outside England, he was able to relax. The normal rules and regulations no longer applied. He wished he didn't have to return home yet, but money was the big decider. Still, at least he had a plan. He had an escape route worked out. Like in the Second World War films. Except the POWs were heading in the opposite direction.

Vince sat on the beach for a long time before giving up his daydreams and heading for the bar. On the way he saw a place to sleep, under the promenade, tucked out of sight. Lovers sat on the wood, while a group of people had started a fire on the sand and were cooking fish. The darkness covered his wrecked appearance and it wasn't till he was back on the road, with the lights shining, that he felt like an outsider again. It was nowhere near as bad as Madrid, but that had been something new, going into an angry city where the looks told him he was inferior. It was the first time he had been on the receiving end of racism, and the old men in the square where the English went to drink had been one hundred per cent fascists, supporters of Franco who saluted Hitler at the England versus Germany game when the national anthem was played. It was odd, conjuring up old grainy film of Nuremberg, and made the mocking, cartoon salutes of the English pointless.

He would have to get used to the feeling, because he was going to see the world one day, and if things went really well who knows, maybe he would never go back to England. The thought made him jolt, though it was all in the future. He was hungry but had to save money, have a couple of drinks and get a decent night's sleep. It would be good in its own way, sleeping on the beach alone in a foreign land. Now he fancied an ice-cold drink. He entered the bar.

– Alright Vince? We thought you'd forgotten about us. John was propped against the bar looking scrubbed and polished, even if the clothes he was wearing were creased and unwashed. Tomorrow he would look the part. Or so he hoped.

– Did you find a place to stay? Gary was in a round with the other Southampton boys, and he ordered a bottle of piss water for Vince, who gave him the money. They were sticking in small rounds because none of them had much cash. Buying your own drinks was unheard of at home, but these were difficult times. Vince told them he was sleeping out.

– I didn't think of the beach, John said. It's a good idea. You'll save a bit. But the shower was fucking heaven and there was hot water. Haven't felt that for three weeks. You wait till tomorrow.

– Decent bogs as well, you can have a nice sit down without some bender peeping through holes drilled in the walls.

– You remember when Sean was sitting there reading that dirty mag he got off that old boy in the square? He's sitting there having a wank and then he looks up and someone is watching him perform.

Sean looked embarrassed by John's story. He sat on a stool with the other Southampton lads Gavin, Tony and Gary. He was always calling John a chirpy cockney, and the Londoner was doing his best to live up to the pisstake. They'd known each other since their arrival in Madrid on the same train. The others just laughed.

– He comes running out with his jeans round his ankles with a hard-on and the watching eye has legged it, but one of the old dears is passing and she stops and just stands there staring at him. He turns and runs back in the bog with his arse hanging out.

– Those old girls were alright, said Vince. Nice ladies. What a place to live, though. Smack in the middle of the red light. They weren't bothered by it much, were they, and they were off to church every evening as well. The Spanish are a bit funny like that. They have Franco in charge all those years, and their coppers are nutters who must've been trained up by the Gestapo, and the Government's worse than Parliament, and then they all march off to church together.

– It's like the Mafia films, said Gary. You look at a film like The Godfather and they're cutting bits off each other and shooting people for fun, and then they're there in front of the old cross giving it a load of chat, asking God for forgiveness.

Vince drank from the bottle of lager. It was freezing cold. He was used to the taste of Spanish beer now, but couldn't say it was that good. He tried not to moan too much, because all the other lads were always going on about drinking piss water, but he told them he'd never drunk piss before so didn't know what it was like. It got a laugh.

– It makes you think about the old Catholics, doesn't it, he said. You look at it, and what countries were fascist before and during the last war? Italy had Mussolini and Spain had Franco. Germany ran the show with Adolf and he got a lot of his support from the Catholics in the south, in Bavaria and thereabouts, while the Croats and Ukranians both joined up. The French split in half and shipped their Jews off to Germany, while the Poles didn't exactly love them and if they got out of the Warsaw ghetto they had the Polish partisans to face. Then you've got Latin America and all the dictatorships. They're all at it, aren't they?

– How do you know so much? asked Sean.

– I read the occasional book. Watch documentaries on the telly and things like that.

– What about the Irish then? They weren't a fascist country, were they? My mum and dad are from Ireland. They would've told me if Hitler had been in the running over there.

– The Irish are different.

– How's that then?

– They're Gaelic. They only became Catholic because the Scots that the English brought into Ulster were Protestant. They just went for the opposite. That's what it was like then. And anyway, the Irish aren't exactly the most open-minded people in the world, and they didn't back up England in the Second World War either.

– Why the fuck should they back them up? What did the English ever do for the Irish?

– We gave them Oliver Cromwell, said John, laughing, trying to calm things down.

– Yeah, right. Oliver Cromwell. Murdering bastard.

– I'm not having a go at the Irish, said Vince. I was just saying it's a bit odd how the Catholics seem to go towards right-wing leaders. I'm not saying whether it's good or bad or whatever, I'm just saying it's a bit of a coincidence.

– It's because the Jews killed Christ, said Gavin. Yiddo bastards killed the Saviour. That's why they all hate the Jews. You look at the Catholics and they're fanatics, aren't they? You saw how they were in Madrid. It's buried in their heads. They don't know why it is, but they have to obey the leader. They obey God or Franco or Hitler or Mussolini or who fucking knows who. It doesn't matter. It's built in. Comes with the religion.

– The Irish aren't like that, said Sean.

– They're different. An island race. A different tribe. Gaelic like Vince said.

– Why does everyone hate Spurs then? asked John. They're the yids and every club hates those bastards.

– That's because they're flash, Vince answered, laughing now. It's there, but not the same. There's no religious mania in England, just a few vicars man-handling their flocks. A few old spinsters in the shires wishing they could get a length off the farm hand, but knowing they can't and pointing to the Bible and saying if they can't get a good poke then why should anyone else?

They were all laughing now. It was an interesting point, though. Vince had never thought it all the way through before. He would have to give it some more consideration in a quiet moment. He finished his drink and got a round for John and himself. A couple more bottles and he would piss off for the night. He was looking forward to a hot shower tomorrow, but had to make the best of tonight first. There were some nice birds in the bar, though he could tell they were well off and the English boys were a bit cut off from the rest of the people there. It was mostly men and women in their early twenties. The majority were dressed in white and had scooters parked outside. He paid the barman and took the bottles.

– That bar was great in Madrid, wasn't it? he said, when he turned back to the others. Poor old Lurch didn't know what was going on half the time. Poor bastard just stood there trying to keep tabs on what we were eating and he had no chance.

– It was a lot cheaper than here, Gary said, looking at his beer. And there was all that food up for grabs.

The Madrid bar had been near the pension where they stayed.

It was the first one they went to in the evening and the last after they'd been for a wander. They generally polished off the evenings with a couple of hours drinking the dirt cheap wine and beer Lurch served. The counters were covered with big trays of food, everything from battered fish and chicken wings to paella and bread. It was greasy, working man's food, and the idea was that customers helped themselves and paid their bill at the end of the evening. The English, as was the custom when following England away, just jumped in and helped themselves, then denied any knowledge when it was time to pay. They figured that the Spanish treated them like dirt, as though they were the scum of the earth, so they went for the herd approach and reasoned that if they weren't seen as individuals then the locals wouldn't be able to tell them apart.

Lurch ran the bar until one in the morning and then he was off, an older, fatter man, who owned the place, arriving to take over. Lurch was alright, and got his name from the typical horror film butler, tall and leaning forward, never showing much emotion. Occasionally he would smile as the England boys went about their business, and though there were no big conversations between the two sides, they always paid for their drinks and he rarely lost his temper. Maybe he decided that it wasn't his bar, Vince never worked it out. It was a strange situation because they were back there night after night, thirty or forty pissed-up English lads in shorts and T-shirts, singing songs about the Falklands and chatting with the prostitutes out on the pavement.

– Remember when we were coming back from that shitty disco and those street cleaners came along and hosed us down? We were pissed up on cooking wine and they soaked us and then just drove off.

When they left the bar, Vince turned towards the beach while the others made a big fuss about the crisp white sheets waiting at the pension. Vince could handle the pisstake though and walked through the near empty streets to the spot he had lined up for the night. A breeze had picked up and he took his jacket from the bag he'd brought to Spain. It wouldn't give much protection if the wind really got going, but he would survive. He got on all fours and crawled under the promenade, smoothed the sand and put the bag under his head. He raised his legs up into the foetal position.

The drink would help him get to sleep. It had been a good idea. Mind you, he was hungry, fucking starving if he was honest, but there was no chance of any food now. He wished Lurch was running a bar in San Sebastian.

Vince was soon drifting away, shifting his position in the sand, which wasn't as comfortable as he had imagined. It was a different texture to the actual beach. This was a mixture, with heavier earth and stone from the promenade's foundations. The sea was faint at first and he enjoyed the idea of water moving up and down the shore, the steady rhythm which would rock him to sleep. This was what living was all about. He was seeing a bit of the world. The sea would eventually become faint and then disappear, but it wasn't working out that way, and after half an hour the noise was deafening, a dose of Chinese water torture which wouldn't let him sleep. The wind was getting stronger and he was cold. His mind raced. Thinking of Madrid.

There had been a bad atmosphere in the city. That night they were in the square drinking at three in the morning, going from bar to bar, thirty or so English singing songs about the Falklands, using the term Malvinas so the Spaniards would understand. Three English lads had been beaten up pretty badly by a gang of fascist blue shirts armed with iron bars while asleep in the park. Then a Derby fan was surrounded by a big mob of the bastards and stabbed through the heart outside the Bernabeu. They were scum. Knife merchants the lot of them. He hated people who used knives. Some of the English started arming themselves for their own defence. Then a mob of Spanish came to the square where they were drinking and piled in. The English ran them all over the shop. A bunch of shitters. That's why the Spanish used knives and needed numbers of twenty or thirty to one. The Derby lad was lucky to survive.

That night they got back to the square at two in the morning and for once weren't going to end up in Lurch's bar. They were sitting at tables when the waiters started pulling out guns. They all had pistols and suddenly the square was full of police carrying machine guns. The English were lined up against a wall and the old bill went along searching everyone. Two men stood behind the person they were searching. Vince felt a muzzle in the base of his back. Hands worked up and down his body looking for something. He wondered if it was drugs. If they were going to plant something nasty on a select few and bang them away for ten years. Then they were surrounding the three German skinheads knocking about with the English. The police were screaming at the Germans and one of the bastards was cracking Jurgen, the leader, in the jaw with the butt of his gun.

Vince remembered the Germans had a pistol and gas cartridges. They were going to let them off in the subway after the Spain-Germany game. He figured it out. Someone had reported seeing a gun and the police had gone into action. They must have been watching all the time and had lined it up. The Germans were getting a battering while the rest of the police kept the English faces to the wall. It was a flies round shit job. Then the skinheads were bundled into a van which skidded off with lights flashing and sirens cranked up doing their best to wake the locals. Coppers loved making a drama out of nothing. It was the same all over the world.

It was only a flare gun or something similar, and the gas would have got a few people coughing but wasn't going to cause mass death. The Germans were daft flashing it around. They had all the skinhead gear, bought in The Last Resort shop in Petticoat Lane, and the first time the three had come into the square Jurgen stopped, pointed to his DMs, and called them nigger kickers. They had the clothes while the English were more of a scruffy casual crew, and this was a time of skinhead revival in London and English club sides in charge of European competitions. He wondered if the Germans would get a sentence or be on the first plane back to Düsseldorf.

The sea was driving Vince round the bend. He wondered what the time was but didn't have a watch. He'd sold it in Madrid for a giveaway price, needing the cash. Some of the lads went to the embassy and pleaded poverty for a ticket home, but Vince was making his time last and wanted a few days away from the football. Scousers were best at getting a long way on zero resources. The Liverpool fans especially, who had been following their club around Europe for a number of years, had it down to a very fine art. They paid for near enough nothing, with stories of blokes travelling under the carriages of trains, and they robbed any shop going. It was established that when Liverpool played in Europe the scousers would hit the clothes shops first and then the jewellers. The Swiss and all those rich, decent-minded countries didn't understand this mentality. They had polished streets and intense discipline while the young men arriving from the English estates were robbers and villains on an early Eighties free for all.

The scousers were leading the trends in football when it came to gear, and they nicked all the expensive sports stuff, wearing some and flogging the rest. They made a decent amount from their raids on jewellers' shops. Get a riot going and the scousers would loot the jewellers and stash the stuff in railway station lockers. They'd return to England for a few weeks and then go back to the Continent and bring the valuables home, where they'd make enough to keep themselves going for a couple of months. The Manchester lads were next in line, and had started boasting that they were better robbers than the scousers.

Vince wasn't a good robber. He could nick a bit of gear, but wasn't dedicated. It was more when he was a kid and it was something to do because it impressed. But he wasn't bothered about England games now, he'd had enough and just wanted to sleep. It wouldn't come. The hours passed and he was floating when the smash of glass woke him with a bang, and he was under the promenade as a group of drunks threw bottles against a wall. He had the image of himself in a hole, like a mole or frightened rabbit, but it was just annoying. They banged their feet on the wood and eventually were gone, shouting into the darkness at nothing in particular. He tried to sleep but couldn't. The dark began fading and the sun was just below the horizon. He knew it was going to be a beautiful sunrise, but didn't care.

A tramp crawled under the promenade early in the morning with the sun starting to rise. He was drunk and surprised to find anyone, let alone a famous English hooligan, asleep in a pot hole under the promenade, there in San Sebastian. He blinked and thought he was hallucinating. Too long sleeping rough. Too much cheap drink. Then he accepted Vince was real and tried to teach him the essentials of the Spanish language. A half hour of this and Vince had to leave. He didn't want to move but his head was banging. He was hungry. And tired.

He walked along the beach and laid out on the sand. This was better. It was much more comfortable and soon fitted the shape of his body. The sun was warming things up quickly and then he was dozing. Later he took off his top and replaced jeans with shorts. He fell asleep. A deep sleep. And when he woke it was with a shock, his head buzzing. People were talking. He opened his eyes and looked around. The beach was full. He looked to his right and two topless teenage girls were eating ice creams. He looked to his left and a body-building Spaniard passed by with some kind of G-string half covering his vitals. Everyone was tanned and saw themselves as beautiful. Vince moved and felt the pain. He looked at his chest and legs. He was red. It hurt. He had fallen asleep and not felt the sunburn. He pulled his shirt on and walked up to the road. It hurt more when he moved. He asked a woman the time and it was eleven. It was painful but it could have been a lot worse. He could have slept till three.

The rest of the lads were sitting outside a café sipping coffee. They looked refreshed. They were wearing familiar, shabby clothes, but it was great what a bit of soap and effort could do. He went straight to the pension and the woman started making a fuss when she saw his burns. She took him to the room he would be sharing with John and gave him some cream. He eased back on the bed and looked towards the open window. Everything smelt so good. There was the same scent in the air he noticed coming up on the train. He wondered what plant or flower it was. He closed his eyes and went to sleep.

– You alright Vince? John was sitting at the end of his bed.

– What time is it?

– Nearly two o'clock. The others are down on the beach.

– I just lay down for a minute and I was out.

– You should see some of the crumpet down there. All a bit young, but they don't mind stripping off. Very nice. The others have got their Union Jack out and put it on the sand. They've dug a trench around themselves and built a castle. The kids love it. They're heroes.

– More like freaks.

– We're a bit different. It's the sense of humour. There's no aggro in this town. Even the body-builders in their plaster-on suntans are laughing.

– England on tour.

– You coming down? The woman who runs the place says we

can have a special rate if we stay three days longer. What do you think? It's a rest after Madrid. I'm in no hurry to get back to England. My job's gone anyway so I might as well get the most out of it now.

– I haven't got much money left. I'm skint.

– Me neither. But I thought we could bunk the train back to England. Enough people seem to be doing it.

– Could do I suppose. We could use the money now and worry about the ride home when the time comes.

– Have a think. I'll be down the beach. Turn left out of here and we're straight ahead. You can't miss us. We're the white-skinned bastards with club crests on our arms sitting on a Union Jack.

When John had left, Vince went for a wash. The sunburn didn't seem as bad as he'd feared. There was a bath and he filled it up with warm water. He sat in it for half an hour. There was nothing like it in the world. He thought of the tramp and wondered when he'd last enjoyed something so good. Poor old sod. He dried off and put on some cream. His clothes were still dirty, but it was hot so a T-shirt and shorts would do. He washed his gear in the sink and hung it out on the balcony. Then he went to find the others on the beach. It wasn't difficult. Just as John had said.

– Alright Vince?

– You fancy a drink? I'm not sitting in the sun right now. I don't want to die on the first day.

Gary and Sean followed Vince to a bar along the seafront. They ordered beer. Piss water. But it was cold piss water. They sat in the shade and Vince watched the waiter and thought of the undercover police in Madrid. It must have been a bit mental for the blokes working there full-time when the old bill arrived and told them they were taking over. They even had striped shirts on, or so he thought. He was pissed at the time but was sure they were dressed like the bicycle-riding, onions-round-the-neck caricatures that screamed out from every tabloid whenever there was a cross-Channel disagreement. There were probably enough police on the lookout around San Sebastian. The Basque separatists didn't sit about waiting for the Government in Madrid to get generous. They planted bombs just like the IRA. Except Vince understood the Basques much easier than the IRA, even though he didn't know anything about the history of the conflict. The IRA were too close to home.

– Dear oh dear, look at the tits on that, said Gary.

– Not bad. You should watch what you say, though. Walls have ears and so do women in shorts.

Gary laughed and looked away. They'd been sitting in the square in Madrid in the afternoon watching the time pass, waiting for the England-Germany game the next day. A nice looking woman in tight black shorts passed their table. The shorts ran up the crack of her arse. She was dark skinned with blonde hair over the collar of a short-sleeved shirt. She was a cracker and Gary, sipping his lager, casually asked if she took it up the bum. The other lads at the table laughed. The woman turned round and came up to them.

– What did you say, you filthy bastard?

The accent was educated and English. A school teacher working for the British Council maybe. Gary squirmed in his seat. His face went red. Like Vince's sunburn.

– Who do you think you are, talking to a woman like that? You bloody animal.

The woman lifted a jug of sangria from the table and tipped the contents over Gary's shirt. Then she stormed off. Total humiliation. The three of them laughed remembering her lesson in good manners.

– That was a nightmare. Why did it have to happen to me? I didn't know she was going to be English and understand. None of the people in Madrid speak a word of English and you can say whatever you want and they just scowl at you. Trust me to choose her. Nice arse though. Has to be said.

They passed the afternoon in the café and Vince filled up on a couple of long bread rolls stuffed with cheese and salad. He was going to stay the extra days and bunk the train back. It was a good idea. The fare saved meant he could enjoy himself. When he returned to the hotel John was just getting back. A couple of blokes he recognised from Madrid were standing outside the pension. John had had a run in with them the week before.

– What are you two doing here?

– We're looking at the accommodation. You staying here? What's it like? Looks like a free bed to me.

– It's an alright place. Nice woman runs it.

– Likes her sex does she?

– If you fancy fifty-year-old women she's okay. Old enough to be your granny I expect.

– I don't mind. I'll fuck anything.

John moved towards the kid doing the talking and leaned into his face. They were a few years younger. Skinny runts. The silent youth moved forward looking to have a go and then saw Vince approaching.

– Listen to me you cunt. You can fuck off somewhere else. You're not staying here. You try it and you're in the fucking hospital. We've got a nice little place. No problems. No aggravation. The woman's alright. She's not some rip-off merchant. You fuck it up for us, you'll have your mate's trainers sticking out of your arse with your mate still inside them.

They moved away. They weren't going to risk a kicking. They'd been round Europe on the blag and would probably be going home with a profit out of nothing. Vince had even seen them ponce a couple of drinks from a Scrooge of a barman in a bar outside the Bernabeu. Wankers were nowhere to be seen when the trouble started though. Spics with English passports those two.

– See you later boys.

Vince had a sleep till nine, then the Southampton lads were knocking on the door and he was washing his face, lining up a few beers and some food. He wasn't out to get pissed like back home. It was a different approach in Europe. Better licensing laws for a start and there wasn't that need to get down the pub in the evening and shove as much beer down his throat as possible before the barman did his town crier impersonation and started ringing last orders. True, you could go on somewhere, but most clubs were interested in fashion victims and silly little disco girls. A bunch of lads on the piss meant trouble and they were generally left out in the cold to fight and break a few windows. In Europe you could take your time.

They were soon in another bar on the seafront, the best place they'd been so far, with a mixture of locals and pretty young Spanish holiday-makers. They got the usual looks and the clothes horses kept their distance. Vince didn't care. He wasn't looking to get his end away. Certainly not here with one of these pin-ups.

What was the point trying? They were like the clones who entered Miss World competitions. Perfect tans, capped teeth and no personalities. Still, at least these kids were one up on the Miss World girls. The lager was good in the bar. It was on tap and hit the spot. They were soon getting pissed. A Man United fan they'd met in Madrid saw them through the window and came in. He was a big, friendly bloke. Hands twice the size of Vince's and a gentle way of talking. But he was well into a bit of aggro after a few drinks. If the situation was right. He hated scousers. Vince was starting to feel a bit sorry for the old scousers. It seemed like the whole world was against them.

– Me and my mate were coming back from Liverpool last year, and the scousers had been singing about Munich during the game, and the two sides just fucking hate each other. You know what scousers are like. Anyway, we're coming onto the motorway and there's this bloke hitching. We thought he was a Manc so we stopped to give him a lift and he gets in the back and he's only a fucking scouser.

– He doesn't realise and starts going on about how he was with this other lot who gave these Man United boys a kicking. Really going on about it, laughing and boasting, but he's wedged in the back and I haven't said a word yet so he hasn't heard my accent, and he's saying they really hurt them badly, no ordinary kicking. I let him go on and I looked at him and told him I was Man United. His face froze. I battered fuck out of the cunt and we pulled up on the hard shoulder and I threw him out. We started driving away and his leg was stuck in the door, caught up in the seat belt, and he was bouncing along the hard shoulder for twenty yards or so. The wanker got what he deserved. He shouldn't go around beating up Man United fans, should he?

– You know what it is tomorrow? Sean looked round, waiting for an answer. Nobody spoke.

– I heard it from this Spanish bloke selling ice creams and souvenirs in a jockstrap. It's the running of the bulls in Pamplona. He said it's not that far away. You can easily do it on the train. We should go down and have a go.

Vince felt the strength of the drink inside him. The others were well on their way already, the effects of the sun and lazing around. They started making plans. It would be something different. They all felt confident. People got killed running the bulls and bull fighting was a crime the English couldn't handle, but they were convincing themselves Pamplona was okay. It wasn't like the bull in the ring, where the creature was castrated and mutilated and had spears stuck in his shoulders, just so some flash poof in a cape could ponce himself up and torment the poor animal.

They decided they'd leave early next morning. Talking about bull fighting had raised a few doubts, but it would be okay. It was a bit of a laugh. A couple more beers and they'd be fine. A mob of bulls didn't hold much threat with a belly full of lager. They were more like friendly English dairy cows than rampaging killers. It was the chance for the bulls to get their own back. It was survival time. They would have to be able to shift though. True, none of the English lads were particularly fit, and they would be going into the thing blind, but who cared anyway? None of them after a few drinks.

– It goes a bit against the grain, though, doesn't it? Vince said when they were about to go back to the pension. They were drunk and had to get up early next morning to find a train for Pamplona.

– I mean, it's not like the English to run, is it?

The others laughed. It was a good line, used by everyone at some time or other. They went back to the pension and told Man U they'd meet him and his mates the next day. Back in his room, Vince dipped his face in the sink and when he got in bed the idea of running the bulls had turned bad. He smelt the blood of the animals as they were slashed, and then he smelt the clean sheets and fragrance coming in through the open window. There was no way he was going to get up early in the morning and torment an innocent animal, and maybe get his back broken. What was the point? Ten minutes later he asked John what he thought. Vince reckoned it was the drink talking. It was a waste of time and effort. And anyway, the English were supposed to love animals. He asked John if he was definitely going in the morning.

– No chance. Everyone will accidently oversleep. I bet you a curry when we get home.

WIMBLEDON AT HOME

I WATCH THE game but don't see the football. It's a fucking sad effort in the rain and the flu's cutting through me like nobody's business. I should be at home in bed with a bowl of soup and someone to look after me, but when you live on your own and you get sick you take care of yourself. Like when you get past fifty and develop cancer or something. Get a fatal disease and you're fucked. Left to die because you're weak and can't defend yourself.

The secret is don't get ill. You have to stay healthy best you can and be your own person. Shut up shop and don't let anything in. If you've got the will power and resist the dangers lurking round the corner you'll come out a winner. But sometimes you can't fight off all the little germs and microbes waiting to stitch you up. Like the cunts going through my head eating brain cells. The doctor just sits there looking at me doing a Prince Charles imitation, then starts making jokes that aren't funny. All this after I've been waiting for an hour reading dodgy two-year-old magazines full of nonsense about junkie aristocrats and the sex lives of pop stars. Fashion models with capped teeth straight from Bugs Bunny's worst nightmare. Truth revealed in yellow newspapers packed with football rumours that never happened.

I don't really dream, but the flu makes up for all that deep sleep. It's like I'm tripping. Not that I'm into crust mode, but my thinking's muddled. It's a bad world when you're sick watching life pass by and Wimbledon bypass the midfield with their long ball game. They're backs to the wall that lot and you have to admire them on the quiet, doing so well with zero resources.

The wind's blowing a gale and even though my hands are buried in my pockets they're frozen. I try and move my toes to keep them from snapping off but feel nothing. Mark comes back with a cup of tea and I hold it with dead stumps. Like I'm an out-of-work bomb disposal expert signing on for my weekly reward. It's a shit crowd and shit atmosphere. All those cunts in warm television studios insisting football hooligans aren't real fans don't know what they're on about. No clue. They're licking the arse that feeds them. Saying what they're told to say by the money men behind the camera. It's true there's blokes who only turn up for big games when there's the chance of a ruck, but they're a minority. Of course there's hangers on. There's hangers on in every walk of life. But not that many at football. Just like the nutters. There's a few of them, and a lot of fans who if there's trouble outside run around and swap a few punches, but most people just don't want to know.

– You look bad, Tom. Mark's watching me shiver. Look like you've got malaria. You should have stayed at home in bed.

I've been off work four days and it drives me round the bend sitting at home doing nothing. The warehouse can be a boring place, but there's people to have a laugh with and Glasgow Steve to wind up. The flat's nice enough and I've got the heating cranked up full blast, but it's just me and a box full of rubbish. Sometimes there's a good film on during the day. An old war effort maybe. Real propaganda jobs raving about freedom and the right to do whatever you want. But then there's the endless love stories and soap operas doing your head in. Makes you understand why women go off their trolley stuck at home all day with a couple of snotty-nosed, screaming brats. Why they end up in bed with blokes they pick up down the supermarket. Why they batter the kids against the walls.

– I hope it's not catching. Rod leans over. I don't want you giving me any tropical diseases.

– Only tropical disease you'll get is Aids, Mark replies. Six inches up the arse and a dose of blue monkey infection.

– You look fucking terrible. Seriously ill. No wonder you didn't come down the pub last night.

I know they're trying to cheer me up but I'm not in the mood. Get sick and you want to curl up and jump back in your old girl's belly. All your confidence disappears. Your bollocks shoot up into your gut. You don't feel cocky any more. Most days you're giving it the big one because you're in the prime of life, doing well, nothing can touch you, then suddenly it's gone. It's like you're a kid again and don't need the hassle. No fighting or shagging. The whole thing's fucked sitting here with a head full of feedback. As though everything catches up with you in the end.

Guilt doesn't come into it. That's a mug's game just down to education. They train you to obey the rules and regulations. Try to control the way you behave. They do a good job because it's buried deep inside and the cunts running the show get a tidy bonus. You reject what they say but when you get weak all that programming returns. They work their way under your skin but we've got them sussed because we're out on limb beyond their ideas of what's right and wrong. They don't understand and we prefer it that way. I can see the teachers when we were kids. Me, Mark and Rod. Getting the cane and a lecture off the head. All those cunts with their speeches telling us what's right and wrong. They do their best to gear your thinking, but they don't come from where you come from. They get up your nose something chronic. Make you go off and do the opposite to what they tell you.

The three of us have always stuck together. Your mates are what's important. You don't get to choose your family and if you end up with a bird, like Rod has, then it all comes back to men against women eventually. You can con yourself there's something more with women, but it's wishful thinking. Nothing's like the films. People should grow up. Your mates are what count but don't expect too much sympathy when you're ill. There's no shoulder to cry on.

– I'm glad that's over, says Rod when the ref blows the final whistle. Come on. Have something to eat and we'll buy you a pint. It'll help clear your head. Have a couple and go home.

We leave the ground and walk towards Fulham Broadway. It's raining and the street's full of dark figures bundled up against the weather. Few people speak and nobody sings or chants. It's a fucking ghost town. The stench of meat cooking makes me feel sick. I think I'm going to puke in the middle of the street. That would give the lads something to laugh about. We go in a cafe and I order eggs on toast. That and a pile of chips. It's well cooked food and I reach across Rod for the ketchup. We drink coffee and it warms me up. People queue at the counter for chips and pickled onions. Some go for the works with fish or pies. The windows are steamed up and sweating like a monster getting her third portion of the evening. Mascara smeared across her face like an inflatable doll. The bird in question was a right goer. Can't remember her name. It was years ago now. Appreciated the attention because beauty's only skin deep.

When we leave half an hour later the streets are clear. Nobody hangs around for Wimbledon. They don't have many fans let alone a firm. It's all greyhounds and sex killers on the common. There's only a few clubs worth bothering about when it comes to the crunch. Most are useless. We walk past the tube towards North End Road and into some fun pub, with tables for burgers and salads. There's a few birds sitting around and Mark's eyeballing them with all the subtlety of Chelsea bushwhacking Spurs. Rod gets straight in at the bar. We sit at a table and I down half my pint of lager. I shouldn't be drinking with the medicine I'm on but fuck it. It's Saturday night and there's fuck all else to do. I'll have a couple of pints and get a taxi home. Leave the other two to get on with it.

– My old girl's started seeing this fucking Arsenal fan, says Mark. He's ten years younger than her. He's the brother of some woman she works with. I met him when I went round last week. Big cunt with tattoos all over his arms like he's a fucking Hell's Angel, except he's got no hair and talks like a mincer.

– It was bound to happen sooner or later. Rod looks at a mob of girls talking too loud, trying to get noticed. Your old man died three years ago. Not many women would last that long.

– I know all that, and I'm not having a go at her or anything, but it's still strange going in and seeing her sitting on the couch with a stranger watching the telly. Just like she used to do with the old man.

– Your dad would have wanted her to get someone else. She's a good woman. She shouldn't be on her own the rest of her life. Not at her age. She's still young enough.

Everyone likes Mark's old girl. She was good to us when we were kids. Always made us a sandwich when we went round. That and a glass of milk. It nearly killed her when the old man died. He was alright. Never a day's illness and looked younger than his years. Then one day he complains about pains in his head. That night he goes for a piss and falls down dead. Just like that.

Doctors said it was a blood clot on his brain. One day he's there laughing with the family, the next he's down the undertaker's having his blood drained. Whatever you do in life there's always something waiting round the corner. That's why those dozy cunts moaning about football firms rucking each other are out of order. We're only interested in the other team's mob and don't care about anyone else. They let the fucking queers and sadists batter each other, but when it comes to something like a bit of football violence they get on their platforms and start preaching.

What do they think they're going to get for their talk? Do they think they'll go to heaven and live happily ever after? Or live right here for ever like some of those religious nutters who come round banging you up at eight o'clock Sunday morning believe? They're mad the lot of them. When your time comes you'll be sitting in your own shit and piss gagging for breath and everything you've done in life will mean nothing. Those cunts you see Sunday evening polished up for the television cameras in gold-plated churches will choke on their own sick like the rest of us, wishing to fuck they'd had a bit of fun while they had the chance. Imagine being seventy years old watching all the birds passing without a second look for a hunched-up old man who can't get a hard-on any more. End up like that and you've wasted your life. Mark's old girl understands, now her husband's dead and she's left alone. Mind you, she wouldn't say it in those exact words.

– She shouldn't have chosen a Gooner. Mark laughs. That's the main problem. Mind you, he could be a Tottenham yid with the curls and hat. Real Stamford Hill effort.

– Or a nigger. Original Gooner from Finsbury Park.

– Not my old girl. She'd never go with a nigger.

– Might be some old West Indian geezer with a bit of dignity and a sense of humour.

– No. She wouldn't go with a nigger. Not her generation.

The birds next to us are talking louder the more they drink. They're well groomed with long hair. Typical prick teasers. Not bad looking though. Like all prick teasers.

The pub's filling up quickly. I'm forcing the lager down but I'm dead. I was hoping it would get me going. There's something happening but it's no miracle cure. All I can think of is Mark's old girl flat on her back with Tony Adams in full Arsenal kit slipping her a length. A horrible thought. It's amazing what the brain can do. Must be what happens to your serial killers. One day they're good as gold going about their business, the next they're sitting by the radio tuning in to Jack the Ripper. Disease gets into the brain and all the messages get scrambled.

– The old girl's got to have her life but I don't like seeing her with another bloke. Someone other than the old man. It's wrong somehow.

Mark's getting a bit emotional on us and it makes me feel uncomfortable. We're mates and help each other out and everything, but we handle our problems alone. The things that go on inside your head. There's nothing anyone else can do for you. It's down to personal responsibility. You can't show weakness in this world otherwise the virus gets into your blood and you waste away. There's no mercy and my temperature's racing. I'm burning up. It's no ordinary infection. Doctor says it's come all the way from Asia. I think of Mark's old man. About when we were kids. About Rod's family and Mandy at home with a different idea of what the bloke's like when he's out with his mates.

I know he's into Mandy in a big way, but if truth be told he shouldn't be shafting birds behind her back. It's not on really, but I don't say anything because you can't. I'd just make myself look a cunt and what's he going to say anyway? He'd just tell me to fuck off and mind my own business. Mark would pile in as well because he doesn't like Mandy much and reckons all birds stitch you up soon as they get the chance. We've all been through it. You're trained up to believe the films and all that love bollocks but you soon work things out. There's no place for sentiment unless you want to end up a snivelling wreck.

I always wondered the reason Rod got married and one day when we were on a bender I asked. Just said he got lonely. That she was the salt of the earth and he had to grab her while he could. He'd never get something better. Real diamond. Said he knew he was a cunt fucking her about, but one day everything would be fine and they'd live happily ever after. Just like the films. I laughed when he said it, but he wasn't joking. It's all a bit sad really.

– I thought about having a word with the old girl. Mark looks miserable as fuck. Tell her to get herself something better, or do without. Respect the old man's memory.

– I know what you're on about, but the point is she's got to get on with her life. She can't mourn for ever. Nobody can. I wouldn't like the idea of some other geezer shafting my mum but it's a different situation now to when your dad was alive. You say something like that to her and you'll just make a cunt of yourself.

I remember my old man arguing with my mum when I was a kid. Telling her she was a slag. That she could fuck off back to her family in Isleworth if she ever did whatever it was she'd done again. My mum was crying and I asked her what was the matter. She laughed like she was going mental or something and said she'd been peeling onions. My old man pissed off down the pub with a red face. I knew she wasn't peeling onions. We'd already had our tea and we didn't eat onions much. I never found out the truth, but it's not hard to guess. Things like that you have to ignore. Push it down and keep it there on a back burner. Bury the bad times under concrete. What's the point of thinking too much about things? It just fucks you up. Like the dossers you see begging round tube stations and sleeping in doorways.

Usually I'm fine with memories. Just remember the good times. All the Chelsea games we've been to through the years. The laugh we've had. Good times as a kid. Of course things go wrong now and then but it happens to everyone. You can't dwell on it or you'll end up a basket case. I see my mum and dad once or twice a week. There's no bad blood between us. It's funny I should think of that time now. It's the flu that does it. Makes you lose your grip. Everyone has black spots in their lives. Things that go wrong. It can't be denied some people get it worse than others, but most of us just roll along with the occasional hiccup. We've chosen our way and the three of us at this table haven't done too bad. We're working, with money in our pockets. We've got good mates and tight families and we don't go without birds when we want them. We have a laugh.

I suppose we're like niggers in a way. White niggers. White trash. White shit. We're a minority because we're tight. Small in number. We're loyal and dedicated. Football gives us something. Hate and fear makes us special. We have a base in the majority which means the cunts in charge can't work us out. We have most of the same ideas but we've worked them round to fit ourselves. We're a bit of everything. There's no label. We're something the rich cunts hate and slumming socialists can't accept. We're happy with life and there's no need for social workers. None of us are sitting in the freezing cold, lonely and depressed, fucked up on drugs or drink or sex or whatever else is out there waiting to do your brain in. Our heads are together. We're three normal blokes and we go along with the football bit because it's part of our lives. Some people join the army, others the old bill. Some go in for killing people with politics and others finance.

Everyone's in a gang. Everyone has some kind of badge. There's uniforms everywhere you look and they all mean something. Something and nothing. So when the old bill and the politicians and the mindless Joe Public cunt down the high street get together and moan about the scum rioting in their back streets, shaming the good name of England, we laugh in their faces. Laugh in their faces and piss in their eyes. It's not what you say or do, it's why you say and do it. That's what counts. Two people could go out and each of them kill someone and both could have different reasons. One would be right, the other wrong, depending on your viewpoint. It's a hard thing to be honest about. The same if you go out and fuck the arse off some tart. The same with everything. We all think we're right and the other bloke's wrong, that's natural, but listen to the cunts delivering lectures and despite their educations they haven't even worked out the basics.

I'm going back to Hammersmith after the second pint. I leave Mark and Rod getting wound up by the screaming birds and get a black cab home, glad to find a driver who doesn't want to talk. There's a time and place. Sometimes you want to be left alone. We cut through the side streets and along the Fulham Palace Road. I watch people going into pubs and restaurants. An outsider. The cab drops me at the bottom of my street and I go across to the Indian. I drink a pint of Carlsberg as I make my choice, then sit back watching the happy couples in action. Psychedelic music floats in the background while men and women stare into each others' eyes. Waiters push trolleys glad they're serving lovers and not the closing-time drunks they used to rely on before half the curry houses went upmarket, but who will probably turn up later all the same. When the order's ready I finish my lager and go home.

It's cold in the flat so I turn the heat on, put my dinner on a plate and sit on the couch. I flick through the channels looking for something worth watching on the telly. There's the usual blockbuster, murder and mystery in a foreign city. I don't follow the story but it's good having the noise. My nose runs more than usual as the Madras makes its mark. Maybe I'll burn the flu away. It's fucking hot enough. When I've finished I start dipping in and out of sleep. Saturday night and I'm stuck at home like an old man. Mark and Rod will be laughing their heads off, slagging off those birds maybe, or moving to a better pub. They'll be talking football and sex, steaming on lager. It makes you appreciate life when you get sick. All the simple things. That you have a bit of excitement with the football and relaxation with your mates down the pub. It's a shame there's all those poor bastards alone the whole time, with nothing to do but work, wank and worry about the future.

I think of the Tottenham game and it cheers me up. People join the army and sign away three years of their lives just to find a bit of danger. Films can't do it like the real thing. It's the difference between wanking and shagging a bird. We need more than videos. Watching films about psychos isn't enough. Or the cunts going on about sex the whole time like they're dangerous. That's almost as sad. If that's the biggest thrill they get they've got no chance. Not that I'm ready to go without the business of course, but the way some people go on about it you'd think they were going into a war zone. I mean, we're not queers or anything, but you get your sex and it's good while it lasts, then you go away with Chelsea for a high-profile match, when there's the chance of trouble, and the excitement lasts all day.

It's a hard thing to explain. It's not that it's like sex, just that there's a bit of risk involved. People watch horror videos and whatever to feel a bit of danger. The urge is still there even if they live boring, everyday lives. Mind you, service a bird nowadays and you're taking a risk with Aids and everything, but even that's not new. We've never thought about getting a dose more than having to queue up down the STD, but there was enough people died of syphilis in the old days.

When the football finally comes on my head clears and I forget all the bollocks floating around my brain. I still enjoy football on the box. Not like when I was a kid learning about the teams and players, knowing all the line-ups and names of grounds, but it's a Saturday night tradition you don't get when you're in your prime because you're out and about. Maybe when I get older it'll go back to the beginning again. Maybe I'll lose my desires, for violence as well as sex, and make do with the things I enjoyed as a kid. It's all that second childhood stuff. They've got the usual selection of studio experts, some talking sense, others shit. There's a Manchester derby between United and City. They go on about big city rivalry till I get bored, but they're even showing highlights of Chelsea-Wimbledon. I'm like a child watching United and City rip each other apart with their different styles of play. It's a good game, but you don't feel the same watching clubs you don't support.

There's under ten minutes' worth of the Wimbledon game. It's dire football but you have to admire the characters Wimbledon bring up from South London. A few minutes of decent action is what the armchair fans get. It's all they want. All they deserve. The day's been a waste of time but it would have been a total write-off staying away. What's the point sitting at home all your life in a chair with football on the screen when you could be there in person? They show every goal from the division. I've been to all the grounds and see the stadiums as more than the view on the screen. To me they're towns. There's streets, pubs, shops, people. Everywhere has its own character. There's Everton getting stuffed at home and behind the stand full of scousers I know the streets are terraced throwbacks to another era. When Villa go on the rampage through the Coventry defence I imagine the park next to the Holte End and the brickwork of Villa Park's main entrance. And when Norwich put three goals past West Ham I have to smile even though I'm picturing the street behind the stand where me and Rod got a hiding.

All your average bloke sitting on his arse fiddling with the remote control gets is the pitch and three stands. He wastes his life flicking channels, pulled back to the football by the sound of the crowd and the passion that makes the game special. None of the TV companies seem to care about supporters, but without the noise and movement of the fans football would be nothing. It's about passion. They'll never change that. Without passion football's dead. Just twenty-two grown men running round a patch of grass kicking a ball about. Fucking daft really. It's the people that make it an occasion. When they get going it takes off. If you get any kind of passion it spills over. That's what can happen with football. That's what makes it for me. It's all connected. All part of the same thing. They can't separate football from what goes on elsewhere. They can make you stand to attention when you're being watched, but when you get away from the cameras fantasy ends and real life takes over.

POPPY DAY

MR FARRELL WALKS to the newsagent's for his morning paper. He pays his money and takes his choice. He argues over the local election result with Mr Patel. The Tory candidate has been defeated by his Labour opponent, yet neither has much to offer. The BNP has been attracting those white working-class voters alienated by the established parties. Mr Farrell and Mr Patel agree that a right-wing local councillor would mean more racist attacks, and that the bangra kids in the next street should turn their music down after midnight. But there's no telling the youngsters of today. They shake their heads sadly and Mr Farrell leaves.

– A white boy got knifed last night outside the youth club. They say he was stabbed through the heart. If he dies it'll be halal murder. He's on a life-support machine and they don't think he's going to survive. The police are trying to hush the whole thing up so they don't have a race war on their hands, but people should know the truth. People have a right to know what's true and what's a lie.

A woman with curled hair and glasses held together with sticky tape has stopped the old man. It takes Mr Farrell a few seconds to recognise the face. Mary from the White Horse. She's getting on in years now and the joke doing the rounds among the younger men is that she was shagged silly in her youth. Mr Farrell remembers Mary when she was a young woman. He sees her partially naked on the common more than half a century ago. They were teenagers at the time. There was cold grass and the smell of her excitement through the beer fumes. Mary had firm breasts in those days. Rock-hard nipples. A sharp brain that lost the thread during the war. People say it's the effects of untreated syphilis, but Mr Farrell puts it down to the Luftwaffe. Nobody wants to hear about the realities of mass bombing. They just want a soft memory with Churchill walking through the wreckage and the royal family taking enemy flak.

– It's those Pakis again. Hooligans the lot of them. They should send the smelly little bastards back where they come from. Hang the ones who stabbed the white boy and kick the rest out. Put them on a slow boat to Calcutta or wherever it is they come from.

Mr Farrell wonders if Mary remembers their night on the common, but doubts it very much. She has changed. Not so much her body, which is bone white and wasting away, because this is inevitable, but more the eyes which have emptied and sunk into the skull. Gossip says she's a drug addict. A slave to heroin and the men who keep her supplied. He sees little truth in the rumour. Mary is too old for this form of recreation and, more importantly, she doesn't have the money. Unless the other rumours are true. But who would pay to have sex with such a woman?

– Their time's going to come. You mark my words. How much longer do us whites have to get pissed on before someone does something? They give them the best flats and what do we get? Nothing. We get nothing but promises and excuses from the council. This new one will be worse than the last.

Mr Farrell continues. It is Sunday morning but the streets are busier than usual. It is Remembrance Day. A time to conjure up the Mighty Fallen. Friends and relatives rotting in the Channel and mud of France. But the old man won't remember quite yet. Not till he's had his breakfast and read the paper. Then he will let the memories come back. Relive the good old days.

– I've made you a nice cup of tea, dear. Milk and two sugars. I saw you talking with Mary Peacock. I watched you from the kitchen window. What was she saying? She looked upset, but she always looks upset these days. She's not well that woman.

Mr Farrell goes into the kitchen. His legs ache from the four flights of stairs. The kettle is cold. He turns it on and puts a tea bag in his favourite red mug, then gets the milk and sugar ready. He looks at the mug and sees a small crack he's never noticed before. Bangra vibrates through the brickwork. The smell of curry. He likes Indian food. When the kettle has boiled he makes his cuppa. He looks at the old photo, a picture of his wife who has been dead for the last three years.

– There you are. That will warm you up nice and quick. It's

hard this time of year, but we always get through the cold weather in one piece, don't we? There's Christmas to look forward to, and then the new year. A brand new start.

Mrs Farrell had high blood pressure but the doctors operated anyway. They made a mistake. An honest mistake. Mr Farrell has seen death many times and understands, but he loves his wife. He is careful and keeps his wits about him. People can be narrow minded. It makes him happy that his wife is still there, that he hears her voice and sees her face even though her body is in the cemetery. If he didn't have her he would be sad. Lonely even. But he will never be defeated. He has the blood of the bulldog breed flowing through his veins. He will stand tall and see the thing through.

– I hope you're still going to Whitehall. You haven't changed your mind, have you? You always say you'll go, but you never do. You always leave and return before you're halfway there. I've got your medals ready. Let me see you wear them. Go on, put them on your chest. They should have you laying wreaths. Poppies for your friends. How many of those bastards lost people on D-Day? Politicians start wars, they don't fight them. They cause the trouble and sign the forms and hide when the bombers come. How many of them suffered like I did? Answer me that.

When Mr Farrell has finished his tea he takes the medals from his wife. He doesn't like it when she swears and never uses bad language in front of her. She saw and heard enough before he found her. They made her suffer and then he played the hero. The medals gleam and he is embarrassed, but somehow proud at the same time. His wife's eyes light up when she sees the ribbons pinned to his chest. Most of his mates sold their medals to collectors to help pay the bills, while some threw them away in disgust, but Mr Farrell kept his for a rainy day. Mrs Farrell admires her soldier. Her knight in shining armour. The Englishman who looked for her two months after the concentration camp was liberated, to find if she had survived.

– I hate that woman. Mary Peacock is a fascist. An English Nazi. Whenever I speak with her she is criticising the blacks and Indians. And me with my accent and history, though she'll never know everything that happened.

Mr Farrell stands behind his wife. He runs his hands through her hair. The same now as it was a year after they were married. After it had grown. She was beautiful with long hair. So much different from the shaven skull. He remembers the texture of her head when he helped lift her into the truck. The stench of death is overpowering. Mortal flesh and broken limbs. He sees a coffin disappearing beneath the soil, but the Nazis didn't waste money on wooden boxes. He wonders how many times she was raped by the Ukrainian guards. He tells her that Mary Peacock is a sad and bitter woman. That life has been cruel to her in its own way. That she needs something at which to direct her hatred. It is not right, but it is the truth.

After reading the paper and eating a breakfast of egg and toast, Mr Farrell smartens himself up in front of the mirror. He spends time on his hair making sure it is combed properly. His wife is sitting at a window staring towards the common. She will stay at home while he attends the ceremony. She prefers to stay indoors these days. Three years since she last left the flat. He kisses her on the cheek and she pulls him towards her. There are tears on his cheeks. He smells the salt and disentangles himself. He must go. He doesn't want to miss the train.

Fifteen minutes later Mr Farrell is standing on the platform at Hounslow East. A train arrives and he chooses a seat. The carriage is almost empty. Two youths in leather jackets sit opposite a man with two young children. They are the only others aboard. The youths consider themselves patriots and verbally abuse the man and his children. They are smelly Paki bastards. They should be exterminated. Wiped off the face of the earth. The only good wog is a dead wog. Adolf Hitler had the right idea. There ain't no black in the Union Jack. The holocaust is a myth. A blatant lie put about by the Jews who control the media. Part of a Jewish Bolshevik Asiatic Zionist world conspiracy. Look at what the Zionists have done to the Palestinian people, though they're just a bunch of smelly Arab shit-stabbers. Nothing's as bad as a Paki though.

The Indian leads his children to the doors at the next station. The taller of the boys stands, follows, punches the man in the face, splitting his lip. He laughs because the blood is red. The doors open and he kicks the kids onto the platform then turns back to his friend, the father torn between his children and the kind of violence which goes against his nature, opting for the crying kids.

The youths share a joke and feel good together. The doors close and the train gathers speed. Mr Farrell is alone in the carriage with the two boys. He feels no fear. He is a white Anglo-Saxon Protestant male. He served in the war. An old soldier with the mark of the bulldog on his forearms, cut into the skin and filled with blue ink. He has killed for England and the English way of life. He is proud of his identity. He wears his poppy with honour.

Mr Farrell is saddened by the changes destroying his country. Things aren't what they used to be. Foreign influences have eaten away at the fabric of the society he once knew. Hospitals, schools, social welfare, unions, industry, everything has been obliterated by transatlantic dogma. England has changed and changed for the worse. Nobody takes a stand against the invasion. A revolution has occurred which Mr Farrell doesn't understand. He has been left behind by the acceleration of change. But he has his pride. He looks at the boys in leather jackets. More people should stand up for what they believe in, but nobody does because they feel there is nothing worth believing in any more. The majority have little genuine pride in their national identity.

He sits back comfortable in his seat and thinks of the war. Only those who were alive at the time care. Everybody else has forgotten. Politicians make noises which mean nothing. They use the annual occasion of Remembrance Day for their own ends. Individuals don't matter because the greater good is what is important, but the greater good has been redefined by arrogant men in expensive suits. Pride has been reinvented as cash flow charts and excessive profit margins. Mr Farrell pictures a young German recruit in a nameless village. Younger even than his killer. The mad rush of war. How many men did he kill? He isn't certain. Six or seven for sure, probably a few more. There are no regrets, he did his job. It was their lives or his. But the boy was different. In an ideal world he would have reasoned it out. The lad was badly wounded but still had a gun in his hand. There was a possibility he would have shot Mr Farrell, though in hindsight it was unlikely. There was no time to think. He blew the boy's head apart. He remembers clearly.

He tells himself that people are the same all over the world. There is good and bad everywhere. He tends to believe human beings are essentially well-meaning, that evil is conditioned by fear. Men raped Mrs Farrell while children were incinerated in nearby ovens. Maybe even they had their reasons. But the next station has arrived and he has no time for such emotion. He ignores the smell of dead flesh and burning hair. Walks towards the door, catching the two boys off guard. He breaks the first one's nose with a straight punch. He is a strong man who boxed in the army and worked outside till retirement. He is reminded of the young German soldier with half a head, face down in the dirt, brain mixed with mud. The second youth is surprised by the assault and Mr Farrell has time to deliver another punch, sending him onto the floor, blood coming from his mouth. Mr Farrell stares at them for a moment and sees the cowardice, nothing more than stupid kids repeating slogans and picking on an easy target. He wishes he had a gun in his hand. Then the anger is gone.

The station is busy and the youths don't follow. It is the Lord's day of rest and Mr Farrell is a dark shape walking with his head down. Nobody really notices the elderly. They are considered an outdated irrelevance. Even hospitals shun them for fear of wasting money as they strive to hit financial targets. The world has moved forward. He will leave Remembrance Day until next year. Mrs Farrell will be disappointed but the good old days can wait a while longer. She will make him a nice cup of tea when he gets home. With milk and sugar. Nobody makes tea quite like Mrs Farrell.

MAN CITY AT HOME

THE CUNT GETS me round the neck and jams my arm behind my back. Pulls me over to the van where one of his mates pokes me in the balls with his truncheon. The pain shoots up through my gut, a short sharp shock to the system. I say nothing because I'm not giving them the satisfaction. The old bill hate it when they can't get a reaction. This is bad news, but I'm not getting into a discussion on the subject. They can make up any story they want. My lips are sealed.

– In the van you fucking animal. They pull and push me into the transit. I make it as difficult as I can, without actually resisting arrest.

The one with the truncheon pokes me again. This time harder. More a stabbing movement. My bollocks jump into my body and my eyes are watering. I don't want them thinking I'm crying like some ten-year-old wanker. Your balls are sensitive and getting wacked with a truncheon hurts. It's a chemical reaction. There's nothing worse. It's fucking agony. They bundle me into the van and I can smell the copper's breath he's so fucking close. He's put his truncheon away, sweating, and I reckon his face is going to melt if he doesn't calm down. A waxwork with an erection. He loves the image. A hard man. Someone to be avoided. Keep your head down when you pass him in the street. Keep on the right side of this cunt.

– You're scum. He leans into my face. Breathing all over me. The smelly bastard should brush his teeth if he wants an answer. I look out the window.

– You lot should be lined up against the wall and shot, then hung up from lampposts between here and the ground and left to rot. They shouldn't cut you down till you're a pile of bones.

I watch Mark and Rod further down the street. Moving away

from the old bill. They're acting casual, melting into the crowd. Getting lost in the mass of people heading towards Stamford Bridge. Two more innocent faces among thousands. Half of me is glad they're getting away, the other half a nasty bit of work wishing they'd got nicked as well. It's no fun getting done, but it's worse when you're on your own.

The old bill are excited. I keep my eyes trained out the window and don't answer when they speak, knowing the more I do it the more it's going to wind them up. It's not a good idea, to be honest, but there again neither is getting yourself nicked in the first place. It's turning into a bad day. I should bow down and act humble, show how fucking sorry I am, admit what hard bastards they are, but they can fuck off. Coppers love showing off their power. They want me to act gutted, come over all repentant like, but I'm not. I'll survive. I should get some kind of connection going because they've still got to write their reports, and even though they're thick as shit and twice as smelly they have a way with words. Know how to tell a good story. Over-active imaginations and a mean streak that runs through the system, right to the bone. The courts believe what they say without a second thought. I should play the game. Play the white man. But I'm not interested. I'm narked with myself more than anything, but I still hate them.

– Wait till we get you down the station. You won't be so fucking cocky once you're in a cell. Scum like you are destroying this country. You give the rest of us a bad name.

I wait for him to go into one about that golden age of law and order when everyone did as they were told. Never questioned anything that happened to them. When people were happy with their lot and front doors never got locked. Back in Toytown the Englishman never stepped out of line. There were no pissheads, nutters, perverts, junkies, killers. There was no sex and everyone was a virgin. Walking around with swollen balls hanging down to their ankles. It's a miracle the race didn't explode in a puff of smoke it was so fucking pure.

– They had the right idea in the old days. They should bring back flogging. That would make you think twice about breaking the law. The Arabs have the right idea. An eye for an eye and a hand for a crime.

There's nine of us in the van. Six Man City and three Chelsea as far as I can make out. The City lads are mostly sloppy geezers who've been doing some serious drinking by the smell of them, though there's a black boy who looks a bit out of place. They're fat cunts with red faces and bloodshot eyes. The biggest one's got love and hate across his knuckles. Real wank job that one. Should have a bit of respect for himself. Born in Strangeways the way he's decked out. But now we're nicked there's no trouble because we're separated and the old bill are in the middle keeping the peace. The moment's gone and I'm feeling a right cunt letting myself get pulled into a punch-up round the corner from the tube. That kind of behaviour gets you nowhere and belongs in the days of fifty-thousand crowds when the old bill had better things to do and the Government was more interested in keeping the country running than fights at football.

We're walking down from the Maltster and there's ten or so Manchester lads pissed up and mouthing off. Walking around our streets like they own the place. They're not a firm or anything like that, but they're not exactly peace and love merchants either. A few Chelsea beer monsters start having a go at them, and before I know what's happening I'm joining in. Nothing serious, but well fucking stupid. We weren't looking for City and had been down the Maltster to see a mate of Rod's. We hung about too long and got stuck drinking. But the sight of a ruck just sucks you into the centre. Specially after a few sherbets. That's what too much lager before a match does. It's rubbish and nobody has to tell me. I've messed up and let my standards slip. I've been pulled into the gutter with the chancers and pissheads. Bad news all round and now I'm sitting in the van like a prat.

– We'll book you down the station, but the cells are getting full so we'll be taking you over to Wandsworth nick.

I want to laugh in the man's face. He thinks he's getting us worried. I want to look him in the eye and tell him he's wasting his time. That he's a cunt and I hope his family dies before he gets home. There's no way the cells are going to be busy against City and I've heard the line before. Why does he bother?

The bloke doing the talking has a thin face and bulging eyes. Bullfrog breed. There's a dedicated look about him. Believes in what he's doing. Wants to make the streets safe for pensioners and kids on their way home from school. Probably collects stamps in his spare time, but the fat cunt he works with is more into hardcore porn and fifteen pints of lager. They should fuck off and hassle some real criminals. The rapists, muggers, nonces. Instead they're wasting their time at football. They're missing the point. But they're also taking home a healthy wage packet for having some fun at the taxpayer's expense. I reckon some of them love it more than us lot.

– You won't get much joy in Wandsworth lads. The fat cunt joins in. Better make sure your arses are ready because they don't like football hooligans in the nick. You'll be walking with a wiggle by the time you get released tonight. Shitting yourself something rotten because your arses have been split.

The man's a hundred per cent wanker. Who does he think he's conning? Just because a bloke goes down doesn't mean he turns into a fucking iron. The copper knows he's talking bollocks, but he has to try it on. It's part of his thinking. All that wanking in Hendon as a boy recruit. He's repeating the same nonsense trendy lefties like to put about. All that bollocks about everyone being a bum bandit on the quiet. They fucking love it those cunts, with their scabby clothes and wishful thinking. Their world revolves around the male arsehole. They lecture the rest of the country about equal rights for queers and how shafting other blokes is natural, then rant on about prison bum bandits to try and prove the point. If it's no big thing like they say, on all those late night programmes on the telly, where the cunts sit around slapping each other on the back trying to be all unemotional, then why go on about it like it's some kind of exclusive?

Basically those cunts know fuck all about reality. They get their piece of paper and think that's it. They get a plush job and retire to the TV studio to continue their lectures. Cradle to grave. That's why nobody in London wants to know about today's Labour Party. They should roll up their sleeves and get their hands dirty. Build up a sweat. A day's hard graft would kill them. They're the cunts who wash their hands after they've had a piss, never before.

– Right, Bob, let's get this rubbish down the station. The fat copper shuts the back doors as he calls to the driver. I need a cup of tea and a cheese roll. Put your foot down will you, I'm starving.

The van starts up and we're crawling through traffic for the short ride to Fulham Police Station. I've been there before. I think of the time against West Ham. Got nicked when West Ham piled in the pub we were drinking in and it went off right there in the door. I'm standing around minding my own business and the doors burst open and a mob steams in bopping up and down like jumping jacks. I turn round and I've just got this whistled Bubbles going through my head before one of the cunts smacks me in the mouth. It was a split second thing with no time to react. The pub was packed with Chelsea and West Ham were there for five seconds before bottles, glasses and some chairs and tables sent them back into the street. West Ham piled out fast as they'd arrived and the old bill took their place. They steamed in with truncheons and I was one of the unlucky ones. The copper who nicked me just grabbed the nearest body. Just like this one now.

That was a wicked day with West Ham causing havoc all over the shop. The cells really were full, and the old bill were giving it the big one then about putting us in Wandsworth, but nothing happened. They got us down the station and moved us to a truck with cells. We sat there for two hours. Real premature burial effort. Half of us needed a piss and kept asking the coppers, but they were laughing like the cunts they are, telling us we'd get a kicking if we pissed ourselves. There were three of them sitting at the front telling stories. One with a bigger mouth than most going on about a queer he'd nicked down some bogs who wouldn't go in the cell. Said he was scared of being in a small space. The bloke promised he wouldn't close the door. Soon as the queer goes in, bang goes the door. Said the queer was screaming and going mental when he turned the key. Frothing at the mouth like he'd picked up a dose of rabies and the copper just laughed and walked off. There was a bit of laughter from the lads in the cells. The old bill liked that. A show of unity.

– What are you looking at, you black bastard? The fat copper gives the City nigger a bit of verbal. You don't come down here causing trouble in the white man's streets. You should've stayed in Moss Side where you belong with your drugs and whores.

It's a slow ride. The traffic's diverted away from Stamford Bridge causing a jam. All the people on foot move in one direction. Off to football like they do every Saturday. It's like those fish that go back to where they were born. They have to return. Something inside forces them back. It's in the blood.

Upstream all the way, but you just have to get there. It's going on all over the country and Chelsea's one of the bigger clubs. I think of all those shit teams who will never do anything, only get a couple of thousand through the turnstile, and know that if Chelsea were the same I'd still be there.

– You lot don't care about football. You just come along because you want a fight. You should piss off and let the other idiots get on with it. If they're stupid enough to come along every week they should be able to watch the game in peace and quiet.

He doesn't have a clue. He's talking to himself repeating the rubbish he hears on the telly and reads in the paper. Five minutes later the van arrives at the station. Things have quietened down because the old bill get bored when no-one answers back. The day's grinding to a halt. For me it ended getting nicked. The City fans have come a long way and they'll be into their hangovers soon. A wasted trip. Manchester to London for a few hours in a cell and a date in court. Now it's just down to procedure and the petty digs. The endless wind-ups and irritation.

– Right, out you get. The coppers are outside standing by the doors. Hurry up. We haven't got all day. Sooner you get in and we check you out, the sooner you can go home.

I expect a kick or punch but they're standing back bored out of their skulls. The excitement has quickly died down and they've realised it was a small scuffle and not the start of a major riot. It's not like the system's going to be overthrown or anything. You'd think after all these years policing football they'd understand what goes on, but they still haven't got a clue. It makes you wonder where they dig them up from. And who's in charge of the operation? Probably some old geriatric with a cabinet full of recommendations he never did anything for and a brain rotting with the clap.

We're led inside to be charged. The bullfrog copper holds my arm like I'm going to do a runner or something. Public enemy number one. Don't make me laugh. I take my turn and give my details. Tom Johnson. No previous. Just say what's necessary and the copper behind the desk writes it down as though he's on a go slow. He's got glasses which keep slipping down his nose and a bald patch at the back of his head like a monk. Doesn't look at me the whole time. Just stares at the forms. I'm not important enough.

Another statistic. He takes his time and the bullfrog next to me shuffles his feet getting impatient. That makes two of us. They take me to be photographed and fingerprinted. It's a load of shit and I've told them I've never been nicked before because, who knows, maybe nothing will show up on record. It happens sometimes, or at least that's what I've heard, so it's always worth a go. I haven't been in trouble with the old bill for a few years so it won't count when the case comes to court. That's the theory anyway. But a simple lie keeps them off your back.

The copper leading me round tries to make a bit of small talk now the commotion's over and the paperwork's got to be done. I'm just looking at him thinking I'd like to nut him. Break the bridge of his nose and see those eyes pop out of his skull. Or stick a banger in his mouth, watch the fuse burn and his head explode. Wanker. Why don't they turn a blind eye now and again? It's not like it's anything serious. A few punches and a bit of shouting. Nothing more. A scuffle which generally looks worse than the reality. Major efforts like Tottenham only come around a couple of times a season.

I'm led to a cell and put in with some other Chelsea lads. City get their own accommodation and that's the last we'll see of them. I nod to the others and sit down. Time to go through the boredom of waiting till the game finishes, the old bill check my details and decide to let me out. Then I'm going to be down Horseferry Magistrates listening to three old squires who should be six feet under telling me what a fucking evil bastard I am. I'll have to stand there listening to the usual bollocks and, worst of all, I'll have to pay the cunts a fine for the privilege.

– I'm just standing there trying to keep out of the way and I get arrested. A skinny kid looks to the rest of us for a reaction. There's these blokes having a go at each other and I'm trying to find a way past and suddenly someone thumps me from behind. Right across the back of the shoulders and I feel him against me and I use my elbow to get him off. I thought it was a City fan and when I turned to get away it's a policeman.

– That's bad luck, says an older bloke trying not to laugh. You're a football hooligan now.

– It's not fair, though. I'm not like that. I've never been in trouble before and I'm going to plead not guilty. I'll say it was an accident. Do you think they'll believe me?

– You've got no chance, but have a go if it makes you feel better. There's no such thing as accidents when it comes to the old bill. You can do fifteen years for nothing, because the bastards decide to stitch someone up, but they never apologise do they? Look at all the cases that get shown up years after the event. It's no honest mistake. They need a conviction and they grab someone off the street. They just want to look good. They're not interested in minor details like innocence and guilt.

– I spat in the gutter outside the ground and a copper on a horse tells me I'm nicked. Another bloke joins in the discussion.

– I just laughed because I thought he was taking the piss and he calls his mate over and here I am. They'll nick you for anything. They're probably on a bonus scheme and get so much for each arrest.

I listen to their stories. The skinny kid getting charged with assault when it was me and the others to blame. The young lad spitting in the gutter. The other blokes swapping punches with Manchester drunks. A man in an anorak like the trainers wear, pissed and bleary-eyed. A bunch of losers. Me included. It's all minor league stuff and just goes to show how the old bill waste time on trivia. What are they bothering with all this for when they could be putting themselves about where it counts. This is the easy option. Get hold of some bystander and spend the rest of the afternoon writing it up. I pay my taxes and this is what I get in return. Mind you, I reckon a few of them agree, just following the political line wasting resources. Rod reckons there's more people employed monitoring football hooligans than there are tracking down child-molesters. Don't know if it's true, but if it is then it's got to be down to politics.

– My brother's mate was in Belize, says the pisshead. He says he was on a bounty for the guerrillas he shot. Bounty-hunting in the army. Says he bagged five of the bastards. He was stationed in Belize City. When he wasn't training he spent his time with the whores, getting drunk or in the jungle killing guerrillas. Says it pissed all over patrolling Belfast.

The drunk must be lying. Either him or the soldier. Can't imagine the army paying bounties. There again, when you stop and think about it, that's what the blokes who sign up are doing anyway. Then they slag off mercenaries. Everyone has a go at us lot as well, but what's the difference? Only ones I can see is your average bloke who gets in a fight in his own time doesn't get paid and isn't killing anyone, but maybe I'm missing something.

– City got a kicking before the old bill got there, says one of the two blokes with a strictly casual appearance. More of a nutter than the others, though I don't know his face. They were sounding off and you don't have to take that from anyone. Serves them right.

I start thinking about that bird Steve battered in Manchester. Now that's the kind of bloke who should be sitting in here. Not us lot. Steve should be in Wandsworth or Brixton or some other hole getting a hiding from the other prisoners. Nobody likes a nonce. They reckon there's honour among thieves. Maybe there is, maybe not. Depends who you're talking about. But one thing's for sure, sex offenders and queers are the scum of the earth. More so inside because there's got to be some kind of standards when you're being treated like shit. If the cunts aren't sectioned it doesn't take long before they get carved up.

Mark did three months for assault after he hospitalised some bloke outside a club in Shepherd's Bush. He was out with his older brother Mickey and some of his mates. Must've been twenty at the time and he was the only one got done. Said it wasn't as bad as he thought because there were some interesting men inside. Old-time crooks and apprentice hoods. As long as you didn't show any weakness you were okay. Mind you, it's no way to live, and he swore he'd never go back. Not that Mark's changed his ways, he's just a bit smarter than the rest and keeps his wits about him.

Mark kicked the fuck out of this nonce one time. Says the screws stood back and watched. Laughed as he sorted the bloke out. Didn't give a fuck. Says the bloke raped a kid or something and deserved what he got. Says the blood was thick like he'd hit an artery and he got a bit worried because you can't hide a murder inside. The screws told the bloke to get up and shut his mouth. Took him off to see the doctor and sectioned the bastard. It made Mark feel better because he was boiling up and had to take it out on someone. I suppose there's a pecking order everywhere you go. People follow the same rules whether they live in a fifty-room mansion in Kensington or five hundred to a cell in Brixton. Everyone's trying to better themselves. We all want to get another rung up the ladder and make ourselves feel important. There's always got to be some cunt worse off because if you reach rock bottom you're fucked. Mark says he has no regrets.

– Chelsea are getting stuffed, lads. A copper looks in through the hatch and laughs. City scored three times in the first twenty minutes and your new goalkeeper's busted his leg.

It's hard to know if he's telling the truth. They get a thrill out of winding you up. It's all cat-and-mouse once they've got you under lock and key. It keeps them on their toes. It's all mind games and though you blank the comments and insults it starts to get on your nerves after a while. One time I got put in the cells overnight for being pissed on a Friday night in Hammersmith. I woke up with a hangover and a copper said I'd raped some bird. He said I followed her after she'd got out of a taxi and fucked her round the back of the optician's. I was so pissed I went for some chips and they caught me. I couldn't remember anything and was shitting it. I'd lost two hours of my life and only just remembered getting nicked. Everything else was blank.

The copper went off and I was sitting there for half an hour. I saw myself sent down for ten years ending up like the nonce Mark battered. I wanted to tell someone it wasn't me responsible. That I must've been on remote control. That I didn't remember anything, so how could it be me? If you don't have a memory of what you've done then how can they blame you for the crime? I was sitting there feeling like shit. Knew that's what nonces say. That they hear voices, or can't help themselves, whatever. I could see it all coming my way. Up in court and the shame, everyone turning against me and then the years inside. I'd rather have topped myself. Then another copper comes along to give me a cup of tea and I ask him what happened. He said I kicked some dustbins over and was singing football songs in the middle of the street dodging traffic. I was drunk and disorderly but they weren't going to charge me. Just give me a warning and send me home. I was so happy I could have hugged him. My hangover disappeared as I drank the tea. He was alright that one.

I sat there waiting for them to let me go home and the bloke in the next cell had killed his wife the previous night. I could hear him crying. They had an argument and he knifed her. Just went mental according to the policeman. Said the bloke didn't know what happened. One minute his wife was there shouting at him, the next she was going stiff. I felt bad for him. Life is shit sometimes and there's always going to be someone round the corner waiting to take advantage. Slip up and every cunt's on to you before you've hit the pavement.

– What's the score at the game? The drunk asks a copper passing the cell.

– One nil to Chelsea.

Silence.

– Has the Chelsea keeper broken his leg?

– Not as far I know. He just saved a penalty. Radio said it was one of the best saves seen at Chelsea for years.

BOMBAY MIX

THEY PROBABLY THINK Vince Matthews went a bit mental when he left England, that he came back a shadow of his old self, but it doesn't bother me because I view everything from a different angle now, seeing things in perspective, skinheads running over the bridge heading for Hayes with a big mob behind them, locals outnumbering the shaven-headed aliens ten to one, and they're big blokes with machetes and those kung-fu sticks Indians use when they're looking for trouble, and then there's this nuclear explosion as the pub blows up, or petrol bombs inside more like, popping glass, and everyone sort of hangs in the air for a second like the film's been stopped and someone in a recording studio's chopping up the negatives, but then their brains click into what the noise is, because, after all, they were there a few minutes before watching the Business 4 Skins Last Resort play, or in the case of the locals armed and called out for duty, probably angry because of the NF march when Blair Peach got a pasting, and that sort of thing sticks in the memory, so when a mob of skinheads comes on your manor you're not going to muck about asking questions, because tabloid pin-ups go a long way, read your papers and every skinhead is a white fascist who hates brown and black faces, never mind the JA music and clothes, the old rude boy style, and anyway, there's stories going round about these East London hooligans thieving from shops and slagging off Indian women and girls, someone's mothers and daughters, and if you do that you're asking for trouble because, the thing is, white blokes from outside the area think Indians and Pakis can't look after themselves, which is a load of shit, and everyone goes along with the easy image that blacks and what have you, even the Greeks and Turks up in North London, are so fucking hard that the Indians just follow in the wake of their mums and dads and inherit all the cornershops and cash-and-carries, but if you knew some of the blokes in Southall, like George, who got embarrassed when his old man stopped to give him a lift home after school when he was with his mates, when it was summer and he had the windows open in his Ford Estate, playing devotional sitar music you usually hear down the temple, yelling at his son to be careful crossing the road, and George knew a load of blokes in the local National Front, or at least blokes who said they were NF but understood none of the politics and wouldn't believe Martin Webster was bent, just thought the NF badge made them hard and got the Socialist Workers Party and Anti-Nazi League going, the same kind of thinking that makes the Union Jack an anarchist symbol, and George said he saw their point of view, in a funny sort of way, and he was like an honorary white boy though he was no Uncle Tom doing tricks in the white man's circus, a hooligan who worked as a hod carrier for a while in Hanwell then built himself up with weights and did some kind of training so he was hard, one of the martial arts, maybe it was kung-fu, and nobody would push him because he'd been inside, did borstal and was never that bothered, but fuck knows where he was when the skins got steamed in Southall, he'd been around a few years before when the NF tried to march through and the whole area got mobbed up and there was a right royal riot and Blair Peach, a red teacher militant or something according to the papers, got killed, battered to death, and a lot of people say it was the SPG, they've changed their name now, big deal, and the studios of the Ruts and Misty In Roots got trashed, black and white united, the West London punk and reggae bands, and George and his crew were down there that day, rioting along the Uxbridge Road, he kicked a copper in the bollocks and his extended family were straight in, all that lot, real Indians without the cropped head and natty clothes George wore, but when there was trouble they'd turn up with ceremonial swords in the boots of their rusty imports and do the business, I got a kicking a couple of times off Indian gangs, after dark at closing time, it was just part of the landscape, but Southall was rioting in broad daylight and the police steamed into everyone in sight and George and the family nicked a bus, gave the driver a kicking, bit out of order that but bad things happen in times of war, people go too far and commit atrocities, it's always the innocent who get lumbered, and George himself was up behind the wheel, putting his foot down racing through the streets, a double decker 207 I think it was, but who cares about numbers, they never paid the fare on that trip, Southall looks after itself and you go down there it's another world with people all over the place and the shops full of food spilling onto the pavement, there's always something happening, a different kind of culture which younger whites find it hard to get into because the blacks have their own thing and the music lets whites get in on their life a bit, but the Indians, they're another story, just do it and live it and there's a single attitude and that's why West London is a different place to South London, or even North London, because it's got that history, that punk flavour, whether it's the Ruts or that Oi riot, two strands of the same thing, and I think about all this sitting in the cafe I use, the most authentic Indian cafe in the whole of Southall, a bit unusual for this part of the world because it's mostly South Indian food, massala dosas and thalis, even idlis in the morning which I have on the way to work if I've got the time, but this place is the business, because when I say authentic I mean the real thing, the best way to spend Saturday evening is sitting in here, I haven't been in a Southall pub for years because they're all shit, basically, and who needs drink when I can come here and have my food then wash it down with a bang lassi, the original item, the bang lassi is a lassi with a bang, and the bloke who runs the place remembers me from when we were kids, I knew his cousin, George, the hooligan who went back to India and runs a guest house in Bombay, some people reckon he's a fool because Bombay's full of junkies, others say he's into the old export business, maybe he is, maybe he isn't, could be he just wants to live there, I don't know the truth about the situation, don't ask me, I haven't seen the bloke for a good ten years, maybe longer, he's like two different people, and the bang lassis take my head off and the prices are authentic as well, or near enough, a special rate because I'm a familiar face, one of the old herberts, thanks for the cocktail of drugs mixed in with the lassi, and it's Saturday night and I'm watching the people pass outside, like I'm back in India, the other side of the globe, and I don't have to move from this place to see the world, just let the lassi take effect and look through the window, and it's a good mix tonight, the chaps have done me proud, a jug of water on the table with dents in the metal, and my hearing must be going because I can hear the voices change in the background, the sound of punk, a good memory, from the Ruts to the 4 Skins, but at least it seems to have quietened down these days, though you go across London to Bethnal Green and Whitechapel and it's another story, another story altogether, and you'd think it would have sorted itself out by now, especially after the Trafalgar Square riot, that was the last punk riot, and there were a few political groups there but there was a lot of everyday people as well, everyone up for a go at the police, and that was the dirty side of punk after it went underground, animal rights and squats, white dreadlocks, but a lot of ordinary people, because how I remember it that was what punk was all about, ordinary people with nothing to say about fashion, except that it was shit and a con and a giant rip-off, morons, and Trafalgar Square was surreal, whatever the word means, South Africa House on fire and bongos vibrating through Nelson's ears, smoke everywhere, horses and riot police, bricks and truncheons, and the police lost control that day and it was the big restaurants in the West End that got wrecked, must be a good feeling putting bricks through the windows of McDonalds and steak houses, and none of the Indian restaurants got touched, just the big corporations and banks, serves them right, all that bad investment and manipulation, and I'm moving now, my head working in a lot of different directions, the peaceful bustle outside has the same kind of electricity as those riots, somehow, shouting voices and political violence without the organisations, youth rivalries, the race question which those at the top keep using, and I wonder where these people come from, they should try living round here for a while and they'll know what's what, because they always go for what they think is the easy option, and that's why the Indians get attacked so often, because of that belief that they're somehow incapable of defending themselves, that they're weak, that they're all peace and purity, a punch bag for the rest of the country to have a go at when they need to unload a bit of frustration, but it's not like that, I know that from growing up in the area, it's bound to happen, different groups maybe but you're living in the real world, not some whitewashed Tory idea of a constipated paradise or socialist ideal of good-natured underdog, just people, that's what it is, just people, and this bang lassi is doing my brain in, and I see Rajiv coming in now and he's sitting down opposite with the small wooden chess set, Punjabi-made he tells me, and he's knocking back his bang lassi talking quietly, too quietly, and I know what he's saying but can't get to grips with the words, funny that, and he's setting the chess pieces up and there's no place for violence and riots any more because it was a long time ago and we've all grown up and, anyway, chess is a gentleman's game, a bit of logical thinking and calm, fucking right it is, and we're starting with a bang, big bang theories, the Saturday night ritual for the last six months now, and my mind's set on the king and queen, washing away the aggravation, something inbred and part of the culture, my life story, something that gets dismissed and ignored and it's easy to see how history is just the winners telling everyone how bad the losers are, Johnny Rotten said that, should call the boy Lydon I suppose, classic line which sums the whole thing up, and even he's got another life now, maybe that was what started me thinking about all that punk stuff, how everything's gone back to square one again, and then those stories on the telly, about the BNP in the East End, and the NF have changed their name as well, just like the SPG, and I would have thought that was all in the past now, that we'd gone through a bit of a breaking point with those two Southall riots, and I grew up with Indians and Pakistanis and know the difference, two separate countries, they killed hundreds of thousands just to get that border, and don't forget Bangladesh, and that was the starting point, knowing the difference, and maybe there was a bit of aggro now and again, but that was just different gangs of kids, even Paki-bashers used to be black and white, that was bad enough, sad bastards, but not like this new stuff, young kids getting stabbed to death, what's going on, and even that Oi riot, who's to say those skinheads were racists, I don't know, it's all up in the air and there's accepted stories about history, invented by those in power who weren't even there in the first place, and I can't get my head round it, can't get my head round this game of chess, three moves in now and I'm looking down through the board, down through the white squares and they're tunnels drilled through the table, except there's no bottom and the sides are red, marble instead of wood, a translucent red haze, very odd, some significance I suppose, symbolic maybe, or just confusion, I don't care, I've got to make the next move, another step forward in the evolution of man, this man, move a piece forward and put the opposition under pressure, shift the emphasis to Raj so he has to work out a plan, and it's all about clear thinking and seeing beyond the initial action, making the right decision when there are so many different versions of the truth, getting beyond the generalisations and having respect for the opponent, and chess is more than competition, of course it is, that's why me and Raj play the game, every Saturday without fail, George's cousin brings a massala dosa over and Raj is getting stuck in and, I can't remember, I just can't remember, trying to think whose go it is and I don't want to ask, there must be a bit of something special in this lassi because I'm having trouble keeping my thoughts together, pulling the different strands tight adjusting the contradictions, like the information has got tangled together and my brain is being squeezed by the rush of images, and I'm thinking back again into the past, trying to remember if Raj made the last move, or was it me, I just don't know, I can't ask, can't ask the question, I can't fucking speak, just can't get the words together clearly, no such word as can't, that's what they say, a full steam ahead attitude, and Raj is sitting dead still with a chunk of dosa in his hand and sambhar sauce dripping onto his plate, just silence now, then the sound of the Ruts in the background, I can hear ghosts, Malcolm Owen singing H-Eyes, poor bloke, and it's all there in the song, no need to say anything else, imagine writing a song about your own death, how did his mum feel, poor woman, and his dad, it makes me miserable, such a waste of a good life, and then his voice is fading and the 4 Skins are singing Wonderful World, going on about the suss laws, and it's a strange moment because the Ruts had a song called Suss, imagine that, never thought of it before, not till this second, but you'd be hard pressed to find anyone who wouldn't consider the two groups on opposite ends of the political spectrum, but maybe they just don't understand, I don't know, it's just a thought, and what has he put in the bang lassi, I've got that paranoid feeling, like everything I think I'm saying out loud, that there's no secrets, and I've got to ask Raj whose move it is, the words are there now, full frontal delivery, he's lifting his head looking up from the board telling me that he doesn't know, he can't remember, and there's a bit of a gap in the conversation as we both try acting with a spark of dignity, the clatter of plates as the cafe closes up for the night and the plate cleaning gets under way, they always let us keep playing till we're finished, but we have to know whose turn it is to make a move so me and Raj start playing backwards, trying to retrace our steps and see how we ended up in the present situation, making slow moves on the board so we don't forget, looking back on choices, turning time upside down and shaking it so the answers fall out, I must remember my original position, but after a couple of backward moves I've forgotten, I hope the same goes for Raj, that he's not carrying the image in his mind, I don't want to look stupid but somehow I know he's in the same state, those bang lassis, talk about value for money, that's what we're getting, no doubt about that, because this is the authentic India right here in this cafe, and we could be in Rajasthan right now, sitting in a desert town confused by the Golden Crescent's finest export, brought across the desert by bandits, the Thar Desert here in Southall except there's no Pakistani border to cross, and it's magic because I don't have to leave London for a taste of the East, all that travel overseas, the clatter of plates in the kitchen, water running, and we're sitting here staring at the chess board, lovely colours too, pulsating and swaying, wooden fractals going with the grain, and there's not much to say, it's all quiet, just my heart thumping, nothing to think about but the next move.

THREATENING BEHAVIOUR

I SIT IN a cafe watching people pass in the street outside. Monday morning and they're hurrying to their offices. The men are identical with black suits and noddy haircuts. The women don't vary their style much either, but there's some nice birds around. Dirty office girls. Just like the one serving me coffee and a Danish. She walks around with her nose in the air like she's renting a room at Buckingham Palace. Can't be more than twenty-two but thinks she's a cut above the rest. Birds like this are easy to work out. They come from money and are bred to be arrogant. They look down on ordinary girls. Slag them off as common. But get one of these stuck-up birds between the sheets and they're away. It's all down to upbringing. They're arrogant like nobody's business, but arrogant makes for a good shag. They don't care about anybody but themselves.

I smile at the girl as she gives me my order. She lifts her head and turns away. She'll get a fucking nose bleed if she's not careful. Her nostrils are up there in space denting satellites. Real Himalayas job. But I let her think I'm hooked. That I reckon she's a cracker. That somehow the fact she's good looking and well groomed makes her more than another snotty nosed slag. She stalks off rolling a shapely arse and I keep my eyes on her. She can't resist looking back. When she catches me staring she marches into the back of the cafe. I want to laugh. It's a classic.

I've got half an hour before I'm due in court and I'm killing time round the corner from Horseferry Magistrates. I've been in these courts before I got wise. I know the place well enough, but it's a good job time has passed since my last visit, otherwise the magistrates might even be looking at something more than a fine. I bite into the Danish and wish it was a proper cafe with decent food. Not a greasy spoon, just somewhere that doesn't have its head so far up its arse it could get some decent food together. Danish pastries, croissants and all the other European shit leaves me cold. That's the kind of rubbish you have to put up with when you go abroad. What the fuck is it doing here? It's taking over in the rich areas because every cunt thinks the Frogs and Eyeties are better than us. It's because they don't belong in the culture around them that they have to look over the Channel.

When it's time I give the waitress a big friendly smile and ask for the bill. She's toned down a bit now and when I've paid I leave a fiver in the dish. I make sure she sees it then flash my teeth at her like a prize wanker. Real devil worship stuff. Done up in my best gear for the magistrates she might even reckon I'm worth a few bob. She's sweet now because a whore's a whore wherever you go and whatever the accent. Only difference, birds on street corners are up front about what they're doing. The girl returns the smile.

I walk round the corner and up the steps leading to the court. The foyer's full of nervous first-timers and cocky pros who think the whole thing's a joke. Sick humour. The other Chelsea boys are up as well and to make things interesting there's four Millwall lads down the corridor. I know they're Millwall from the crest and slogan sweat shirt one of them's wearing. They're scruffy bastards. Haven't made any kind of effort. No respect for authority. We'll be down there in the League Cup in a couple of weeks and it'll be mental. They're ragged and even if they didn't have the cunt with the shirt it would still be easy to tell them apart by the rest of the gear. It's easy working out where football fans come from. It's not even the style. That spreads fast enough. There's something more. Scousers look like scousers. Geordies are geordies. Forget the clothes and look at the haircuts and tashes for Northerners. Their heads are a different shape. The faces look like they belong to another race. Must go back to tribal times.

Take London. Go to any derby game and you can tell different firms apart. It's not just the niggers at Arsenal and yids at Tottenham, it's something more. You know from experience where they come from. West Ham and Millwall are tatty even when they're looking smart. There's common blood with West Ham and Millwall, and the difference from living on opposite sides of the river. Same with Arsenal and Tottenham. Then there's

Chelsea and nothing clubs like Rangers and Brentford. The Millwall boys are giving us the eye and there's no love lost. Chelsea generally have a bit more cash because West London's a classier place than the likes of Peckham and Deptford. Acton and Hammersmith piss all over the Old Kent Road. I feel a bit of a cunt in my Sunday best but that's why they're on a hanger in my cupboard. Weddings, funerals and court appearances. All the sad occasions. If you can save a hundred quid dressing up for a couple of hours then why not? The waitress was obviously impressed.

I look at the sheet pinned to the wall. It's a mix of drunk driving, theft, assault, the standard football charge of threatening behaviour, and a rape. Bad news that last one. People mill around talking. A cross section of everyday blokes, though the men doing the defending all come from the same classrooms. They're easy to tell. No need to look. They're the cunts with the clipped accents. Stroppy the lot of them. Relations of the bird in the cafe. It's all men as well, not a woman in sight. Suppose it's true what they say. It's a man's world when it comes to crime.

The kid on the assault charge talks with his brief. Shitting himself. He doesn't belong here and it's out of order they put that kind of bloke through the grinder. Shows what cunts the old bill are when it comes down to it. They stitch themselves up in the end because they turn everyone against them. I think of Tottenham. Anything they give me today will be okay because I'll be watching the coppers, magistrates and all those other snides sitting around wanking themselves off. I've been in there with the lads doing some of their own and they haven't got a clue.

I haven't bothered with a brief. No point. Just plead guilty and get it over with. Nobody saw me do anything, but bollocks, why bother? The first time I got nicked I'd done fuck all. I was just a young lad into football, a drink and a quick punch-up if one came my way. The old bill turned up after a bit of trouble and I was straight in the van even though I was just passing by. I was down Fulham nick in ten minutes and when I got to court I pleaded not guilty, which was a big mistake. Whatever they say about the British legal system being the best in the world, it's shit. They say you're innocent till proven guilty, but the first thing the magistrates did was order me to sign on every Saturday when football was on till my case came up. I waited two months and learnt a lesson from a bloke up on the same charge. He was another teenage bystander who'd done nothing, but he was smart. Pleaded guilty. Paid his fine and took his chance. Said he couldn't be bothered and didn't want to miss Chelsea.

It was funny that one. He's telling the magistrate what happened and the old cunt is looking into him like he's a nuclear scientist gone mental. Says that if what the kid's saying is true then he should be pleading not guilty. The bloke knows that if he does that he'll have to sign on like me. He wants to watch Chelsea. They've got some good games coming up. He tells the magistrate he just wants to plead guilty. Everyone knows the score. It's a lottery. The kid's almost begging the bloke to accept he's guilty even though his statement says he's not. The magistrate convicts and fines him.

For two months I signed my name at three o'clock while everyone was down Chelsea. I could have shot down the ground for half-time but what was the point? It was a miserable time. I was shitting it as well. It was like being a virgin or something, not knowing what to expect. I got myself a brief and he was a plonker if ever there was one. I'm standing outside waiting to go in and it's the first time I've seen him face to face. He says a few words and makes a crack about not liking Saturdays because all the riff raff comes in for the football. He lives in Fulham. One of the cunts who pushed house prices up and gave the area a dodgy reputation. Wanker with a plum in his mouth.

Having said that, I went in court and the copper who nicked me must've been brain damaged at birth, though that's being unkind to flids. The bloke representing me did a good job. I got Mark and Rod to give evidence and the arresting officer mucked up his story. The magistrates didn't like it, but they couldn't really get away with a conviction. The old bill were gutted. It was a good moment. My brief asked for costs and the cunt in charge snaps at him and says no. Says I shouldn't have been where I was when I got nicked. I can't dwell on the past, though, because what's done is done. But it shapes you for the future. When my turn comes I plead guilty and tell the three waxworks staring at me that I regret my actions and was only defending myself. I wait for the speech. There's a lot of cases lined up, so the man in the middle, a prat with greasy black hair who looks like he hangs around schools at closing time, gets to the point and says I should be ashamed of myself. He asks me what my parents and friends think about me being in court?

I have to tuck my head into my chest so I don't burst out laughing. He probably thinks I'm ashamed. I should tell him to shut up and stop molesting kids, but what's the point stitching myself up? I've got to keep quiet, take my punishment and come out smelling of roses. I look up quickly and see the fat woman next to him nodding her head. Real dyke prison warden effort in desperate need of a length. The third magistrate wishes he was inspecting his stamp collection. He wants to go home and seems a bit embarrassed by it all. Like the rest of us.

I walk out with a two hundred pound hole in my pocket. It's a con but I've seen it before. I don't hang about. There's no point trying to say anything because it's meaningless and I've got nothing worth saying. These people are scum. Everything's sorted before the accused arrives. Sometimes you get lucky but even then you still have to put up with the hassle. There's never an apology. Look at all those Paddies who got stitched up by the old bill, not to mention all the other bastards through the years. There must be loads of poor sods rotting away inside framed by bent coppers. I've got the old bill's number. Just keep away from them and live your life on the quiet. It's only wankers who get done. Wankers like me.

I walk away from the court and remember the waitress. I look at my watch and it's half-twelve. It's worth a try. I head back to the cafe and go in. Sit at the same table. The bird sees me come in and though she tries to hide it I see she recognises me. When she comes over I tell her I've had a hard morning. Been busy signing a big contract. Made five grand in my pocket but it took a bit of doing. She raises her eyebrows. I tell her life is hard on the streets. She nods and says she knows what I mean. I want to crack up but keep a straight face. The slag walks to the back of the cafe to get my order. I sit back and watch the people outside. The streets are getting busy with office workers running around looking for food. The fine doesn't phase me. It's a risk you take. I don't like the law or any of those involved, but there's no point getting wound up. Two hundred quid's a drop in the ocean. The amount of gear I sell on the side from the warehouse keeps me going. That and a modest wage. It's always the fringe benefits that see you through. Leave it to management and you'll lag behind all your life.

I drink more coffee and eat a sandwich. Life's okay if you know how to handle yourself. Horseferry Magistrates is a minor inconvenience, not the end of the world. Just keep your chin up and they can't touch you. I'm thinking how to spend the rest of the day but have a good idea the way it's going to go. I'm on a near enough cert. There's no point going into the warehouse this afternoon. I told them I was going to a funeral. They won't miss me at work. Everyone respects death. I don't fancy a day off my holidays for the old bill. Far better to invent a family tragedy.

When I start getting bored I catch the waitress's eye and she comes over. She's a good looker and has that rich bitch sleaze about her. This is the fucking class war. Not a bunch of cunts dressed up thinking they're hard when they're more into their clothes than getting stuck in. If they want to go on about class they should have a bit of this bird working out my bill. Or just give up the notion and get stuck in at the football where you avoid the limelight and do the business without justifying yourself. Aggravation without the excuses. I ask her if there's a decent pub nearby. She gives me directions. A five-minute walk. I ask her what time she knocks off. Half-two. Ask her along for a drink and she says yes. Not a second's hesitation. I think about giving her another hefty tip but decide against the idea. A bit obvious that one and I'm into her for a fiver already. We give each other the eye and I watch her arse move all the way back to the kitchen.

I find the pub easy enough and sit down with a pint of lager and the paper. It's one of those Central London pubs done up nice enough but without much character and hardly any locals. The dinner hour mob are clearing out when the bird from the cafe turns up. She looks fit without her uniform. A nice body with good legs and a healthy pair of lungs. She's got a short haircut which suits her bone structure. I know she's going to be a dirty cow. Everything about her spells it out in giant letters. She's got a strong line in confidence and gets the drinks in, then sits down at the table. Her legs brush against me straight off breaking down space.

Her name's Chrissie and she lives in a flat in Westminster.

Belongs to her parents. They live in the Far East and she gets the place for nothing. They're into drugs, the legal variety. It works out well for her because she doesn't have to worry about rip-off rents. She tells me London's full of high prices for studios in dodgy areas. We have the one drink and then she's taking me back to her flat. There's an entry phone downstairs and a video camera bolted to the ceiling. We get in the lift and Chrissie's sticking her tongue down my throat while I'm still swearing at myself getting caught on film. What happens if I want to come back another time and turn the place over? I'm on a mission, doing my bit for the workers. Muscle relaxation after the tension of a court appearance and maybe the chance to make good my losses.

We go into a luxury flat on the eighth floor. There's a view of the surrounding buildings running down to the river. I look out and it's a nest in the clouds. You don't imagine this kind of world exists. I mean, I've seen the sights from tower blocks, but there's an atmosphere to this place. It even smells different. This part of Westminster means money. Big money. There's no rundown cornershops or takeaways. Nothing but luxury flats and Government buildings. The flat's in the middle of London but it doesn't belong here. It's another dimension. A world without people. The place is massive. Three bedrooms, Chrissie tells me. Decked out with paintings that look like they're worth a bomb. There's pictures from all over the world and the carpet must be a good inch thick. There's even a leopard skin on the floor with glass eyes. What a way to end up.

I feel like James Bond or some other upper-crust playboy as Chrissie starts kissing me again. She has me out within seconds and she's got a grip like a pro. I can see us in a big wood trimmed mirror and imagine a camera on the other side with MI5 agents recording the details. Like I'm important or something. Not just a football hooligan fighting my own kind. But Chrissie's groaning like mad and I haven't even got inside her top yet. She's got me stripped in a couple of minutes and she's down to her bra and pants. She won't let me take them off which is getting me wound up. She gets down on her knees and starts in and I have to make do watching her in the mirror. Then she's on her feet going to a bedroom. I'm told to wait a minute before following. I feel like a right cunt standing in the middle of the room with a hard-on, stark bollock naked.

I'm summoned by her highness and Chrissie's on a giant bed with a vibrator wedged up her. She's still got her bra on but I can't see her pants. She's saying she wishes one of my mates was along so we could do her in tandem. I'm smiling but she's bad news. I'm not that kind of bloke. The very idea makes me feel like throwing up and turns me right off. What's the point? It's supposed to be some kind of turn on this line of chat. Breaking down barriers she says. But all I'm interested in is a bit of one on one. I pull the vibrator out and we're going at it, but when it comes to the business Chrissie starts prick teasing. You can usually tell when a bird gets mouthy they're not going to deliver. Same with blokes. The ones bragging about how many birds they've had are the same ones wanking their lives away.

I get her worked up and she lets loose. Makes a liar of me. She's pulling a condom over my knob which I hate but this bird prefers burning rubber to riding bareback and the woman always knows best. I'm banging away for a while but the delay's blocked me up which isn't a bad thing I suppose. Means I last a bit longer though I'm not that bothered either way. She starts telling me she wants it from behind so I have to pull out with this fucking robber's mask over my knob while she gets on all fours. Chrissie assumes the position and raises her arse in the air. She leans over and picks the vibrator up from the floor. She starts sucking on it, groaning like she's auditioning for a film. I start laughing but she doesn't hear. I'm glad I've got the rubber on now because if this bird wants a threesome then fuck knows what she's been up to over the last few years. She's getting well horny and it's no problem keeping her going. Then I'm giving her the business with just the back of her head for company realising that this isn't any kind of revenge, just a good one off.

I shoot my load eventually and roll off. We lean against the pillows with nothing to say. It's that moment of truth after you've done the business with a stranger when you wish there was a button nearby. Hit the switch and the bird disappears. I'm James Bond again. Activate the ejector seat and you're alone to carry on down the road without the model. In the films the woman always gets killed off so Bond never has to bother about small talk after he's done the business. I hate the after-shag chat. I want the bird to disappear so I can be on my own. I nod off for a while and Chrissie's dozing as well. It's an easy option because you wake up later all refreshed and you've got the urge again. There's no need for idle words.

I'm drifting, half asleep, feeling I've let myself down. It's alright when you're going for goal because you've got a bit of steel in you and this kind of shag's about invasion. Instead of sticking the boot in you're using your knob. An invasion of privacy. But once you've delivered you look at what you've done with a bit more vision and see it's shit. You've opened yourself up just to exploit someone else. Violence and sex. Sometimes there's little difference. Not like cutting someone up or torturing them, but it's all about boosting the ego. At least when you get in a punch-up it's power pure and simple. You keep your identity. It's more honest somehow. Not like this set-up where you're conning each other the whole time. Talking shit just to get your end away.

I get up and go for a piss. Chrissie's asleep. It's a palace of a flat and I help myself to a drink from the fridge. A bottled import. All the nobs drink this kind of lager. I sit on the couch and put my feet up. My flat's not bad but it doesn't get near this place. I must have dozed off again because next thing I know it's dark and Chrissie's dressed up in red stockings. The TV's on and there's a bird on the screen getting serviced by a nigger. It's a bleary recording but I recognise the body. Chrissie's smiling for the camera as Dildo Boy does his duty. It's a rich man's paradise and she's telling me nobody does it better than a black man. She's looking in my face for a reaction probably thinking she's radical or something. Probably is for her line of thinking. Chrissie can't compare two different cultures.

It's all a bit of a comedy. The faces are so serious that I see the angle. I feel like a vicar because I'm supposed to be impressed and turned on more than usual. Chrissie looks at me again for a reaction. She starts lecturing me on racial equality and sexual freedom in her pinched upper-class voice. I hate the accent. I realise that now. Maybe that's what does me in, even though she starts sucking my knob again telling me she loves the taste of rubber. Half of me is laughing, the other narked. Suppose I thought I was going to get one back on those miserable cunts in court. Thought I was going to stitch up one of their own. Get the business and turn over a stuck-up slag's flat next time she's selling over-priced coffee. It's no victory. I'm getting a lecture on niggers by a slag in an ivory tower using a black man for her own ends. Arrogant brat's setting herself up as some kind of expert. Actually thinks she's dangerous.

Mind you, I can't get too upset because she gives a good blow job and I'm happy enough shooting off in her mouth. She chokes a bit and I cheer up because she's pissed off. Tells me the one thing she doesn't like is a bloke spunking up in her mouth. At last I've got a blow in against the magistrates. She'll take anything shoved her way but doesn't like a mouthful. Too fucking bad darling. What's she's doing down there in the first place? Chrissie storms off to the bathroom to rinse her mouth out with disinfectant and I go to the fridge for another bottle of lager. I'm sitting on the couch dressed when she comes back, wondering what the fuck I'm doing here. It's raining outside and it's a long way home. The day hasn't really worked out. That's what happens when you get involved with the law. They come at you from every direction. They pull all the strings and have their way every time. The cunts are everywhere.

I watch Chrissie walk in with her cockiness and set ideas. She goes on about niggers but how many mates has she got who are black? Shafting a black man doesn't prove anything. She uses her sex like a hammer and it's me that's being used here. At least I got a shot off in her mouth, though, so something good's come of the day. That and six inches of Chelsea aggro. Expensive though. Two hundred and five quid for something I should be getting for free.

BOMBER COMMAND

The picture flickered for a fraction of a second, causing Matt Jennings to lift his head from the newspaper he was reading, a plastic mug of steaming tomato soup frozen halfway to his lips. He concentrated on the screen that had attracted his attention, eyes trying to make out a vague object in the darkness. It was nearly two in the morning and the conditions outside were fair for the time of year. It hadn't rained for three days and the wind had calmed after its earlier rage. There was something in the shadows on the far side of the car park, though he couldn't see more than a faint quiver on the rolling film. Jennings put his mug down and was tempted to pour the soup back into his flask, but kept his gaze on the dark corner, automatically switching the angle of camera 6.

He punched the correct buttons and achieved the desired view. A jolt of recognition identified a human form. Jennings zoomed in, wondering what he would find in the recesses of the car park, up against the wall, fearing the worst as a reel of psychopath blockbusters hovered. Day followed day, weeks turned into months and years, and now he was cruising down a tunnel into God knows what. Cushioned by warm air and surrounded by high-tech surveillance gear, he didn't really want to know what went on in the depths of night, the endless repetition of empty car parks and sidewalks, metal gates and driveways suddenly appealing in the face of murder and mutilation. Despite himself, he felt the anticipation of puberty, a twinge of excitement penetrating thirty-five-year-old bones, adrenalin flowing as a ghost began to form. He felt exposed as the camera hit its target and a face looked straight back.

A drunk glanced over his shoulder, the stream of hot liquid running back between his legs across the patterned concrete, harmless dregs, a million miles from the torrent of thick jugular blood Jennings had feared. Disappointment gave way to joy, embarrassment replaced by a sense of the absurd as the drunk walked back towards a small side gate dedicated to those who had fallen in the Falklands, out of the company car park, off along a side road towards the train station. The figure swayed gently from side to side and Jennings imagined him singing a song, a happy song of dancing and love, on his way to the all-night kebab house for a large donner with chilli peppers and chilli sauce. That would sober him up quick enough.

Jennings clicked into the various cameras and enlarged images flashed across the bank of screens surrounding his desk. He was safe and sound, a politician in his nuclear bunker immune to the outside world, removed and cut-off with a one-way view of life that strayed across his line of fire. But he could do nothing other than pick up the phone and call the police station. He was a peaceful man. Violence scared him and, despite the repetitive nature of the buildings he had watched over for the last three years, he was content with the safety of his hideaway, the consistency of the work, the chance to read newspapers and travel magazines, and dunk the sandwiches Pat made him each evening into a mug of soup while planning for the future. Tomato was his favourite flavour and he had this on Tuesdays, Thursdays and Saturdays, while chicken filled in the gaps on Wednesdays and Fridays.

Jennings was thorough in everything he did and had great pride in the knowledge that nothing would ever get past his command post. But there were no bitter winds blowing across his face and no searchlight with which to examine the surrounding jungle. He tried to picture himself with his finger on the trigger of a machine gun, smiled, glad that he wasn't hoisted up as a sitting target for Iraqi commando raids or South American peasant rebellion. He was happy with the warehouses and concrete walkways, the passing cars and drunks emptying their bladders when they thought they were safely hidden from prying eyes, the prowling cats and stray dogs.

Once his shift was finished, Jennings exchanged brief pleasantries with Noel Bailey and was straight out of the door. His replacement would go through the formality of checking the cameras and have an excellent view of his colleague crossing the car park. It was six in the morning and still dark, but Jennings was conscious of the lenses. He didn't like being watched. He got into his car and was soon home, the journey taking ten minutes, the roads practically empty of traffic. He walked through the small front garden and was safely behind the front door, bolt in place and chain hooked. His sigh of relief was audible in the silence of the hall. He was king of the castle once more, back in total control.

He went into the kitchen, took a carton of grapefruit juice from the fridge and filled a tumbler. He drank slowly balancing calories with vitamin content, rinsing the glass when he had finished, leaving it to dry in the empty rack, changing his mind and wiping it with a cloth before putting it back in the cupboard; then tiptoeing upstairs to the bedroom he shared with his wife. He could see the outline of Pat's body under the duvet, the friendly smell of sleep and perfume, earrings and bracelets on the bedside table. The door clicked when it was closed and he listened for the sounds that would show he had woken her, but there was nothing. He went directly to the boxroom at the end of the landing which had been converted into a small office. This was his workshop and the nerve centre of their future success. Jennings plugged in his Macintosh and switched on, a crack of light burning through the screen, the mouse tight in his right hand, finger on the button.

The man from the surveillance unit was soon surfing the Internet, information setting wires alight, ridding him of the need for conversation and puerile social skills, the warehouses and empty car parks blasted into the void, technology maximised. It was so easy on the superhighway, the world at his fingertips waiting to be explored, and all for the price of a local call. The only light came from the screen and he was all-powerful, sitting back in the dark, a white knight in the London metropolis, the figure lurking in the shadows serving humanity. His fingers pounded the keyboard, eyes flitting up and down, left and right.

The downloaded image of a red-headed woman filled Jennings with great expectation, the transparent negligée and welcoming smile a subtle turn-on, the red painted nails long and exotic, text running ragged around partially concealed breasts. He felt guilty and turned to look towards the door, fearful Pat would wake and find him examining other women. It wasn't right, but he was curious all the same and there could be no real harm in looking. He knew there were harder services available, that he was a child in the world of international pornography, a naive boy scout in a web of middle-aged perverts.

With a burst of decision Jennings cancelled his last command and dragged the image to the dustbin, then confirmed the option. He switched off and sat in the dark, thinking and plotting the future. He was ambitious. A winner. He was a clean-living man with morals and a beautiful wife, a woman he loved dearly, someone to cherish and respect. He didn't urinate on private property and hated the thought of having his soul caught inside a surveillance camera. He let his mind race, living the future, then started dozing, dreams setting foundations, jumping awake and going to the bathroom, ripping the woman's memory into tiny pieces and flushing her away. He looked at his watch, mouth watering as he realised it was almost time for breakfast.

Jennings waited for the bacon to crackle and the tomatoes to melt, the smell of fresh Colombian coffee filling the kitchen. He had always wanted to visit South America. Brazil, Colombia, Peru, Bolivia. The names were magical, but a fear of disease, filth, macho violence meant he would make do with glossy magazines and the Sunday papers. Pat was still asleep and he would eat his breakfast and watch twenty minutes of morning TV, wash the dishes and take his wife a cup of coffee in bed. She wasn't working today, but rarely slept in. She was at her best in the morning whereas he was the kind that enjoyed the evenings. The night-shift suited him and it gave them both the space they needed, which in turn helped to keep their marriage fresh. He was a lucky man.

Jennings had plans. Big plans. He was working for the future, clicking into the modern age, his computer a lifeline, a connection with the rest of humanity. Technology was making world travel redundant. Everyone wanted to watch satellite TV these days. The planet's population was tuning into the same news broadcasts, while personal computers would soon be as essential as electricity. Virtual reality was the new reality and Jennings was smart enough to adjust his thinking and move with the times. He was progressive.

– Are you awake, dear?

He saw Pat's bare back in the half-light of the curtained room. He slipped into bed next to her and she turned around, healthy breasts pressing against his sweater. A wedding photograph on the wall showed family and friends, a country church, flowers and confetti, smiling faces.

– I didn't hear you come in, Pat said.

– I've had my breakfast already. It's only half-seven though.

Pat sat up and took the mug of coffee, shifted over a little so that her husband would be more comfortable. The coffee quickly had its effect and Jennings felt his wife's hand moving across the inside of his thigh tugging down his zip. He took the mug of coffee, careful not to spill it on the bedspread as Pat moved nearer, placing it on the bedside table, mildly irritated he had forgotten to bring one of the Windsor Castle coasters to protect the pine. Jennings watched the motion of the bed clothes and noticed the freckles on Pat's face and shoulders. He loved his wife. She was everything a man could wish for in a woman.

– Come here and kiss me, he said gently.

Husband and wife kissed with the solid romance of companionship and ten minutes later he was moving softly, timing his run, high above the clouds riding on pure oxygen, bringing her to climax with his precision performance. When he had finished he timed the withdrawal perfectly, simultaneously positioning his discarded briefs below his wife's buttocks, thereby avoiding stains on the sheet. They lay in each other's arms and rested. Soon Pat was quietly snoring and Jennings began drifting, musing over the wonders of his invention, Smart Bomb Parade, and the deal he was about to sign with a major video games manufacturer. Youngsters would love Smart Bomb Parade. It would satisfy their natural instincts and make him a rich man. He would move out of London and enjoy some clean Gloucestershire air. Perhaps they would try for a child once they were financially secure. He knew Pat was proud of his inventiveness and technological know-how. They were going to be rich one day.

He imagined amusement arcades full of Smart Bomb fanatics splashing out on merchandising. Living rooms echoing specialist sound effects. Personal computers pulsating to the red and yellow flashes of incendiaries. He saw that kid Dave from next door hooked and benefiting from a healthy outlet for misdirected energy. The game would wean him off ecstasy and channel his thoughts. It was good, clean fun and the boy would look good with a short RAF haircut and Smart Bomb T-shirt.

Jennings moved towards sleep, Smart Bomb Parade playing in his mind. There was a hum deep inside the machine and a blaze of ticker-tape street scenes. Blonde virgin girls waved white handkerchiefs and a stern middle-aged man wiped a tear from his eye. The graphics were excellent. A brass band played a familiar tune and this filled the combatant with hope and glory. The sound effects were perfect. Jennings was a fighter bomber pilot for the New Economic Order; power of decency pitted against the evil General Mahmet. He was ready for take-off. Red digits flashed across the screen counting down seconds. The computerised faces disappeared as he prepared for the dangerous task ahead.

An electrified crucifix melted through fading street scenes as the military took charge of the operation. To progress through the ranks he needed a high score. It was a question of discipline and the will to win. Individual thoughts had to be controlled and his life donated to the greater good. If he lived he would be a hero with all the benefits such selflessness brought. If he perished, he would be a martyr, and his memory live forever. His family would quote Shakespeare, the message flashing briefly across the screen in a font he had designed himself, that a coward dies many times but a hero dies just the once. He was proud of the artistic touch. He was a man of culture.

Jennings took his place in the massed ranks of fundamentalist crusaders. Modern weaponry was quiet and efficient and only punished the guilty. There was a rigorous points system that recognised decisiveness in battle and the ability to smart bomb a nation's infrastructure back to the Stone Age. He felt the thrill of conflict. He was on the march, part of an organisation based on chivalry and the highest moral principles. He was justified in whatever actions he was forced to take to save his way of life, community, nation. His finger tingled on the mouse deciding life and death. Although strategic missiles and smart cluster bombs were readily available, there was a bonus for decisive strikes. Waste not want not was the NEO motto.

The score was scaled according to a target's military importance. A secret bonus scheme operated, details unknown. Schools and hospitals recorded points, though this was officially denied for reasons of political politeness, while other more complicated factors were also taken into account. Kill ratios were broken down and categorised. The player would never question the machine. Deep in NEO circuits the publicity network protecting Jennings from mass opinion called for extra memory. Nothing was left to chance. Lights flickered and the eyes of the General burned communist red. A blood red craving for infidel babies and homosexual deviance. The General was flanked by sadistic mullahs, Korans held to the sky, thunderbolts cracking the minarets of the East. There was no need to consider the strange mixture of Islamic and communist ideas. As far as the game was concerned they belonged together.

Rockets spat flame and Jennings was soaring through the skies on the crest of an adrenalin rush, thoughts sucked towards the hard disk. He crossed parched desert landscapes and spotted a Bedouin camel train, insignificant and unarmed. He considered a strike but would be wasting time and ammunition for a low points return. He switched to control frequency, briefed by a computer programmer tapping into detailed information banks, digitised kill potential passed to a gunslinging pilot. Righteousness flooded his brain. He was a prophet in steel casing, a clean-killing European superman. He launched his craft in a calculated arc, technology confirming creative genius. Missiles burnt beneath an Arab sun. A row of slum housing exploded in dust storms. Colour was added to a drab world of hunger and disease. The gleaming dome of a mosque stretched outwards and then melted back into itself. He hit the water works, score rising as black ants ran beneath falling debris. Chemical weapons were the reward for experience. Death better than continual poverty.

The Smart Bomb pilot turned in semi-consciousness, bumping his wife, turning for home with joy in his heart, knowing he was safe from ground attack. He had one rocket left and turned a victory roll, spotting a bazaar on the outskirts of town, a tangle of bright stalls and frantic insects. He clicked the mouse then shouted into his radio as a school exploded. The score increased, machine buzzing with complicated equations. It was an easy ride back to base, but he had to keep his wits about him. He was ecstatic with success. Mundane existence was transformed.

The score was high and Jennings translated the success of the software into hard cash. There would be steak on the menu and congratulations from his comrades. He would drink cold American beer and listen to relaxing mood music, take a shower and enjoy the praise. He was a credit to his country. He timed his approach and felt the bounce of touchdown. Pat was awake and getting out of bed, on her way to the bathroom to clean up the mess. He hoped she hadn't leaked on the sheet.

VILLA AWAY

WE'RE STUCK IN traffic on the motorway looking over Birmingham. It's a fucking horrible place. Ties with Liverpool as the worst place I've been in the last few years. That's saying something because the North is stacked with dead industry and ghost towns where the kids are deprived and the parents depraved. The traffic's died a death and we're pissed off because it's getting late. Half-one and we're still on the flyover. There's cars and coaches and lorries backed up. The cars carry happy families and decent football fans. There's Villa, Chelsea, Arsenal scarves hanging from windows. A couple of other clubs I don't recognise. All the colours of the rainbow. Rod says Arsenal are playing Everton away. Wankers wearing colours.

Birmingham stretches as far as you can see. All the way to the horizon. There's no colour, just grey warehouses and derelict buildings dwarfing identical houses full of Jasper Carrot Brummies. There's mist floating around but it's no natural beauty, more like poison from the traffic clogging the motorway. Traffic speeds in the opposite direction while we sit tight like a bunch of cunts. Coachloads of grannies and Paki pilgrims head south to London. Can't blame them wanting to enjoy a bit of civilisation. Anything for a break from a lifetime stuck in a slum clearance like Birmingham.

We're not going as far as Spaghetti Junction, turning off for Villa Park before we're sucked into that particular abortion. But we've been through enough times going to away games to know about the jams and fumes. Space Age gone wrong. When we go away it's either coach or train travel and both have their advantages. At the moment we're using coaches a lot because you avoid the aggravation and expense of travelling on British Rail. There's no coppers standing at the barrier watching you from the moment you pull out of Euston or King's Cross till touchdown in Manchester or Leeds. There again, when you go by coach you end up tied to the fucker. That's if you want to get back to London without forking out for train fares. Nothing's perfect in this world.

The old bill have Saturdays sewn up and are always on the lookout for coaches, so you have to work things out in advance. The more they install cameras and set up cordons around grounds like it's some kind of war zone, the further away they push the problem, stretching the Harris imagination. That's all anyone really cares about, keeping their patch tidy. No major disturbance translates as a clean bill of health according to those in charge. But nothing gets solved ignoring the problem. It just sets up shop somewhere else. It's human nature and that's why banging someone up never does much good, because even though it's no picnic inside, the causes are still there bubbling away.

– Mandy thinks she's up the duff. Rod's been a miserable cunt since this morning and now it's easy to understand why. He sits there looking at us like a stray dog feeling sorry for itself.

– What do you mean? Mark looks puzzled.

– What do you think I mean?

– What do you mean she's up the duff?

– Well, mate, it's like this. Blokes have this lump of meat between their legs that fills with blood when it sniffs a bit of gash. The bird gets greased up when she sees the bloke. The man shoves this stiff object into the hole between the woman's legs, moves back and forwards for a while, in your case a couple of seconds, and shoots off this white washing-up liquid. Nine months later, if the timing's right, a screaming brat pops out and the cunt responsible gets to pay for it for the next sixteen years.

– Are you serious?

– That's how it works Mark. I wouldn't lie to you. Not about something that important. It's in all the medical books and most of the programmes on telly, though they don't show all the details. It's the birds and bees. Watch them next summer if any of the cunts get lost and fly down your street and you still won't have a clue what I'm on about. I'm surprised your old girl didn't tell you when your balls dropped. They taught us at school when we were kids, but you were always skiving so you were probably down the arcade or something fucking about with the Space Invaders.

– Very funny. Are you sure about Mandy?

– She's two days late. Didn't seem bothered when she told me this morning, but it felt like she'd kicked me in the bollocks. I'm getting dressed ready for a day out and she comes back from having a piss and breaks the good news.

I tell Rod that two days isn't a long time. Birds can be a lot later than that. Some are so fucking dozy they can't count past ten so they never know what time of the day it is let alone the month. I can see he's gutted. It's there in his face carved in deep like he's been glassed by some headbanger. Even Mark sees it and he usually misses the subtle things in life. Like his time in the nick. He's always been like that, even as a kid. He's thick-skinned like a pissed water buffalo. Just says what comes into his head and doesn't give a fuck if it winds people up or not.

He's leaving well alone at the moment. It's a good idea, because though Mark can be a nasty bit of work sometimes, with a mean streak that makes you think he's a closet psycho or something, Rod can be a bit naughty himself. If Rod gets pushed far enough he snaps. Goes mental and then he's worth two of Mark. I remember him at school in the playground when some kid picked a fight, said his old girl was a prossie, and Rod went off his rocker like someone had pulled the plug. Had the bloke on the ground with his shoulders pinned down, smashing his head on the concrete, again and again. I had to pull him off in the end before he killed the cunt. It's not part of his basic character, but it's there all the same. Everyone has a breaking point. I can't imagine Rod being a dad.

– What are you going to do if it's true? What if Mandy is in the club? Mark looks worried. Kids are bad news all round.

– Don't know what I'd do. Mandy wouldn't get rid of it and it's not like she's some slag I've serviced in a doorway after one pint over the top. She's my fucking wife. I suppose I'd end up being a dad. Either that or kick her down the stairs.

– That's a fucking stupid thing to say.

– I wouldn't do it. Don't know why I said it. I'm a cunt, alright?

– You could buy it a Chelsea shirt and bring it to games. You wouldn't be out with us lot much, would you? You couldn't go out steaming Tottenham with a kid sitting on your shoulders.

I start laughing and Rod gives me a nasty look. He asks what's so funny. I tell him I'm imagining him kicking some Spurs cunt in the head with a kid on his shoulders directing operations. He could be the firm's mascot. He doesn't see it himself and shakes his head. The idea starts growing on me but I'm not telling Rod. He'll end up like one of those blokes you see on a Saturday with messy grey hair walking down from Fulham Broadway, who goes in the ground and has to sit in the family section surrounded by brats while the lads are having a good time. If Rod ends up like one of those cunts I'll get a shooter and put him out of his misery. Play the vet doing the decent thing for a poor dumb animal. Otherwise he'll end up another one of the walking dead. The people milking the game say football should be family entertainment and all that nonsense. They say more birds should go to football. There's enough of them there already and who wants a stand full of screaming kids like at England home games?

We cheer up as the coach pulls off the motorway heading towards Villa Park. We've got a different driver with Ron Hawkins off with the flu and he doesn't take long to get lost in the traffic, missing the signs, and the old bill are dozing and don't see us go past. We end up on the other side of the park backing onto the Holte End. He's a fucking wanker this driver. Doesn't want the ticket Harris always gets Ron for the game. We get the bloke to drop us off. Tell him we'll walk and he can meet us at the same place after Chelsea have stuffed Villa.

– You'll be alright, Mark says, trying to cheer Rod up. I wouldn't worry about it too much. Not yet anyway. Every bird is late now and again. That's how it goes. She could've had a shock or something, or not been feeling well. Maybe she was frightened when that thing you were talking about filled up with blood and hit six inches. Fright of her life after getting used to six centimetres.

– Mandy looks after herself. Rod laughs despite himself. She knows what's going on inside her gut. Mind you, she said she didn't think she was in the club. Reckoned she'd be able to tell though fuck knows how.

– Forget it. Maybe we'll find some Villa fans. That'll cheer you up. Batter a few Brummies and you'll be smiling.

– Some chance. Remember how they scattered that time on

the pitch? Last game of the season and they get steamed by fifty Chelsea and do a vanishing act.

– Bunch of cunts.

– Thought I'd been slipped a nasty chemical. One minute they're standing there like they want to know, the next there's nothing but thin air and a pile of steaming shit.

We walk down a terraced row of houses. There's two beat up cars and a load of kids playing on the sidewalk. Small scrawny bastards shivering in the cold. There's a Paki shop on the corner with bare metal shelves and a few tins in the window. Curried beans and chopped mushrooms. A rack of newspapers with a bird on the front in suspenders and a headline accusing a leading politician of adultery. A gang of black kids stands around the corner watching us. Must be eight or nine with oversized coats and trainers. They've got flash bikes and bobble hats as well, so they must be doing something right.

They're waiting for cars coming to football, trying to make a bit on the side, offering protection from other kids they say are going round slashing tyres. You have to admire their understanding of the free market. It's basic economics, because you take something like a major war and it's a money spinner. Bomb the place till there's nothing left standing and then a few years later put in bids for work rebuilding the place. There's big money in sewage systems and fresh water. It's sound business sense. Build and destroy. Or when you can't go out and smash it straight off, put a timing device inside so after a few years the fucker breaks down.

We head off across the park. A coachload out for a stroll and it must be an odd sight. It's a mild day in the park with green grass and trees, and a loving couple walking their dog take one look at us and head in the opposite direction. It's funny, but I feel uncomfortable. We're out of our surroundings and must look a right bunch of cunts. It's like when we stopped for a piss on the way to Sunderland for the Newcastle game and Facelift was doing his best to pollute the English countryside with an Agent Orange piss attack. We didn't belong and now we're taking it a stage further. The fat cunt's not with us today, but Harris is up ahead getting muddy, looking left and right like one of those bouncing toy dogs Pakis carry round in the back of their Datsuns.

There's a smart red brick building to our right and we're coming over a ridge walking through dead leaves. Like a tribe of Apaches on the skyline. There's locals heading in the same direction, little knots of teenagers who you know straight away have never been in trouble in their lives. We come to the street along the side of the ground and turn right into the buzz of Saturday afternoon. The main entrance to Villa Park is impressive. It's old brickwork from another era, a nice bit of history. Classy but ancient. It's two o'clock and the place is packed with people walking up and down, a lot of them wearing Villa tops. We go towards the Holte End, a wedge through the middle of the street looking for reaction but not expecting much. The crowd melts away. They know we're Chelsea and know we're a firm. No colours or shouting, but it's obvious. Any cunt could tell us apart. Harris slags off a few blokes walking the other way but it's a waste of time, they don't want to know.

– What's the matter with these cunts. Mark is laughing because it's a bit of a joke.

– They're not interested. They just want their football.

I look at the blokes walking along holding the hands of small children, making sure their kids don't get lost in the crowd and trampled underfoot. They look at us sharpish with a bit of dread mixed with disgust. They're older and not exactly trainspotters, but they're on their own with the kid and we're just another problem along with the bills and dole queue. They want to watch the football while they can still afford to get in the place.

We're outside the Holte End and nothing's happening. There's no Villa mob in sight and even the groups of three or four young lads hanging around look like the last thing on their minds is a row. We walk back the way we came with Villa fans hurrying the other way. They're real Brummies this lot with their dodgy gear and accents. It's obvious we're ready for a bit of conflict, but for something to happen you've got to have opposition. We're up here for the day, all the way from London, ready and willing, but there's no-one worth steaming. We're walking up and down the street outside their ground and it's up to them to do the business. They should be having a go at us. We need a Villa firm to make things work. These cunts around us with their programmes and rip-off club shirts don't count.

– Don't know what's the matter with them. Harris is laughing because if you make an appearance there's nothing more you can do. You've done your bit and it's the other side that looks bad.

– There's a few pubs round the back of the away end, says Billy Bright. Let's take a stroll down there. See if we can flush the wankers out.

– They'll be shut up, says Mark. Worth a try though.

We turn through a set of gates leading to the away end. There's a mesh fence with a crowd of people peering through waiting to see the players. I hate that kind of thing. Real hero worship. I mean, I support the team and everything, but I don't want to talk to the players. At least not through a fence with my tongue hanging out like a demented polar bear in the zoo, like the players are something better than me. You get enough of that during the week. It's bollocks and we keep going through a small car park and down to the away entrance. Suddenly it's all Chelsea and it's good how you just walk round a ground and the people all have a different accent and way of dressing.

– Down here. There's a couple of pubs at the bottom of the street. Billy Bright plays the Pied Piper and leads the way.

There's a transit with a riot shield across the window full of old bill. They watch us pass in silence. Make no move to interfere. We're going against the flow of Chelsea coming the other way. It's sunny out, but cold as well, and the area around the ground is dead. No character till we come to a stone pub on the corner which is closed and then a junction that's more Midlands depression, crumbling in front of our eyes. There's a pub across the street with a couple of police horses and a transit van parked outside. There's the sign HOME FANS ONLY in the window. Now and then some cunt in an anorak knocks on the door and goes inside. It's not exactly going to be a major Villa firm inside so we take a wander. There's nothing. All the pubs are closed and there's no Villa in sight. We've done our best and turn back to the ground for the kick-off. Have to admit I didn't expect much. We have to queue for ten minutes and there's some kid copper explaining that having too much to drink before the game means you're pissed and not allowed to watch the football.

I get a cup of tea inside and we sit in small plastic seats waiting for the match to start. Villa are singing in the Holte End but

Chelsea always give it some good vocals when we play away. It's all end to end stuff which warms us up and takes Rod's mind off Mandy's missing period. I start thinking about this bird I went out with when I was a kid. Two years it was before I found out she was knocking off some bloke from Kilburn. Claire thought she was in the club one time and I made the mistake of telling Mark, who passed the news on. Soon I was getting the piss ripped out of me left, right and centre. She was black and they were giving me stick asking what the kid was going to look like, whether it was going to come out half man, half baboon.

I was shitting it because I didn't want to be a father at fifteen and they were trying to ease the agony with a bit of humour. It turned out alright in the end because she came on and we went out and got pissed on snakebite. We were out of it and I shagged her in the back of some car we broke into and the next morning I was red as a beetroot. She was alright Claire, really into the old music and that, and became a dancer when she grew up. She moved out of the area years ago and went up to North London. Moved in with some kebab merchant. She was one of those birds who if you met her twenty years later you'd probably end up staying with. I remind Rod about Claire to get him looking on the bright side.

– She was a cracker, he says. Well tasty.

– I'd have fucked that if I'd had the chance, Mark joins in.

– Fit body on her. She made a bomb as a dancer, didn't she?

Chelsea break clear of the Villa defence and we're on our feet. The ball hits the net and we're jumping up and down going mental and Claire and Mandy are forgotten. It's a good game of football and when the ref blows the whistle at the end we leave happy. The dark's starting to come now and we're going back across the park with a good chunk of the crowd. Billy Bright stands against a tree having a slash and a woman coming the other way looks at him like he's committing a major league crime. He flashes at her and she runs off.

The coach is waiting and we're ready for the trip back to London, planning a stop in Northampton. The kids guarding cars are still there, but don't look like they're doing much business. Times are hard and those at the bottom of the pile are always first to feel the pinch. Harris has slipped the driver twenty quid to stop in Northampton so everything's sweet. We move slowly through football traffic. Once we get to the motorway we're off with everything moving nicely. Should be in a Northampton pub within an hour or so. Now the game's over Rod sits frozen looking out the window watching the world pass in the opposite direction.

– Phone Mandy when we get to Northampton. Mark is sitting next to Black Paul, leaning over the seat. She'll have come on by now. She's got you worried so she'll start bleeding.

– I'll phone her but I'm not holding my breath.

We're soon pulling off the motorway and stopping at a pub we've used several times before. We're straight inside lining up the drinks. Rod fucks off to the phone. I watch him and he looks like he's talking but comes back and says there's no answer. He's been chatting with himself. Mandy must be round her mum's, but there again she could be doing a Claire. You can never trust a bird because they give it the big one about honesty and everything, then soon as you turn your back their pants hit the floor and they've got their ankles digging in some other bloke's arse.

– I fucking need this, says Rod, lifting the glass to his lips. Beautiful.

– That'll sort you out. Black Paul is next to him drinking orange juice. It's thirsty work waiting for women to get their act together.

– Why don't you drink then?

– Don't have problems with women. Treat them like shit and they love you. Give them a bit of leeway and they'll take liberties. It's a fucking war.

– Mandy's alright. She's straight. Solid.

– She might be, but what about you? Mark joins in. A few beers in your belly and you're sniffing round anything that moves.

– It's different. It doesn't count.

– How's that then?

– Don't know, it's just different somehow. I know I don't mean it I suppose. It's just the alcohol taking charge.

– You drink it in the first place, says Paul coming on like a fucking agony aunt. You want the effect otherwise you wouldn't get pissed. You go to football and you lay off it because you know you'll get out of hand. Go out in the evening when you're socialising and you don't give a fuck.

– I don't know. You can't think about these things too much.

– It's war. Just remember that. But it's a psychological war. Lift a hand to a woman and she'll never forget it. You can treat them like shit, but show respect when you're doing it. Lose your temper and it means they've got under your skin.

– Paul's right in a way, says Mark. Getting pissed is no excuse. Everyone says it is, but it's a bottle job. But who needs an excuse in the first place?

Rod gets the drinks in and we're knocking them back fast. After five pints Rod goes over to the phone and tries again. I watch the bloke and know he's not talking to himself any more. There's a big grin on his face. Ear to ear job. Real Joker effort. He puts the receiver down and comes back. He's got a result and Mandy's got a Tampax earning its keep. He clenches his fist like he's just scored a goal.

– One-nil. Came on this afternoon.

– Told you it would be okay. You shouldn't worry.

– I know. But you do, don't you? You just see your life going down the bog with the used rubbers. You know you'll never fuck off out of London or do anything different with your life, just keep on going till the day you die, but you like to have the option. Kids stop all that.

– Depends how you look at it, says Harris. I've got two kids myself. It doesn't change anything. It's all in the mind, like everything else. I see them twice a week and everything's okay. I wouldn't swap them for anything, even though me and their mum don't live together these days. We get on alright and the kids are the most important thing in your life once you have them.

I look at Harris a bit different. I'd never have guessed it, but that's not unusual. You see some blokes at football and you'll only ever know some of them one way. Then they melt into everyday life. They don't walk around with a sign round their neck telling everyone they're the hooligan element or anything. They've got their jobs and their loves, though that's not to say they're saints. Football is just a focus, a way of channelling things. If there was no football we'd find something else. Probably be a lot more indiscriminate as well. The aggression's got to get out some way and the authorities know the score and want you signed up, standing to attention killing Arabs or Paddies or whoever's flavour of the month on their behalf.

– I'm a free man, says Rod. I feel like I've been let out of the nick. Ready to pass go and collect my cheque.

– No you don't. Mark speaks up. That's something you've got to go through to understand. It's a different thing being inside, like nothing else. Take my word for it.

– You know what I mean.

The night passes quickly and we're hammered by ten. The coach driver says he's leaving at eleven. We're trying to persuade the cunt to stay on, to come along to this club we know, but he's not interested. Says he's got a wife and kids at home waiting for him. We're undecided, not fancying the hassle of trying to get back to London at three in the morning. Rod makes the decision. Says he fancies a bit of bloodsport when he gets home. It's the man's night so we let him have the final word. He tells us to drink up. We've still got another hour till we head back to London.

ASHES TO ASHES

A CHEERFUL YOUNG man said a few words, the mourners sang a song of remembrance without musical accompaniment, and the deceased's remains were sent below to melt into nothingness. Mr Farrell caught his line of thought, stopped it dead. It wasn't emptiness but a new beginning; if that's what Albert Moss really believed, then why not? He had no deep-rooted faith of his own and doubted whether his Spiritualist friend would have trusted in a greater, all-loving creator if he'd been inside a concentration camp, but that was the democratic way.

With Albert's corpse went visions of Mrs Farrell. Her husband was finally at rest; one day he would visit the headstone, read the inscription he had chosen after much careful thought and days of indecision, then trim and arrange her favourite red and white carnations. He saw flesh slowly rotting, skin sucked into itself and wrinkles exaggerated, below ground with the sewage pipes and broken bones. A shudder passed through his body, starting at the shoulders and racing down to his feet, forcing him to lean forward in his pew. Nobody paid attention. They just saw an old man expressing his grief.

When the congregation filed out of the chapel, Mr Farrell stayed behind, sitting with his head in his hands. Tears trickled beneath strong fingers but didn't reach his lips. He hadn't cried properly since he was a child, though he couldn't remember even that, and he wasn't exactly sobbing now. He was sad but at the same time relieved. He remained solid for a long while, flashbacks coming in bursts then slowly melting away, the stacked corpses and rotting bodies of his army experience swamped by happy memories; family and friends and a pride in his role in the war.

While others his age fumed at antagonists who had only ever known peace, Mr Farrell just didn't care. Perhaps Bomber Harris had been wrong about Dresden. There was no glory in fireballs and burning human beings, how could there be, yet he couldn't see what could be gained attacking pensioners who had done what they thought best. They had been kids at the time. Teenagers in uniforms. But he marvelled at the spiral of history, rewritten and revised and turned inside-out. He was living history, for as long as his memory held, and he would be dead in a few years, perhaps sooner. Then it would be left to books to tell the story secondhand.

Eventually Mr Farrell stood up and pushed through the weakness, because that was all tears could ever be. His sex and class meant he was denied the right to act soft, to shed tears and openly mourn. That was for the privileged, with time on their hands and a need for excessive psychology. He wasn't complaining, because you needed an inner strength to get through life, the ability to face everything and come out on top. The weak sank into depression, names unknown and reason lost. Perhaps he'd been on the brink himself, suffering hallucinations and seeing his wife where she couldn't possibly exist, hearing her voice in his head, allowing himself to drift towards Albert's way of thinking. But he was finished with all that now. She was dead.

He didn't care for religious ceremony or images, the only reality body fat melting in intense heat, bubbling up and dripping from the oven, turning to stone. Deep down he envied Albert his Spiritualism, yet could never become immersed himself. Belief was ingrained. If a person created their own afterlife then who was to say it wouldn't come true; like wishing on a star. Time was the crux and while the past was reinvented daily it was too hard an exercise for him to follow at his age, all the bickering back and forward, the future an easier and more positive option.

– How was it? Vince asked, his grandfather opening the passenger door and getting into the car.

– A funeral's a funeral, though this one was better than most because there was no organ player going through the motions and hitting all the wrong notes, and they kept the speech short. At least there wasn't the fuss of your gran's burial. I remember everything like it was yesterday. The organ blasting away out of tune and echoing through my head driving me mad. Then the vicar rabbiting on about someone he'd never met, not even knowing she was born a Jew in Budapest and died an atheist in London, that she was a million miles beyond his forgiveness and taking a plot in his graveyard. I swear if he'd gone on much longer I'd have swung for him.

Vince Matthews nodded his head, not knowing what to say. He turned on the ignition and pulled to the edge of the road, looking for a way into the traffic. The old boy'd had a rough time of things since his wife died, but seemed to be pulling through now. He found a gap and put his foot down, leaving the crematorium behind as quick as possible. The lights were rolling in his favour and before long they were cutting along beneath the Chiswick Flyover gunning towards Kew.

– You should come out to Australia when I get set up over there, Vince said. Give me a few months to get things going then come and stay for as long as you want. I'll get work no problem, I know enough people, and we can drive into the outback and see the sights. It's relaxed and you don't have to worry about politics and getting mugged, or how much the council's going to tax you next month.

– I could have gone years ago you know. A mate of mine emigrated after the war and wanted me to try my hand, but I didn't fancy it somehow. Mind you, maybe I'll take you up on the offer, though it'll cost a bit to get over there. I didn't know what was going to happen after the war. It was an exciting time in its own way, coming out of something like that with all your limbs and half your mind left, then after a while the relief just turned to sadness. There was no help in those days. Nobody you could go and talk to about what you'd seen and done, and your gran was such a mess after everything that happened to her. You got through it though. You had no choice. It was either that or the madhouse. Maybe we were stronger then, I don't know. Not like you nancies today with your counselling and social workers.

They both laughed. Vince wondered if he'd killed anyone during the war, but would never ask. Even as a kid he had known enough not to put the question. That would be hard to handle, even though it was war and a fight for survival. He thought about the punch-ups he'd been involved in when he was younger. He couldn't link the two characters even though he was the same person. If he got himself in the situation he would fight for survival, but he preferred overseas travel to a trip up to Liverpool or Manchester. Losing his head over a bang lassi was better than a two o'clock kicking outside some dodgy club with your eyes bleary from the drink and your brain about to get another pounding from some nutter out to do you serious damage.

– I'll pay your flight over, don't worry about that. You've done enough for me in the past, when I was a kid and all that. You just get yourself down Heathrow and enjoy the ride. Don't let me down either. Mum and Dad said they'd be over but you come on your own and we'll have a good laugh. You drive out in the desert over there and there's nothing to see but sand and the horizon, burning mountain ranges the Aborigines say are sleeping animals that created the world. It does something to your head. There's no crowd mentality in the desert, just kangaroos and maybe some Aborigines out in the heat living the dreamtime.

– It'll be my second youth, let alone childhood, my first time abroad since 1945. I've never been on a plane you know. They say it's an experience, a bit better than jumping out of a landing craft with German machine-gunners trying to cut you in half if you get to the beach and a bastard of a sergeant at your back with a machine-gun threatening to chop you down if you don't get out quick enough. It was like that, you know, because if you didn't shift you risked the other blokes as well as yourself.

– You get treated with respect when you travel to Australia because you've paid a fair bit for the seat. It's not like some two-hour tube trip to Spain or Greece. You go long-haul and they look after you. Free drinks, meals-on-wheels and films. You get some crackers working as stewardesses as well.

– Maybe I'll find myself a dolly bird and get her to look after me, you never know. I'm not past it. Even when you're old you still get the urge now and again.

Vince was embarrassed. He didn't want to think of his granddad on the job, shagging some British Airways bimbo on Bondi Beach, giving her a nice line of chat, pulling the rubber on and spreading the woman's legs, dipping his winkie in a piece of BA hardcore, bony arse moving up and down in time to a brass band, voices in the distance, the blonde with blue eyes captivated by the pensioner's charm, the medals he rarely wears because he thinks they're rubbish, digging ten-inch purple fingernails into sand-paper skin, coming in a groaning tribute to age and experience, the skeleton shag-machine from West London on tour down under, bikini blondes flocking around the pre-war model sex instructor tucking into his early morning breakfast. Vince shook his head. That lassi must be lingering. It was disgusting. Child-molesting in reverse. He took the techno tape his brother had made up and slipped it into the cassette-player, Spiral Tribe, turned the volume down so it was just about audible.

– You get high above the clouds and next thing you're flying over all these places you hear about on the news, Kuwait City, New Delhi, Singapore, the works, right there in space looking down on everything, the shapes of the clouds, and when the sun comes up you look through the window and you can almost see a curve in space. It's like you're halfway to being an astronaut riding with the gods. You feel special. Nothing can get near enough to harm you.

– It sounds good. We'll see about it later. You might not go back.

– I will. Give it another six months or so. I love England and everything, but it's shit really. It's all the stuff you have to carry on your back. I mean, I know it's the same anywhere you go, but I'd rather just be on the outside looking in, keeping my head down, rather than in the middle of things getting battered all the time.

Vince crossed Kew Bridge, indicated right and stopped, waiting for a gap in the South Circular. He pulled off towards the front of Kew Gardens and easily found a place to park. At this time of year there was always free space around the common. The houses were more like mansions and he wondered what it would be like living there. Not bad probably. It wasn't London really, at least not the London he knew. During the summer there was a cricket pitch and the old church opposite served tea and cakes. It was more like a country village. They got out and walked to the main gates, Vince's treat as it was expensive to get in Kew Gardens these days.

It had been five years since Mr Farrell's last visit, a summer's day walkabout with his wife, his former occupation adding to the attraction of the botanical gardens. Vince had been as a child with both his parents and grandparents. He especially remembered the time his brother got lost in the trees off towards the river. Their dad gave him a hiding when they found him. They went straight then turned left towards the lake, the Palm House to their right. As a kid Vince was convinced it was a spaceship, the shape and glass panelling elegantly contoured and maintained, as big now as it had appeared then. They stopped by the water. There was an elderly couple on the opposite side and three Japanese tourists, but this time of year saw only a fraction of the summer rush. The earth was black and rich, clouds blocking the sun, a relative solitude and promise of life under the soil waiting to rise up and take over.

They went to the Palm House, heavy doors sounding behind them. It was warm and humid, the glass sections above just visible through lush foliage, a regular hiss of sprayed water. They were transported to the Amazon, the rainforests of Asia, around the globe in minutes. Everywhere there was exotic life and lush vegetation. They climbed circular stairs to the walkway above, stopping to look down on enormous leaves and intricate bark formations, lost in a Victorian jungle.

– They did some good things in the old days, didn't they, Vince said, finally breaking the silence, footsteps on metal. It wasn't all blood and theft. You know, I read that they used to castrate Aborigines and bet on how long it took them to die, but you come here and see what other people built and it's another story. You look at this place, the parks in London and all the museums, and you don't see anyone doing that nowdays. It's all cutting back and closing down, and if they could get their hands on Kew the developers would chop down the trees and flog the land as prime real estate.

– Things get better in some ways and worse in others, Mr Farrell replied, the load just gets shifted around. Look at my day. World war and millions murdered, raped, tortured. That was Europe and now we build the guns for others to do the killing, but there's nothing on that scale. It depends which way you look at things.

Mr Farrell was glad when they left the Palm House. The humidity was affecting his breathing. Vince enjoyed the fresh air as well. It made him happy seeing the old boy in a positive state of mind. He was always talking about his wife in the present, like she was still around, sitting at the table in the flat maybe, or resting in the bedroom, watching through the window for her husband's return. It was a bit sick somehow and Vince was thinking of his gran, the way she laughed deep in her throat, but now his granddad was talking about her in the past tense. It made him feel a lot easier.

They went towards the river, past the second lake with ducks on the water and duck shit on the bank, circling around so they eventually arrived at the Evolution House. Vince read about asexual and sexual reproduction, the roles of bats, bees and butterflies in pollination, the extra strength to be gained through sexual production, the addition of new genes which made for a better chance of survival. It was all there in the bang lassis, the great British mega-mix.

– I'm glad we came, Mr Farrell said, sitting in the nearby restaurant half an hour later, a squirrel sauntering up for a piece of cheese sandwich. It gives you a lift, somewhere like this. This is the real world, what it's all about, trees and plants and flowers and scientists looking at the medicine we can get from nature. It's all this that you never hear about. You just get the negative angle the whole time.

Vince nodded. He was right. Kew just meant happy memories as far as he was concerned, but there was something even more positive about the place now. It was more sophisticated, like they were trying to get people involved in the work, attempting to educate as well as everything else. Maybe he'd just not been looking before. But how were you supposed to know the truth about the past when on the one hand you had stories about Aborigines getting castrated for a wager, yet at the same time there were naturalists and horticulturists travelling the globe fascinated by trees and plants and the benefits they offered humanity, trying to preserve nature.

– What do you want to go to Australia for when you've got this? Mr Farrell laughed. It might be nice over there but it's never going to be home, is it? That's probably why I never went and tried my hand over there, I remember now. It would have been admitting failure, that a part of me was no good, that the country that made me was nothing. The future's got to be worth seeing, just finding out what's going to happen next, even ten or twenty years down the road. That's what keeps you going. You sit in the past and you never move forward. It's half and half. Keep the good things and add to them, but throwing it all away and starting again is as bad as never changing anything at all.

– You sound like a politician, Vince said.

– I've never heard a politician worth listening to, and I've heard a few.

Vince was in Australia, north of Sydney along the Great Barrier Reef, sheer beauty beneath a clear blue ocean, diving down into another universe of fish and coral, shoals of minnows darting back and forward, thousands of tiny lives, bigger multicoloured fish looking at him with enormous eyes, a harmless shark in the distance. Below the surface life was vibrant and alive, finding its own way to survive, all the colours mixed in together, and he was thinking about asexual and sexual reproduction, vindicated in his role, thick sand and the Italian girl he met diving, that evening sitting on the beach looking into the darkness, the outline of her long black hair against a cloudless sky covered in stars and trailing meteors, waves crashing on the shore taking him back all those years to San Sebastian, trying to sleep under the boardwalk with drunks smashing bottles up above, and he'd done what he planned, got out of the rut, out of his environment, so now he could see what was under the surface, deep down, all the colour and movement, people like himself too far into their world to see there was something outside, something bigger, and the great thing was that it didn't really matter one way or the other, just that Italian woman was important, total beauty, a soppy way to describe a human being but that's what it was, pure magic, the realisation that he, Vince Matthews, had made it to the other side of the planet and had seen more than seven wonders on the way, almost laughing out loud thinking of the lads in San Sebastian, the bulls they were going to run and the sunburn, where were the poor bastards at that precise moment, the bulls dead, what about John and Gary and all the others, then they were gone again, as Vince focused on the red burns of space rock millions of miles above his head.

– There's one or two politicians who made the effort, but they got shouted down, so now none of them bother any more and make do looking after their own little bit of power. They blend in with popular opinion and settle for an easy life. Suppose we all do. Not you and me though. We've been outside and seen the options. I had no choice and didn't like what I found, but you had the nerve to do it on your own and you'll probably be going back for some more. What are you smiling at Vince?

– Just the thought of those explorers and how they must've travelled. There were no round-the-world airline tickets or backpacker hostels in those days.

When they'd finished their coffee and Mr Farrell had attracted another couple of squirrels with hand-outs, they started walking again. The clouds had gone and it was a fine day. They passed through a ruined brick arch and were about to pass the Marianne North Gallery when Mr Farrell caught Vince's arm. Neither remembered the building and they walked inside, reading the details of a Victorian artist without formal training who had travelled the world painting plants and scenery.

Hundreds of brightly coloured pictures covered the walls, each with a black wooden frame holding it in place. There was no space between individual paintings, the walls literally covered. There were details of plants, their intricate forms painstakingly recreated, and wider more general views. There were few people, just plant life and incredible scenery. The woman who painted them looked dour in a long dress, round glasses and hair held in a scarf, but that was just her appearance. She had been everywhere; Borneo, Java, Japan, Jamaica, Brazil, India, Chile, California, New Zealand, more places than either of them could absorb. There were plants and flowers and trees, seascapes and volcanoes, snow-capped mountains, kangaroos in the outback, walking from picture to picture, a monkey eating fruit, the mass of colours a kaleidoscope of impressions.

Vince had never been inside an art gallery before. Art was something for the people who lived in Kensington and Hampstead. Mind you, there'd been that time with the school when they'd gone to the Tate Gallery, but they'd had a fight with some kids from Lewisham, even at that age West London fighting South London, and Vince had hit one of them. A teacher saw him and he'd got the cane, then been banned from the next trip, a visit to the seaside which he'd have liked seeing as he didn't go on holiday very often. But he'd done well when he grew up and had been to more places than most people managed and wasn't finished yet, a bit like the woman in the photo at the front of the museum or art gallery or whatever they called the place. He bet she didn't care about Victorian bullshit when she was off travelling, fighting back against her set role in society, refusing to be ground down, showing more bottle than he ever could, and he had total respect for Marianne North, though he knew nothing more about her than what he saw on the walls. She showed what was possible.

– She saw a lot didn't she Granddad?

– Just saw the beauty. That's the way to do it.

Mr Farrell went briskly from one picture to the next, matching images with the text below. They were nice enough though a bit close together. She was an example, someone who had a passion for a subject and really lived. That was all you could do. Then he was finished and outside waiting for his grandson, ready to go home and sort out his wife's clothes and give them to the jumble, clear out and start again, wash the floors and scrub away any lingering scent, the wind cool on his face, refreshing and invigorating, like he was waking up after a long sleep, his grandson inside still, looking at volcanoes in Java and then a picture of a plant whose name he couldn't pronounce, thinking of that Italian girl on the beach, an old Spanish tramp trying to teach the Englishman his language, glad they'd left the bulls alone, something worthwhile that, knowing some people were more up-front and took protest further, something beyond class, like Marianne North, daughter of an MP, just people in the end, looking inside the plant past the shape and seeing all that detail, Vince wondering whether its genetic survival depended on a bat, bee or butterfly.

MILLWALL AWAY

WE'RE HARD AS nails going into the Lions' den, warming up on a couple of slow pints, enough to get the courage flowing in this nothing pub, something to dull the blows if things turn bad. The kids are bragging and singing while the older blokes play it calm knowing mouth and action rarely go together. It all comes from experience. Apprenticeships have been served and lessons learnt. There's no room for chancers tonight. Everyone here has got to stand up and be counted. There's a lot of pride at stake and self-respect is all important. If anyone bottles they better not show themselves again.

I look at familiar faces. Mark and Rod standing next to me. Harris with Martin Howe and Billy Bright. Black Paul putting coins in the fruit machine acting casual and pulling it off. Black John lucky to be back in Victoria after West Ham. Facelift and Don Wright. Everyone is primed ready to get stuck in. Doing their duty when it matters most. Behind the scenes maintaining reputations and promoting the good name of the club, our select club. We'll put on a show tonight and if we're the only ones who see it then so fucking what. It's not one of those things you do for someone else. You do it for you and yours and we're peering through the pub window seeing what's what in the station.

There's not a lot of drinking going on because two pints is the limit if we want all the benefit and none of the weakness. A lot of the lads make do with soft drinks. Alcohol dims the brain and kills discipline. If you want a punch-up and not just the chatter you've got to watch what you drink. You can't afford to get careless away to Millwall. Make a mistake down there and you're dead. There's no second chance against that lot. We have to keep alert and see what's going on. Act straight till the second it goes off and when we get stuck in take no prisoners.

Harris stands at the corner of the bar with his squad taking the nod from new arrivals, clocking faces knowing who's who, wary of outsiders more than ever since Newcastle. We're a tight mob tonight and it's only the full-timers who make the trip to Millwall because it's major aggravation down in South East London. True, there's one or two kids knocking around, youths pushing into their twenties, but they know the score and are older than their years, keen to prove themselves and move up the pecking order. It's games like this when a kid can arrive, getting stuck in with the best of them, building the base of a reputation that will see him alright if he stays solid. If a bloke does the business when it counts then it doesn't matter what else he's about.

We're building up for Millwall away and it's going to be nasty, yet we respect Millwall somehow, deep down, though we'd never say as much, knowing New Cross and Peckham are the arseholes of London. The Bushwhackers have been making people take notice for years. As far back as our memories go Millwall have always been mad. Something special, mental, off their heads. They've got the reputation and they deserve it, raised on docker history spanning the century. A hundred years of kicking fuck out of anyone who strays too far down the Old Kent Road.

Their old men were doing the business chasing visitors around Cold Blow Lane when we were kids into toy soldiers, before they moved up the road to Senegal Fields, and before that their granddads were handing out sewing lessons when West Ham strayed too far through the Isle of Dogs, bringing in bad habits from Poplar and Stepney. Knives, bottles and running battles before, during and after the game. All that before my old man was even born. Back in the good old days when Britannia ruled the waves while parts of London were no-go areas for the old bill on Bank Holidays, when the locals went on the piss in a big way.

Human nature translates as human nature, and if the old bill nick you and worst comes to worst and you go down for a couple of years, banged up for affray, then your mates will come along to wherever you end up for a visit, and when you get out you'll be made. That's how legends happen. Names from history that mean more than all your Nelsons and Wellingtons put together.

Millwall, West Ham, Chelsea. F-Troop, the ICF, Headhunters. Waterloo is just the name of a train terminus and the best the blokes who died for their country got was a station named after the place where they fell. Going to Millwall is what it's all about today and it makes more sense than fucking off to France to get your head blown off.

We're killing time in the pub, stronger by the minute as fresh faces arrive, keeping things tight, being discreet. There's no need to attract attention, tonight more than any other time, the old bill primed for trouble with their riot gear and half-starved Alsatians tucked away down dark side streets on standby. There's expectation and it's a balancing act keeping the momentum flowing in the right direction, looking for a result. Harris tells the kids to lay off the noise and they respond straight away, toning down the songs, tight lipped, understanding that Millwall away is the big one and no time to lose control, the majority of the firm older with a few well known faces who only turn up for major aggravation.

We leave it till half-six, then Harris starts moving and we're following him out of the pub, through buses packed with silent citizens into Victoria. We're remembering West Ham briefly but it's in the past now filed away and we're into the moment looking at the departure times, Harris knowing where we're going, the plan to get a train to Peckham Rye. We want to avoid New Cross and South Bermondsey, where most of our support will arrive. If everything goes to plan we'll be walking around Millwall without an escort while the old bill are focusing their attention elsewhere. They'll be lined up doing their duty while we're wandering around out of sight looking for a good night's entertainment.

The mob's filled out by now and there's a good three hundred of us. There's a lot of muscle around, the older element, some nasty cases straining to hold back the violence. Every firm needs numbers for major games like this. You're no good with twenty or thirty headcases, however tasty, and we're having a laugh thinking of Pete Watts, how he got thrown through a pub window at Millwall fifteen years ago, another slice of Chelsea myth, knifed in the leg before the police pulled up and nicked him. Cost him fifty quid that one.

We're on the train filling the carriages knowing other

passengers fear us, but we're not interested, keeping our affections for Millwall, not wanting trouble, none of that juvenile hooliganism throwing light bulbs on the platform and touching up office girls. Millwall's a corner of London where time stands still even if they do have a plush new ground. The streets and people remain the same and Cold Blow Lane was a wicked place full of nutters, and the New Den may look flash but it's full of the same old faces standing in the background waiting patiently.

Those days of everyday Millwall theatre riots are part of the past, our fun out in the streets, as it's always been anyway, year in year out, away from reporters and photographers. What do they expect the old bill to do? Put cameras on every roof of every house in every street in every city hoping to get a recording of the latest assault? They're not interested. It costs too much and they're only moved to act when it gets in the public eye, a dead fly irritant washed out with a good caning and some outraged words from the tabloids.

The doors close and we're moving away from Victoria and the plastic Disneyland of the West End. We're moving through London with its granite blocks full of official secrets and money managers, arms dealers and legalised drug barons. There's glass offices reflecting light and buildings, empty of life, full of advertising strategies, the river a great sight this time of night, a harsh city London where the lights are the only thing that stop the place exploding. We gradually pick up speed, train rocking gently side to side with flashes of electricity on the tracks and the whole thing could grind to a halt at any second. The windows are full of reflected faces and soon we're rolling through Brixton and Denmark Hill, travelling in silence. Turn the lights off in London and the whole place would go up. They've got to keep the fires burning no matter how much it costs. Pull out the plug for more than a few minutes and there'd be nothing left.

Harris starts talking in his precise way, giving instructions and warnings, his reputation sound despite Newcastle, that wasn't his fault, beyond his control, but he still has to deliver because the rush is there and we're ready for it to go off in a big way. There's been too much frustration over the last few weeks, the old bill sticking their noses in all the time, doing their job, messing things up. Tonight has to happen. It's vital for confidence. Suppose we're like junkies in a way. Clean-cut junkies looking for the kick of a punch-up. Except we don't take the easy option sitting in our own shit jacking up, out of sight trying to impress the neighbours. We get out there and put ourselves in the firing line. It's a natural high. Adrenalin junkies.

The train pulls into Peckham and we pile onto the platform. Queen's Road is nearer the ground but it means hanging around waiting for a connection and it only takes one phone call and we'd be lumbered with an escort. It's looking good though and we don't see any coppers. Looks like we're in the clear until some wanker nicks the ticket collector's small change. The man's a Paki or something and he's shaking a bit, obviously shitting himself. Don't blame him really. But Harris shouts at the bloke to give the money back and the British Rail man seems happy enough, not wanting trouble, doing his best, earning a crust, Harris coming on like some kind of Robin Hood, and we're laughing inside knowing he doesn't give a fuck.

We're just keeping our noses clean for the moment. Petty theft and vandalism are the mark of a cunt, and Harris doesn't want the ticket collector on the phone. That's the last thing we want. We pile out of the station and are on our own, spilling into the road, geared up because we're steaming, moving away from the station, over the street not waiting for the traffic lights to change, energy flooding our brains and we're on their manor now strutting along and we know the bastards will be around somewhere with their scouts out, mobile phones in small fists for a quick call to the Bushwhackers switchboard.

We look at stray males with suspicion and head towards the ground, buzzing inside the whole time. It's going to go off in a matter of minutes rather than hours. It's a fucking unreal feeling getting into a place like this knowing there's another mob nearby looking to do the same thing, and the fact they're Millwall makes the whole thing major league. This is top of the table. Millwall and West Ham. But we're united, all together in this, and we're telling ourselves that Millwall are mental, but we're mental as well, like we were against West Ham at Victoria, and it's all about pride and self respect. Traffic piles up as we cover the street, taking over, total control, a shot of power. We're on Millwall's manor and it's up to them to stop us taking the piss otherwise they won't be able to hold their heads up till the next time the two clubs meet and they get the chance to try and turn us over.

We're taking liberties but they're smart cunts, it can't be denied, like the time they mobbed together and cut a tree down blocking the Leeds coaches heading back to Yorkshire, or the two thousand a side they had against West Ham. That takes organisation. The tension rises. We're nervous and cocky at the same time. Somehow we've got to control the nerves and make it work for us. It makes us more violent. More determined. When it goes off we'll have to be brutal if we're going to survive. We're putting ourselves on the edge and when you're in South East London it's a fucking long way to the bottom if you get thrown off. It's like we're on the edge of the world sailing along with Christopher Columbus against the tide and you have to keep your momentum otherwise you're fucked.

There's not a copper to be seen, only Peckham locals and flashing amusement arcades. Every pub holds potential as we pass, Millwall holding up somewhere trying to find us, playing the same tracking game, cat and mouse, hide and seek, through streets they know like the back of their hands. This gives them the advantage because you could get lost for days in the blocks, houses, empty yards. There's no colour in the buildings, bricks identical and wasteland overgrown, rows of broken walls and barbed wire, smashed glass and rusted metal, dull new houses that remind me of Bethnal Green. It's a fucking joke thinking about Millwall's flash stadium set in among this shit. Makes you think about priorities in a dump like this. We turn right at a set of traffic lights moving with more of a swagger because we're pumped up to breaking point, Harris shouting at a few lads to tone it down. Keep calm and hang back. We've got to behave ourselves for a bit longer.

We can hear the crowd singing in the ground streets and estates away through the darkness, the station way behind us now, mist coming off the river drifting across the rubble, a white chill infecting dead homes. It's fucking eerie this place. Full of decaying dockers in flat caps bombed and left to rot under a collapsed London. People talk about concrete jungles and that's what this place is, a perfect description, a fucking nightmare world without any kind of life, but we know once we find Millwall that's all going to change, that they'll come out of the brickwork and then disappear into the tunnels when the job is done like they were never there in the first place. Fog drifts through blocks of flats in and out of stairs and balconies, a mugger's paradise, the chance to earn a few bob carving up a skint granny, scum of the earth niggers. The air is cold and evil and it's only our energy that keeps us warm. London's a ragged place now, full of mute pensioners and sullen rappers, past and present melted down and spat into the gutter.

We turn a corner and there they are. Millwall up ahead. There must be a good five hundred of the cunts and they've got the numbers and we could be on for a kicking. But there's quite a few kids with them, though there's a few niggers as well and they're always carrying. They're mobbed up in a patch of wasteland the council calls a communal garden, in among a tunnel of concrete blocks, and they start moving our way slowly, coming down from the New Den maybe, or just standing around out of sight, waiting for the right moment. Time gets lost as the clocks don't matter any more and we're shouting Chelsea as the bricks come raining in, bottles lobbed by kids on the balcony of some overlooking flats.

Millwall are moving faster now, getting things going and we can feel the hate coming our way like they're gasping for air or something they're so fucking wound up, and you can understand the thinking of these blokes nailed into a slum like this, but we're strong united, and we're Chelsea, and this is what we've been looking for, out to settle a few scores, showing our bottle, making a point that we're here at all, and we don't feel Millwall's hate any more because we've got enough of our own.

We return the bricks and steam in. There's a roar that sets heads racing and we feel the rush, the buzz of fighting shoulder to shoulder, for status and our mates, the first punches and kicks landing, both sides piling straight into each other. We've got the front in this slum they call Peckham, New Cross, Deptford, wherever the fuck we are, who knows where we've wandered, trading more kicks and punches in a madhouse, the usual gaps appearing in the street as the two sides clash, the crack of glass and a couple of men going down on the concrete, immediately set upon kicked black and blue from head to toe, and some poor bastard's going to have a serious headache in the morning.

There's no time for fear as we kick out and six or seven older geezers into their forties come through the crowd at us, real old-time street fighters these ones in their donkey jackets, with scarred faces and poxed skin, uneven haircuts and dead eyes even in dim street lights, but they get bricked and hammered. One bloke's on his own with everyone scrambling to kick him and use up some of that energy, threatening to break him in half, send him back to his family and friends in a wooden box. But Millwall act fast and he's dragged back along the concrete unconscious by some of his mates, Millwall winding themselves up, an uncoiling spring with a sharp edge, Millwall going mental, Chelsea going mental.

We're holding our own, but there's just too many of the bastards to run them right off, fights breaking out back and forwards through a kiddies' playground, bottles smashing against the climbing frame. One day we'll think back and see it as a bit of a laugh, if we can think straight, because there's swings bouncing around and some kid trying to get up the slide, pulled back with his head slammed into the metalwork by a couple of older blokes taking turns, Chelsea boys battering the Millwall kid's head trying to dent the fucking thing. It's mental rucking in a playground, seriously funny when we think about it later, reminiscing over our Millwall trip. Childhood fucked up by grown men who should know better.

More Millwall start appearing through the concrete like soldier ants, flooding through the precise angles and stacked piles of rubbish. Battles are kicking off towards the ground, houses and flats around us coming alive with old men hanging out of high-rise windows cheering Millwall on. Their bitter voices echo through the concrete, locked in cells with only the telly for company, taking their hatred out on West London. The roundabout in the playground is spinning with an unconscious youth bent double like something from a war photo. He could be Millwall or Chelsea. Nobody knows what side he's on, or what he's called. What's the fucking difference anyway? And it's all there, the generation gap closed, with the swings and slides and men in their prime cheered on by men ready for the grave.

The fighting's confused now, Chelsea and Millwall getting mixed up. The sound attracts more people coming over from the direction of the ground, but there's still no coppers in sight. It's a kind of heaven this, even though it looks more like hell with the low wattage lighting and dirty mist turning everything inside out. We can feel the anger and hate coming out all around us, flushing out the locals, dragging them from their caves, their kingdom under attack, moving through the age groups, women's voices screaming from the balconies up above now as well as the old boys, the sound of fighting cats late at night, shrieking like babies, a seriously sick sound, turning the air blue with the best Queen's English.

Things are getting worse and we look down the street and there's a few of the lads getting the shit kicked out of them. They're too far gone and we're unable to do anything to help. There's no mercy on sale and we're yelling at each other to stick together, loving every second of what's going on, and Harris starts going mental with his hunting knife, a six inch blade and a dark wood handle, it sticks in my mind, time stopping for a second then speeding up again, didn't know he was tooled-up, his arm moving forward slashing some Millwall cunt across the face, the bloke in shock, expression frozen, a thick groove across his cheek, jaw to the edge of his eye, those Millwall around him holding back as he staggers.

There's Millwall everywhere now. Must have been waiting mob-handed further down the street. It's out of control and they're coming for us desperate for blood, kicking to kill, more bricks and bottles landing on our heads though fuck knows from where unless the pensioners on the landings are dismantling their flats. We don't know what's going on up above because our attention is on the aggro two feet in front, ears burning with the din, the movement and dull blows, the thud of fists and kicks, an iron bar or something catching me across the side of the head.

Suddenly I'm on my own. Isolated. Face down in the street eating dog shit. Forehead in a puddle. Grit cutting my hands. Up against a wall. The smell of crumbling brick and wet concrete. Weight of numbers forcing the main battle further along the street. Off to the football. To the Millwall-Chelsea match. A game of football. It's only sport. Should be an attractive match between two sides who love to go forward. But I don't reckon I'm going to make it because the kicks are coming in, a mob of blokes surrounding me, kicking to cause maximum injury, numbing my body, digging in, breaking blood vessels. I feel the kicks bouncing off my head and shoulders, along my spine, the crush to get stuck in my only protection as Millwall get in each other's way, kicks aimed at my bollocks and I'm tight in a ball trying to protect myself best I can.

There's a ringing sound all around me as most people move off down the street taking that deep roar with them, individual words coming through now, just nonsense, and hatred, fucking Chelsea cunt, fucking cunt, fucking Chelsea cunt, fucking cunt, fucking cunt, fucking cunt, the kicks slowing down but better placed, evil bastards picking their spot, the numbers thinning, leaving the sicker ones to work me over, probably scrawny kids with no bollocks. Seconds turn to minutes and I have no idea to get up and run away, because I'd never make it and only open myself up, expose my balls and face, escape impossible not even considered, must take my punishment like a man, like I'm taught in school, by my mum and dad, hit them harder than they hit me, don't cry, don't tell tales, stand up for yourself, be a man, have a bit of pride, some self-respect, violence without a happy ending.

There's no way out of this and I want to shout but nothing comes out. My throat is bruised and the chords rigid. I'm scared like never before as I realise it's me against the whole of South East London, less than ten of the cunts left now I suppose, and they're hammering me into the concrete. Trying to force me through the gutter into the sewer. The kicking doesn't stop. I feel sick. Like I'm going to die. I'm shitting myself and it's turning to panic. Sheer blind panic which grips me inside as the kicks bounce off my head, spine, even my bollocks as I roll over opening up. I taste sick in my mouth as I try to keep the ball shape. Protecting my bollocks. Hiding my head. But the blows crack against the back of my skull and along my back. I imagine myself in a wheelchair, in a coffin rolling down the chute, burning in the furnace paying for my sins, corpse melting like a waxwork puppet, strings cut one last time.

Where the fuck are the others? Where's the rest of the lads? Why don't the cunts help me? I shouldn't be left alone like this. It's not supposed to be this bad. Football should be about running punch-ups and a few bruises. Nothing too serious. A quick ruck and some mouth. I've been left to fend for myself. I'm losing my grip, going into some kind of junky dream world, thoughts cracking up and drifting along, floating, and I can feel the blows but none of the pain, just numb now, like I'm pissed or something. But through it all I've still got my dignity, a dull voice in my head telling me that we did the business. We've done ourselves proud showing we've got the bottle to take on Millwall and we've held our own against superior odds. I can hold my head up high if I get out of this, but my legs have gone dead and my skull's aching. I've had enough. Thank God for the sirens.

LIQUIDATOR

The editorial team was in place and ready to get down to the evening's business. There was a lot of planning to do for the next issue and once the content had been decided on there wasn't going to be much time left to write, edit, design and get the pages down to the printer. If they missed their allocated slot it would mean a two-week wait, and a lot could happen in that time. It was the difference between a well-run operation with its finger on the pulse and a cowboy outfit that trailed in the wake of its contemporaries.

The editor came into the room with a wooden tray, carrying mugs of steaming hot coffee. Maxwell was a big man with badly cut hair and a chubby face. He had bushy eyebrows and a square mouth. He placed the tray on the table and the rest of the editorial team took their drinks. Maxwell lowered his bulk into the editor's chair and picked up his clipboard, paper and pen which had been cast aside in the rush to make coffee. Maxwell was one of the troops and didn't want his colleagues to think he was taking the piss. There was a chocolate cake and plate of crackers for those who fancied something to eat. Maxwell had already cut himself a slice of cake and took a big bite, then leant over and added three spoonfuls of sugar to his coffee. He stirred the mixture and marvelled at the whirlpool effect.

– Issue two sold well, said Vince, who was new to the team. Two thousand copies is a lot of magazines to shift in two months. You must have been so busy flogging them I'm surprised you had time to see any football.

He had been introduced to the others by his younger brother Chris, and they found him an interesting character, having spent two years in Asia before travelling to Australia where he'd worked on the railways. He was a bit older than the rest of the squad and had a good knowledge of Chelsea history. He was planning a return to Australia at some point so his contribution wasn't going to be long term, but the more people they could get interested the better. The editor had been going through the mail before the rest of the lads arrived.

– We're picking up momentum, said Maxwell, who had been nicknamed after the slightly more famous Robert. We doubled our print run for the second issue and sold out. We'll be challenging the other Chelsea fanzines soon if we keep going at this rate. We've got twice as many letters as for the first issue and there's still a couple of days left till the deadline. We've also had three articles sent in that aren't bad; one on the Rangers-Chelsea connection, another moaning about the lack of skill in your modern professional and the last one going on about the club in general.

No Exceptions had started up in the wake of the more established Chelsea fanzines *The Chelsea Independent* and *Red Card*. There was no serious sense of competition despite the editor's remarks, but more an attitude of if-they-can-do-it-then-why-not-us? Maxwell was the first to acknowledge the *Independent*'s determination at getting the punters a say in how their club was run. Indeed, he had every issue lined up next to his programmes. Like many others, he strongly believed that the club belonged to the supporters, because the players, chairman and backroom staff came and went through the years, but the hardcore fans were there from child to pensioner. The name of the fanzine had been Maxwell's idea and he was proud to have come up with such a clever title. It had been lifted from the club's own terminology when telling people about ticket arrangements. To buy tickets for big games there were often long lists of conditions and qualifications with NO EXCEPTIONS tagged on the end to prevent further discussion. The lads felt it summed up Chelsea's attitude perfectly.

As well as the Matthews brothers, Tony Williamson and Jeff Miller were also making the most of the coffee, cake and crackers, both of them long-time mates of Maxwell. The core three had inevitably been strongly influenced by *When Saturday Comes*, and their broad socialist/anarchist approach to life meant they appreciated the worth of fanzines such as the *Independent* in reflecting the natural grassroots acceptance of black players within the English game. All three had been at the Crystal Palace-Chelsea match in the early Eighties when Paul Canoville had been booed by a big chunk of the Chelsea support when coming on as a substitute. The arrival of a black face in the Chelsea first-team had upset a lot of people and many had walked out, the three of them talking about it in the pub later that evening.

Maxwell had argued that it was a beginning, though, and Canoville soon won over the majority of Chelsea fans, his performances on the pitch and some vital goals putting an end to the abuse. Since then numerous black players had become big crowd favourites. The editorial team believed that football more than any other area of society, with the possible exception of popular music, had accepted the shifting make-up of England's working-class population. It had done this without the help of any of the latter-day interest groups which, now that they felt safe to get involved in football following a middle-class media-inspired acceptance of the game as something other than the domain of Neanderthals, had jumped on the gravy train ten years after the event. Maxwell, Tony and Jeff agreed that those who had founded fanzines such as the *Chelsea Independent* should be getting the credit, not people within the media establishment who had spotted a good career opportunity.

–How about a cartoon strip? Vince asked, shifting the conversation. I'd be up for doing it. It would be this character Liquidator, after the song. He'd be this bloke with a mean streak mixed with a Robin Hood sense of justice, and he'd go about righting wrongs at Chelsea and within football in general.

– We need a few images, said Chris. It's all text and a few lifted newspaper photos at the moment, which never show up all that well. It's either arguments about team selection or club politics. We need to lighten up a bit and keep expanding without losing the edge. After all, two thousand happy customers can't all be wrong.

Maxwell nodded and heaved himself up from his chair, then walked to the bathroom for a piss. He left the door open a bit so that he could hear what the other lads thought of the idea. If Vince was good with a pen then why not? He made sure he hit the side of the bowl and avoided the water. The rest of the editorial team seemed enthusiastic, discussing various ideas and laughing as they pictured Liquidator in action. Maybe they could do something about Dean Saunders. Liquidator could take Paul Elliott along with him on the mission. Maxwell shook himself dry and washed his hands. He examined his face in the mirror. He was an ugly bastard and hadn't been near a woman in five months.

This made him feel like a professional publisher, or maybe a journalist working on one of the tabloids or a shitty football magazine. They were the scum of the earth, some of them at any rate, and he was happy enough as he was, driving a delivery van and taking the *No Exceptions* pages down to the cheap printer they'd found in Crystal Palace. They used paper plates which meant costs were kept low and the manager even looked a bit like Dave Webb, which was a bonus. It was fine as a hobby but he wouldn't want it as a job. Maxwell was honest if nothing else. He turned away from the mirror in disgust.

Vince, meanwhile, was busy giving life to his creation. Liquidator would be a bit of a boy, he wasn't going to make him into one of these TV celebrities who went on about football but when questioned a bit more closely knew few of the specifics and skirted the issues. Liquidator would have a semi-aggressive appearance and would go to the heart of things. Perhaps he would be half-man, half-machine. There would be no trial by jury and his justice would be instant and final. Vince tried to think up a story-line, veering from the hypocrisy of politicians and those running football to the money-madness the game had developed. All the time he was looking at the wider angle, football a microcosm of society.

– I reckon something about football's pricing policies would be well appreciated, said Tony. Everyone I speak to thinks they're being stitched up, no matter what club they support. It's going to hit breaking point and then they'll just give up.

Jeff was weakest on this angle, trying to convince the others that while he didn't agree with the price hikes, if English teams were going to compete with the big boys in Europe, the Italians and Spanish clubs which were backed by corporations and seemed to have their own mints built into stadiums that easily held a hundred thousand people at a go, then money was needed. There would only be a drain of talent to Milan or Barcelona and where would that leave the English game? Top players were going to go where the money was and, if they were honest, wouldn't any one of them jump at the chance to live in Italy and earn twenty grand a week? The others nodded, quickly pointing out that from Chelsea's point of view the argument about a player drain didn't hold. The Italians and Spanish wouldn't want any of their lot.

Maxwell said it was sickening the amount footballers were paid. How could anyone justify ten thousand pounds a week and up? Vince agreed, though they weren't exactly going to turn it down. But it was a subject that needed addressing and Liquidator would deal with a couple of well-paid Tottenham stars and their agent, but first he was going to settle old scores and pay Thatcher and Moynihan a visit. Vince let the story develop, the pictures he would draw already forming, revenge the driving force as he thought about identity cards and expensive seats in all-seater grounds.

Liquidator was on a train south to Dulwich, bunking the fare and covering the walls with marker-pen graffiti. He'd heard Maggie was at home after her latest world tour and would probably be suffering from jet lag. He knew the address, found the house and climbed over the back garden fence. He broke a window and was soon inside. Denis was crashed out on the couch with an empty bottle of champagne discarded on the floor. Liquidator kept moving. Thatcher herself was upstairs in a deep sleep. The house was expensively decorated and ornaments from all round the globe were positioned in strategic places. Vince was impressed by the Iron Lady's choice in artefacts, but Liquidator told him not to be such a prat, that they were on a mission. He told a humble Vince that they were probably fakes and the originals stashed in a bank vault. Maggie would be saving her treasures for a rainy day.

Liquidator was looking good. Vince had the curves of the face and the assassin's expressions perfectly formed in his mind. He thought about doing something with the eyes, making them oversized or filling them with reflected images, but decided it would just make the CFC superhero look a plonker and anyway, it would be too difficult. He didn't know how good his drawing was going to be yet. Liquidator was casually dressed in jeans, trainers and black jacket. His hair was short but not shaven. All he had to do was transfer this mental prototype to paper and he would be away. That was the hard part.

Liquidator led the way upstairs and stood over the former Prime Minister, the woman Vince whispered would have been Queen if the Queen had allowed such a constitutional oddity. She was bald and a wig rested on the bedside table. The Iron Lady was getting old. Now that Liquidator was in a position of power Vince didn't know what to do. Murder and torture could well upset those readers who had an inbuilt respect for the fairer sex, not to mention age, so instead he chose a tattoo. Using chloroform to anaesthetise her, Liquidator added the original club crest to the Iron Lady's right forearm. The next time she shook hands with a foreign dignitary it would catch the cameras, the Chelsea lion wrapped in a Union Jack. Thinking about it, the flag probably wasn't such a good idea, only adding to the nationalistic mystique. On the way out of the house Liquidator ransacked Denis's drinks cabinet.

Vince knew the plot wasn't strong enough. His audience would demand a more decisive thrust if the Chelsea hero was going to live up to his name. That was the modern way. Things had to be clear-cut, with good and bad aspects separated and no common ground in between. Moynihan was next. Perhaps he could do better there. Moynihan was working as a newspaper boy in Surbiton and Vince decided on a puppet characterisation. Once Liquidator had recovered from his Thatcher-fuelled hangover, he tracked Moynihan down and, using the chloroform, bundled him into a suitcase. He would keep the former Parliamentarian in cold storage until the Millwall-Chelsea game which had just taken place. Then he'd take him down to South East London and at the exact moment when the two mobs were about to steam into each other he would produce Moynihan and, in a frenzy of working-class recognition of a common enemy, they would join forces and rip him apart.

Maxwell came back into the room and took his place. He felt like a major publisher right enough and wasn't there something about the big boys being able to do whatever they liked? Imagine having that kind of power, influencing and deciding democratic elections, forming opinion in millions of people around the globe. What would Rupert Murdoch do next? He only had the job for a year and then it was going to switch to Tony or Jeff. They'd adopted a democratic approach to *No Exceptions*. Maxwell cleared his throat and prepared to speak. He was gearing up for something profound, about to stun his comrades with insight and publishing acumen, but bollocks to all that, it was only a bloody football fanzine, it wasn't like they were trying to bring down the Government or something. He was thirsty despite the coffee.

– Does anyone fancy going down the pub for a bit of inspiration? We can continue the editorial meeting down there. The Harp does a decent pint and they've even got Liquidator on the jukebox. Anyone thirsty?

The team collected their coats and Maxwell switched off the lights. Everything was going well. He could murder a nice pint of Guinness.

SOMETHING SPECIAL

THE NURSE ADJUSTING my pillows smells of roses. Something like that. Some flower melted down and turned to liquid, stuck in a bottle and flogged for a small fortune. She's a nice looker. The uniform does her no harm either. Not that I'm into birds in uniforms in the sense of shafting them just because they've got the official stamp, but this one makes her different. Something a bit special. Nurses serve time helping the likes of me and that makes her more a woman than the mouthy regulation slags you pick up, shag, then never see again.

Mind you, there was this time in Chesterfield, coming back from a game up north. Can't remember where, though it might have been Oldham. We ended up at this club full of off-duty coppers. I was pissed, drinking shorts, past the point of no return, and I'm sitting at a table talking to this woman in a black pencil skirt with fishnet stockings wedged up her arse and Gary Glitter heels on her feet. She wasn't bad and I was getting in there. Then she leans over and tells me she's a copper. Tells me she loves being in the force because she can sit back watching the world go by, knowing she can nick anyone, anytime, anywhere.

I was gutted. She was filth and I was lining up a good bit of sex and I find she's got the plague. But I got myself back in the swing and started thinking what a laugh it would be shagging a copper. It would be a crack telling the lads I'd knobbed a WPC. I tried to imagine her in uniform, but it didn't work. She looked like any other Saturday night bike ride. Then she starts going into one about how she's got the cuffs tucked away in her handbag and if anyone starts anything she'll be over in a flash, kick him in the balls, then nick the bastard. She says she's not scared of anyone tonight. She's got plenty of work colleagues around to back her up.

My head was spinning and I went into one saying how much I hated the old bill. That I'd love to fuck one up. Luckily the music drowned me out and she just smiled and rolled her eyes like any other bird looking for a bit of stiff. She was pissed as well, so nothing was making much sense. I realised what I was saying and toned it down, still thinking I was in, but ended up getting blown out. It would have made a good story, but soon as she pissed off I had a word with Mark and Rod and we got out sharpish. That's all you need, socialising with the old bill on a Saturday night. I'll have a drink with almost anyone, but there's a limit. You have to have standards.

The nurse asks how I'm feeling. Not too good, I'm afraid. Still, that's what happens when Millwall get hold of you. I tell her I must look a right state with two black eyes and cuts and grazes all over. My body aches from head to toe. She says I look worse than I am. I've got three cracked ribs, a fractured cheek bone and bruising over a good chunk of my body, but I'm lucky it isn't worse. She says there are some sick people in the world. That she can't understand why a gang of men would attack someone just because he supports another football team. I shrug my shoulders. The slightest move hurts. I say I don't know either. It doesn't make much sense. She tells me I probably owe my life to the policemen who got there in the nick of time.

– There's so many people come in here suffering, really suffering, that when drunks arrive with sick down their clothes and their heads split open from fighting each other, I feel more angry than anything. They've got their health and money in their pockets, and yet they go out and get into fights for nothing.

Her name's Heather. Comes from the West Country. I think of Bristol City and Rovers. Always football. Heather is a Lady With The Lamp throwback. Suppose all the nurses are really. A romantic view because there's no glory emptying bed pans and scrubbing the incontinent, but maybe there should be, because the cunts who get the headlines and congratulations deserve sweet FA, earning more in a week than nurses do in a year. It's all about public service.

– You get kids come in here with cigarette burns all over their bodies, where the parents have stubbed them out, tormented all their lives. Little bodies covered with cuts and bruises and hair pulled out in lumps. Then you get the men at closing time full of beer and filthy language. You hate them because they just see themselves and nothing else. They're angry but they don't know why. They don't try to work anything out. They spend a fortune on drink and drugs and where does it get them? Their Saturday entertainment is damaging people.

Heather has a chirpy voice despite what she's saying. It's positive. She's tidying my bed, clearing away a plate and cup. Keeps moving, doing things the whole time, twisting her body, almost breathless the way she darts around. No pause for rest. Nurses don't have time to hang about talking rubbish. Every second counts. They have to keep cheerful otherwise they'd crack up seeing all that misery and shit every time they come into work. There's no way I could handle it.

– Try and get some rest. The doctor will be along to see you later. You'll be fine after a couple of weeks doing nothing. You've got to give yourself time to heal. You'll be right as rain and we won't have to see you again.

Heather walks down the ward. She's got a nice body. I think what it would be like if we were tucked up in bed together. She stops at a middle-aged man with a sad dog look on his face. Don't know what he's in for, but it's not going to be anything good. I can't hear what she's saying and he just nods his head up and down. I'm not interested in what the man's about, keeping my eyes on Heather. She doesn't look back the whole time she's with him, then she's moving further down the ward out of sight. She's a nice lady, Heather, real class act, but I know I'm never going to get near her.

We're moving in opposite directions and if I'm honest I have to admit she's got it sussed. But it takes all sorts, and I'm not going to sit around thinking I'm shit because thinking too much can seriously damage your health. Like the official Government warning. I've enough to get on with at the moment. My right arm is bandaged along with my ribs. I'm a mess. Heather says I've got enough bruises to open a market stall. She's got a sense of humour. They've done X-rays and given me a brain scan. I'll be okay. Got to stay patient. I'm better off than some of the poor cunts in here. I try to keep still. Feel like a geriatric confined to bed for the next twenty years. What a way to spend your life. I feel bad as fuck for all those poor sods stuck at home from the day they're born to the day they die. Worse than the physical side, it must seriously mess up your thinking. It's the boredom that would do me in. Even now I want to get up and move about, but at least I know that if I keep my head down for a couple of weeks or thereabouts I'll be on my feet and out the door. Good as new in fourteen days.

– She's lovely that nurse. She can come and give me a blanket bath any time she wants. I won't disappoint her. I may be getting on but I still know what it's for.

I say nothing and pretend to sleep. The ward goes about its routine and I'm not interested talking with the bloke in the bed next door. He's one of those cunts who's into every little detail. Talks all the time but says nothing. Reads all the papers and knows a million facts and figures. Reckons he's the dog's bollocks when it comes to politics, with the brainy papers stacked next to the comics. I don't give a toss about committees and arguments between party leaders. They're a bunch of wankers and their publicity stunts do nothing for me. He's welcome to them. I keep my eyes closed. Start drifting off.

– Wake up you ugly cunt. Rod's voice makes me start. Pain racing up my spine. Foot on the accelerator. His words a kick in the balls.

– You can try hard as you like but you're never going to fool anyone you're Sleeping Beauty. No nurse is going to creep up and give you a kiss, hoping you'll wake up and save her from all this. Not looking like that she won't.

Mark and Rod stand over the bed looking down on me with a plastic bag of biscuits and Lucozade. They look fit and healthy, prime of life, though Mark's got a bit of a shiner where his right eye used to be. Apart from that, not a scratch. Shows it can be done. You can go to Millwall and come out in one piece. Even do well out of the experience. Learn a few things without paying for the lesson. It's the luck of the draw. They're a couple of pretty boys looking the part. Making the effort because this is a hospital. Real end of the line job.

– Come on, Tom. Mark is eating biscuits from one of the packs they've brought along. Speaks with his mouth full. Fucking slob.

– Pull yourself together. It's visiting time. The nurse said we've got an hour if we want it. Said you're going to live and that you're lucky to have come out of it with your head still on your shoulders. Silly cow. What does she know? She needs a good six inches up the arse. That would sort her out quick enough.

They pull up chairs and sit down either side of the bed. I prop myself up feeling a bit useless and reckon they should give the nurse a break. I feel like I'm a pregnant housewife or something waiting for the kid to drop. Or some invalid with disease eating my insides away, working itself up to the brain so I end up a haggard old dosser talking to chocolate machines down the tube. It's the same feeling you get with the flu but a hundred times worse. It's being out of circulation with your defences down. At the mercy of something beyond my control. Something I made for myself.

– We just lost you. Rod shakes his head and forgets to hand over the bag he's been carrying. Just puts it at the foot of the bed. Two unopened packets of biscuits spill out. They don't notice. Rod continues.

– It was mental, Tom, fucking chaos, and you're just thinking about what's going on in front of you and you don't see anything else. You know who you're with and everything, but it all gets mixed up and confused because you can't be looking over your shoulder every other second.

– We didn't know you were getting a hiding till we saw Millwall kicking the shit out of this ball of clothes on the ground, and even then we weren't sure it was you. Mark looks at the ground. Focuses on the tip of his right foot.

– There was no way we could get to you. Rod looks guilty and I know they think they've let me down.

– There's a hundred or more people in the way and it would've been like going into a tidal wave. It was just the numbers. Millwall were everywhere, but we did the business alright.

– One minute you're there, the next you've gone. Mark looks up. It all happens so fast you don't have time to think.

They're acting like a couple of grannies because I know the score. They'd have done whatever they could. There's no need for explanations. Most of the blokes there would have as well, but in that kind of situation there's no organisation and little chance going against the flow. The whole thing's a lottery and if you're unlucky enough to go down you're fucked. I tell them to leave it out. It wasn't their fault. Nothing they could do. Diamond blokes. Bit of emotion. Embarrassing really. We avoid each others' eyes. Get into that kind of position somewhere like Millwall and you have to take what you're given. Take it on the chin.

The cunts in charge say there's freedom of choice, but the options are lined up before you start. You don't get to pick and choose. A bit of luck and you're king for the day. Fuck up and you're straight down Emergency. Mark and Rod look relieved. Like it's been on their minds. I can understand it easy enough because the big thing isn't really winning or losing, it's having the bottle to have a go in the first place. It's about sticking together. About getting onto Millwall's manor and making your mark. It's pushing yourself a bit further showing what you've got inside. But there's been no overall winners or losers anyway, just a good row, though considering the odds I reckon Chelsea came out looking pretty good.

– After we lost you it went on for ages, says Mark, cheering up, turning the Millwall game into a bit of history, something that'll develop and grow through the years.

– Millwall are fucking evil, but we didn't put up too bad a show considering. Facelift got four stitches in his head where some cunt lobbed a brick. Blood down the front of him like the fat bastard had puked up. Except it was red. Thought the cunt would have blue blood or something. He was well narked about the mess. Said he'd send the bill to Millwall.

– It was a bit tense inside but apart from a couple of scraps down the side of the ground not much going on, says Rod. But afterwards Millwall went mental and had a go at the old bill.

– We come out of the ground and we're held back by vans and dogs, says Mark. They've been at the stores and the shields are out and the truncheons oiled. Half of Battersea Dogs Home was on overtime working for their extra tin of Chum. Alsatians everywhere and vans packed with psyched-up coppers. They looked nervous as fuck. Millwall were off down the end of the street and they were going mental trying to get at Chelsea.

– All you could hear was smashing glass and riot police legging down the road to get stuck in. We were penned in and the old bill shunted us down to South Bermondsey and sent us back to London Bridge. They were on the trains, everywhere. Up at

London Bridge in case Millwall followed us and tried to have a go there or we tried to double back. We hung around for ages but nothing happened. A lot of Chelsea got the tube from New Cross and it went off at Whitechapel.

There's a sudden silence and they're thinking they shouldn't be going on about Millwall, especially the buzz they got out of it, because in the end it was me who got a hiding, me sitting in hospital suffering, me who Heather reckons owes his life to the Metropolitan Police. I'm not bothered. It gives it a bit of meaning and when I'm fit it'll be another story. But last night, when I'd got my head together, I was in bed looking at the ceiling with the breathing of all these sick, sad men around me, wheezing and coughing and half drowned with disinfectant, and I started thinking about Millwall. Like it was a nightmare but real.

I was fucking scared when I went down, though I feel a bit of a wanker now and wouldn't tell anyone. Never known anything like it. Norwich was a playground punch-up in comparison. At first I was thinking I must be a bottle merchant, but it wasn't that, not really. You just realise you could get yourself killed, crippled, blinded, brain damaged, something that would stay with you your whole life. Suddenly you don't want to be there any more. You want to turn the telly off and tell everyone that it was only a joke. One big grin. No hard feelings. Why take life so seriously? Because, after all, we've heard the soundtrack and football's only a game.

– How long before they let you out? Rod moves the conversation on. You look a mess. That yokel nurse told us she thought you'd get better quick. She said you're young and strong so you've got a head start on the old men. Nice bit of skirt. Reckon she fancies you the way she was going on. You should get her out for a drink. When you get yourself fit. They reckon nurses are dirty as fuck. They see so many bodies and that, they're not scared of getting stuck in.

I think about what Heather was saying. Men kicking lumps out of each other and she has to put the pieces together. I know what she says is right. I understand the argument. But it can't change anything. She'll never know what it's about because her thinking is different. Suppose the whole country works along a million different wavelengths. Getting battered at Millwall was bad news, but I know why it happened and it's not a surprise. Other people would feel disgust. I just feel the pain through my body. Head to toes kicking. Right now I care because I'm hurt. In a couple of weeks, who knows.

– I spoke to that Scottish bloke at the warehouse, Mark cuts in. Told him what happened and he said he'd pass the message on. The foreman phoned up and said anything he can do I've only got to let him know. He said some of the lads would try and get down to see you. Seemed like a decent enough bloke.

– Your old girl phoned up as well. Wanted to know what happened. Then your old man got on the phone. They came down yesterday but you were out of it. Said they'd come again tonight. They were worried.

I wonder how they found out. It's not the kind of news you want the old girl hearing secondhand. When I was a kid and the old bill came round my dad used to give me a whack, but Mum just cried and drank half a bottle of whatever was handy. Went on about how she'd failed her kids. That was the only time I felt guilty. Like if I got done as a juvenile for nicking a car or something she was gutted like it was her fault. It's a dumb way to think and it makes you feel a cunt. I never forgot that, but you get older and you don't want your parents involved.

Mark and Rod stay until their time's up. The hour goes by fast. When they're about to leave they remember the biscuits and Lucozade. Hand it over a bit embarrassed because they say they should have brought some porno mags and lager to ease the pain. I tell them the biscuits and Lucozade will do fine. They laugh. I watch them walk down the ward. They look back and give me the wanker sign. Laugh again as they turn the corner.

I'm soon dozing. Down in South East London again. It's six o'clock Sunday morning and the streets are empty. The sun's shining so hard it must be summer. There's this gold plaque on a wall that's just been rebuilt. The only clean bricks in the area. The plaque reflects sunlight. I have to cover my eyes to read the words. I'm an old man. My hair is grey and I walk with a limp. I'm suffering from arthritis. I've got a walking stick with the Chelsea crest painted on the handle. The name on the plaque is mine. Says I died for my country and have been buried where I fell. I look around but there's just concrete and a cross in the street.

I jolt awake. Remember the dream. A load of old bollocks. I drift off again and I'm with Heather in the nurse's hostel. She's got a room on the tenth floor overlooking London. I watch trains cutting through houses like mechanical snakes. There's no sound. It's late at night and the lights make the trains stand out. I can see miles of vague terraces. No detail. The Post Office Tower in the distance with a flashing light on top. I'm in the spotlight but nobody can see me. I like Heather. She's different. I turn around and she's naked, her back to me, opening a cupboard full of whips and vibrators. She reminds me of that posh bird after Horseferry Magistrates. She lies on the bed and tells me I'll be fine in a couple of weeks. Mark and Rod are laughing on a television screen. They tell me she's just another money grabber. In it for the dosh. That there's good money in bed pans and shovelling shit. Cold hard currency.

– Tom. You alright son? I jolt again. It hurts. My old man's standing next to the bed. I look past him and it's dark out. Must have been asleep for ages.

I've got a depressed kind of hard-on under the covers because Heather's turned out different to what I wanted, but I'm expected to perform. It disappears in seconds. Heather is forgotten as I get accustomed to the light. The old man's got a pile of newspapers under his arm. Something to read, he says. A good draw in the next round. Home to Derby. He smiles a bit uncertain and sits down. Stands up again to take his coat off. Lays it across the bottom of the bed. He starts talking to me a bit nervous like, but his eyes are checking the bandages and bruises. After a while he gets used to the scenery and I don't feel so awkward.

– Your mum was going to come down with me, but we didn't know how well you'd be, and she's got some overtime tonight, but she'll come along in a couple of days. We were here yesterday but you were sleeping, then we phoned up this morning and they said you'd be alright.

The old man looks healthy. His eyes are burning like he's been on the piss. Silly old sod probably thought I was going to snuff it or something. Suppose you worry a bit when it's your kids. Least he knows not to go into any lectures or anything. Unable to move much you've got no chance getting away.

– I spoke to a couple of the nurses and they said you'll be good as new in two weeks. We heard from Gary Robson's old man. Gary heard it off Rod. We got a bit worried at first. We thought you might die or something. It was a shock. Still, you don't seem too bad. I mean, I know you're not in perfect health and all that, but at least you're not maimed or anything.

For some reason I think he should be more upset. Don't know why. A bit daft really. I mean, I don't want a fuss or anything, and I'd prefer it if he didn't come along at all, but now he's here the least he could do is see that though I'm still alive I've been through the grinder and it's going to take a while for the pain to go away. Mad I know, but these ideas spring up from fuck knows where and before you realise what's happening you're thinking gibberish. Must be the drugs. Dad stretches his legs out. He's going to tell a story. Give me a few pearls of wisdom. Real father and son job.

– There was this time when we were kids. Me and your Uncle Barry. We went down Acton to this Irish pub with a load of lads from the area. A couple of them had been in a bit of bother down there and these Paddies knocked one bloke's teeth out with a hammer. We took the train down and had a drink in a pub round the corner. We knew what we were doing. We were in the pub for three hours and when we came out we were raring for a punch-up.

– We got to the Mick's pub about closing time. They were coming out blind drunk. Real hard bastards they were. Navvies the lot of them. They beat the shit out of us. I got stabbed in the stomach and lost two pints of blood. I could have died but I survived. Someone got an ambulance and the hospital stitched me up. I remember the doctor. Indian he was. He said he was from West Bengal. There weren't that many of them around then and he stood out. Looked a bit like Gandhi. It's funny the things you remember. They're good people.

I look at the bloke a bit cockeyed. I'm surprised. Couldn't imagine him doing the business like that. It's not that I'm amazed those kind of things went on, and you always know your parents weren't lily-white like they try to make out when you're a kid growing up, but even so. I wonder what he's telling me for now. Probably his way of saying that he understands. I don't care if he does or doesn't, but he keeps going. It's all good stuff, and I'm interested now, but he doesn't need to say anything. Some things don't have to be said. Families and mates don't need big speeches.

– Then I was in the army. We were doing our basic training. It was down near Salisbury and it was hard work, but it toughened us up. There was this bloke from North London, Edmonton I think it was. He thought he was the king. He was a bit of a spiv but liked having a go at the boys who were easy targets. He tried it on with me once. He just went on all day, taking the piss. He said I had no guts. I was frightened of him. I don't mind saying it, but by evening I'd had enough. Something in my head clicked. It was like I'd got a big dose of strength from somewhere. It's like the stories you read in the papers about crack.

– He went out of the barracks and was shining his boots round the back. I walked straight up behind him and put my knife across his throat. I had him in this lock they'd taught us in training. I nicked his throat with the knife and the blade was over his jugular. It was just like they taught us. I wanted to kill him but held back. If I could've got away with it I would have done it and been pleased, but I controlled myself. He started crying. I told him if he hassled me again he was a dead man. He was sobbing and said he didn't want to die. He said he was sorry. I walked off and he never spoke to me again.

I'm trying to work out why he's telling me this. If it has some kind of hidden meaning or whether he's just trying to show me he was a lad in his own youth, in his own way. He smiles when Heather walks past and says hello, doesn't make any comment though I can see he's watching the way she moves. He asks me if I fancy a drink. He's bought a small bottle of gin with him. I shake my head and laugh but tell him to go ahead. He makes a big deal of keeping the gin secret, so that if anyone was bothered they'd work him out straight away.

He says he feels better. A bit of gin and old stories to tell. Says he never liked Millwall. They were always a bunch of hooligans. He'd thought trouble at football was a thing of the past. You don't see it much on the telly these days. He seems happy. He's actually smiling which is unusual for the old man. It's a bit of a funny situation. You'd think he'd be gutted, but for some reason he's really enjoying the visit.

DERBY AT HOME

I FEEL LIKE a kid. Full of life and raring to go. Nothing can touch me. Millwall's another story to tell in the future, again and again, over and over, small boy sitting on my knee watching the old geezer with drink on his breath, dentures chattering, gasping for air; but for now I make do with thirty of us wandering the streets between Earl's Court and Fulham Broadway. A Derby firm has been spotted and we've had a call on the mobile. If we find them it's a chance to make up for lost time. I'm in the mood. Feel good. Derby may be fuck all when it comes to football, but they've got a few faces prepared to do the business. These midweek Cup games in winter are ideal. There's added needle because of the competition and darkness for cover. As long as it doesn't get too cold and freeze your bollocks off it's a good night out.

We're walking down from the Jolly Maltster. A couple of the lads go inside the first pub to check for Derby. They're straight back shaking heads. The pub's full, but it's all Chelsea. We keep moving. Going against the flow of decent citizens coming out of dead back streets, heading for Stamford Bridge. Eyes full ahead, inspecting concrete as they pass. But there's no pavements of gold, just fag ends and old paper. Even Dick Whittington gave up when he got to London. Made do with shafting his cat. They're looking to get in early and beat the crowd arriving just before kick-off, lapping up the atmosphere like we all did when we were kids with big eyes believing we'd be out on the pitch playing some day. No chance. We check another pub round the corner. It's my turn, and I go inside with Mark. Nothing happening. Just a crowd of men with papers and programmes talking football. We go back out.

– Let's have a drink and wait here for a while. Harris takes command once we're back outside. I fancy a pint. It'll warm us up and get the blood flowing. If Derby walk down from Earl's Court they'll have to come this way. Either that or North End Road, and that's the long way round. Chances are they'll come to us whether they know it or not. If we sit tight we'll be okay. Everything comes to the man who waits.

Half of us go in through one entrance. The other half the side door. A couple of the younger blokes go off to have a look around. There's no point standing on street corners looking like a bunch of orphans, making cunts of ourselves. We go in the pub and though there's no direct look the volume dips a bit as the men inside keep talking but have a quick glance, working us out. Robot mouths moving in time. All the usual chat. It's obvious we're Chelsea and the noise goes back to normal, a group of men arguing the toss about the England side and what's wrong with football in general. Same old words and opinions, year after year. Daft cunts should let it be. You've got no comeback against the men in charge. Goes for everything in this country. England's feeling the strain.

– What do you reckon on Derby then? Mark rubs his hands together. Like an excited schoolboy who's just nicked a dirty mag from his local paper shop and can't wait to see the beavers tucked in his jacket, burning a hole.

Mark's in a good mood tonight. Haven't seen him this happy for years. He's being made redundant in the next couple of months and is due a healthy pay off. He's done his time and is looking forward to the cheque. Thinks he's got it made, Mr Big, but he hasn't stopped to think about the future. He hasn't planned on what happens when the money's spent. Says he's not bothered. Hasn't given it much thought. Says something will turn up. No trouble. Does he look like a tosser or something? Thinking short term as usual.

– They'll have a few boys down tonight.

Rod pours his bottle of Light Ale into a glass as he speaks. Acting flash like he's a genius on remand. Fucks up the image making me laugh. Swears because he's given the Light Ale too much head and the cunt's threatening to spill over. He puts it on a beer mat and lets the advert take the strain.

– We steamed this vanload of Derby up by Earl's Court, about five years ago, says Harris, coming over with his tonic water. We were on our way back to the tube. Been hanging around for an hour after the game, but nothing was happening so we fucked off to the nearest station. Well pissed off we were, slagging the cunts off, then this van stops at a red light. Right rust bucket. Must've been running on a bent MOT, but it had Derby inside so we tried rocking it over and suddenly the back doors swing open and this tribe of Midland headcases piles out. Fuck knows how they all got in the van. Couldn't believe it. Must've been auditioning for the circus, though they weren't exactly a bunch of clowns or beauty queens practising for the high wire.

– I remember that one, Martin Howe joins in. Don't know where you lot were. They were mental. Big bastards in donkey jackets. Never heard the war was over. Still hanging about in the jungle eating roots for twenty years in gear that went out in the Stone Age.

– About twenty of the cunts steamed us, says Harris, taking over the storyteller role. Must've been hiding under the seats or wired into the electrics. Lary as fuck. Tooled-up with iron bars and baseball bats. Cunts pushed us halfway down the street we were so fucking surprised. It was the shock that did us, nothing else. Didn't run us, more like we moved back to clock the situation. Looked like they lived on shit burgers and twenty pints of stout a night. It gave us time to get ourselves sorted. Lobbed a few bricks and tooled up, then chased those Derby bastards back to their van.

– Billy puts a bottle through the windscreen and the driver's panicking and tries to run the cunt over. Up on the curb thinking he's on the dodgems. There's a bit of a barney and everyone backs off and Derby are back in the van safe and sound and just piss off. Cunts were laughing as they disappeared. Flashing their arses as they went. Fucking irons. Went up in a puff of smoke.

– Must've been a cold ride home without a windscreen, says Rod. Thick bastards probably didn't notice till they got halfway up the M1 and started dropping dead with frost bite.

I knew this Derby nutter a few years back. Met him in Poland watching England. Mad as they come, but a good bloke all the same. Was in the army as a kid but got kicked out after one punch-up too many while he was stationed in Germany. A smart bloke. Read a lot of books and could tell you the prime ministers and wars from a hundred years ago. Knew his history and geography. Any capital in the world. Didn't drink and spoke so quiet you had to stop and listen to what he was saying. Kept himself in good nick and got stuck in at the football. Haven't heard from him for three years now. Last I knew he was inside. Could've been a year. Don't remember exactly though the extra months would've meant a lot to him. A mixture of football, thieving and general mischief. The big one he got sent down for was assault.

He was alright. Sort of bloke you knew was going to do something with his life. He wrote me once when he was inside. Said things were getting wound up tight as a queer's arse at a fascist rally because it was summer and rumours were going round the whole time. Said everyone was on edge waiting for the place to go up. Wrote his letter dead straight. Very factual. Clinical way of thinking and I could see him working his way up through the system, building a name for himself, football a hobby, bit of an apprenticeship even, though probably one of the last ones going because they don't have apprenticeships these days. No cunt running a company's interested in anything but quick profits. Still reckon Derby's done well, whether legit or otherwise.

– You recovered now, Tom? Facelift stares me in the eye. I look at the scar where Millwall damaged his looks. He's ugly and the stitch marks aren't exactly going to turn a mob of screaming birds off him. They're cunts Millwall, but we were there, and nobody's going to take that away from us.

Can't be denied. We were on Millwall's manor giving it the big one, taking the piss, mob-handed walking around, but who was it left behind? Me and a few others. Real brain damage material. Don't remember seeing this cunt much when it went off but it's a bad way of thinking because Facelift's no bottle merchant. He's a nutter. A cunt. A mad bastard. A slob. But he's no shitter. That's all that matters at the end of the day.

– Next time we play Millwall we'll make sure we give some of their boys a hiding on your behalf, Facelift says, smiling, mouthy as ever. We'll do it even if we have to go down there five hours before the game with a shooter. Next time. There's always the next time. Take a shotgun along and blow some Bushwhacker cunt's head off. But it was a mental night whatever way you want to look at it. One to remember.

I think about arguing the toss but what's the point? Now I'm on my feet again, Millwall's something to talk about and look back on. I don't think too deep about it, specially being on the ground with half of South East London doing their best to kick me to my reward, but there again the whole night was mental. It rarely happens that bad. You get a handful of decent rucks a season, but Millwall was something else, and though I got a kicking it gives me a bit of respect from the other lads.

If I'd been hiding, holding back even, then I'd probably never have got done. I suffered, but it gives me something in return. Respect. Bit of a name. That's important. You have to earn respect in this world, unless you're one of those bent public schoolboy politicians. There again, that's just their own idea of respect because every normal person thinks they're scum. There's no way you can con your way through life. Comes a time when you've got to stand up and be counted. You can hide, but if you hide you don't live. Definitely not at football. You get sussed soon enough and if you're a wanker you can fuck off.

– I hope they bomb fuck out of those Arab cunts, Billy Bright's watching the telly propped at the end of the bar. Fucking animals. They should use a warhead on them. That would sort the ragheads out. It's all desert anyway, land's not worth a fuck, so why not drop something special and get rid of the bastards. Just make sure the wind's blowing away from England and you're laughing.

The woman on the box is going on about possible air attacks on a Middle East dictator. The volume is down low but I pick up some of the words. Same old phrases and excuses. Usual bollocks. Like a fucking advert. We're sick of hearing about it. Nothing but the threat of bombing for the last week and it's obvious the Government's softening everyone up so there's no protest when they steam in. Public relations. Stand together. Another showing of Coronation Street or Eastenders. Formula curries. Bulldog breed. We won't see the cunts burn and so we don't care. We've got our own lives to worry about. There's no tin soldier gear or guns for us lot.

– What happened with that nurse at the hospital? Mark waits for a story but there's nothing to tell. Did she spit or swallow?

I asked Heather if she'd come out for a drink. Couple of pints and a meal. Said I wanted to show my thanks for getting me put back together again. My treat. She laughed all embarrassed like and said she had some late shifts coming up, but leave my number and she'd give me a bell. It was a nice way of getting blown out and it made me feel stupid asking her in the first place. Knew inside there was no chance getting in there, but if you don't try then you don't know. Said she'd call this week sometime, but I know she won't because Heather had me worked out by the end of my visit. She was half keen, but knew I was a cunt. And that's the way it goes. You get the kind of birds you deserve. Just another piece of skirt looking to turn you into a Saturday afternoon wanker down the high street shops. Life's a bitch, then you marry one, then you die. Saw a sticker saying that on a Jag once. But only if you're a cunt to start with. Nobody makes you into something you're not.

– There's Derby coming down from a pub off North End Road. Harris has the phone to his ear and is relaying the message. Don't look like anything major but there's forty or thereabouts. Look like they could be up for it with a bit of encouragement. A lot of pissheads but a few boys in there as well. A mixed bag of treats. They'll be here in a few minutes. They're not exactly in a hurry. Taking their time seeing the sights. Terraced streets, cockney dustbins and the like. Should charge them for the tour.

– Give it a couple of minutes and we'll give them a running commentary on the wonders of West London, says Rod.

We're outside and suddenly it's a perfect evening. Sharp but clear, and not that cold. Makes your mind concentrated. It feels good to breathe in and out, without the death fumes and disinfectant of hospital. Rain has washed away the poison. We walk along keeping to the pavement, heads down like decent citizens, near enough silent. We turn a corner and Derby are up ahead. Silly bastards are laughing and joking like they're on holiday with a plate of Spanish baked beans in their guts. We stand back in a junction and wait. They're a bit slow and don't clock us right off. Then they see Chelsea waiting and stop. It's a bit of a comedy really. Like stray dogs with ruffled fur, scratching their heads wondering what the next move is. We're two different dimensions. Chelsea are smart and without colours. Derby old-time drunks with kit tops. Obviously not a serious mob. Just a load of geezers out for the football. They're not the ones we were expecting to find, but still, sometimes you just have to make do with what you're given.

– Come on then, you Derby cunts. Harris gives the visitors a warm welcome. Steps towards them. Best foot forward.

– Fuck off cockney, shouts a big bloke in club top, flanked by the half smart element, backed up by the pissheads with beer guts and bad reflexes.

We laugh and move. It's hardly big time this but it'll do for now because major London derbies like Millwall, West Ham, Tottenham are all about inter-breeding and bad blood. Northerners are aliens and you don't expect large-scale aggravation, at least not for a midweek effort this near the ground. Not with modern technology and everything. Amusement arcade battlegrounds and video cameras on rooftops. It's slow motion again and Harris puts his leadership up front and the Derby cunt with the mouth tries to headbutt him, misses, hits cold air, off balance like the mug he is, gets a bruised jaw for his trouble. There's a brief punch-up, a lot of front and kicks, and Derby do a runner as though it's synchronised. All turn and run at the same time. Should be on a fucking ice rink. We follow at a jog, knowing their hearts aren't really in this, follow the trail of shit for a bit, then give up. We walk back the way we came, Harris shaking his head. We're half sad, half narked we've only found a bunch of drunks and not some decent opposition.

– Shitters. Facelift laughs like a Rampton special. What the fuck are they doing down here if they're going to run soon as it goes off? Makes you wonder, cunts like that. Can understand the old men and kids, but not blokes on the piss on someone else's manor. Waste of effort that lot. Should have stayed in Derby with their whippets and pigeons.

We melt into the side streets away from the busy glow of North End Road. Leave the shop windows for people with nothing to hide. Heads down hurrying to watch a ball kicked up and down a patch of grass, maybe even between a set of posts. Fucking dumb when you stop and think about it, but there's something more for me, Mark, Rod, all the boys here, the whole thing that goes with football, the way of life you can't see changing but know it will eventually, when you get tired and old and a younger firm comes up and makes a name for itself, carrying on the tradition with a new set of rules, shifting the emphasis to avoid detection, always a few years ahead of the old bill and five or so in front of the media and public opinion. It'll either be that or I'll end up like one of those trainspotters who never change because nobody notices them, so they just get on with it day in, day out, undisturbed.

I see kids with their old men down North End Road. Lit up 3-D by street lights, cartoon cut-outs, electricity in the air. There's cold and rain and burning bulbs everywhere, the only bit of warmth during winter, and when they pass the Maltster and get down to Fulham Broadway they'll be nearly home and dry. Then they'll see the floodlights glowing like some kind of spaceship. Get all religious, and it was Bill Shankly said football was more important than religion. A famous quote that one. They'll hear the crowd and it's unreal when you're a kid. Like when I first went down Chelsea and saw the Shed singing its head off moving back and forward, on its feet, and there was that passion all round Stamford Bridge which could spill over into a punch-up or pitch invasion at any time.

It was supposed to be dangerous but somehow you felt safe at the same time, because apart from a few headcases that you get everywhere, there were rules. Even major aggro looked worse than it was. You soon got to understand what is and isn't important, because the people running the show were outraged when shop windows got smashed and a few hundred lads ran onto a piece of grass. But out of sight of the cameras and reporters it was a different story. It's like those monkeys. See no evil, hear no evil. It's all cosmetics which isn't a bad thing really because as long as we keep out of sight we can have our fun and games. Just don't shit on the grass.

I feel like the kid I was, thinking about it all these years later. Must be more than twenty years since I first went down Chelsea. All that time and I've grown into what I am now, and after that first game at home to Arsenal I latched on to the Blues. It's just how it happens. It's part of you and what you are makes you what you are at football. If you're a programme collector you're the same outside. If you're mad you don't turn into a

Samaritan once you walk out of the gates. Makes me laugh the cunts calling it football violence when it's nothing to do with football. Nothing at all. Anyone can work that out if they take the time. But they don't because they don't really care. Just drop everyone in a filing cabinet and give them a label.

Suppose you get cynical and ground down the older you get. England's changed since I was a kid. Sound like a real old geezer ready to collect my pension, so fuck knows what it's like for people who can remember back sixty or seventy years. Change comes gradual and worms its way under your skin, irritates the fuck out of you in your sleep so you start scratching like you've got a dose and wake up with the inside of your legs ripped and bleeding. But it's different now, because when I was a kid there were a few punch-ups and whatever, and it went off inside grounds fairly regular, but today, with everything crushed, and more and more people plugged into their TVs and video games, everything's about having money and doing the right thing. Looking like you're behaving yourself. Least that's what they'd have you believe.

– When I get my redundancy I'm lining up a coach for the first away game comes up. Mark wants to share his fortune. No-one pays a penny. It's coming out of my pay-off. Bit of wealth distribution.

– Look at those cunts getting out of the car, Facelift's butting in, bringing us back to the here and now.

– Who you looking at?

– Four blokes across the street. Just parked up. They're Derby alright. Bit smart like they've got money in their pockets.

I look over and see the four men Facelift's pointing out. Blokes in expensive gear. Dressed to blend into the background with a bit of style. Keeping quiet but not through being scared.

– Oi, you, Derby. Facelift shouts across the street.

One of the men turns. I recognise his face. A bloke who did his time in the services. In Poland when the Poles were going mental having a go at the famous English hooligans, lobbing bricks, bottles, anything you can name. Getting stuck in for England. All grudges forgotten for a while. Another flag to fly. Petty local rivalries suspended.

– Fuck off, you cockney bastard.

No fear in Derby's face. Looks older than I remember. Same close-cut ginger hair. Expensive coat and the look of someone who's made a few bob. And I'm just a cunt working in a warehouse who doesn't do too bad selling gear on the side. But he's got more than me, making me the nigger locked out of the shop again, looking in through the window, denied access.

Facelift walks across the street and Derby stands facing him, his mates on both sides, broad faces, cut faces. I hang back watching, wanting to say something but thinking there's nothing I can do. The odds are stacked and when all's said and done it's one of those situations you swear you don't go in for but with Facelift and Billy Bright around, Black John as well, it'll happen because the rules are drawn a bit further down the line for those cunts. The rest of the firm don't care because these are bad odds, thirty or so onto four if everyone goes for it, though I reckon one or two will stand back. Makes me feel sick inside. The odds and the man.

Derby's a good bloke. I want to say something but don't. Just bottle out. He knows the score. He's no fool. So I just stay where I am and don't bother. I'm not going to cover my eyes like a kid, because you see enough blood and guts on the telly so what's a bit more, except in real life it's always raw and dull. No romance. Not now with Derby about to get a kicking and me keeping quiet. Knowing I should speak up, but telling myself this is no innocent sneering at Facelift.

Suppose when it comes down to it I don't want to look bad now Derby's had his say and no way is Facelift going to back off. Don't want the lads thinking I'm a wanker. I have to belong somewhere and when you belong you don't stitch yourself up. You eat shit and follow the rules, even though you keep telling yourself you don't. But I'm trying to persuade myself that Derby's got it coming in a way. Rough justice. He's been in enough trouble in his life to know what's what. But I'm not in the swing of it so it's going to be worse somehow. Like the cunts who watch life through their videos and TVs and clips of porn. The old bill with their surveillance gear and Marshall with his soldier gang rape show. Rod on stage getting the business off some old slapper. The whole fucking game recorded and examined.

Facelift gets close enough and Derby's arm shoots up from his waist, knife buried in Facelift's gut. I want to hear a popping sound. Like the balloon's been deflated or something. But I just hear someone yelling down the road a bit and a load of men coming our way. I look back towards Facelift and he slumps over a car bonnet. Derby slashes his arse with the knife and I want to laugh because he's going to have a lot of grief when he sits down over the next couple of months. I pity the poor bastard who gets the job of sewing him together again.

I look back and there's the old bill escorting some Derby fans and Harris reckons we should get moving. That it's not the time or place. We melt away and a couple of the lads are bent over Facelift who's bleeding into a puddle. Blood and water mixing patterns. A copper comes over from the firm we must've been looking for originally. We keep moving away because the streets are narrow and we don't want to get boxed in by the old bill. We leave Facelift to himself and I've got away without seeing Derby battered. It makes me feel better. I'd have felt a cunt letting him get done like that. He's moved on himself and I've been saved any feelings of guilt.